# Undo me

*The Good Ol' Boys Series*

*USA TODAY* BESTSELLING AUTHOR
## M. ROBINSON

Marie 10-27-18

xo

To my parents Mario and Carmen

Who always showed me that determination and hard work always paid off, and that I could do anything as long as I tried. To the hardest working people I know and the best role models a child could ask for in every aspect.

I love you more than you'll ever know.

# Acknowledgments

**Boss man:** Words cannot describe how much I love you. Thank you for ALWAYS being my best friend. I couldn't do this without you.

**Dad:** Thank you for always showing me what hard work is and what it can accomplish. For always telling me that I can do anything I put my mind to.

**Mom:** Thank you for ALWAYS being there for me no matter what. You are my best friend.

**Julissa Rios:** I love you and I am proud of you. Thank you for being a pain in my ass and for being my sister. I know you are always there for me when I need you.

**Ysabelle & Gianna:** Love you my babies.

**Rebecca Marie:** THANK YOU for an AMAZING cover. I wouldn't know what to do without you and your fabulous creativity.

**Heather Moss:** Thank you for everything that you do!! I wouldn't know what to do without you! You're. The. Best. PA. Ever!! You're NEVER leaving me!! XO

**Silla Webb:** Thank you so much for your edits and formatting! I love it and you!

**Michelle Tan:** Best beta ever! **Argie Sokoli:** I couldn't do this without you. You're my chosen person. **Tammy McGowan:** Thank you for all your support, feedback, and boo boo's you find! I'm happy I made you cry. **Michele Henderson McMullen:** LOVE LOVE LOVE you!! **Dee Montoya:** I value our friendship more than anything. Thanks for always being honest. **Clarissa Federico:** Thank you so much for coming in last minute and handling it like a boss. Your friendship means more to me than you'll ever know! **Rebeka Christine Perales:** You always make me smile. **Mary Jo Toth:** Your boo-boos are always great! **Ella Gram:** You're such a sweet and amazing person! Thank you for your kindness. **Kimmie Lewis:** Your friendship means everything to me. **Tricia Bartley:** Your comments and voice always make me smile! **Natasha Gentile:** Thanks for being gentle on my children and for all your amazing feeback. **Danielle Renee:** Thank you for wanting to join team M. **Kristi Lynn:** Thanks for all your honesty and for joining team M. **Pam Batchelor:** Thanks for all your suggestions and for also wanting to join team M. **Jenn Hazen:** Thank you for everything! **Laura Hansen:** I. Love. You. **Patti Correa:** You're amazing! Thank you for everything! **Kiki Amit:** Thank you for jumping in last minute! You're a doll. **Amber Hayes:** Welcome to team M! Thank you!

To all my author buddies:

**T.M. Frazier:** I fucking love you, you fucking Ginger.

**Jettie Woodruff:** You complete me.

**Erin Noelle:** I. Love. You!

**The C.O.P.A Cabana Girls:**

I love you!!

## To all the bloggers:

A HUGE THANK YOU for all the love and support you have shown me. I have made some amazing friendships with you that I hold dear to my heart. I know that without you I would be nothing!! I cannot THANK YOU enough!! Special thanks to Like A Boss Book Promotions for hosting my tours!

## To my VIP group

I love you.

I write all my books for you.

Thank you for being YOU.

Oh my God ladies…words cannot describe how much I love and appreciate every last one of you. The friendships and relationships that I have made with you are one of the best things that have ever happened to me. I wish I could name each one of you but it would take forever, just please know that you hold a very special place in my heart. You VIPs make my day, every single day.

**THANK YOU!!**

Last but not least.

**YOU.**

My readers.

**THANK YOU!!**

Without you…

I would be nothing.

# Aubrey

"Ma'am, we're going to need to ask you a few questions."
*Who is she talking to? Wait... who the hell is she?*
I racked my brain, trying to figure out what the hell was going on. A million and one questions started racing through my mind, making it hard to focus on the woman in front of me.

"Ma'am, can you tell me what happened tonight?"
I cocked my head to the side, looking dubiously at the woman dressed in a black suit with curious eyes.

"I'm Detective Monroe and this is Officer Parkins."
My gaze went from her to him within a matter of seconds.
*What are they talking about?*

"Aubrey," he announced. "Do you remember me?"
I just stared at him not saying a word or making a sound. Trying to find my clarity.

"Can you tell us what happened last night?" Detective Monroe repeated, bringing my attention back to her.

"We're here to help you," she added.
*Help me? What the fuck was going on?*

Their imposing figures loomed in front of me, as if they were villains from a fairytale.

"Aubrey," he coaxed, suddenly raising his hand toward me. I instinctively flinched, leaning back as far as I could, a reaction that had become second nature to me.

He grimaced, pulling back his arm. "I'm not going to hurt you. You're safe. We're here to help you," he repeated again.

I narrowed my eyes at him and then her, trying to take them in.

"Do you know where you are?" she followed with concern etched in her tone.

I glanced around the room, my eyes not knowing where to look first.

I was at a loss.

"You're at the hospital," she said as if reading my mind. "We can't help you unless you talk to us. Do you understand? I need you to at least nod."

"No... No... No... I hate hospitals, I hate hospitals," I panicked, vigorously shaking my head.

She put her hands out in front of her in a surrendering gesture. "Jeremy Montgomery," she coaxed.

I scooted back, practically ripping the IV from my arm, hugging my knees to my body. Still violently shaking my head back and forth.

"No, no, no, no, no, no," I chanted over and over again, rocking back and forth. Trying to comfort myself like I had done countless times before.

"Aubrey," he soothed, touching me.

I swatted his hand away, covering my ears now. "No! No! No! No!" I endlessly yelled out as loud as I could.

"What are you doing in here?" someone shouted out, making me cover my ears harder, firmer.

I tucked my head in my lap, curling up like a ball.

"I'm the doctor in charge and no one gave you permission to come in here!" she yelled again.

Hands touched me everywhere, and all at once, causing me to fight harder. Pain coursed through my entire body, my head throbbed and my vision blurred.

"She's going into shock. Get the hell out of here now! You're not helping anything."

"We're trying to help her. We have a Detective behind bars and a man who—"

"Nooooo!" I cried out. "No... no... no... no... no..." I sobbed, my body shaking uncontrollably to the point of pain.

"Get out! Now!" she ordered. "Aubrey, Aubrey, sweetie, you need to stay with me. You need to calm down," said the woman in scrubs and white coat.

*She seems so familiar? Do I know her?*

I shoved their hands away, pushing at the grips they all had on me. At anything near me, at anything that was touching me.

"Don't touch me! Don't fucking touch me!" I screamed, violently thrashing my body around. Causing even more pain. The sounds of the machines beeping all around me were deafening. "Don't fucking touch me!" I repeated, yelling out bloody murder.

"Grab her legs!" someone demanded above me. "Help me grab her arms."

Their hands were everywhere, trying to control me, trying to restrain me, trying to undo me.

"No! No! No! No!" I whipped around every which way, but they were too strong for me.

They were always too strong for me.

"Please... please... please..." I bawled like a baby, my emotions overtaking me, smothering me in nothing but a sea of despair and loneliness.

"Shhh... shhh..." they coaxed and I immediately pictured Dylan's face, Dylan's voice.

I instinctively placed my free hand over my heart, taking in their words, "Shhh... shhh..."

My body felt slack, heavy, foreign, as a warm sensation began surging through me from my head down to my toes.

"Shhh... go to sleep. Close your eyes and go to sleep, Aubrey..." I heard them faintly say as an echo in the distance.

I shook my head, desperately trying to keep my eyes open. I couldn't fight it off. I never could. I closed my eyes against my will, welcoming the darkness.

*Silence.*

Always numb.

Always alone.

Always afraid.

I secretly prayed that I would never wake up or that I would die. Knowing in my heart...

I was never that lucky.

# DYLAN

I walked into Alex's restaurant like a man on a goddamn mission.

"Fuck, man, what the hell happened to you?" my friend Jacob asked, taking in my bloody lip, bruised eye, and cut up knuckles.

"Bad day at work," I simply stated, grabbing a beer from the bar.

"No shit," was all he could reply.

"Happy birthday." I pulled his girlfriend Lily into a hug.

"Thanks, are you okay? Do you need me to get you something?" She looked me over. Concern and worry etched in her knowing eyes.

"Don't fuss over me. I'm fine. Comes with the job."

"Okay."

Family and friends all gathered around celebrating Lily, my best friend Lucas' baby sister's twenty-fifth birthday. Everyone was so goddamn happy and there wasn't anything to be happy about.

At least not for me.

Not ever again for me.

It didn't take long to hear my other friend Austin yell out, "What the fuck?"

Everyone turned, following the direction of his gaze.

Everyone but *me*.

Three police officers walked in, heading towards us. I was sitting down at the table beside Jacob and Lily, sipping my beer like nothing was going on, as if my life wasn't about to get shit on and disposed of as if it meant nothing to begin with.

"Detective McGraw, we hate to have to—"

"Just fucking do it," I interrupted the officer, standing to look at all of them.

The rest proceeded in slow fucking motion and trust me if I could have sped it up, I would have.

"Dylan McGraw, you have the right to remain silent. Anything you say can and will be used against you in a court of law. You have the right to an attorney. If you cannot afford an attorney, one will be provided for you. Do you understand the rights I have just read to you? With these rights in mind, do you wish to speak to me?"

I nodded and Jacob who was a lawyer immediately jumped into action like I knew he would.

"What's going on?" he asked. "Dylan, do not say a word without me present. Do you understand me? Do not open your mouth for nothing."

I nodded again.

They finished handcuffing me and escorted me out of the restaurant with everyone's prying eyes on me. Shoving me in the back of a cop car as I had done to so many people before, too many damn times to count.

The irony was not lost on me.

I was fingerprinted, a mug shot was taken, and I was stripped and searched before they pushed me into an empty cell as I waited for Jacob to make his presence known.

I took a deep breath, sitting on the bench with my head leaning back against the wall.

My entire life flashing before my eyes like a goddamn movie reel I couldn't pause or fucking stop.

I heard footsteps down the hall and I didn't have to wonder who it was.

"Come on, your lawyer wants to talk to you."

He handcuffed me once again and led me down a narrow hallway into a room with a large rectangular table that had chairs scattered along it. Jacob was sitting at the far end of the table, exactly how I assumed he would be. I took the seat on the opposite end from him, mostly because I didn't want to walk that fucking far to be closer to him.

I was exhausted and I'm not talking about physically.

They shut the door and left us alone. Neither one of us spoke for I don't know how damn long. We just kinda stared at each other, waiting to see who would make the first move. I sighed, leaning back into my chair, trying to get comfortable with the goddamn cuffs cutting at my wrists.

"Jesus Christ, McGraw, what the fuck did you get yourself into?"

I didn't say a word. I didn't even fucking move.

"What? You're just going to sit there and stare at me all damn night?"

"I ain't got nothin' to say."

"Cut the shit," he gritted out.

"What do you want from me, Jacob? A fuckin' bedtime story?"

He leaned into the table with his arms resting in front of him.

"Listen to me, you stubborn son of a bitch. You need to start talking and you need to start talking real fucking quick. The charges you're up against are going to take a goddamn miracle from Jesus himself appearing in the courtroom to get you off. Now, you need to tell me what the hell happened so I can do my job and save your sorry ass from becoming someone's bitch in a jail cell for the next decade. Do you understand me?"

I cocked my head to the side and spoke with conviction, "Where? Where would you like me to start?"

He didn't falter not that I expected him to.

"The beginning, Dylan, start from the fucking beginning."

# Chapter one

# Aubrey

"You're such a fucking asshole!"

There I was, yelling at a dude I knew by reputation only, out in the school parking lot by his Jeep. Both my fists remained at my sides while I tried like hell to keep my cool, to maintain my composure and act like the lady I was raised to be, but you wouldn't know it by my actions in that moment. Uncontrollable anger toward him took over my entire body, and I fought the urge to punch him right in his damn mouth.

*Dylan McGraw.*

Just his name made me want to throw down.

I hated guys like him.

I didn't know much about him, but the fact was I didn't need to. Boys like him were all the same, every last one of them. Acting as though they were hot shit and owned every place they walked into. With their my-shit-don't-stink kind of attitude. They knew how to flash their boyish grins and show off their dimples just the right way to grant them access to all the lust-infested girls' panties. Their mere touch, the calculated romance or with their slick lines had those stupid, naive girls spreading their legs faster than I could say, "Open sesame."

It was so cliché.

All of it.

I had heard enough to know that I needed to steer clear of Dylan McGraw and his asshole tendencies. I was only a few months into my freshman year at a new high school, but his reputation preceded him.

Dee was the only girl to approach me on the first day of school, and we quickly became friends. She was sweet and funny in an innocent kind of way. When she told me she was hanging out with Dylan McGraw, I kept my mouth shut. If I was aware of his reputation, I was sure she was aware of it, too. Especially with both of them being natives to Oak Island. You'd have to live under a rock to not know that no good came from that boy.

The rumors were everywhere.

Dylan turned from his Jeep with an overconfident arched eyebrow, narrowing his stare on me. He stood there with nothing more than a mischievous smirk. It was the first time I had ever been around a guy who screamed sex. It radiated off of him, he had this cocky demeanor without even trying. I slowly licked my lips, my mouth suddenly drying up. I felt like I was under a spell. His gaze immediately followed the movement of my tongue, and I subconsciously took a step back, folding my arms over my chest to stand my ground. I shook my head, ridding myself of the uneasiness I was immersed in because of his slightly intimidating composure that unexpectedly seemed to loom over mine.

"You're an *asshole*," I repeated.

He folded his arms over his chest and his face didn't falter. I tried like hell to ignore how his stance only emphasized his tall, muscular build as he leaned back against his black Wrangler with one leg propped over the other.

Cocky and confident as ever.

The parking lot was empty. Everyone had gone home for the day. Everyone except me. I had to listen to Dee cry for an entire hour in her car about Dylan and how he had used her. How they had sex a few times, and now he didn't want anything to do with her, tossing her away like I had heard he had done to so many other girls. Treating them as if they were disposable.

Fuck 'em and chuck 'em was his style.

*Asshole.*

After she finally calmed down and drove away in her car, I started to walk back toward my house, but then I saw Dylan throwing his textbooks in the backseat of his Jeep. I don't know what came over me. I just made my way over to him and shouted the first thing that came to mind. I had never been that close to him before. I'd never even looked his way or said a single word to him before that moment.

"How could you do that to Dee? She doesn't deserve your bullshit. She's a nice girl. She's not like the girls you're used to, okay? You owe her an apology," I ordered.

He grinned.

He. Fucking. Grinned.

"Is this amusing to you? Do you like hurting girls? How many notches do you need on your bedpost, Dylan? What's a few more right?"

He bit the side of his lip in a charismatic and magnetic way, and it was my turn to arch an eyebrow. I hated that he was trying to use his so-called charm on me.

"What? You're just going to stand there and not say anything? That's really mature, asshole."

He scoffed. "I'm not the one throwing a temper tantrum, now am I?" he finally spoke with a rough yet smooth tone.

His voice was deep, deeper than I expected, with a bit of a Southern drawl. It was the first time I had ever heard it, and I would be lying if I said it didn't catch me off guard. Everything about him did. I thought I knew what to expect when it came to him, but he proved me wrong. Which didn't make any sense. I was supposed to have the upper hand, not him.

My eyes widened in shock. "This is not a temper tantrum, *asshole*. This is someone calling you out on your shitty behavior. Own up to your whorish ways, apologize to Dee, and we won't have any problems."

His patronizing eyes scanned the length of my body, starting with my pink toes, lingering on my breasts, and coming to a stop at my eyes. His expression was hard to read, and it did nothing but confuse me even more. I thought I was prepared. I thought I knew everything there was to know about him. I thought a lot of things, but I would learn soon enough that I had no idea what I was getting myself into.

It was one thing to think you knew, to assume, but when it was staring you right in the face, when *he* was looking only at *you*, it changed things.

It changed *everything*.

The way his eyes barred into mine ignited a fire deep within me. He wasn't looking at *me*. He was looking *in* me. And that I hadn't expected.

That I wasn't prepared for.

His reality being much more intense than my assumption, I never wanted to be one of those girls.

*Especially not now.*

The awkward silence was finally broken by his condescending tone. "Problems with you?" he stated as a question with a crooked grin and a cocked head, eyeing me up and down once again.

I watched as he slowly engulfed every inch of my body, making me feel naked and exposed. He bit his bottom lip again when he sensed what I was feeling.

"Yes, that's what I said."

We locked eyes.

"I'll take my chances," he retorted with an arrogant tone.

"Oh my God! You're such a fucking asshole."

"Darlin', I think you've already pointed that out."

"I'm just stating facts. None of which you're denying."

"Darlin'-"

"Stop calling me that."

He pushed off his Jeep and strolled over to me with such purpose that I felt it down to my bones with each step he took. He stood right in front of me, lowering his face too close to mine.

"Darlin'," he drawled. "I don't know your name, and although Crazy Bitch seems fitting, I figured you'd appreciate Darlin' more." He smiled, breaking the harshness of his words.

Something about the way he was looking at me made me more uncomfortable than I already was, if that was even possible. I had never been that conflicted around a guy. I realized right then and there that Dylan McGraw was different, I just didn't know in what sense, at least not yet. I could feel my guard escalating higher and higher as the seconds passed between us.

"I mean if we're calling a spade a spade, I'm not the one who came at you, am I?"

I said nothing because honestly, what could I say to that? My outburst was spontaneous. I just wanted to rectify the Dee situation and his demeanor ruined my momentum.

*Bastard.*

"I didn't think so," he added, as if reading my mind. "You've called me a fucking asshole more times than I care to count in a matter of five minutes, and I'm still not clear on what I did wrong? Try again."

"I already told you. What you did to Dee. You used her."

He shook his head, narrowing his eyes at me. "I used *her*? That's not the way I remember it. I would get your story straight before I go playing martyr, sweetheart."

"Unbelievable, you're going to try to deny it?"

I don't know how long we stayed frozen in that moment but he suddenly leaned forward, closing the gap between us and bringing us back to reality.

"I don't think we've been properly introduced," he added. His cheek grazed mine as he moved closer to my ear. I faintly felt his breath on my neck.

"You smell good," he whispered, lightly brushing his lips on the sensitive area just below my ear. Shivers rippled throughout my entire body. The rhythm of my heart escalated, betraying my mind from the asshole before me.

"What the hell?" I snapped, roughly pushing back off of his hard chest. He didn't budge.

"Who the hell do you think you are? You can't just go around sniffing girls!"

"I believe I just did."

"So is this how it works, Dylan? Am I supposed to spread my legs open for you now that you introduced yourself to me? Just like every other girl?" I crudely mocked, letting him know that he couldn't intimidate me. "I will tell you one thing... I'm not impressed. You're a boy trying to be a man, and not even a good one at that."

He snidely chuckled, "You have no idea, suga', what I'm capable of. How about I show you just how much of a man I am? I have something right here for that pretty little mouth of yours that seems to know everything." He gestured toward his dick.

"You cocky son of—" His finger came up and pressed against my lips, silencing me, and I barely resisted the urge to bite it off.

"Sticks and stones, suga', you best remember that." He playfully tugged the loose ends of my hair that were lying across my cheek. "I paid you a compliment, it would do you some good to say thank you." And with that he turned around and got in his Jeep.

I was dismissed.

# DYLAN

"Woo-ooh-eee!" Jacob hollered beside me as I threw the Jeep into reverse.

"Someone just got chewed up and spit the fuck out," he laughed, clapping his hands over and over again obnoxiously. "Damn, I would pay good money to see that again, bro!"

"Shut the fuck up," I snapped.

"What pussy did you piss off this time? Two? Damn, this is a new record for you." He just didn't know when to quit, and that was always the problem with Jacob. "Who was that anyway? Is she new here? Maybe I should show you how it's done, fucker. I'm marking today as the first time Dylan-fucking-McGraw couldn't seal the deal."

Jacob was my childhood friend. He was more like a brother to me. I knew he would be running his mouth to Austin and Lucas as soon as we stepped out of the Jeep. I had known these guys since birth, our parents had been best friends since before we were born. They took any opportunity to fuck with me, as I did with them.

And this gave them the perfect ammunition.

I hoped Half-Pint would be around to stop them before I had to do it with my fists. Half-Pint was Alexandra, Alex for short. She was the glue that held all us good ol' boys together since we were kids. She was younger than us by two years, but you'd never know that. She was much wiser than all of us put together. She was a true lady, the only one besides my mama I had ever met.

That chick from the parking lot was right about one thing…

I was an asshole, I owned it, and made no excuses for it.

There was no reason to try to deny it. I accepted that title a long time ago. I spoke my mind, I didn't sugar-coat shit. Whether it hurt someone's feelings or not, that was their goddamn problem, not mine. Life was too damn short to pretend to be something I wasn't.

Now, did I use girls?

*Fuck no.*

They knew what they were getting themselves into. My reputation followed me everywhere. I got more pussy thrown at me because of it. See, girls loved the bad boys. The ones they thought they could change, the challenge, the rule breaker, the game changer. The ones that fairytales were made of, the happily-ever-after's where Prince Charming swept you off your feet and you rode off into the sunset looking deeply into each other's eyes or some shit like that.

*Bullshit.*

Every last bit of it.

I was sixteen years old. My parents just got me a brand new Jeep Wrangler. I came from a home with a loving mom and dad who went above and beyond for me. I had a group of boys that were like brothers to me. I didn't need a girl to love me. I didn't need a girl expecting things from me. I just needed my cock played with because the best part of being me was that I was hung like a goddamn horse.

Now if you were in my shoes, would you settle for one girl?

*Yeah, that's what I thought.*

I did what any normal teenage guy would do. The only difference was that I wasn't subtle about it at all. Why hide it? That's what got you in trouble.

End of story.

But having a stranger, a hot-as-fuck stranger, call me out on it was completely new territory for me. Yet there I was, lost in thought about her. Except, I wasn't thinking about her ridiculously, curvy figure that would usually have my cock standing at attention. It was the way she came at me with no fear that had my interest piqued. She had the damn balls to call me out on my shit. What people I've known all my life said behind my back, she had the backbone to say it right to my face.

*Honesty.*

A guy like me could appreciate that, yet I was labeled an asshole for it.

Not that I didn't enjoy watching her pouty pink lips pucker every time she tried to hide the fact that I had an effect on her. I would even go as far to say she had an effect on me as well. Too many adolescent years spent stroking my dick to images of women that were shaped just like her in Playboy magazines. Her blonde hair lay perfectly against her huge tits. She tried to hide them with a modest-cut shirt that did nothing but the opposite. She stood her ground and glared right fucking at me, making me take in her bright green eyes that had a hint of brown in them. Not once did she cower or lower her intense stare from mine.

She smelled good enough to fucking devour. Honey and vanilla mixed together. My favorite.

The girl was a paradox of contradictions. Her demeanor screamed she hated me, but her body, her body liked me just fine. Which only made me want to get to know her that much more. I loved a challenge as much as the next guy.

"She got to you, didn't she?" Jacob asked, pulling me away from my thoughts. "Well, I'll be damned. I never thought I'd see the day. Someone got through to your icy prick—"

"Jacob, stop watching all those Disney movies with Lily or I'm going to have to start buying you tampons. I'd really hate to have to punch a girl in the face," I mocked.

I may have hit a sore spot there, bringing up Lily. She was Lucas' baby sister and seven years younger than us. I swear the girl was a spitfire. She was a kid, a youngin', only nine years old, who was desperately in love with Jacob. Had been her entire life. Jacob though, was oblivious to it. It was his subconscious way of protecting himself from the little girl in pigtails in front of him. The same little girl, that would one day turn into a woman right before our very own eyes and eventually carry Jacob's balls in a jar.

In the years to come, it would be like Lucas and Alex all over again, history repeating itself, and karma knocking Jacob right in the fucking mouth.

"Her name's Aubrey," he announced out of nowhere.

"What?" I glanced at him, pulling into Alex's parents' restaurant to meet up with the rest of the boys and Half-Pint.

"You heard me." He grinned like a goddamn fool. "Aubrey Owens to be exact, according to Kayla." He showed me his text message. "Oh, she's a freshman, fresh meat just the way you like them, asshole. She moved here from California with her mom or some shit. Do you want me to get her address too? Maybe you guys could braid each other's hair."

I chuckled. Everyone fucked with me because of my hair that sat just above my shoulders, especially my mom. I'd had long hair ever since I could remember. It was blonde, but turned white over the summer from surfing and constantly being in the sun and salt water.

"I get plenty of pussy on my own, Jacob, which is more than I could say for you."

"What can I say? I have high standards. I don't go around and fuck everything with a hole. By the way, tell your mom I said hello."

"Not before you tell your sister Amanda she's the best I've ever had, you sick son of a bitch."

"Touché, motherfucker. Touché."

Lucas and Austin were already surfing by the time we walked into the restaurant. Alex sat at a table with her notebooks spread out, writing in her binder. On a Friday afternoon, it was normal to see Half-Pint doing her homework like the good girl she was. She was very bright.

All of us boys were like brothers from different mothers. Alex being no different, but there was no telling her she wasn't one of us boys. She was like our little sister. We all looked out for each other, even when we didn't need to. Old habits die hard, that was true when it came to meddling in things that were none of our business to begin with.

Jacob and I were definitely the closest, since we were the oldest and our smart-ass personalities were somewhat the same. Both of us acted like we owned the damn beach and our little town. And in our minds, we did.

Lucas was a few months younger than us, but you'd never know it by looking at him. If you told that boy no he would do it just to spite you. Stubborn, hardheaded, and a temper that would make anyone think twice about ever crossing him. That didn't stop us from fucking with him though since we were all a bit like that, growing up together made it easy to fall into similar patterns, our personalities rubbed off on each other whether we liked it or not.

Alex was adamant she would be one of the boys from the second she popped out of her mama's belly. She came out screaming and kicking, a force to be reckoned with. Hell would freeze over before she would act like the girl she was. It was only a year or two ago that she actually started wearing dresses and make-up. Before that she dressed exactly like us, begging her mama to buy her cargo shorts and loose-fitting shirts to blend in with us boys. And like Lucas, we picked on her every chance we got. She hated being called a girl, or being treated like one. Though she was tough. Tough as nails, we made her that way, and you better believe that we were overprotective as hell of her.

Despite her tomboy tendencies, I meant it when I said Alex was a lady through and through. She never cussed, she didn't hang out at parties with us, and was polite to everyone, even if we didn't like them or talked shit about them. She never cared to get involved in gossip or school drama like most girls did, keeping to herself or hanging out with us. Except she wasn't very bright when it came to her choice in guys.

We all realized it before it even happened.

Case and point... Lucas and Alex aka Bo and Half-Pint.

Those two had always shared this special bond between them that didn't include the rest of us. They were separate, but still a vital part of us. We ignored it for years, blew it off, thinking it was the best thing to do at the time. We all hoped it would magically go away on its own or some shit like that. Until one day we couldn't overlook it anymore. When shit went down it was like a goddamn avalanche occurred, and it impacted all of our lives in ways we never thought possible.

Austin was the youngest among us boys, a year younger than Lucas to be exact. He was trouble with a capital T, in every sense of the word. He was the good ol' boys wild card. The older he got the worse he became, and there was nothing any of us could ever do about it. It wasn't from lack of trying on our parts either. He was out of fucking control.

Jacob headed toward the beach, saying he was meeting up with someone, probably some new pussy he was trying to get a piece of. I walked over to Half-Pint.

"Hey," she greeted, looking up at me. I pulled a chair over and swung it around to sit on it backwards.

"Whatcha workin' on?"

"Algebra," she sighed.

"Ah shit. Your worst subject."

She peered at me, wide-eyed and confused. "I think I'm going cross-eyed trying to figure out these formulas."

I nodded at her. "Scoot over, sweet girl."

She smiled, pushing back her chair to give me some room to sit beside her. I grabbed her algebra book, skimming over the chapters she was working on. Numbers and statistics were always my best subjects in school. It was easy for me to remember formulas and rules. Numbers stayed consistent. I grabbed her binder to help explain an easy way for her to remember the patterns.

"See, here's your problem, Half-Pint. Your Order of Operations is off. You need to do the parentheses before your exponents or else it's going to mess you all up."

"Ugh, I always forget that. It's so hard to keep them in order and remember which goes first."

I grabbed her pencil from her. "Remember it like this: Parentheses, exponents, multiplication, division, addition, and subtraction. Please Excuse My Dear Aunt Sally. You remember that phrase, you'll always remember the rule, guaranteed."

She nodded, looking at what I just wrote. Whispering, "Please excuse my dear Aunt Sally." She glanced over at me. "Good to know. Got it!"

"Knew you would, you're smart, darlin'."

"Okay, what about these?"

I sat there for the next hour, explaining numbers, shootin' the shit, and simply laughing. I helped her with everything she needed. It didn't take long for Alex to catch on to what I was explaining. I told you she was bright. That girl could take on anything, and she did, in more ways than one. When I got up to head out to where the boys were, I never expected to look up and lock eyes with my destiny and quite possibly the girl who would undo me.

*Aubrey.*

# Chapter two

# Aubrey

My mom wasn't aware of the fact that I walked home from school everyday. She didn't need to worry about me anymore than I knew she already did. I was supposed to get on the school bus, but the noise and rowdy kids were too much for me to handle.

I hated it.

Walking was my peace, a chance for me to clear my mind from the chaos all around while listening to my favorite playlists. I loved to get lost in the songs, letting them take me somewhere else, anywhere but here. Back in California we had a steady routine that no longer existed. My mom dropped me off at school and my dad would pick me up everyday. Sometimes afterwards we would go for ice cream or a cup of coffee, as I got older. I miss that time with him. I miss our conversations, and most of all I miss laughing at his lame jokes. He was a great father. It was obvious to me even from a young age.

My mom up and moved us clear across the country when she decided we needed new scenery and a fresh start. I couldn't blame her, not after what my dad did. That's how I ended up in Oak Island, North Carolina.

*Our new home.*

My mom never talked bad about my dad even though she had every right to. She never uttered a single negative thing about him in my presence, not even once. I respected her so much for it, not all parents took the high road like my mom did.

I saw the pained look in my mother's eyes…

It was always there.

*Haunting me.*

But at the end of the day, he was still my father and I loved him.

She bought us a cute house in a nice neighborhood that reminded me of Pleasantville. Oak Island was a small beach town with a country feel. I quickly learned that everyone knew everyone in this town. I secretly kind of loved that, an extended family of some sort. Polar opposite from the hustle and bustle of LA, where everyone kept to themselves, absorbed only in their money and looks.

My mom was an ER General Surgeon and Chief of Medicine back in California. She ran the entire ER unit. When she decided to move us, a friend of a friend had some connections, and she was lucky enough to get a contracted job running the ER at Dosher Memorial Hospital in South Port, which was only a town over. She worked all sorts of crazy hours here like she did back in California. I barely ever saw her. I was alone in a new town, so far from my home.

The more things changed.

The more they stayed the same.

My dad worked from home designing computer software for a telecommunications company. He had only been working for TLCOM the last few years after he went back to college and got his degree. He said he wanted to better himself, but I often wondered if it was because my mom was the breadwinner of the family. I wondered if he felt emasculated.

For most of my life, my dad was a stay-at-home parent. He raised me along with my mom's sister, Celeste, while my mom worked her life away to provide for us.

It was never a problem.

Until it was.

We got to spend a lot of time together, but unfortunately he also had more time to dwell on the fact that it was usually only him and I at home. There were plenty of times he had to take on both the "mom" and the "dad" roles since my mom was working all those insane hours.

There were instances when my dad was simply not enough. My first period, my first crush, my first kiss, getting ready for my first date, things that only another woman would understand. That's when my aunt stepped in, picking up the slack for her absent sister. My

Aunt Celeste was like a mom to me and still is. I could see the hurt on my mom's face when I told her about something that she should have been apart of, that she should have witnessed. It was a memory that only a mother and daughter should experience, bonding the connection of parent and child for years to come.

She always listened, though.

I guess that was her role.

I could hear the strain in her voice when my aunt or my dad told her about all the other milestones that she should have been apart of but wasn't.

Nothing ever changed.

My mom lived and breathed her job. She always said she loved helping people, that it gave her a purpose in life. I couldn't fault her. She spent years in school, and half of her life was consumed with her head in the books. It was just who she was. My aunt would often tell me stories about how my mom missed out on her childhood, teenage years, college, and all the normal stuff that people should experience because medicine was in her blood, she got her first medical kit for her sixth birthday and it was like a light bulb went off in her head. I once read that doctors were born, they weren't made.

I never wanted for anything. I opened my mouth, and I had it the next day. Growing up I always had the best toys, best clothes, best everything. That wasn't my

father's doing. He often fought with her about how she was spoiling me too much. That I needed to earn things, not just have them handed to me every time I wanted something. I never understood how she found time to buy me everything I asked for, but barely found time to eat dinner with us, or even watch a movie.

Little did she know I would have taken an hour with her over any fancy toy.

I thought with the move that maybe things would somehow change, that maybe she would make time for us now. I had no one here. But I couldn't have been more wrong.

She started working the day after we arrived in Oak Island, which left me to do most of the unpacking. Even though it was tedious going through all the boxes, I was grateful for the distraction. My mom's inconsistent hours were starting to get to me, I was lonely, and this time around I didn't have my dad or my aunt to fill that void. I never said anything to her because I knew she had enough on her plate, and I didn't want to add to it. As much as she tried to play it off, I knew our current situation hit her harder than she liked to let on. That burden just added to the reasons she drowned herself in her work, more so than before.

Which was another reason I was grateful for my friendship with Dee, I spent a lot of time at her house with her family. They took me in like I belonged. I think her parents took pity on me since they knew I was by myself most of the time. Maybe they just assumed my mom was a struggling single parent who needed to work all the time to stay afloat since I never went into details about her position at the hospital.

I was alone with nothing but my thoughts, desperately trying to ignore my feelings about Dylan. I couldn't believe he had the nerve to just turn his back on me as if our conversation was over because he said so.

*Arrogant asshole.*

The whole encounter was kind of a blur. I was so worked up I hadn't even realized someone was in his Jeep watching us argue until Dylan backed out of the parking space and I heard his friend's voice full of laughter. I instantly felt a sense of pride coming over me that someone had witnessed him getting knocked down a few pegs by a girl. I wouldn't be surprised if someone told me that I was the first girl to ever do so. That alone gave me a feeling of satisfaction.

It was a long time coming for a guy like him. Walking around school like he owned the damn place, with a certain swagger and his stupid, long blonde hair that fell perfectly on the sides of his chiseled face, as if he was some sort of Greek God or something. He was tall for sixteen, way taller than my five-foot-four frame. I assumed he was probably a little over six foot. His intense hazel eyes had a hint of green running through them that I imagined would really pop when he wore green. Not that I was imagining him in any way other than annoyance.

He was built like a man. He could definitely pass for someone much older than he actually was. Needing to stop all the thoughts I was having about him, I shook them away before they consumed me again and took over. That's when I realized I was lost. I looked around for a sign, but instead saw a restaurant on the beach. I decided to stop in and ask for directions and maybe grab something to drink or a bite to eat while I was there.

As soon as I walked in, there was a warm, welcoming feeling in the air. The restaurant was beautiful and homey with an open view of the beach. All you had to do was walk across the open floor plan and your toes would be in the sand. There were tables everywhere. The smell of delicious food assaulted my senses, making my stomach growl. I knew right then and there it would become one of my new favorite places to eat. The hostess said I could seat myself, so I decided to walk towards the back to sit by the deck where I could enjoy the warm, salty air of the ocean when I came to an abrupt stop.

*Dylan.*

I rolled my eyes when I noticed that he was with a girl. Shocker. I had just called him out on all his bullshit, and there he was already sitting with another girl. I shook my head in disgust, but it was suddenly replaced with curiosity. This girl was tiny and not his usual type from what I had heard. She didn't look familiar in the slightest. Our school was small enough to know most of the students, even if only by appearance. She looked too sweet and innocent for the likes of him. I had the urge to go over there and warn the poor girl to stay away from him, that he was nothing but trouble. He would dispose of her like she was yesterday's trash once he got what he wanted.

I didn't.

I couldn't.

I just stood there unknowingly, staring at them without even realizing I was doing so. He was helping her with her homework. Now that didn't strike me as the Dylan I encountered and heard of. He was attentive with her, patient. They appeared as if they had known each other their entire lives. I knew it couldn't be his sister, they looked nothing alike, but he was treating her like she was. And what really shocked the shit out of me was that he looked at her with love and adoration. Even respect. Which was completely different from the guy who stood in front of me, less than an hour before, the same guy I confronted in the school parking lot who didn't seem bothered by what I was accusing him of in the slightest. I don't know how long I stood there watching the two of them. Taking in every laugh and smile. They seemed so carefree, their banter effortless.

He unexpectedly looked up, as if he felt my presence from across the room. Our eyes once again tethered, and for a moment, I saw a certain vulnerability pass through him that I could feel deep within my core. However, just as quickly as it appeared, it was gone. Whatever it was had me questioning my beliefs about him. His gaze immediately made me peer down, shutting off the connection that we briefly shared for just a few seconds in time. I walked to a table on the other end of the restaurant, needing to get as far away from him as possible.

I ordered a drink and food, and then started playing with my phone, when I felt someone crouch down beside me. There he was, balancing on the balls of his feet, just a few inches from my face, in all his glory. For the first time it made me nervous.

"You stalkin' me now?" he asked with a grin.

I resisted the urge to smile. "I'm not the one sitting at your feet, am I?"

He grinned, wider, putting his dimples prominently on display. His jaw was clenched and there was a gleam in his eyes like he was amused with my banter.

"Well, sweetheart, you are the queen and I am the asshole, as you pointed out earlier, so it seems as though I am right where I belong."

"Who's the girl?" I blurted out of nowhere. The words were out of my mouth before my brain even registered what I asked.

He smiled, his straight white teeth shining with the glare of the sun. "Jealous?"

"You wish, buddy. I'm not one of your minions."

"That you aren't," he replied with a hard edge.

"What do you want anyways? Need me to call you out on more of your bullshit?" I snidely questioned, ignoring his last remark.

"Can't a guy just say hello to a friend?"

"We're friends now? When did that happen? I don't even like you."

He narrowed his eyes at me as if he was calling my bluff.

"That really hurts, suga'," he replied with a smirk, holding his hand over his heart in a dramatic gesture.

"You're full of it."

"And you're beautiful," he asserted, not missing a beat.

I couldn't help but smile. "So this is how it works, huh? I don't know if I should be offended or flattered that you're already hitting on me. An hour hasn't even gone by since I chewed you up and spit you out, and you're back on the horse again?" I mocked, throwing the same statement that I overheard his friend say while he was pulling out of the parking space.

He chuckled, a throaty sound escaping his lips. "If I had to choose I would prefer the latter."

"Well, thank God you aren't then."

He slowly nodded. "This how you gonna play it? Cuz I'm fixin' to be a gentleman here, but that sassy lil' mouth of yours is makin' me all sorts of crazy, baby."

"A gentleman?" I looked around, pretending to see if someone else was there. "You might want to look it up in a dictionary because you are doing it all wrong," I said, feigning shock on my face.

He shook his head, flashing me that boyish grin before tugging on the ends of my hair like he had earlier.

"As always, it was a pleasure." With that, he stood and left.

I was dismissed once again.

# DYLAN

"There's a spot open over there." Austin pointed to the only available parking spot on the grass.

The empty land by Ian's house had turned into our private parking lot, it looked like a small car dealership. From Mercedes to beat up Hondas. Our little town was diverse in almost everything, but you wouldn't know it by looking at our groups.

It was Saturday night and Ian was having one of his signature parties at his parents' house. His parents were known for always being out of town, traveling around the world and letting someone else raise their kid. That was the beauty of living in a small town, everyone knew everyone else's business, and gossip spread like wildfire. We tried not to pay attention to it, but it was hard to ignore when everyone's dirty laundry was aired out in the open for everyone else to see.

Like any dysfunctional family, we always took care of our own.

Ian's place was fucking huge, and the best part of it was its location. Private beachfront property, where there was so much distance between houses, the cops were never called on us for disturbing the peace. It was the perfect place to let loose and not have to worry about the consequences. His parents never found out or maybe they just didn't give a fuck. Everyone partied near the pool where country music blared through the expensive speaker system. Later in the night, the party would move down to the beach for a bonfire.

I was surprised we even found a free spot tonight. We usually had to park down the street and walk our happy asses to the house. It was almost seven by the time the boys and I made our way to the beach. Of course, Alex was home, she didn't do the party scene. I'd bet my right nut that Lucas wouldn't stick around for long, making some lame excuse and casually leaving the party to go over to her house. He never stayed for more than one drink.

*Pussy.*

Time just sort of seemed to fly by at these parties. Before you knew it you were there for hours, drinking and fucking around with everyone.

"So… is it my turn to have a chance with the famous Dylan McGraw?" Chloe purred. At least I thought her name was Chloe. Faces and names seemed to blend together over time for some reason.

"I've been told about you and your skills. When am I going to get a turn to show you mine?" She pouted.

I smiled wide. "Why don't you enlighten me on what you've heard? I do enjoy a good bedtime story," I baited, knowing my words would have an effect on her.

She took a deep breath, trying to play her part. "I'm just saying that I've been told, you're quite the ladies' man, and that you know your way around a girl's…" She raised her eyebrows. "*Heart.*"

I sucked in my lower lip and narrowed my eyes, letting them wander to her hair that was long enough for me to pull nice and hard as I was slamming into her from behind. To her mousy face, down to her perfect tits that would fit in the palm of my hand. She would do just fine for the night.

"I'm going for a walk. Would you like to... come? Because I'd really love to see you come..."

Nothing excited me more than a girl's response to my touch.

She nodded, trying desperately not to seem easy, but failing miserably in her attempt. I leaned forward, my mouth close to her ear.

"Besides everything you've heard," I whispered, pausing while my lips lightly brushed the nook of her neck, my trademark move that drove girls wild, her chest lifted, flushed, but she tried to remain in control.

"I'm also an asshole," I added, kissing the same spot that got their panties wet and their hearts racing, knowing I was getting the reaction I craved.

It worked on every girl.

Except Aubrey.

I extended my arm and she followed suit, linking her fingers with mine. We walked hand-in-hand as I took her down to the secluded part of the beach that I was very much familiar with. But I stopped dead in my tracks when I saw her.

Speak of the devil...

*Aubrey.*

## three

# DYLAN

There was something about the way she was sitting on the sand, looking out at the water with her hair blowing in the light breeze. The sight of her literally took my breath away. That had never happened before, me taking an interest in another human outside of my family and friends, especially some chick I had just met. I'd only had two conversations with this girl, and yet I found myself completely mesmerized by the vision that sat in front of me. As if she appeared out of nowhere.

So consuming.

So blinding.

So real.

She was like a mythical creature that was luring me toward my destruction. In that moment, in that second, there wasn't even a choice to be made. For the first time in my short life I wanted to blow off the opportunity to get my dick wet in favor of just a conversation, and it didn't faze me in the slightest. I found myself gravitating toward her. Before I even registered what was happening, I pulled my arm away from the blonde girl who was ready to spread her legs open for me like so many had before her.

I glanced at her. "Run along, sweetheart."

She jerked her head back, looking in the direction of my stare, realization quickly claiming her face. "You ass—"

"I do believe you were warned, darlin'," I simply stated while walking away from her and towards Aubrey. All the snide comments coming from behind me were trivial.

Wasn't the first time and it sure as hell wouldn't be the last.

As I got closer I realized she was crying. A sense of curiosity piqued my interest, but it wasn't only that. An unfamiliar emotion of wanting to know her reasons and caring to make it better came over me. My feet shuffling in the sand broke her trancelike state, she immediately peered up and over at me, wiping her eyes, camouflaging her distress before recognition settled in.

She scoffed and stood to leave as I gripped her wrist, stopping her, and for some unknown reason, she let me.

"What's wrong?" I questioned, sincerity laced in my tone, surprising us both.

"None of your business, McGraw." Her face frowned. "I saw you come out here with one of your hussies. You should probably head back to seal the deal. I'd hate to be the reason your dick doesn't get wet tonight." Her voice was laced with an equal mixture of anger and sadness.

*Was she jealous?*

Her response stung a bit, but didn't shock me in the least. We were strangers, she barely knew me. She had only heard awful things about me. I couldn't blame her for not wanting to open up. If anything, I was happy that her first instinct was to protect herself from assholes like me. At that moment, all I craved was to break through her icy demeanor and bring down a piece of her wall.

Most of all, I wanted to see her smile.

I wanted her to let me in.

"If you wanted to hang out with me, all you had to do was ask, maybe even throw in a please for good manners, though I am enjoying your stalker tendencies."

She smirked.

"I'll settle for that smile." I paid her no mind and sat in the same spot she just stood from. "You know, I was born and raised in this town. Actually born at Dosher Memorial Hospital in South Port," I disclosed, catching myself off guard. I never opened up to anyone. "This beach holds a lot of fond memories for me. I rode my first wave—" I nodded toward it, "— at that peak point past the breaks when I was six. I got tossed off my board for the first time when I was eight at that same exact spot. I had it coming to me 'cause I was a cocky little shit and had to show off to my boys. Getting caught inside the wash of the wave is like unexpectedly being thrown into a washing machine, not knowing when the cycle would end and let you go. I was scared shitless. I didn't know which way was up and which way was down. I thought I was going to drown. Damn," I chuckled, shaking my head. I never admitted that to anyone.

"The boys were terrified for me, it was written clear across their faces. I still remember opening my eyes and seeing Half-Pint crying for the first time, when the white-wash dragged me back onto the shore."

"Half-Pint?" she asked, finally taking a seat beside me.

"No, suga'." I turned to look at her. "Your turn."

I walked down the beach to be alone.

Finding a spot on some rocks nearby, I sat watching the sunset over the horizon. The sky always made a scenic panoramic view over the water. All the beautiful colors blended together preparing to shift into night. Mother Nature's private work of art. Sitting there listening to the soft lull of the waves dragged me into its calming rhythm, bringing a sense of peace over me.

The ocean was my happy place.

It was one of the things I missed most about being back home. We lived within walking distance from the beach, but here in Oak Island it was a car ride away. It was another reason I couldn't wait to get my license. Watching the waves reminded me of my dad, he was a surfer. That was how my mom met him actually. She used to tell me the best stories of how he tried to impress her and ended up eating shit. Nevertheless, she loved his efforts.

Being lonely was the hardest pill to swallow. I missed California. I missed the house I grew up in and the friends I'd known since childhood. I missed every sight, smell, and sound. I had lived there my entire life.

*Home.*

The familiarity of it all.

The comfort.

Most of all, I missed my aunt and my dad.

In the blink of an eye, nightfall was upon me. The stars that shined bright above, illuminated against the darkness of the sky with the moon smiling high like a Cheshire cat. The ocean breeze brought a slight chill to the air. I hugged my knees to my body in a reassuring gesture, shielding myself to create some warmth around me. I sat there alone thinking about how much my life had changed in such a short time. I didn't even realize I'd started crying, spilling tears over everything, over nothing.

A wave of emotions took over, mimicking the ominous waves in front of me, one right after the other. I looked back toward the party that seemed so far away, but still so near. I caught sight of McGraw parading another one of his conquests. All that came to mind was *man whore*. Rolling my eyes, I looked away from what was about to go down.

Seconds later I heard the shuffling of sand beside me. I immediately locked eyes with him and stood to get away. Wiping away all my tears, he's the last thing I needed right then.

*Except he wasn't.*

He grabbed my wrist to stop me and took a seat where I had once sat, after he made me smile with his relentless flirting. I couldn't have left even if I wanted to.

*And I didn't want to.*

I listened to him describe his childhood with the same sense of longing that I was feeling for my hometown. The sincerity in his tone had caught me off guard, making me feel like I was the only person he had ever shared these memories with. For the first time since we had moved to Oak Island, I didn't feel so alone anymore. It shocked me that it came from the boy I had convinced myself I needed to stay away from.

The irony was not lost on me.

"Half-Pint?" I interrupted, sitting beside him. I wondered if it was the girl from the restaurant I had seen him with the day before.

"No, suga'." He turned to look at me. "Your turn."

I stared into the eyes of the guy who was a walking paradox of contradictions. I was seeing a side to him that he wouldn't show anyone, and I had no idea why...

All I knew was that I liked it.

I wanted more.

I needed more.

Something deep inside told me I could trust him. I was the first to break eye contact, looking back toward the ocean trying to reel in my emotions that seemed to be taking over, contemplating if I was really going to do this. I could still feel his gaze on the side of my face, burning a hole into my skin, and a part of me knew he sensed that.

The effect he had on me.

Taking a deep breath, I opened my mouth and murmured, "I'm lonely," just loud enough for him to hear. My eyebrows rose, surprised with my own revelation. I finally admitted my truth out loud.

"My mom and I moved here from California a few weeks before school started. She packed up the only life I've ever known in one week, and we drove across country in a few days. I didn't really have time to process the severity of the situation. I think I was in a state of shock from the news of our upcoming move that I didn't think of how much my life would change," I paused, needing a second to gather my thoughts and regain the courage for what I was about to say. For what I had never told anyone, not even my closest friends when they asked why we were moving.

"My dad filed for divorce. I wanted to hate him, I tried to hate him, but I couldn't. I felt so helpless not knowing whose side to be on or what I was supposed to do. My world was ripped apart because my dad decided he couldn't do it anymore. Yet, I still love him. I felt like I was in the middle of a storm, not knowing which way was out. I had to choose a side, and in the end, I'm sitting here missing my dad. The same man who ripped my life to shreds, but I can't fault him because my mom worked all the time. He was pretty much a single parent, we were lucky enough to have my Aunt Celeste, who would step in and help as much as possible. It's comical how two sisters can be so different. My mom is a general surgeon. Back home she was the Chief of Medicine and ran the ER unit. She now runs the ER unit at the hospital in South Port. The one you were actually born at," I chuckled, trying to break the tension in the air.

His stare never faltered. He just sat there patiently listening to every word, never interrupting me. I instantly looked down when I felt him gently place his hand on top of mine in the sand. It was a soothing gesture, reassuring. Maybe to show me he cared.

A little part of me…

Soared for the first time in months. A real connection was felt with another human being. With a boy who didn't even know me.

"I'm by myself a lot. More than I should be at my age. My mom works more at the hospital here than she did back in California. Sometimes I think it's easier for her to not look at me. I remind her too much of the man who broke her heart. A part of my father staring her in the face every time she looks at me."

My eyes were still fixated on his hand that never left mine. In the dark, our hands were one, extensions of each other. His rough, calloused fingers were so comfortable resting over mine that I wanted to turn my hand over to feel him. When he reached over and lightly grazed the side of my cheek with his other hand…

*Was I imagining this? Was this happening to me?*

…his fingers moved to tug on the ends of my hair that framed my face. This simple yet meaningful gesture was the first crack on the wall I had built up against him. His knuckles grazed my cheek again, and I nervously licked my lips, peeking up at him through my lashes.

"Shit happens," was all he said.

Nothing overly descriptive, nothing emotional, nothing loving, just, "Shit happens."

"You make life, Aubrey, it doesn't make you."

And in that moment, it was the right thing to say.

It was exactly what I needed to hear.

Never in my wildest dreams did I think it would come from the mouth of the boy I needed to stay away from the most.

# DYLAN

A few weeks had gone by since that night at the beach with Aubrey. Our paths always seemed to cross, but our interactions were nothing like that night. They were flirty with playful jabs at each other.

I thought about her more than I should, which was funny because I had no idea who she was prior to her ripping me a new asshole in the school parking lot. The memory of her confronting me that day caused me to smile every time it crossed my mind.

Which was more than I cared to admit.

"You ready?" Austin asked, walking up to my locker.

I nodded, throwing in my last textbook. Christmas break was officially upon us, two weeks of nothing but surfing and girls.

"Hurry the fuck up. Colleen is waiting for me at Half-Pint's restaurant."

"Colleen?" I asked, shutting my locker. "Who the fuck is Colleen?"

"Is the pot calling me black?" He raised his eyebrow in a challenging manner.

I couldn't help but laugh. "Just looking out for you, brother," I replied.

"I don't need you to look out for me, Dylan. I can look after my damn self."

I put my hands in the air in a surrendering gesture, backing away from him. Austin was barely fifteen and had already made his rounds in and out of our school. Shit, I may be chasing my fair share of tail, but I was always careful. Something told me Austin didn't give a fuck as long as he got his dick wet. The last thing he needed was to knock up some random. He had his whole life ahead of him. I bought him condoms every chance I could, but the older we got, the more he would tell me to mind my own damn business.

"You ready or are you going to keep pussy footin' around?"

"Jesus, hold your shit, I'm almost done."

"Isn't that the girl you're trying to nail?"

"What?" I turned in the direction of his gaze.

Aubrey was leaning against her locker with Kyle, the star quarterback, standing in front of her.

I cracked my neck and cleared my throat, my body suddenly becoming stiff. "Ready."

Austin grinned, shaking his head, knowing exactly what I meant. Aubrey and I locked eyes right before I body-checked Kyle into the lockers as we headed toward the parking lot to leave. Her eyes widened in disbelief, but there was also a hint of amusement behind those pretty green irises of hers.

"What the fuck?" Kyle roared, turning to face me.

I smiled. "Ah, man, I didn't see you there."

He casually nodded, his demeanor drastically shifting from cocky to cowering. "No worries, man." He looked at Aubrey, backing away. "I'll see you around."

*Pussy.*

She slightly smiled, surprised that Kyle left so quickly. Frowning, she peered over at me. "Are you for real?"

I shrugged. "I'm not the one running away with my dick tucked between my legs, now am I? I'm as real as they come, suga'. Wanna touch me? Make sure you're not dreaming?"

She sighed, folding her arms over her chest, making her perky tits stand at attention. I almost didn't notice.

*Almost.*

"No. You're just the one who chased him away."

"Semantics," I contended.

Austin looked back and forth between us with a pleased look on his face that I wanted to knock the fuck off.

"I'd love to continue to stand here and watch this foreplay between y'all, but I have somewhere to be. So do me a favor, either seal the deal or move the fuck on." He smiled. "Please."

She blushed, the crimson red peeking from her nose to her cheeks. I shook my head, ignoring my cock-blocking friend.

"That shade of red looks really good on you," I acknowledged instead in a teasing tone. "Don't mind my friend Austin here. He's not much of a gentleman."

She scoffed. "And you are?"

"Only with you, darlin'."

"You just have a witty come back for everything, don't you?"

"What can I say, pretty girl? You bring out the best in me."

She smiled, a real smile that time, tucking her hair behind her ear. I instantly reached over and pulled it back out to tug on the ends of it, letting my fingertips graze the soft skin on her cheek. She leaned into my touch for a split second before I stepped away.

"I'll see you around," I mocked in a condescending tone, using the same words Kyle did.

Walking away from her...

Even though I didn't want to.

I spent the rest of the day at the beach with the boys and Alex just like any other ordinary day. I was trying like hell to keep my mind from wandering back to Aubrey and that fucking douche bag from earlier today in the hall to no avail.

*It is what it is.*

As usual over Christmas break, the boys and I spent all our time at the beach and Alex's parents' restaurant. Oak Island got cold during the winter, but that year it was surprisingly warmer than normal. The water could get chilly, but as long as you wore a wetsuit you'd be alright.

Surfing, soaking up the sun, and hanging out. Shooting the shit was exactly what I needed.

*Santa wasn't the only one saying, "Ho ho ho."*

I saw Aubrey around here and there, but she was always with that damn chick Dee... at least I think that's what her name was. Apparently, I fucked her over, so I kept my distance. The last thing I needed was some chick getting her panties in a twist and going ape-shit on my ass around Aubrey.

I never saw her with Kyle again, but word around the beach was the new girl in town had gone on a few dates during break.

*Who really dates in high school?*

I couldn't believe guys my age were actually dating. What a bunch of pussies. Aubrey was getting hounded with douche bags because the boys smelled fresh blood. Give me a break, they didn't wanna date her, they wanted to fuck her.

*At least I kept it honest.*

That's when I realized I had a real problem with Aubrey being touched by anyone, including *me*. Call it what you want, jealousy or plain ol' stupidity, I despised it.

*What was I supposed to do about it?*

I kept my distance, listening to what people said about her, watching her from afar, and fighting away any sentiment to actually do something about it.

When a fucker touched her, I bit my tongue.

When she smiled in the direction of a guy that wasn't me, I clenched my fists.

When I heard a douchebag talk about her, I gritted my teeth and walked away.

The urge to be possessive circulated all around me. I was drowning in it. I had become one of those clichés, the guys that I made fun of. I grew a goddamn pussy overnight. I barely knew this girl, and yet I couldn't stop thinking about her.

She was consuming me and she didn't even know it.

Christmas break came to an end all too soon. A new year always meant new class schedules, but I couldn't complain. Aubrey and I shared the same homeroom now, since all grade levels were mixed. I got to spend the first thirty minutes of my day checking her out. It was the best damn half hour of my day. She sat a few desks in front of me. I could watch her every move. The way she twirled her hair when she was deep in thought. Or how she bit her pencil eraser when she didn't think anyone was looking. Her damn clingy clothes that hugged her in all the right places were my undoing.

She was fucking gorgeous. The girl didn't even have to try.

She never truly realized the affect she had on me and that stayed true throughout the years.

*Or maybe she did.*

We never had more than one full conversation with each other. That night at the beach had been the first real conversation I had ever had with any girl besides Alex. As much as I tried to forget about that night…

*I couldn't.*

I've never had a girlfriend, I've never wanted a girlfriend, and all this emotional bullshit with Aubrey was starting to scare the shit out of me. So I did the next best thing I could do, I showed Aubrey the real me. This time I was going to do the right thing. I wouldn't hurt another girl, at least not one that mattered.

I'd rather make her hate me since I couldn't stay away from her.

It was late afternoon. School was done for the day and most of the students had gone home. The teachers were all in their classrooms, grateful the day was over and getting ready for the weekend ahead.

"Is that right?" I taunted close to Bristol's ear, caging her in with my built frame. Her locker was right next to Aubrey's. Maybe I chose Bristol on purpose. Maybe I didn't.

*Who the fuck knows what I was thinking?*

All I knew was that her body pressed up against mine didn't do one thing for me.

Not one twitch from my dick, the fucker wasn't cooperating.

*That* pissed me off more than anything.

I tried harder, deliberately pushing my cock against her muff, her legs pretty much wrapped around mine. I sensed Aubrey the second she walked up behind me. I felt the hole she was burning in my back, searing into the empty space where my heart should be. I continued my little show, taking it a step further. My hands started to roam from her hip up her side, grazing her tit, causing a moan to escape her mouth. Aubrey made her way to her locker. I could still feel her stare now and again while Bristol melted into everything I had to offer, which was no surprise there.

I heard a loud slam and looked to where it came from. Aubrey looked straight into my eyes, going toe to toe. She didn't back down, not that I expected her to. I could read her like an open book, and it didn't make any fucking sense.

The connection that we shared.

We were so young, but none of that mattered. Not when she was looking at me like that. It seemed like she hid her emotions from everyone, except me.

*Why?*

She looked back and forth between us, almost as if she knew what I was doing all along. I thought if she watched me with someone else, if I hurt her, it would make it easier to forget her and move on.

*It didn't.*

It made it harder.

*What the fuck is wrong with me?*

I played the games.

I set the match.

I made the rules.

I wasn't used to feeling out of control. I wasn't used to feeling anything other than my body rubbing up against some random chick and my cock sinking into her welcoming heat. I didn't do emotions, I had them under lock and key but this girl seemed to have the key, causing me havoc.

Bristol giggled, dragging me away from my thoughts to look at her.

"Dylan, you're going to get us in trouble." She rocked her hips, pressing her pussy further against my dick that still refused to react.

All I felt was...

Remorseful.

The entire time I spent chatting with the chick in my arms, I pictured Aubrey's face, and for some fucked-up reason, it made me feel better.

"Hey, where did you go?" she purred in my ear, nudging my neck with her nose.

I cleared my throat, gazing back to Aubrey who was gone. I stepped away from her. The craving for Aubrey became too overwhelming. Filling the hollow space in my heart with bullshit I didn't want or need. I unintentionally followed the subtle sway of Aubrey's hips as she walked passed us again and out to the parking lot. The backpack she had swung over one shoulder looked as if it weighed more than her. She walked fast and with purpose. She obviously needed to get away from me.

"What just happened?" Bristol cooed, trying to wrap her arms around my neck.

I held them back. "Darlin', desperate isn't a good look."

She jerked back, offended.

"I'm done here," I stated.

This was the second time I walked away from a sure thing because of Aubrey. My reactions to her were unfamiliar territory, uncharted emotions were taking over, and I wasn't sure I wanted it to stop. I sure as hell didn't fight too hard to control it, that's for damn sure. This energy took over my entire body when I was around her, and I wanted it to.

I got into my Jeep and started driving, going nowhere in particular or so I told myself until I saw Aubrey walking on the other side of the road.

"Keep driving, McGraw. Keep fucking driving your car, you pussy," I reasoned with myself, casually looking into the rearview mirror.

There was no argument to be made.

The choice was never mine.

"Goddamn it," I yelled out, popping a sharp U-turn. Cars slammed on their brakes, honking their horns and shouting obscenities of where I could go and how to get there. The commotion stopped Aubrey dead in her tracks. She turned around to find out the source of all the chaos.

Not even a second later I pulled up next to her.

"Get in."

# Chapter five

## Aubrey

I hesitantly smiled, debating whether or not to get into his Jeep. I could have kept walking, but the way he was staring at me, with such...

Desperation.

Confusion.

Longing.

Had me questioning my resolve.

*How many times would I have to see him trying to get in another girl's panties before I'd get it through my head that the boy was no good?*

"Get. In," he repeated in a commanding tone. He reached over the console to open the door for me. His open palm extended, beckoning me to take it. I peered from his hand, to the door, back to him again, sighing. Something about his stare made me give in. I threw my backpack in the backseat. My foot hit the running board and my hand landed in his. We pulled in unison, Dylan, helping me with the leap up.

He glanced behind him, accelerating on the throttle. "Put your seatbelt on," was all he said, keeping his intense gaze on the road in front of him, not saying another word. The uncomfortable silence hammered all around me, tearing into my insecurities that this was a bad idea. I shouldn't be in his Jeep. I shouldn't be talking to him. I shouldn't be feeling anything for him other than what I'm supposed to.

What was good for me...

I think he sensed I wanted him to say something.

Anything.

Instead he turned the radio back up. Bill Withers' "Ain't No Sunshine" assaulted my senses, shocking the shit out of me, and clouding any doubt. Before I opened my mouth to call him out on it, he put his finger up to my lips and rasped, "Don't."

We locked eyes for a few seconds, but he quickly broke our connection. I decided to look out the window. It was easier that way, to pretend this little encounter didn't mean something.

*To the both of us.*

I listened to the lyrics of the song, trying like hell not to read too much into it, while he tapped his fingers against the steering wheel to the beat of the music. When you're fifteen you feel everything so passionately, so deeply, it burned all around, leaving behind a wake of ashes that you gathered near your heart.

Making it all that much more real.

Chalk it up to hormones, or maybe it was *me,* desperately wanting to form a connection with anyone. In that moment, sitting beside him with nothing but my thoughts and the lyrics of the song, I felt like he was showing me a piece of who he was. Letting me in the only way he knew how, by exposing a side to him that no one knew about, possibly not even him. Something told me that this gesture was his way of extending the olive branch.

*The question was, would I take it?*

I already knew he didn't have any friends outside of the boys and that girl Half-Pint, but for whatever the reason...

He liked me.

We drove in silence for what seemed like forever, lost in our own thoughts that were shattering with the turmoil on our minds. When he pulled up to my house, I realized that I never told him where I lived.

"Stalk much?" I teased, not being able to help myself as he parked in my driveway.

He visibly took a deep breath as he shut off the Jeep. Wanting no sounds to interrupt what he was about to share with me. It seemed as though he needed to get out whatever he wanted to say before he lost the courage, but he didn't falter. He shifted in his seat to look deep into my eyes, searching for something I couldn't quite put my finger on.

A war was raging in his eyes. He was becoming undone.

An internal battle took place as if what was right and what was wrong had been sitting directly in front of him this whole time.

*Me.*

The serious expression on his face captivated me in a way I had never experienced before. Which only added to the plaguing emotions that were placed in between us.

Then he admitted, "Been thinkin' about you, suga'. Ever think about me?"

Just. Like. That.

So forward.

So direct.

So unforgiving.

I learned right then and there that there was no gray area when it came to Dylan McGraw, only black and white. He got right to the point, it was yes or it was no. Never maybe. Never somewhere in between. The crazy thing about it was I had only gotten to the tip of the iceberg when it came to him, and like the Titanic, I was sinking fast.

So, I shrugged in response because I couldn't say what I was really thinking. What I really wanted to.

*I. Like. You. Too.*

"Go out with me," he followed up with as a statement, sensing my reserve. I didn't know what bothered me more, the fact that he could read my mind, or the fact that I could read his. From everything I heard about him at school, I knew one thing for sure, I was definitely the first girl he ever asked out. He chose me over every other girl.

That simple fact overwhelmed me more than it should.

Shoving away the fluttering feeling his question triggered inside me, I shook my head no. Scared that if I opened my mouth the response would have been different because at the end of the day, I didn't trust him.

He countered, tugging on the ends of my hair, "I won't beg. I also won't ask again, suga'."

For the second time in a matter of minutes, I appreciated his sincerity. "I'll make you a deal," I challenged, throwing his abrasiveness back at him.

He cocked his head to the side, riled by my proposition.

"Keep your dick in your pants for one month and we'll see about a date."

He laughed big and throaty, it echoed all around us. "You gotta be shittin' me? You know who I am?"

"I do." I opened the door to step out, pausing for affect. "But I also know I deserve way more than what you're willing to give me." I got out of the Jeep, grabbing my backpack from the back seat. "Thanks for the ride."

I walked away without looking back. Leaving him with my conditions, silently hoping that he would follow through, but not stupid enough to believe that he would.

# DYLAN

"Hell has officially frozen over ladies and gentlemen!" Lucas hollered from the beach for the rest of the boys and Alex to hear.

"Shut. The. Fuck. Up," I gritted out.

He put his hand up to his ear. "Excuse me? What was that? Can you say that one more time? I don't think I heard you the first time."

Alex tugged on his shirt. "Bo, leave him alone. You're being mean."

"Yeah, Bo," I mocked. "You're being mean," I repeated in a high-pitched voice.

"Oh come on, Half-Pint, this is monumental. A fucking universal standstill, pigs are flying all around us!" Jacob proclaimed, pulling Alex to his side. Austin rolled around in the sand, laughing his ass off.

"You miserable fucks! Enough!" I shouted to all of them, except Alex, hauling her in front of me to block all the remarks from my so-called boys.

"At first I thought you were pulling a fast one on us. Then, I thought you were trying to prove something to Half-Pint, like you're really not an asshole and actually a nice guy. But now... well shit, now, we know it's about a girl," Lucas laughed, testing my goddamn patience.

"And get this, not just any girl but the new girl. The one that no one has gotten their hands on yet. Which could only mean one thing, McGraw, you don't like to share," he added, making me realize that maybe he was right.

*Was that why I liked her?*

"The plot thickens… dun dun dun! Did you not realize that little fact?" Jacob interrupted, baiting me.

Alex met my eyes for a split second before she peered back over to the boys, standing up straighter and putting her hands on her hips. "Enough, you idiots. Why does it matter why he likes her? Bottom line, he likes someone. If you know what's good for y'all, you'll leave him alone," she warned, and I loved her a bit more for it.

"Half-Pint, let's face it, we all know Dylan tames his true colors when you're around. Are you seriously going to deny you're not a little surprised by the fact that the last time he didn't have a girl attached to his hip, was when we were all in grade school?" Austin chimed in. "And even then he was still getting in trouble for kissing girls behind the slide. This was the same guy who brought a Playboy magazine into our third grade classroom and flipped off the teacher when she took it away from him and called his parents."

I decided to live up to Aubrey's challenge, I wanted to spend time with her and what she said struck a cord in me. She did deserve better than what I had to offer. It had been a few weeks since she challenged me, and I had managed to keep it in my pants.

"What's it been now, McGraw, three, four weeks? How's your hand, buddy?" Jacob taunted, mimicking a jacking-off gesture with his fist.

Half-Pint looked down at the sand, kicking it around beneath her, a soft red glow creeping up her cheeks. I glared at the boys who all nodded in recognition. We all respected Alex too much to continue the conversation around her.

I grabbed her hand. "Come on, Half-Pint, let's get away from these dickwads. My virgin ears can't take anymore."

She giggled, following close behind me. We all headed up to her parents' restaurant to grab some food. Just as we walked through the glass sliders, Lucas smacked me in the chest.

"Speak of the devil, isn't that your girl, McGraw?"

There before my very own eyes was…

Aubrey.

With a motherfucking guy.

Of course, the boys busted out laughing and Alex reassuringly squeezed my hand. Aubrey looked over toward our direction and our eyes locked for a brief moment. It took everything inside me to not walk over there and make my presence known. Out of respect for Alex's parents, I restrained myself. They were like my own parents, and they didn't need me causing trouble.

"Let's go sit down. I'm kinda hungry," Alex announced, leading us to the corner table in the back. I knew she did that for my sake. They all ordered some food except for me, my appetite suddenly disappeared. I pulled out my cell phone and sat it on the table.

*Waiting.*

It was all I could do. I had to sit there and endure his unsubtle longing looks. He was devouring her body with his eyes and his constant touches made me want to break his fucking fingers. Our eyes connected several times, it was like she was doing it on purpose, to get a reaction out of me but for what?

I couldn't be around them much longer, I was going to snap. Jealousy washed over me.

I saw her get up, making her way across the room, into the hallway. Before I knew it, my feet were moving forward as if being pulled by twine with the rope she was holding. I found myself following her as she made her way to the restroom. I was grateful it was secluded in the back of the restaurant, because I waited for her.

"You tryin' to make me jealous, sweetheart?"

She gasped, placing her hand over her heart. "Jesus! Are you trying to give me a heart attack?"

I cocked an eyebrow, leaning against the wall with my arms folded over my chest. Her eyes followed my every move.

"No, just trying to make you scream… anyway I can, but you see, I have this wager going with a feisty blonde to keep it in my pants."

She grinned.

"At least one of us has kept up their end of the bargain," I snidely stated.

She shrugged. "I don't remember making a deal that concerned me."

"Is that right?"

"Damn straight."

I nodded, narrowing my eyes at her. "Let me refresh your memory then."

"By all means," she threw back at me.

I scowled. "You sure you have time?"

"What's that supposed to mean?"

I pushed off the wall, walking toward her. "Oh, you know, your date is out there. I wouldn't want to keep him waiting." I tugged on the ends of her hair. "Boy's probably lost without your tits sitting in front of him." Releasing her hair I continued my assault, grazing her collarbone. "God knows he hasn't been staring at anything else."

She shoved my hand away. "You, asshole!"

"Never claimed to be anything but."

"I'm going to go now."

"Ain't no one stopping you, darlin'."

Her eyes widened in shock, making those beautiful emeralds of hers shine bright as they tore into mine. I tugged on the ends of her hair again.

"But if you really wanted to go, you would have already left."

Her chest heaved. I was clearly getting to her.

"What you want and what you're going to get are two different things, suga'." I reached for the side of her face, my knuckles caressed her cheek, tucking a misplaced hair behind her ear. Her lips parted.

"I've been a good ol' boy playing by your rules." I slowly moved my fingers to her mouth. "Watching you these past few weeks is doing me no favors, baby I know you enjoy seeing me getting tortured and sporting blue balls for days. I see the looks you throw my way and the way your pretty little mouth smirks every time you see me shut down another girl." With my thumb I rubbed her bottom lip for a few seconds, she stirred and I immediately took my hand away, slipping it in the pocket of my cargo shorts. Making her miss my touch.

She cleared her throat, shaking her head. "I know," she said out of nowhere.

My eyebrows rose.

"There haven't been any girls crying in the bathroom in weeks."

I chuckled.

"So, I'll bite. Congratulations, McGraw, you do have self-control."

"And…"

"There's more?" she challenged, cocking her head to the side.

"Don't dig, sweetheart, you might not like what you find."

She dramatically sighed. "Go one more week, and I'll give you the benefit of the doubt. I'm still not impressed." She stepped aside. Looking back she informed me, "By the way that's just an old family friend, he's staying with us for a couple of days and he's like my brother. But thanks for your friendly concern."

She left, leaving me with nothing but fucking blue balls for another week.

# Chapter six

## Aubrey

My phone pinged with a new message. Swiping the screen, I didn't recognize the number.

*Tomorrow. I'll pick you up at eight.*

**Aubrey:** *Who is this?*

*Your Prince Charming.*

I laughed, I couldn't help it. This could only be the one asshole I knew.

**Aubrey:** *I'm not having sex with you, McGraw.*

**Dylan:** *Good, no one else has either.*

My entire body shook with laughter as I typed.

**Aubrey:** *You're funny tonight.*

**Dylan:** *I'm also charming.*

I rolled my eyes.

**Aubrey:** *I didn't say yes to a date.*

**Dylan:** *I didn't ask. I'll pick you up at eight.*

I started to type no.

**Dylan:** *Please.*

Of course he knew what I was thinking.

**Aubrey:** *Wow. Dylan McGraw said please. I'm glad I have proof.*

**Dylan:** *Wear something yellow. You look pretty in yellow.*

I grinned at his subtle change in subject.

**Dylan:** *I'll see you tomorrow.*

I took a deep breath.

**Aubrey:** *Don't make me regret this, Dylan.*

**Dylan:** *Duly noted, suga'.*

**Aubrey:** *Night.*

I threw my phone on the nightstand and fell back onto my bed, peering up at the ceiling.

*What the hell did I just get myself into?*

I tossed and turned all night, not getting much sleep. My mind raced with all the *what-ifs*. I woke up early letting my mind win the battle. Needing to clear my head, I decided to go for a run. I use to run all the time in California. It was one of my favorite things to do. I hadn't run once since we moved to Oak Island. My running shoes were still packed at the bottom of a box, along with a few wedding photos of my parents.

They looked so happy and in love.

I woke up one night after my dad had moved out to the sound of crying. I found my mom on the kitchen floor sobbing. She was hugging a book of some sort tight against her chest. The green spine of the book was the perfect background to her white knuckles. I didn't interrupt her private break down, all I did was watch with tears that threatened to spill like hers. Every one of them was because of the pain my father inflicted on her, on us. His decisions not only shattered their marriage.

They destroyed our home.

Our family.

She finally lifted herself off the floor to go into her bedroom, throwing the book in the trash as she walked by. I waited till she was gone before I went to look at what she threw away. It was their wedding album. I looked at every last picture, for some reason touching their faces in each one. When I heard a noise coming from the direction of her room, I impulsively ripped out a few photos and scurried back to my bedroom before she caught me.

I ran faster.

Harder.

And with more determination.

My feet burned through the pavement with each stride and each memory, sweat dripping from every inch of my body. My heart pounded against my chest, echoing through my body and making me feel alive. My head started getting fuzzy with little specs of dots clouding my vision. My vigorous breathing escalated higher and louder. My ears started to ring. I needed to slow down before I passed out, but I couldn't. The adrenaline coursing through my bloodstream had already taken over.

Finally my legs gave out on me, causing me to fall over onto some grass, hyperventilating deeply and profusely. I closed my eyes, riding the wave of euphoria that only running could ever bring me.

*Why did I stop doing this?*

I breathed in and out, my breaths per minute leveling out with each second that passed. I got up on my hands and knees to stretch my neck and back.

"Couldn't wait to see me, huh?"

*Oh no...*

"You didn't have to run all the way here, suga'. Our date's at 8pm not 8am."

I reluctantly opened my eyes. Dylan was sitting on the steps of his patio, hunched over with his elbows resting on his knees.

"Don't flatter yourself, McGraw."

He grinned, devouring me with his eyes. "You cold, suga'?"

I lowered my eyebrows. "What?"

He nodded toward my chest, and I peered down.

*Shit.*

My yellow sports bra was soaked with sweat, making my nipples stand at attention.

"I do love that color on you, baby."

"Shut up. You know if you were a real gentleman you wouldn't have pointed that out. Let's add *pig* to the list of insults, Dylan."

"I can't help it, sweetheart, they're pointing right at me."

I instantly crossed my arms over my exposed chest, blushing.

"Now that red is my second favorite color on you," he rasped, standing up.

I stood up too, looking everywhere but at him, trying to avoid his stare. A bottle of water appeared in front of my face. I mistakenly gazed up, locking eyes with him. I reached out to take the water he was offering. Our fingers lightly brushed longer than I wanted to, but he wouldn't let go of the water.

I scowled, pulling it harder in my direction. His face didn't waver along with his grip.

"Thank you," I appeased, and he immediately let go.

*Asshole.*

He grinned, tugging on the ends of my hair.

"What's with you and the hair pulling?"

He stepped back, engulfing me with his stare again. He turned to walk back up the stairs, completely ignoring me.

"You didn't answer my question!" I shouted

"I'll see you tonight," was all he said.

I walked the entire way home.

Not needing to run away from anything that time.

# DYLAN

I knocked on Aubrey's door at five minutes till eight. Alex said I needed to arrive early to show that I was serious about this date.

"You must be Dylan," an older lady greeted me, opening the door. I assumed it was Aubrey's mom since she looked like an older version of her. They say daughters turned into their mothers and if that's the case, I fucking approved.

I smiled. "Nice to meet you, Mrs. Ow— Ma'am."

*Shit.*

Her parents were divorced, and I had no idea what her mom's maiden name was. She must have noticed my not-so-subtle pause because she instinctively narrowed her eyes at me, tilting her head to the side.

"Aubrey told you—" it was her turn to hesitate. She casually smiled, recovering quickly and shaking her head. "You can call me Jane."

*What was that?*

She stepped aside for me to come into the foyer.

"These are for you." I handed her flowers.

"For me?" She smiled for real that time. I instantly felt at ease.

"Of course, mama's deserve flowers, too. These are for Aubrey." I winked.

"Why thank you so much, Dylan. This is very sweet of you."

"Not a problem, ma'am."

"Ma'am? I told you to call me Jane."

"With all due respect, ma'am, I appreciate that, but that's not how I was raised. I'm justa good ol' country boy. Here in Oak Island, we respect our elders."

I could tell she was impressed with me. Honestly, I wasn't blowing smoke up her ass. I may be an asshole, but I still had manners. My mama did raise me right. She would have my balls if she ever saw me disrespecting an adult.

"Aubrey is almost ready, she should be down any minute. We can wait for her in the living room."

I nodded and followed her lead. I could hear some music playing, but couldn't make out what it was. It had to be coming from Aubrey's room.

Works of art scattered on the pale yellow walls here and there. A flat screen TV was sitting in the middle of the room on top of a modern entertainment center. The couch in front of it looked like one of those sofas that you could sink into and not want to leave. The room was bright and open with a bay window that looked out to their front yard.

Their house had a cozy and inviting feel, similar to mine.

"Would you like something to drink?" she kindly asked.

"No thanks, ma'am, I'm good."

I walked toward their fireplace by their dining room, there were pictures of Aubrey displayed on the mantle and I wanted a peek into her childhood. I found it odd that there weren't any pictures of her and her mom, but there were a ton of her and another lady who looked like she could be related to her mom. I assumed it was the aunt she mentioned the other day. There was only one picture of her and her dad. They were on the beach building a sand castle, looking as happy as could be. I saw the love and devotion in her father's eyes from that picture alone.

If I thought she resembled her mom that was quickly shot to shit seeing what her dad looked like. She was the spitting image of him, which reminded me of what she shared that night on the beach when she told me she thought her mom worked so much because it hurt to look at her.

*Aubrey might be right about that one.*

"She was a very beautiful little girl," she spoke in past tense, pulling me from the memories of that night.

"She still is," I honestly spoke, turning to face her.

She affectionately nodded, glancing at the picture of them that was prominently placed behind me, with a sense of longing in her eyes. It was quick but I saw it.

"Why don't you make yourself at home, have a seat."

I walked over to the loveseat positioned in front of the window and sat down.

"How are you liking Oak Island? Seems like you've settled in well," I stated, looking around the furnished room.

"I wish I could take the credit, but I'm afraid Aubrey is responsible for all this." She gestured with her hand towards the open space.

I nodded in understanding. Aubrey was the one that put the picture of her dad on the mantle, along with all the pictures of a woman that *wasn't* her mother.

"I'm happy to finally meet one of Aubrey's friends," she breathed out. "She said you guys share a homeroom. You're a sophomore, right?"

"That's right."

"She didn't tell me how you guys met, though. I'm assuming at school?"

I nodded in response.

"Aubrey says track season doesn't start until spring. Do you run track as well?"

"No. I surf."

As soon as the words left my mouth I regretted them. Her face frowned. Something I said resonated deeply inside her. It pained me to see such hurt in her eyes. I couldn't help but want to make her feel better. I felt connected to her in a way I couldn't explain or even understand for that matter. Maybe it was because she was Aubrey's mom.

"I can't wait to watch Aubrey run track in the spring. I got a glimpse of her this morning. She's fast. I'm sure she will win all sorts of awards. Our track team actually went to nationals last year," I rambled, changing the subject.

She nodded, knowing what I was doing but appreciating it nonetheless. "Aubrey must love that you surf. She used to go with her dad back home. She's actually pretty good at it. Her dad had her on a board by the time she was five. He had her in the water before she could even crawl, she loves the beach."

It was plain as day to see. This woman was still very much in love with her ex-husband. The mere mention of surfing had shaken her to the core.

"Good to know. I'll have to take her surfing sometime. Maybe you'd like to come and watch?"

"That would be great," she stirred with her face lighting up.

"Have you been able to head out to the beach? Oak Island is known for its beaches. We get tons of tourists during the summer, it's the only time of year that you will see the beach packed with people from all over the world. The rest of the time it's just us locals. Maybe I could show you and Aubrey around town sometime? I bet she'd love that... to get to spend time with you and all," I pressed.

There was no way in hell that her mama didn't want to spend time with her. I could tell by the way her face lit up every time she talked about her. But there was also remorse on her face and traces of guilt in her voice. If there was anything I could do to make it better, I would.

Sometimes people needed to see the light before they could get out of the darkness.

"That would be lovely, Dylan. I might have to take you up on that offer."

"Not a problem, ma'am. I'd be honored, two pretty girls on my arm... can't ask for a better day."

She smiled. "I'm glad Aubrey has a friend like you here. Are you sure I can't get you something to drink? I need to get ready for work, but I'm so glad I got to meet you," she repeated with the same enthusiasm as the first time.

"I'm—"

"Hey," Aubrey announced, stepping into the room, surprised. "Mom! I didn't think you were still here. I thought you had to go to work?"

"I do." She looked down at her watch. "I'm actually going to be late. I just wanted to meet one of your friends."

Aubrey nervously looked over at me, and I arched an eyebrow. "You look beautiful, *friend.*" I grinned, taking in her yellow dress that I knew she wore for me.

They both smiled at me, but when they turned back to face each other I could sense the tension between them, and it killed me to see Aubrey struggling with her emotions.

Especially since she never did that with me.

Although, I was sad for them, I was happy that I got to see the vulnerability between them. I got a deeper look into Aubrey's life, learning something new.

"Well, you kids have fun. Aubrey, please try to be home by eleven, okay? I'll be home early in the morning to make you some breakfast," she said with a strain in her voice.

She nodded as her mom leaned into her ear to whisper, "I like him," I overheard her say as Aubrey locked eyes with me.

"It was nice to meet you, Dylan. Maybe next time we could plan that day?"

"You can count on it," I declared, my stare still fixated with Aubrey's.

Her mom excused herself to go get ready for her shift, leaving Aubrey and me alone in the living room.

"Are you ready to head out?" I asked, cocking my head towards the front door. She nodded in response, a little taken back with what her mom said to me before she left the room.

"Lead the way, suga'."

A smile spread across her pretty face when she realized there were flowers in my lap.

"Are those for me?"

"No, I don't buy my *friends* flowers," I replied with a smart-ass grin.

She took the flowers out of my hands and said, "Thank you." Not bothering to acknowledge my retort.

After she put the flowers in water I grabbed her hand, helping her down the stairway as we left the house.

"Hey, I'm really sorry about my mom, I didn't think she would be here. What was she talking about back there? What day?"

My fingers brushed hers when I reached to open her door, purposely trying to be a gentleman. Another one of Alex's quirky little tips. The smirk on her lips told me she knew what I was up to. She didn't comment on it, but I was hoping my efforts were going to be appreciated. I closed her door with the same affectionate smile she'd given me.

I jumped in the driver's seat and cranked the engine, thinking about what she had asked. She flinched when I swiftly moved my arm over to her and grabbed her chin. I watched her lips part and her tongue moisten them, expecting a kiss that she didn't get. She got a delayed reaction to the question she'd made with great conviction.

"Your mama loves you."

Her eyes widened, she wasn't expecting me to say that.

"But just so we are clear, suga', this is a date and we are not friends."

She also wasn't expecting me to say that.

# seven

# Aubrey

"Why are we at the marina?" I asked, shutting my door.

He waited for me by the hitch of his Jeep, extending out his hand when I got close to him. I cocked my head to the side, raising an eyebrow not budging until he answered my question.

"To find a fucking mermaid, let's go," he snapped with a straight face.

I tried to keep my amused expression to myself as he tugged me toward him. We walked hand-in-hand down the dock, strolling past one boat after another. When we reached the end of the boat slip he stepped over the railing onto a sailboat that had a blanket spread out on the bow. I was careful to step over the riggings as he led us to the front.

"Wow," was all I could manage to say as I slowly turned in a circle, taking in my surroundings.

The sun had just set and every star shined bright above the water. I took in the blanket and picnic basket that were perfectly placed in the center of the bow.

"Do you bring every girl here? No wonder you get laid as much as you do," I chuckled to no avail, taking in his stern expression.

"Let's get one thing straight."

He placed his finger under my chin to get me to look up at him. I peeked through my lashes, anxiously waiting for what he was going to say next.

"I've never brought a girl here before."

I shyly smiled, his words warming my heart. Making me feel like shit for what I said before.

"Now, that boat right over there." He jerked his neck behind me, and I turned to see.

"I usually use that one," he added with a neutral tone.

I gasped with my mouth wide open. "You asshole!"

He laughed, big and throaty.

"Oh my God! You actually had me going! You're such a dick, McGraw!"

He laughed harder, his head falling back. It shook the entire boat. "I never smile unless I mean it," he confessed out of nowhere.

I lowered my eyebrows, confused by the turn of events. I instinctively peered down at the makeshift picnic he had made for us…

*For me.*

"As a matter of fact, I don't do anything unless I fucking want to. I don't care who you are," he said with a thick Southern accent, running his hand through his long hair. I noticed his twang came out more when he really meant something. When he was passionate or determined to get out what he needed to say.

I licked my lips, carefully listening to everything he was sharing. My heart fluttering faster with each word that left his mouth.

"Since I met you, I smile a lot, and I find myself doing all sorts of shit I never have before."

"How do you do that?"

He knowingly arched an eyebrow.

"How can you make me so mad, and then make it go away as if it was never there in the first place?"

"It's a curse, darlin', I have that effect on girls."

I shook my head, smiling.

"What's your favorite color?"

"Pink," I replied, confused. He seemed to be full of surprises.

"Food?"

"Chicken wings and pizza. Where is this going?"

"Movie?" he followed, ignoring my question.

"Boondock Saints."

He grinned, surprised with my answer.

"I love an asshole hero," I sincerely stated.

He smiled big and wide, knowing I meant that in more ways than one.

"Best childhood memory?"

I frowned but quickly recovered, simply stating, "Surfing."

"Last question, what's your biggest weakness? What do you hate?"

"That's easy. I hate being tickled. I cannot freaking stand it."

"You mean like this?"

It all happened so fast I never saw it coming. His arms wrapped around me before I got the last word out, locking me in place against his hard, firm chest.

I gasped. "Dylan…" I warned. "Let go! I don't want to play with you anymore," I argued, pathetically fighting his hold.

The boat wobbled more, adding to my weak attempts of breaking away from his tight grasp. The water smacking hard against the sea wall, mimicking what I wanted to do to him at that second.

"Oh really, where are you the most ticklish? Here?"

I started squealing, struggling, and hysterically laughing. My body violently shook as he tickled me everywhere. Finding my sweet spot almost immediately, right under my ribs. I shuddered, falling to the ground with him pretty much on top of me. Except he didn't stop, if anything it gave him more leverage to do what he wanted…

*To torture me.*

"Stop!" I screeched out, squirming and kicking every which way.

"Suga', now's not the time to pretend like you don't like my hands on you."

"McGraw! I mean—"

"You mean what, suga'?" he taunted, stopping his assault with his face mere inches from mine.

"Tell me, what do you mean?" he baited, inching his face closer.

I have never wanted someone to kiss me more than I did right then and there.

I watched the way his lips moved.

I watched the way his hair blew in the wind, framing my face.

I watched the way his chest heaved up and down, mirroring mine as if they were in sync with one another.

I especially watched the way he looked at me. No one had ever looked at me like that. I wanted to engrain it in my memory. To take a piece of him home with me.

When he brushed the hair away from my face he didn't say a word. His eyes spoke for him.

The way he affected my mind and my heart was petrifying, but it was so real.

The emotion…

I could touch it.

I could feel it.

I could taste it.

It surrounded me. It undid me.

"You're trouble, McGraw. You're so much fucking trouble," I murmured, loud enough for him to hear.

"Baby," he huskily groaned, placing his forehead on mine. "You have no fucking idea."

He wanted to kiss me.

By the look on his face, he knew I wanted it, too. But what he did next surprised me more than anything.

He sat up.

Breaking the strong connection that held both of us captive for just a few minutes. I cleared my throat, sitting up with him. Pretending like I wasn't hurt by his rejection.

"You hungry?" he asked, walking over to the picnic basket, breaking the thick air between us.

I nodded, not being able to find my voice. He handed me a sandwich before he headed over to the edge of the boat, sitting with his feet dangling in the water.

I watched him from afar without him noticing, which was odd because he seemed to notice everything.

An old blues beat unexpectedly filled the silence. The first few lyrics described a man that was running, hiding, and then running and hiding again, not knowing what the girl wanted him to do. I couldn't help but laugh and smile.

I smiled so wide that it hurt my face.

He was trying to tell me something again. Letting the music express what he couldn't say himself.

I paid attention to every word as the enticing beat rocked through me, and I felt the need to be close to him. Closer than I already was, and I meant that in more ways than one. I took off my sandals and scooted to the edge of the boat where Dylan sat, letting my feet sway to the music in the warm ocean water.

His fingers strummed to the beat of the music on the side of the boat, and I placed my hand close to his.

"You like blues, huh?" I questioned, pulling him away from his thoughts.

He nodded, glancing at the side of my face. It didn't take long for his hand to find mine, and he lazily drew circles to the rhythm of the music. Shivers coursed through me even though there wasn't a chill in the air.

"Who is this?" I asked out of curiosity. I really liked the man's voice. It did something to me.

"Jimmy Reed. Do you like it?"

"Very much so. What's the name of the song?"

He looked back out at the water, hesitating to answer my question, like he was contemplating if he was going to tell me or not.

When all of a sudden he turned and leaned forward close to my ear, whispering,

"Baby, What You Want Me to Do."

# DYLAN

She grinned and it lit up her entire face.

It lit up the entire boat.

I sat back up, gazing out over the water once again. "I love blues music. I have ever since I was a kid. I guess you could blame it on my dad who was constantly playing it as I was growing up. I can't tell you how many times I've walked in on my parents slow dancing to it. It's the only music you can feel in your blood, it vibrates and bleeds into your body. You can appreciate the pain in every lyric like they're telling you a story about a significant time in their lives. Whether it was good or bad, it didn't matter. It happened."

Her toes skimmed mine in the water.

"Your parents are still married then?"

"Happily."

I took her hand and placed it on my lap.

"Is your dad an asshole like you?" She smiled, nudging my shoulder.

"I'm one of a kind, darlin'."

Leaning forward, she swished her feet back and forth with the current.

"Ain't that right," she giggled, and it was the sweetest sound I ever heard.

"Are you close to your parents?"

"As much as any son can be close to their parents at sixteen," I chuckled, tangling my foot with hers.

"Do they know about all your extra-curricular activities?" She peered over to me with laughter in her eyes.

"What is this, twenty questions?" I teased.

"Oh, McGraw, you can get your questions in, but I can't?"

"I wasn't after the questions, suga'. Back to your question though, who do you think handed me my first condom?"

She raised her eyebrows, surprised. Her cheeks turned a soft red.

"I also love classic rock. Throw in a little country, too," I said to change the subject. I didn't want to talk about myself anymore. I already knew about this fucker, I wanted to know about her.

*Just her.*

She scoffed. "You're just a good ol' boy, aren't you, Dylan McGraw?" she baited.

"You are a pretty thing, aren't you?" I tugged on the ends of her hair, ignoring her question.

She blushed again.

"That red is surely becoming one of my favorite colors, suga'."

"You can be quite charming when you want to."

"Nah, you just caught me on a good night."

She snuggled into my shoulder, inching closer to me. We sat in comfortable silence with our feet rubbing together every few seconds in the water. I could have stayed in that moment with her forever.

It was perfect.

With the music, the boat rocking softly, and the moon shining bright above us, something came over me. I stood, pulling her up with me. I took one of her hands and placed it on my shoulder then intertwined the other in mine, placing it near my heart. I grabbed her waist with my free hand and hugged her close. Her face conveyed so many emotions in a matter of seconds, and I paid attention to every last one.

We swayed to the music as I hummed the melody. She placed the side of her face on my chest and I knew what she was trying to do, but it didn't matter because I already felt everything she was trying to hide.

"You want to know something, McGraw?" she whispered in my ear.

"I want to know everything, suga'."

She wasn't caught off guard with my statement, and quite frankly, neither was I.

"I'm not so lonely when you're around," she chuckled.

There was nothing funny about her statement. Not even a little bit. I looked down at her, and she stared up at me. She had this pained look on her face, and I wondered if I wore the same expression as we continued to move.

"My mom likes you. Don't let it go to your head or anything though. She's hardly met any of my friends. Even back home in California. She's my mom and I love her, but my Aunt Celeste filled her shoes for most of my life."

That explained the mystery woman in the pictures, I thought to myself.

"She's my mom's sister, she couldn't have kids. I don't know if it was intentional or not, but she kinda raised me as her own. Doing the things my mom should have done. I miss her as much as I miss my dad," she muttered.

I unexpectedly spun her around, dipping her, catching her off guard with my nose practically skimming hers. I wanted to ease her sadness so I said,

"Life is simple, darlin', it's just not easy."

# eight

# DYLAN

It had been one month.

One month of *dating* Aubrey.

Three months since I met her.

Over two months of no sex.

I held her hand, I tugged on her hair, I kissed her face, and I listened to everything that came out of her mouth as if she was telling me the world's biggest secrets. I hadn't kissed her. I hadn't even tried to kiss her. Being around her was enough for me. To be able to be with someone, to really be with them on a level other than physical, was something I had never experienced before. Something I had never had.

I was officially pussy-whipped and sporting the worst case of blue balls known to fucking man.

I didn't understand any of it, the need to be around this girl was throwing me off-kilter. Every waking moment I thought about this girl. The next time I would see her, talk to her, hold her…

The list was endless.

Our connection was flawless and fluid, we didn't have to work at it. It wasn't a burden or a struggle to be with her like it was with the others. I used to get bored the minute the sex stopped, fucked 'em and dumped 'em, moving onto the next. Not with Aubrey though, everything with her was easy. It flowed seamlessly, the conversations, the chemistry, and the *friendship*. The subtle looks she would give me when she didn't think I was looking.

She was perfect.

She came into my life like a riptide, taking down everything in her path and dragging me right along with her. I couldn't remember the last time I came up for air, took a second to breathe, a moment to catch my bearings and try to fight against her pull. Her current was strong and growing every time I was with her. I was lost in the waves of everything she had to offer. I never expected to fall for her. I wasn't even looking for anyone, but there she was, this girl with such a force, such a drive. It was so fucking powerful that I never stood a chance.

There was no push and pull.

*At least not yet...*

Every single time I told myself that today was going to be the day. The day that I would make my move, the day I would kiss her, the day I would touch her, the day I would move on from this PG-13 bullshit or whatever the hell it was that was going on with us. That I would show her who I truly was, what I could truly offer her, what I gave to so many other girls...

I couldn't do it.

Just. Like. That.

Dylan-fucking-McGraw couldn't seal the deal.

No room for maybe's or possibly yes, it was a dead no, and I had never been happier. I looked forward to our next conversation, the next time I would get to see her smile, or make her laugh, but I still loved making her mad, pissing her off and seeing that feisty temper come out as much as possible, so I hadn't become a complete fucking pussy.

I kept going back to her, wanting more.

Wanting everything.

Nothing or no one stood in my way.

I'd like to see them fucking try.

I started to bring her around the boys and Alex a few weeks ago. Alex loved her right away. They got along like two peas in a pod. The boys welcomed her into our circle with open arms, but that didn't stop them from giving me shit.

We had just finished surfing. It was pouring every afternoon for the last few days and a mean swell would kick up before the storm.

"My aunt's going to be calling soon, and I forgot my cell phone back at my house. I gotta get going," Aubrey said, walking up to me with Alex close by her side.

I stuck my board in the sand and shook out my hair.

"McGraw!" Aubrey squealed, blocking the water with Half-Pint giggling.

I grinned, tugging on the ends of her hair. "Don't pretend like you don't like me gettin' you wet."

She chuckled, "You're such a dick."

"I'll take you home." I looked at Alex. "Make sure Lucas doesn't go back out there once the storm hits. I see it in his eyes, he's thinkin' about it."

She rolled her eyes. "Of course he is."

"Come on." I grabbed her hand and led her up to the restaurant, placing my board in Half-Pint's parents' backroom.

We'd been leaving our boards in there since we were kids, it was easier than lugging them around everywhere. I think our families appreciated that we still surfed near the restaurant just in case. Surfing was like freefalling with no parachute, you respected Mother Nature because she could kill you if you didn't.

I opened the door for Aubrey to get in, shutting it, and walking to the driver's side. I grabbed my cargo shorts from the backseat and opened my door, depriving the bystanders from my naked glory while changing. I didn't give two shits if Aubrey could see. To be honest, I wanted her to. I watched Aubrey from the corner of my eyes, while she watched me from the corner of hers.

"You can look, sweetheart, he's not shy."

She turned beet red, making me laugh.

It didn't take us long to get to her house, she lived a few blocks from the beach.

"Can I use your bathroom?"

"Sure."

I followed her inside, taking in the way her hips swayed as she walked.

*Damn, I loved her ass.*

"Down the hall, first door on the left." She pointed. "Can I get you anything? Sweet tea?"

"Nah, I'm good, thanks, darlin'. I'll be right back."

I made my way down the hall to the bathroom. I took care of business and walked back out to the living room where she was sitting on the couch with her legs tucked underneath her.

*She was so damn beautiful.*

"Do you want to watch a movie? My aunt's going to call in a bit, but we could watch one after if you want to stay."

"We're alone?" I blurted out, surprising myself.

She peered around the room, confused, and I felt like a fucking idiot.

"Um, yeah. My mom's working like always." She smirked, with a twinkle in her eyes that I recognized all too well.

I didn't even have to give it any thought. There were zero fucks given.

"Maybe some other time."

"Oh..." she breathed out, scratching her head. "You got somewhere to be or something?"

"Or somethin'." Avoiding eye contact so she couldn't see right through my bullshit.

"Right. Okay. I guess I'll see you around then," she nervously stated.

"I'll call you later." I tried to reassure her, walking to the front door like the pussy I had suddenly become, not bothering to look back at her hurt face.

"Dylan."

I stopped dead in my tracks, knowing exactly what she was going to ask. I turned around to face her, still giving her a questioning look. No matter what she had to say I wasn't going to do a damn thing about it. That much I knew. She was standing by the archway, looking gorgeous as ever, her vulnerability radiating all around her that I suddenly found it hard to breathe.

"We've been hanging, you know... for like a month or something," she muttered. "I mean... do you... I mean... you know..."

"Just fucking say it, Aubrey," I interrupted, harsher than I intended.

She took a deep breath, slightly annoyed with the tone I dealt back, but the doubt was too big for her to swallow.

"Do you not like me?"

I wasn't surprised in the least by what she wanted to know. She knew who I was, my reputation with girls. I'd become my worst damn nightmare overnight. I opened my mouth to say something, but for the first time in my life I didn't know what to say.

"It's okay if you don't like me and just want to be friends. I could use more of those. I really like Half-Pint and your boys. Everyone has been really nice with welcoming me. I would hate to lose that if you don't like me more than… a friend. I mean, I know I'm not like the girls you're used to and I guess… that would be hard to let go of and stuff…"

I let her ramble, mainly because she seemed like she really needed to get it out. A part of me, the asshole part of me, thought she looked so fucking adorable being all exposed and shit, that I let her continue with her little monologue. If this was any other girl something like   this would have had me running for the door and slamming it in her face, but not with her, she was different.

*Never with her.*

"Darlin," I rasped all too soon, not ready for what I was going to confess. "I'm only leaving because I do like you."

"What—"

With that I opened the door and left.

I drove around for I don't know how long, listening to "The Thrill is Gone" by B.B. King on repeat. Etching the lyrics and beat into my mind as if I were the one singing them. It was dark by the time I made it back to the restaurant. I sat on the beach instead of going in to face the boys and their ridicule. The storm had come and gone, but the wind remained. I welcomed the cool breeze coming off the ocean. The sand was wet and hard beneath me, but I didn't pay it any mind, there was too much on my mind to care.

"Hey," Alex greeted, sitting beside me. She put a blanket around the both of us. "You're going to get sick if you sit out here. By the look of the clouds, it's going to rain again any second."

"A little rain ain't ever hurt nobody."

I continued to stare out into the night as she glanced at the side of my face.

"What's wrong?"

"Nothin' to worry your pint-size head about."

She fell quiet for a few minutes, leaning against my arm with her head on my shoulder.

"You remember that time you boys finally let me up into the tree house? When I found your stash of nudie magazines?" She blushed, saying the last part.

I chuckled, "Yeah."

"The first time I saw Aubrey I thought she looked like one of those girls. I thought she was going to be a complete spoiled brat from California, or she was going to be dumb as rocks... you know, your usual type," she teased, breaking a smile. "She wasn't though. I liked her immediately. She was so sweet and down to earth. I've known you my entire life, I've never seen you look at anyone the way you look at her, Dylan."

I peered over at her for the first time, taking in everything she was saying.

"Your face lights up like in one of those movies you always make fun of. I like seeing you with someone who actually likes you too. Those other girls, they're just using you. You're as much of a game to them as they are to you. You do know that, right?" she questioned, her tone laced with determination.

I slightly nodded, my face suddenly serious.

"It's okay to get to know someone before you sleep with them, Dylan."

"What the fuck do you know about sleeping with someone, Half-Pint?" I roared, jerking back surprised.

"Nope. Not a chance. You do not get to flip this around on me. I know who you are. I know who all of you are. Let's not pretend, okay? Not now. Out of all the boys, you have always been the one to hide yourself from me. I haven't let it bother me. Do you know why? 'Cause you love me. You love me enough to respect me."

I pulled my hair away from my face, holding it back on the nook of my neck in a frustrated gesture.

"You respect her, too."

We locked eyes.

"You respect her enough to not kiss her. To not touch her... to not do any of the things that make up who you think you are, Dylan McGraw. You may be crass and blunt, not caring about hurting other people's feelings, but you're still a good guy. We all know that, especially me."

"How did you—"

"She told me."

"What?" I narrowed my eyes at her with an intense stare. "She told you what?"

"She told me what I already knew. What I've always known. You do have a heart, but I'll still pretend like you don't already know that."

I shook my head, letting a heavy breath escape. Finally admitting out loud and to myself, "I don't want to hurt her. She's been hurt enough but I also can't stay away from her, Half-Pint. So I guess I'll take her anyway I can."

She stood up, hovering above me.

"Why don't you let Aubrey decide that?" She reached for me.

"What if you're wrong, Half-Pint? What if you're wrong about me?"

She squatted in front of me, placing her hands on the sides of my face and spoke with conviction,

"I'm not."

# Aubrey

"I'm sorry, honey, I got stuck in a meeting. I know I was supposed to call you hours ago. How are you? How's everything?" my Aunt Celeste asked when I answered her call.

"No worries. I'm fine. How are you?" I asked, trying to divert her attention away from my lie.

"Girl, don't even try to pull that one on me. I know you better than that. What's wrong? What happened? Who do I need to come beat up? Is it your mom? Honey, you know—"

"It's not my mom," I interrupted.

Getting off the couch, I muted the TV and began to pace the living room. I knew this was going to be a long conversation.

"Oh… it's about a boy," she stated with understanding.

I shook my head even though she couldn't see me. "How do you know that?"

"Oh, honey, psssh, in life it's either our moms or it's our men. Now, come on, tell your favorite aunt what's going on?"

"I wish I knew," I grumbled, walking in the kitchen to grab a soda out of the fridge.

"Start from the beginning."

I took a deep breath. "He's an asshole," I laughed.

"Oh, honey, they all are. That's part of the appeal. Better for you to find that out sooner rather than later, when it hurts more. Now, keep going."

"No, I mean like a real *asshole*, Aunt Celeste. He uses girls, sleeps around with everyone, and make's no excuses for it. He's blunt, rude, crude, and cocky as shit."

"You just described my last few boyfriends. Any relation?"

We laughed. I knew she was trying to make me smile. I hopped up onto the counter, took a sip from my soda, and continued to describe Dylan.

"But he's also deep in a weird, mysterious way. There's so much more to him than what he lets people see. He says everything I need to hear in a few words. He's honest, caring, and he doesn't sugarcoat shit. He says what he needs to say. He's the most real person I have ever met."

"Then what's the problem, honey?" she questioned, not understanding the issue at hand.

"I don't think he likes me."

"What do you mean? What's not to like?"

"We've been hanging out for a month and nothing has happened. He holds my hand, opens my door, and kisses my forehead. He talks to me all the time, whether it's at school, over the phone, or texting. Aunt Celeste, I think I'm in the friend-zone now or something," I confessed.

"First off, since this isn't about me, I'm going to let go of the fact that you've been hanging out with this boy for the last month, and I'm just now hearing about it. We will come back to that later."

I chuckled. She always knew the right things to say to me, to get me to laugh and make me feel better.

"Honey, he definitely likes you plain and simple, no doubt about it."

"Then why hasn't he tried anything? He sleeps with anything that has a pulse, but he hasn't even kissed me. He hasn't even tried to. He has to know by now that I want him to!" I exclaimed, getting worked up over the whole situation again, like I did when he left. "He's sending mixed signals, and I called him out on it. All he had to say was and I quote, 'I'm leaving because I do like you.' What the hell does that even mean? He wouldn't even let me ask before he turned and left."

"Your house?"

"Yes."

"Your mom's working?"

"You know she is. She's always working."

"Oh, honey, he is a keeper."

"What?" I asked, utterly confused and surprised with her response.

"Long story short… he can't keep his junk in his pants. Never has, am I right? He respects you enough to not tempt himself to not keep his junk in his pants. Understand?"

"That makes no sense," I simply stated.

"That's because you're seeing it like a hormonal teenager. Take a step back. You're different, honey. He knows that."

"Oh…"

"There's your crash course into a man's psyche. You're welcome!" she laughed. "Look, honey, I have to go. We're on deadline with this marketing campaign, and my boss is riding my ass. I'll be in meetings all night, so I'll call you tomorrow. I'll come to visit as soon as this merger is over in the next few weeks."

"Okay. I love you. Thanks for listening."

"I'm always here. No matter what, you know that. I love you, too. Tell your mom I said hello. Talk soon."

"Bye."

I hung up, and not even a second later the doorbell rang. I didn't even have time to contemplate or take in what my Aunt Celeste alleged. I looked down at the time on my phone and it read almost ten pm. I hopped off the counter and made my way to the door.

"Who is it?" I called out.

"Your Prince-fucking-Charming."

I chuckled with a confused expression on my face. Opening the door, I said, "Did you forget—"

The air was immediately knocked out of me from the impact of Dylan's lips on mine. He didn't falter, he parted his lips, beckoning me to follow and I did. His hands were on the sides of my face, pushing me back until I felt the stairs. My body fell back on them with Dylan's falling on top of mine.

He wanted me.

He needed me.

He consumed me.

It was the scariest but most liberating feeling I had ever felt. Like I was standing at the edge of a cliff, looking down, ready to jump. Not caring if there would be land or water beneath me.

I was ready to take the plunge.

With him.

My mind was scrambled with thoughts and emotions I couldn't control, label, or even understand. It was one giant cluster-fuck of weeks of wanting to feel his lips on mine. I put my arms around his neck as he pushed me further into the steps, kissing me deeper, harder, and with more determination. I had never been kissed like that before. The passion radiated off of him. I didn't even know kisses like that existed outside of the movies.

Something told me he didn't either.

My chest rose and fell faster and faster with every slip of his tongue in my mouth. With each deep breath I took, with each caress of his fingers along my face, with each groan that escaped his mouth, with each heartbeat I felt against mine, with each… with each… with each…

I felt *his* a little bit more.

I wasn't imagining it. He matched every beat, every moment, every feeling and emotion times ten. I was putty in his hands. He could mold me, build me, and roll me however he wanted.

In that moment, I would let him.

He suddenly lifted me off the stairs and carried me through the archway to the living room, gently laying me on the couch. His body hovered over mine, our lips never leaving one another's. They continued to move together as if they were meant for each other.

It was unreal, but so fucking real…

He kissed me one last time, letting his lips linger for just a few seconds on top of mine. I instantly felt the loss when he set his forehead on mine. I could barely hear our heavy panting over our escalated hearts and minds.

They took over.

His hair framed my face again like it did on the boat. I knew right then and there that it was going to be my favorite thing ever. Feeling as if we were in our own little world, surrounded by nothing but our feelings for each other.

Where nothing else mattered.

No one.

He pushed the hair away from my face, and I desperately wanted to return the favor, but I didn't. I wanted to stay lost in his eyes in that moment, savor the way he was looking at me, the way he felt on top of me, the way he pulled every sentiment from my body as if it belonged to him.

I never wanted it to end.

With his hands framed around my face, he kissed me again, slower, more delicate this time, less frantic and desperate, but with the same intensity and passion. When he pulled away, I whimpered as he let out a loud, massive groan, feeling his absence. I felt like I was going to scream, my mind already shouting on the inside, over and over again. It echoed through the walls, making its way into our hearts where we would forever remember this moment.

He took one last look into my eyes and leaned in toward my ear.

"You're going to undo me," he huskily whispered, rubbing his lips below my earlobe, causing tingles everywhere.

"And I'm going to let you."

# nine

# Aubrey

A few months had passed and spring was finally here.

Dylan and I were officially dating, spending every second we could with each other. We seemed to learn something new about one another with each passing day. It was interesting to peel back the different layers that made Dylan McGraw.

What made him happy, what made him smile, what made him laugh.

My personal favorite…

What pissed him off, which was pretty much everything. The boy had the temper of a two year old, making it known what he liked, what he tolerated, and what would make him flip the fuck out.

*Alex* was his Achilles heel, and I felt bad for whomever that girl fell in love with because those boys were going to tear him a new asshole. Never thinking it was *one* of their own.

*The boys* were more like brothers than friends. I had never seen a bond like that before. A brotherhood. They were all extensions of one another, and I often felt like I was dating a bit of all of them with the way they acted when they were all together.

*His parents* were his relationship role models, and I realized that on our first date when we danced under the stars on his parents' sailboat. Moments after he shared how he watched them from afar, dancing to the same blues beat that surrounded us that night.

Then there was *me*…

McGraw was like Jekyll and Hyde. Acting one way when it was just us and another when people were around. It didn't matter who it was. That icy prick demeanor immediately lifted around him as if he was the gasoline that lit his own flame. But when we were alone, he was very charming. He loved to cuddle with me and have his hair played with or his back scratched. Pretty much anything that involved my hands on him, he loved. He was extremely bright, knew all sorts of random facts about anything and everything. He enjoyed watching the news, Discovery or History channel, saying it was good to know what was going on in the world, to be prepared. He hated the unexpected.

He had to be in control.

His dad taught him how to use a gun for the first time when he was five. He told him he would rather Dylan know what it was and the power it had, than to be a curious little boy and hurt himself. It wasn't a toy. It was protection. Dylan could shoot within the bull's eye at a hundred yards without batting an eye. When I told him that guns scared me, he simply stated,

"Best way to stop a bad guy with a gun, is with a good guy with a gun."

The more I was around him, the more I wanted to be around him. He made me feel safe, and for the first time in a long time I wasn't lonely anymore. I once read that some people are born lonely, like it's this predisposition like your hair color, or your eye color, something we couldn't control. Something we couldn't understand.

It was just there.

I often felt I was one of those people, born to be alone in life. But when McGraw was around, the anxiety that I felt deep within my bones that strengthened over time, would disappear like it was never there to begin with.

"Where are we going?" I asked as we drove out of Oak Island.

"To the moon," he said with a dead-serious face.

He loved to surprise me with all sorts of stuff. Bringing me flowers every few weeks when the others had died became part of his routine. When I called him out on it he simply said, "I like to see you smile."

"South Port."

"Why are we going to town?"

"Why is the sky blue, suga'?"

He reached over and grabbed my hand, placing it in his lap. Every time we were in his Jeep my hand was sitting pretty on his thigh. He'd rub his fingers back and forth on the palm of my hand or sometimes he would tap to the beat of the music.

His hands were always on me in one way or another. At times it was subtle, his arm on the back of my chair, rubbing my shoulder with his thumb. Or when we were deep in discussion, he would play with the ends of my hair, listening to every word that came out of my mouth with an intense stare. Or he would draw pictures on my arm with his finger and make me guess what it was, making me miss his touch when we weren't together.

The boys loved to play pool at Half-Pint's parents' restaurant. Alex and I would sit and watch, laughing at their ridiculous egos on who would kick whose ass. Dylan would stand by me waiting his turn, rubbing the back of my neck, right at the nook by the hairline. I would often catch the boys looking over with amused expressions on their faces.

Alex never seemed fazed by the attention he gave me. Her and I became great friends right away. I never felt like she was a year younger than me. If anything she acted much older than her fourteen years of age.

"Are you kidnapping me?" I coaxed, glancing at him.

"Can't kidnap the willing."

We drove for forty-five minutes when he got off at the exit for Ocean Island Beach.

"We're going to another beach? You know there was one within walking distance of our houses right?" I joked.

"Can't surf there."

"I've seen you surf there almost every day since we met."

He ignored me until he finished paying the parking attendant and pulled his Jeep in the parking space at the beach.

"I can surf anywhere," he arrogantly asserted. "You on the other hand, cannot. The waves are less intense here. I don't want you gettin' hurt, suga'."

"I'm surfing?" I asked, taken back. "I don't even have a board. I left it back in Cali."

"We can rent you one," he simply stated.

"Dylan, I haven't been surfing in a long time, I don't think this is a good idea."

"It's like ridin' a bike, darlin', you never forget."

"Have you seen yourself surf lately? You can ride."

He cockily smiled. "I do love when you talk dirty to me."

I rolled my eyes, smirking. "I meant I won't be able to keep up."

"I'll go slow. I know how you girls like it slow."

"Whatever." I opened my door and he caught my wrist before I could leave.

"I know you used to do this with your dad, suga'. I'm not trying to step on anyone's toes. Just thought we could have a fun day together doing something we both love."

*That.*

That's why I was falling for the boy who sat in front of me.

He always knew what I was feeling, what I wasn't feeling, what I wanted to feel. It's like he had a sixth sense when it came to me. He was unbelievably perceptive. I used to think it was just with me, but the older we got, and the more I was with him, I realized he was like that with everyone. You couldn't keep anything from him. When you thought you did…

It was only because he let you.

I sighed, "Fine."

He leaned back into his seat still not letting go of my wrist.

"I got all day, darlin'."

I took a long, deep, sarcastic breath with a fake smile. "I can't wait. I'm so excited."

He caught me off guard when he pulled me toward him, lifting me to straddle his lap. He kissed the tip of my nose and tugged on the ends of my hair.

"Talk to me."

Just. Like. That.

I knew he wasn't going to let me go until I did. His eyes were glazed over, like they were every time he wanted to know something about me. Dylan was one of the most impatient people I had ever met, except when it came to me opening up to him. He would wait till the end of time to get what he wanted to know out of me. He wouldn't give up until I did. He was relentless when it came to something he wanted, especially *me*.

At times I felt our relationship was more than just wanting to be together, it was more than the classic boy meets girl story. What we had wasn't a normal high school romance. It ran much deeper than that. It had been that way since the very beginning, and the longer we were together, the more I realized he didn't just want to know me...

He wanted to *own* me.

"Talk to me," he repeated in a gentle tone. Rubbing my arm in a comforting gesture. I peered down into my lap not wanting him to see my weakness. I knew he wanted me to look him in the eyes.

That was another thing about McGraw...

He wanted to see the truths that most people tried to ignore.

I struggled like hell to let go of my resolve that I had been holding onto since we moved here. To bring down the wall I'd built so high, so thick with everyone except him. I never understood why he was the exception. I used to spend hours thinking about the connection we shared, the intensity of it, the way he looked at me, the way he spoke to me, the way he listened, every smile, every laugh. Every word that fell from his lips meant something.

It didn't matter how big or how small.

It was there.

Etching it's way into my heart where no one could ever come close to it.

Not that I had ever let them.

I wrapped my arm around my stomach trying to hold it together and tell him something I had never told anyone. Not even my aunt. Of course she knew because my mom told her, but I spent days locked in my room, holding my hands over my ears to drain the voices from that day out of my mind. I didn't want to relive it again.

The first time was enough.

So when I opened my mouth and said, "My dad had a teacher conference at my school one afternoon," I shocked myself with what I was about to openly share with a boy that would undo me.

"Except on this particular day, my mom was with him." I bit my lip, trying to keep my voice steady. Already knowing it was no use, the inevitable was going to happen. I was going to break down in the arms of a boy I really liked. I released my arms, picking at the seams of my shirt for a few seconds before I could continue.

My mind was running a marathon, making it difficult to try and find the right words to express how much that day meant to me. "I remember being so happy. I was so happy I could have cried, Dylan," I recalled, shaking my head, almost feeling that happiness again. "I wasn't concerned about my grades, I've always been a good student, but I was thrilled my mom was there to hear my teacher talk about me. I was proud of my accomplishments and maybe she would be, too."

My eyes blurred with tears threatening to surface. I pushed them back, having years of conditioning to do so. Dylan was so attentive, sweeping the hair away from my face and softly rubbing my cheek with his thumb.

Silently telling me it was okay to keep going.

"When my parents' and I got in the car, I was just so grateful that they were both there. How fucking stupid is that?" I wept. I couldn't hold it back any longer. The memory held me captive for so long. It overpowered me.

My emotions ran wild.

"Come here."

He drew me closer, letting me melt into his chest. Rubbing my back, and whispering, "Shhh" in my ear. He allowed me to cry and let go of the dire anguish I've been carrying in me since that day.

"It's not stupid, baby, it's not stupid at all. It's a strong part of you."

I sat up, licking my lips not bothering to wipe away the stray tears. "I hugged my mom. I mean I full-on hugged my mom so tight for the first time in a long time. I wanted her to know what it meant to me that she was there with my dad. That she took an interest in my life, instead of just hearing about it from my dad, my aunt, or me." I sniffled as Dylan caught another tear rolling down my cheek.

"I was hoping that if I showed her how much it meant to me, that maybe it could happen more often, you know, like she would realize how important it was to me for her to include herself in my life and stuff, like my schooling." I shook my head, saddened. "I never said that to her though, maybe I should have. Maybe it could have changed something."

*I knew in my heart it wouldn't have.*

I paused, needing to take a deep breath. I closed my eyes, and I swear I could see the look on her face when I jumped into her arms. It was forever engraved into my mind, a memory I refuse to let go of. No one could take that vision away, even though it hurt me every time I thought about it.

"From school we all went to the ice cream parlor in town. The same one my dad would take me to when it was just us. I loved that he was trying to include her in our after school routine. Show her what we did together." I let out a deep breath I didn't realize I was holding, licking my dry lips and brushing my tears away from my face.

My mascara running everywhere.

"Walking back to the car, I stopped dead in my tracks when I noticed that our boards were on the roof. I eagerly looked over at my dad and he just nodded. Reaffirming what I already knew. They were taking me to the beach. The day wasn't over."

I peered out the window with a sense of longing, looking at all the loving families on the beach, only reminding me that I didn't have that.

That I never did.

"I rode wave, after wave, after wave. I swear it was like the universe knew. The waves would come in sets of two or three, spaced out every couple minutes. There were nice clean breaks. It made it so much easier to paddle when you're not fighting against the current, and the winds were calm and clean," I reminisced, imagining it like it was just yesterday and that I was still there. I could smell the saltwater in the air and feel the warm sun on my skin. Having an out of body experience.

"I know, darlin', there's nothing else like it," he stated with dilated eyes.

My memory was clearly affecting him, too.

"The wave heights were overhead, five to eight feet. To be able to ride a clean wave face down in a long line was like bonding with earth. The power that pushed me right along was amazing. The excitement to get out there, again and again, to catch the next big wave with my dad by my side was awesome. To have my mom watching from the beach made it that much better. We rode the waves all day long, back and forth without a care in the world. Running around in the sand and water carefree and laughing. All I wanted to do was impress my mom, thinking that if I did she would come out to the beach with us all the time. We would be one of those families that I prayed for every night," I paused to gather my thoughts, trying to put my emotions in check, but I was too far gone.

I was physically there, but my mind had checked out.

I was there…

But I wasn't.

# Chapter ten

# Aubrey

"The sun was setting as I sat on my board looking out over the horizon. California sunsets… there is nothing like them. The sky was like a painting of bold pinks, purples, and oranges, all of them meshing into one, getting ready to dive into the water and bring us night. The remaining sunlight sparkled on the water, glimmering on the surface. It was so peaceful. I didn't want the day to end. It was one of the best days of my life," I cried, getting choked up, wanting to swallow it back down, to bury it like I had done my memories and emotions.

"I rode our last wave of the day with tears falling down my face. The sadness that it was over was devastating. I hated feeling that way. I wanted to start the whole day all over again. Put it on constant repeat, so I could play it whenever I wanted to. When I grabbed my board and we walked back to where my mom was, she was smiling. Happy," I wallowed, not wanting to get to the next part.

I fucking hated the next part.

It broke me.

"To have her be part of our family, to actually have a family that did normal things and spent time together, was all I ever dreamt of. It was the family I so desperately wanted."

I failed at wiping all the tears away from my face. They were coming so fast, so hard, so unforgiving, like a faucet I couldn't shut off. I swear he could feel my pain, it resonated that deeply all around us. Stabbing me over and over again, that the Jeep started to become confining, making it harder for me to breathe.

The space was closing in on me and I couldn't move, I was suffocating in nothing but my own misery. My lungs felt as if they had nothing left in them, the air was gone, and I didn't know if it would ever come back. My vision narrowed, and sounds became distant. My heartbeat echoing in my ears.

I needed to continue, to push on, and just when I thought that I couldn't... Dylan grabbed my hand and put it over his heart.

It was so steady.

It was so solid.

It was so safe.

"Breathe, Aubrey. Feel my heart. Feel my breath. Just breathe."

He watched all of this unfold, but he was willing to sit there and allow me to fall apart. Crumble to pieces in his arms. Shatter like glass in front of his eyes.

In hopes of maybe someday being able to put me back together.

I sucked in air that wasn't available for the taking, laying my forehead on Dylan's chest. It was all too much. To relive it all over again and knowing the outcome would still be the same. Nothing would change.

Not. One. Damn. Thing.

The pain...

The hurt...

The loss...

The sensation of my heart breaking all over again.

He rubbed the nook of my neck and I could feel him kissing the top of my head repeatedly, whispering, "Shhh..." again and again.

"Baby, you don't—"

"We sat there for what seemed like forever, but it wasn't nearly enough," I interrupted, needing to get it out.

Needing to tell someone.

Needing to tell h*im*.

Needing him to know I was broken.

"I lied to you, I fucking lied to you," I uncontrollably sobbed, my vision blurred and my throat ceased, becoming so raw, so dry, so torn into a million pieces.

"I'm so fucking stupid, Dylan. So fucking stupid. I hadn't noticed that my dad had barely said one word to us all day," I bawled, shuddering against his chest.

I wanted to hit something, anything, to keep from feeling the emotions that were dragging me down, deeper and deeper.

He gripped my hand, pressing it tighter against his heart, willing me to keep going.

"There we were one, big, happy, fucking family," I sobbed into his chest, his other arm steady around me.

"We went home and had dinner and my mom, my mom… she mirrored all my happiness, all of my joy, all my excitement for the future and the unknown possibilities. I went to bed that night happy, content. The next morning my dad took me to school. He never took me to school… He kissed and hugged me. Telling me that he loved me and I swear… I swear, Dylan, I heard him faintly whisper he was sorry." I swallowed hard, choking back the sobs.

"My mom picked me up from school. It was like they had switched places, but she was so sad. Nothing like the woman she was the day before. Not one trace of her was left. On the way home, silence filled the car. My mom stared straight ahead with worry in her eyes. Something was eating away at her, something she couldn't tell me. Something that would change the rest of our lives. The course of our future. I never saw it coming. When we arrived home, all my dad's stuff… was gone. When I looked back at my mom, I just knew. My dad had left her. Not only her, he left me, too. He left us. My parents' aren't divorced. I lied to you… He just packed up and left without so much as a note. Just like that! It was so cruel what he did… so fucking cruel, Dylan!" I shouted as if he was sitting beside me, as if he could hear me, and it would change things.

As if shouting turned back time and it would make a difference.

As if shouting took away the pain and the hole I felt in my heart.

I tried to pull my hand away, but he wouldn't let me. He held it tighter against his heart. Not one time did his steady beat change. It was so stable, so secure, so calm and serene.

*So Dylan.*

I shook my head into his chest instead, feeling like my skin was burning, as if it was on fire, searing from the inside out. Breaking down with his strong hold around me. Engulfing me with the comfort that I couldn't feel, that I didn't want to feel. That I felt I didn't deserve.

"Why? Why give me hope and let me see what it could be like, only to just rip it all away? Why would he do that to me? Why would he hurt me like that? Why, Dylan, please tell me why? Why would he hurt us like that?" I choked out, the big, huge, ugly tears falling faster and harder.

They were merciless, every last one of them.

I cried so damn hard I was hyperventilating. I had never cried like that in my entire life. I couldn't, I wouldn't allow myself to, because I knew, I knew I wouldn't be able to stop.

It would consume me.

And it did.

It was taking over me in the arms of a boy that I really liked. A boy I wanted a future with. I had never felt worse. Only adding to my tears and the hurt of a day I wanted to forget…

But knew I never could.

# DYLAN

She was in my lap crumbling to pieces before my very eyes.

I hugged her so tightly trying to hold what was left of her together. Comforting her the only way I knew how. I held her as tight as I could, wanting to mold us into one person, lift her up and take away her pain. I never allowed her hand to leave my heart, hoping that my steady beat would calm her. Whispering reassuring words in her ear with my leveled tone to provide her some security.

Some sense of something.

Anything…

I once read that it helped people in distress. It helped take away some of their agony, their grief, their suffering. It was the body's natural way of finding stability, finding comfort, finding hope.

It shattered my heart.

She cried harder.

I had never seen someone sob like that before. Having her tangibly breaking down in my arms was almost too much to bear.

I felt so fucking helpless.

Her beautiful face was filled with so much despair and sadness that it caused a physical reaction from me. The ache that I felt in my heart was so foreign and unfamiliar. It was beyond crippling.

I was at a loss.

At that moment I hated her father *for* her.

I pulled the hair away from her face. She finally looked up at me with a huge hollow vacancy in her eyes. It chipped at my heart a little more. There was nothing left of the strong girl I had known for the last several months. I didn't recognize the person sitting before me.

There was so much I wanted to say, wanted to do.

I wanted to do everything, but I felt as though I could do nothing. She was hurting in a way I never knew was possible. It cut me deep within my core, a place I hadn't realized existed inside me. She was trapped inside her own head, held captive within the memories that she desperately tried to forget. I wanted to make her laugh. I'd kill to see her smile, knowing that in the end it wouldn't matter. She'd let me see a piece of her that she had never shown anyone. The warm light of her innocence was gone, bleeding all over me and I didn't know how to get it back.

Watching someone I cared about suffer wasn't just painful, it was crippling. It took everything out of me. My own body felt unfamiliar with all the sensations she was causing. I never understood the concept of someone else's pain, the way they feel, the harbored damage of one day that could change everything for them. How life might change with a few words, a few seconds, a few moments in time that you wanted to forever change but would never be able to get back.

You would never understand, unless you saw it. It would kill you more than you would ever expect, more than you could ever prepare for.

How was it possible to feel that connected to another person? How was it possible to feel almost everything they're going through? But not once experiencing it first hand.

You're just hurting because they are.

I learned right then and there that the hardest part of watching someone you cared about go through turmoil was how helpless love could make you feel.

Everyone suffers. Everyone goes through shit. At times it's worse than others. At times you feel broken beyond repair, but what

I took from that day, from that second, from that moment, was that we now formed a connection and as selfish as that sounds.

I was happy.

I wanted that with her.

And I knew that at sixteen-years-old.

"Baby, shhh… look at me." I pressed her hand firmer against my chest.

"Feel my heart. Feel all of me. Do you understand? Can you do that for me?"

She absentmindedly shrugged.

"No, darlin. Feel. Me," I urged, placing my own hand over her heart. It was beating fast and hard with each passing second with each passing moment.

"Feel me…" I repeated, pushing both our hands into one another's hearts.

Her eyes widened in recognition with an intensity I had never seen before. A gleam in her eyes that needed to break through all the sadness and despair, all the things that ate away at her. Everything she couldn't change but desperately wanted to.

The memories that made her who she was.

*The loneliness.*

"Listen to me. I will only say this once."

She swallowed hard, less tears falling from her eyes, her heartbeat slowed down, mirroring the rhythm of mine.

"I never understood this saying until right now. Until this very moment."

She sucked in her lower lip and stared into the depths of my soul as I said,

"The deeper the love, the deeper the pain."

# eleven

# Aubrey

"You ready, darlin'?" Dylan asked, lying on my bed with his arm behind his head. He was watching some fishing show that bored the absolute hell out of me.

A few months had passed since the incident from the beach. The one that I cared to forget about, and to my surprise, Dylan never brought it up again.

All our birthdays had come and gone. The boys were seventeen, Austin and I sixteen, and Half-Pint fifteen. For the first time in a long time, I felt like I was part of a family again, and I loved that more than anything. Summer was in full swing and the boys surfed now more than ever, but I didn't mind because I got to spend time with Half-Pint. She began working at her parents' restaurant a few weeks ago. She said she wanted something to do, and that it looked good on college applications. She was starting high school with us and was already thinking about college.

It was a lie.

I knew why she really wanted to work.

"Almost," I replied, trying to figure out what I was going to wear.

"Jesus Christ, suga', fucking put anything on, you'll look gorgeous regardless."

I smiled, placing my hands on my hips. "Say that again, except this time add a please."

"Kiss my ass." He grinned. "Please."

I laughed, rolling my eyes. I looked back in my closet, sliding hangers back and forth, with nothing special catching my eye.

"Is Alex working today?" I turned my head to ask him.

"Yeah."

"Remind me to ask her if she wants to go shopping with me. I could use some new clothes."

Dylan rolled his eyes and shook his head at my overflowing closet. "I'm not going to say one fucking word to that. The boys are meeting us there in a bit. If you would hurry your pretty little ass up, we may get there today."

"I'm sure Lucas is already there," I commented, ignoring his impatience.

That was just Dylan. Patience was not his middle name. I ignored most of the stuff that left his mouth. He was still an asshole. Except now, he was *my* asshole.

"What the fuck is that supposed to mean?" he snapped in a tone I didn't appreciate, which made me turn to look at him.

I cocked my head to the side and arched an eyebrow in a questioning gesture.

"I believe I asked you a question, darlin'."

"I didn't mean anything by it, McGraw." I hesitated a few seconds, debating if I really wanted to go there. I did. "But what if I do?" I challenged.

"Don't talk about things you don't know, suga'."

"I'm not the one that doesn't know," I muttered under my breath, turning back to look in my closet.

"What was that?"

"Nothing."

"Yeah… that's what I thought."

I took a deep breath, annoyed. "You know, sometimes things happen in life that you can't control, Dylan. All that's left is to accept them, whether you like them or not."

I heard the bed dip, and I knew he was sitting up.

"Well, sweetheart, you best be puttin' on your big girl panties if you're going to be throwin' out vague theories like that."

"It's not vague." I shrugged. "You just want to assume it is, and you know what they say about people who assume shit, Dylan McGraw."

"Well, fuck me runnin'. That went over about as smooth as sandpaper."

"Now, that's a vague assumption," I mocked in the same condescending tone.

"Hot damn, darlin'."

He stood, walking over to me all confident, a predatory look in his eyes like he was going in for the kill. I didn't cower when his large, muscular frame overshadowed mine as he pressed me up against the wall, closing me in with his arms on the sides of my face. A bit of my resolve shattered when he leaned forward, kissing my cheek, slowly moving over to my ear, which sent tingles down my spine. His hot breath radiated off my skin, causing all sorts of other sensations. He had me right where he wanted me.

*Vulnerable.*

My heart fluttered, my stomach dropped, and my mouth parted. I hated this.

*No, I didn't.*

He knew exactly what he was doing when he rasped, "If you're looking for a fight, suga', then I'm your man."

He cocked his head to the side and stepped in toward me, it didn't take much for his mouth to be close to mine. Although, he pulled me closer to him by the nook of my neck and I didn't flinch, if anything I stood taller.

I cleared my throat, trying to steady my voice. "All I was trying to say was for someone who's so observant, you're ignoring what's blatantly in front of your face."

He looked me up and down. "You're the only one that's in my face," he groaned, inches away from my lips. "What do you want to do about that, huh?" he added for good measure.

I shoved his chest as hard as I could, but he didn't move an inch. It didn't faze him one bit.

*Asshole.*

He suddenly grabbed my wrists and brought them above my head. Holding them in his tight grasp. I had nowhere to go now. I could barely move. I was at his mercy and as much as it pissed me off, it also turned me on in ways that I never experienced before.

*What the hell?*

"Because I could think of plenty of things to do with that sweet little mouth of yours that knows how to push every single one of my goddamn buttons."

"I—"

"Did I say you could talk?"

My eyes widened and mouth dropped. "Who the hell do you think you are? This is not how it's going to go, McGraw."

His eyes dilated, dark and daunting. "Or what? What are you going to do, suga'? Because I'm not the one that's backed up into a wall, am I?"

I jerked my body around, trying to break out of his hold, but the second I felt his fingers tug on the ends of my hair I froze.

"Sweetheart, you're not going anywhere unless I want you to."

He softly gripped the front of my neck, his thumb and index finger clutching my pulse that only heightened with his touch. He cockily smiled when he realized how much he was affecting me. He moved his hand from my neck down to my inner thigh and slowly caressed the soft skin of my bare thighs.

Dylan had never touched me like this before. We barely made out. I didn't recognize the guy before me, and that thrilled me more than it should. I swallowed the saliva that had pooled in my mouth. My breathing elevated, showing him just how much he was getting to me.

"Does it excite you to be at my mercy, darlin'?"

I clenched my thighs. Even the way he was talking to me was new and unfamiliar. This wasn't *my* Dylan, this was the Dylan that all the girls were talking about, lusting after. He moved closer to my core, and I resisted the urge to moan.

"What's wrong, sweetheart? No witty comeback? No sexy banter? No smartass mouth? Where's my tough girl? Huh? Not so tough when I have my hands near her pussy, is she?"

I sucked in air, startled by what he just said.

He continued his gentle torture for a few seconds, enjoying the feel of my skin against his calloused fingers. Moving closer to where I wanted him to touch me the most. The exact same place his filthy mouth just called it. I hated that word, but you wouldn't think that by the way I desperately wanted him to say it to me again.

As if reading my mind, he tilted his head to the side, tempting me with whatever he wanted to do. I could see, feel his internal struggle. He was fighting something deeper than I could ever truly understand.

"I know where you want me to touch you, baby," he paused to let his words sink in. "But what I'm fixin' to do and what I want to do are two very different fucking things."

He backed away and took his warmth with him. It was like a bucket of freezing cold water washed over me. He turned around to leave but stopped at the last second to look over his shoulder.

"But just so we're clear… I'm not ignoring shit. Alex is too good for Lucas, she deserves better."

I opened my mouth to say something.

"Yes, darlin', I'm fully fucking aware that you're too good for me and deserve better, too."

# DYLAN

You couldn't fault me for who I was.
*For who I am.*

I wanted to touch her so fucking bad. It physically pained me to restrain myself. My cock throbbed and my balls ached to sink into her sweet pussy. I wasn't trying to play mind games or go from hot to cold, but damn I couldn't help myself. Her sassy mouth had been my initial draw to her in the first place. That didn't change just because she was mine now. I hadn't so much as touched more than a hair on her pretty blonde head.

It had been nine months since we met.

Six months since I last fucked someone.

Five months since we started dating.

Trust me… I wanted her. I wanted her so damn bad I couldn't see straight. It took everything inside me to not claim every inch of her creamy white skin right then and there. To get lost in her body for hours at a time, until I couldn't tell where I ended and she began.

Except, I never tempted myself.

I never gave myself the chance to get inside her panties. We barely made out. Even then, I never allowed it to get too out of hand either. I endured the worst case of blue balls every time I was with her.

That's dedication.

And trust me, I knew about Lucas and Alex's feelings for each other since we could all walk. Just like I knew that Aubrey was very much a virgin. She was also inexperienced with everything that happened in between, but that wasn't the reason that I held back. If anything her inexperience was what drove me fucking mad. The mere thought of making her mine, being the first man to claim her, drove me insane to the point of no return.

Alex was right.

I respected her.

That shocked me to the core.

It wasn't as hard as I imagined it would be to keep my dick in my pants, but when she talked back to me… fuck it did things to my cock that I couldn't control.

*I am only human.*

A man used to getting what he wants and never holding back.

I had to walk out of her room and into the bathroom before I did something I knew I would regret. She wasn't ready. That much I knew. Splashing cold water on my face, I gazed into the mirror.

"Jesus Christ, McGraw, get your shit together."

The whole ride to the restaurant Aubrey didn't say one word to me. When I reached for her hand, she immediately tore it away from my grasp. I swore to everything that was holy I almost pulled the goddamn Jeep over on the side of the road and had it out with her right then and there. But, I continued driving. She was out of my Jeep before I even had it in park, slamming the door behind her, and rushing into Alex's parents' restaurant. Not bothering to wait one damn second for me.

Half-Pint peered from Aubrey then back to me as soon as I walked in, a knowing expression written clear across her face. She stepped toward me, and I instantly shook my head no. I was going to let my anger go on the wrong fucking girl if she came near me, and Alex didn't deserve that.

I'm not quite sure Aubrey did either.

I did the only thing I could before I flipped my shit. I grabbed my board and took out my frustration on the water.

# Aubrey

"I. Hate. Him!"

Alex sighed, looking toward the ocean where Dylan had just disappeared to. I followed her worried gaze, except my eyes were filled with fury.

"What happened?"

"Dylan McGraw happened."

"Aubrey..."

"No, Half-Pint, you don't get to take his side without knowing the facts. God! He's such a fucking asshole!"

Her eyes widened, and I regretted the words as soon as they came out of my mouth. Lily, Lucas' baby sister was standing right by Alex's side. She was only ten, but she started to follow Half-Pint around everywhere.

I knew why Lily did that, too. But that was a whole other story that I didn't feel like getting into.

"Yeah, you know he is, Alex!" I pointed to both of them. "You both do!"

"What did he do?" Lily asked with caring eyes. She was the sweetest little girl who I thought would grow up to be like Alex. Boy was I wrong.

*Hell no, she didn't.*

Sometimes I thought Lily was worse than I was.

"What didn't he do? Let's start there!" I argued.

"Calm down," Alex coaxed, her tone laced with nothing but concern. "Tell me what happened?"

I took a long, deep breath, blowing all the air out of my lungs before I started. "We were hanging out in my room. I was getting ready to come here and I said—" I stopped myself.

Alex never told me about her and Lucas, but she didn't have to. It was blatantly obvious. I didn't want to push her to tell me something she wasn't ready for me to hear.

"That's not important," I sidestepped. "He just... God... he just... fuck I can't even explain it." I glanced at Lily. "I'm sorry, Lily baby. I shouldn't say those kinds of words."

"Why?" She shrugged. "The boys do all the time."

I chuckled and Alex just shook her head.

"I don't understand him sometimes. He gives me whiplash. Normally it's a good thing. Today it was not."

"There's this boy at school named Adam," Lily said out of nowhere, surprising both of us. "I didn't like Adam. He was mean to me. He'd pull my hair, he'd cut in front of me at lunch, and he'd take my pink marker when I've told him several times that it's my favorite color."

Alex and I both looked at each other confused and then back at Lily.

"I told my mom all about him. She just said that it was because Adam liked me. That boys don't know how to express themselves, so they act out to get your attention. Dylan and Jacob came to pick me up from school the next day and told me to wait in the car. I waited for a long time. The next day at school Adam was nice to me. As a matter of fact, he hasn't been mean to me since."

Alex and I busted out laughing. That poor little boy probably didn't see them coming.

"What I'm trying to say is Dylan is mean to you because he likes you, Aubrey. But only he can be mean to you because if someone else is than he's going to kick their a-s-s. I'll take a Dylan over an Adam any day."

"What, Lily, how—" I muttered.

"Well... well... well... if it isn't my so-called best friend," I heard a voice snicker behind me. My head whipped around and came face to face with a very pissed-off Dee.

I hadn't been hanging out with her that often since Dylan and I started dating. She always said she was busy. I saw the looks she gave Dylan and I in the hallway. Every time I tried to talk to her about us, she blew me off. There was only so much I could do. She didn't give me a chance to explain myself. I would never want to hurt her. It's not like Dylan and her were ever together in a relationship. I hadn't broken some girl code. I went to bat for her and put him in his damn place.

She never even thanked me for it.

"How's it feel to be his new whore?" she spewed without an ounce of remorse on her face.

"Excuse me?" I jerked back as if she smacked me across my face.

"Oh, come on, Aubrey, you can't actually think he likes you. I thought you were smarter than that. Don't you see he's fucking using you? As soon as you give it up he's going to dump you and move onto the next one. That's who he is. You think you have a wonder pussy or something to change him?"

"You don't know—"

"Oh, I know! Why do you think I can't even talk to you anymore? Because I know! I know what he's going to do to you, and I never thought you would be so fucking stupid to fall for it!"

"You mean stupid like you? What are you more pissed about, Dee? The fact that he slept with you and was done? Or the fact that I haven't slept with him and he's still with me?"

"Girl, you're getting my sloppy seconds. I thought you were my friend, Aubrey."

"I am your friend," I simply stated, trying to not let her vicious words get to me. She was hurt, I got that. "And because of that I'm not saying every shitty thing that I want to say to you, like you are to me. I didn't do anything wrong! What you're doing right now is because you're jealous! You're jealous that I have, what you want."

"God, Aubrey, with friends like you who needs enemies?"

"Dee, I would never want to hurt you. I've been trying for months to explain! I can't help it that he likes me, that we like each other. I'm not going to stand here and defend my relationship to you. I don't owe you anything. You seem to forget I actually went to battle with him for you. Now take a step back before you say something that you're really going to regret. Or before you piss me the fuck off."

"What did he tell you?" She ignored my warning. "You're his only one, you're the most beautiful thing he's ever seen or wait, I got it, that he could make you forget about your pain? Right? Poor little new girl. Everything you wanted to hear, wrapped in a big red bow."

I fervently shook my head and Alex grabbed my wrist, but I ripped it away. "You don't know him. You don't know anything!" I screamed back, letting her get the best of me.

"No, it's you who doesn't know anything." She stepped toward me, getting a few inches away from my face, looking me up and down with a snide glare.

She scoffed in disgust. "He's just like your daddy, Aubrey. He's going to leave you too without so much as a fucking goodbye!"

My arm was swinging toward her face by the time she had the last word out, but someone saw my intention and gripped my wrist mid-air. Before I could turn to see who stopped me, Dylan stepped out in front of me, placing me right behind him.

He cocked his head to the side, and I could physically feel the heat searing off of him.

"You better back the fuck up, *Dee*, right? That's your name?" he sneered in an eerie tone as I watched with my heart in my throat.

"That right there... is how much you meant to me."

My mouth dropped open, nervously looking around me. The boys were standing beside us with a look on their faces that I had never seen before.

*They were waiting.*

Alex's expression mirrored mine while Lily just stood there with a mischievous gleam in her eyes and the biggest smirk I'd ever seen. She would be a force to be reckoned with one day.

"Now, I'm fixin' to let you know, darlin', that the difference between you and Aubrey is that I care about her, she is *my* girl. You... you on the other hand were just a piece of ass I got to tap. And not a very good one at that," he paused to let his cruel words sink in. "Which is surprisin', seeing as you'll give it up to anyone who will give you just a little bit of attention," he jeered as tears formed in her eyes, but he didn't falter. "I would know. I barely fucking looked at you and your legs spread faster than butter."

I felt bad for her. I knew I shouldn't, but I did. I opened my mouth to say something and she cut me off.

"How is she any different from me? You know you're going to get what you want and leave her. It's in your blood, Dylan... it's what you do. She will be where I'm standing in a few months. They say girls end up with men just like their daddy's, well it must be true."

She wasn't backing down. Hateful words just came one after another. The one thing she said that was true, I was stupid.

I was stupid for thinking she was my best friend.

He smiled big and wide, not fazed by her response in the least. "You mention her daddy again, I won't stop her from beating your ass this time."

"What game are you playing, Dylan?"

"That would imply that I don't know what I'm doing. I don't play fucking games. This is your first and last warning. You fuck with Aubrey again, and I'll give you something to cry about."

"Well, I'll be damned. Aren't you just her knight in shining armor? You're a modern day hero. I can't wait until she's the one who's crying and I'm here to pick up the pieces." A combination of anger and hurt came out of her in waves, but McGraw surfed every one of them with ease.

The irony was not lost on me.

"Darlin', the only reason she'd be crying is from fuckin' happiness."

He walked over to her, each step precise and calculated. Each stride more unnerving than the last, his conviction never wavering, right in front of me. He didn't care who saw. He was a man possessed with his heart on his sleeve and I waited, holding my breath with my heart on mine.

"See, you oughta' know that I love her. That I'm in love with her so when you fuck with her you fuck with *me*."

Just. Like. That.

The words fell off his lips for the first time into the face of a girl that wasn't *me*.

"Now scurry along, we're done here." And with that he turned around and left her standing there without a bit of guilt for what he just shared.

I vaguely heard Lily whisper in my ear, "Told you," before Dylan made his way over to me with a confidence I couldn't quite place.

"You okay, sug—"

I. Cold. Clocked. Him.

# DYLAN

"What the actual fuck?" I roared, gripping my jaw, glaring only at Aubrey.

She slowly stepped back with her hand out in the air. "Don't follow me, McGraw," she ordered with a pissed off look on her face.

"You gotta be shittin' me," I gritted out.

"I mean it." She shook her head, her body shuddering with every step she took away from me. "I'm out of here." She took one last look at me and left.

I peered around the beach for the first time. Everyone was standing around with wide eyes, frozen in place.

"The show's fucking over," I growled out to our audience, glancing over at the boys who were grinning like goddamn fools. "You say one fucking word, one fucking word, and I will knock you the fuck out," I warned, my fists at my sides.

I could see it in their eyes, they wanted to laugh and give me shit, but they just shrugged their shoulders not breaking eye contact.

I spun around and Alex gripped my wrist.

"I don't think—"

I glared at her, letting her know that now was not the right time.

She let go immediately, stepping back. "Okay."

I got in my Jeep, throwing it in drive before the door even shut. Tearing through the parking lot and down the street until I saw her. She was walking with her arms folded over her chest, her pissed-off stance still very much alive and thriving.

I pulled up next to her. "Get in!" I barked.

She looked over at me, surprised. "No!"

"Don't poke the bear, sweetheart."

She rolled her eyes, throwing her neck back and screamed, "Fuck. You!"

I snidely grinned, immediately slamming on the gas and veering across the sidewalk to block her path. Throwing it in park, not bothering to turn off the engine, I jumped out before she even saw me coming.

I was sure I'd never seen that look on her face before. She pivoted around to take off in the other direction. I was over to her in three strides.

Face to face.

She stepped back until she was against my Jeep.

Nowhere to go.

Placing both hands on each side of her head, I spoke through clenched teeth, "What the fuck is your problem?" I lashed out, looming over her smaller frame.

"You!" She shoved me and I didn't waver, which only made her push me again.

"You're my problem! Now get out of my damn way."

I could see it in her eyes, she had gone mad. I didn't know what the hell I had done to piss her off this bad.

*I fucking defended her, and this was the thanks I got.*

"I hate you! I hate you so fucking much right now! You're an asshole, Dylan McGraw! You're a fucking asshole!"

I immediately fell back, the wind knocked from my sails. She took the distraction as an opportunity to maneuver herself away from me.

"I can't believe you did that! I can't believe you did that to me!"

I scoffed, "I would do it again."

"Of course, you would! That's who you are! You don't think for one damn second about me. Not one! Now, leave!"

"Fuck you, I'm not going anywhere. If you really wanted to leave... you would have left already, not bothering me with your bullshit," I regretted my words as soon as they came out of my mouth, but thinking before speaking had never been my strong suit.

Case and point, she screeched out, "You asshole!" shouting in my face.

I stepped toward her and she instantly backed away, once again holding out her hand in front of her.

"Yeah! I'm a fucking asshole, but I will die before I ever apologize for defendin' you. Do you understand me?"

"You're such an idiot. You're so blinded by your goddamn pride you don't even see it! You don't even realize it!"

"My pride? Sweetheart, those are fightin' words. You best consider takin' a step back and realize who the fuck you're talkin' to."

She put her arm down and stepped toward me. "I know exactly who I'm talking to, and I don't give a shit. I can't believe you did that!" she repeated with the same stride. "Telling me for the first time, for the first time, McGraw, that you loved me to that piece of shit Dee. How could you do that to me? How could you hurt me like that, you asshole?!"

I caught her open palm that was coming at my face again. "I let you hit me once, darlin', it won't happen again."

She forcefully tried to tug her arm away, but I used the momentum to pull her toward me instead. She lost her footing and began to fall forward. Her free hand collided with my chest, giving her leverage.

I hugged her toward me. "Relax."

*Shit.*

I didn't even realize that. I was so caught up in putting that bitch in her place that I hadn't grasped that it was the first time the words came out of my mouth.

I didn't think twice about it.

"You cannot do this! You cannot manhandle me every time just to get your way! It's not fair, McGraw," she yelled, taking me away from my thoughts.

"Unlucky for you. I don't give a flying fuck."

I leaned her back, putting my hand over her mouth, sensing she was going to scream. I placed her up against my Jeep again not taking my hand away from her mouth.

Her nostril's flared and her chest heaved.

"You are so goddamn beautiful that it hurts to look at you sometimes."

Her eyes widened, not expecting what she had just heard.

"You're not going to talk." I shook my head. "You're going to listen to every word I have to say." I nodded, gently letting my hand fall from her mouth. I had to explain, I knew it was the only way she would ever forgive me.

She swallowed hard but didn't say anything.

"I don't know what happened back there and frankly I don't give a shit. I watched my girl—"

"You were surfing," she interrupted.

"My eyes are always on you, darlin'. I always know where you are."

She bit her lip, surprised by my declaration.

"But if you interrupt me one more time. You're giving me no choice than to cover that sweet mouth again."

She narrowed her eyes at me not saying a word, though she didn't have to, her eyes spoke volumes all by themselves.

"I fucked girls, Aubrey, plenty of them," I simply stated, catching her off guard.

"That's all I've ever done. It made me feel good. It made me happy. It made things easier for me. I used girls, but you want to know somethin', suga', they used me, too. It was a win-win situation. I come from a happy home, my parents' clearly love each other, but I still ran from love. I chalked it up to normal boy bullshit. Ya feel me?"

She didn't move, her eyes intently placed on my face, waiting for the next thing I was going to share.

"I've seen Lucas and Alex... fuck me..." I breathed out. "My two best friends battle this connection they've had since they were kids. Since before I knew what the fuck it even meant. I see Lily. And I know you see her, too. Jacob's never going to see it coming. She's going to hit him like a ton of fucking bricks."

The expression on her face softened and it gave me the push to keep going.

"It's all so fucking messy, so fucking complicated, so fucking forbidden. I didn't want shit to do with that. Not for one damn second. Unlike Austin who has no damn clue who he is, that's the difference between him and I, I do. I know I'm an asshole. I don't pretend to be something I'm not, darlin'. I don't need to and I don't fuckin' want to. Ain't got time for that shit. I never hurt a girl and if they want to claim that I did, it's only because it's easier to blame someone else than to look in the goddamn mirror and realize who they really are."

She frowned, sad for me.

"No, suga', this isn't about you feelin' bad for me. I loved doing it. Sex, fucking, and being with someone was the closest I ever let myself go. It was addicting. My addiction. The feeling of another body pressed up against mine. Well, there's nothing else like it. I did what felt good. No strings. No attachments. No unnecessary bullshit."

I could tell she wanted to say something, but the need to know what I had to say was too strong for her to interrupt.

"For once, baby. For once in my life someone had the balls to call me out. Ain't ever happened before. Especially by a *girl*. A hot-as-fuck girl," I added, grinning.

She hid a smile.

"So, after years of watching my boys struggle with emotions and feelings and who the fuck else knows. All that shit that I ran away from, was staring me right in the face, I wanted it," I paused, gazing deep into her eyes.

"I. Wanted. You."

Her mouth parted, and I swear I could feel her heart beating against my chest.

"Except, I know, baby. I know you're too good for me. I know the first time we have sex, make love... it's going to mean something and maybe, I'm hoping that it'll make me a better man. That you..." I tugged on the ends of her hair.

"That you'll make me a better man."

She jerked back. "Oh my God." She exhaled long and deep.

"I love you, Aubrey. I fucking love you, and I don't care who knows."

Her eyes swelled up with tears and I leaned forward to her ear and groaned,

"I. Love. You."

# Chapter thirteen

# DYLAN

"What do you want to watch?" I asked from her bed. Grabbing her around the waist, pulling her toward me.

She came effortlessly as if she weighed nothing. I lifted her up and placed her on my lap with her legs straddling my waist. She put her finger up to her lips and hummed.

My cock twitched.

Ever since I told her I loved her, our make-out sessions were becoming hotter and heavier. Every time I pulled back, stopping them from going any further, I could see her impatience growing more and more. Though she hadn't called me out on it.

Summer was almost over and it had been over a month since I told her I loved her. She had yet to say it back to me. My impatience to hear her say the words was increasing by the minute. I knew she loved me, it was written clear across her pretty little face. Especially when she was in my arms, which happened to be more often than not. But I needed her to say it out loud, to validate our relationship and how far we've come.

"Why are we going to pretend to watch a movie, McGraw? Aren't we a little old for make-believe? You know what's going to happen?"

"Is that right? Remind me then."

"Yes, sir." She kissed along my cheek, moving down to my neck.

Her mom was never home. She was always working. There was no point not to hang out in her room.

On her bed.

Alone.

I said I loved her.

Not that I was a fucking saint.

I wrapped my hands around her waist, sliding them under her shirt to feel her soft skin against my fingers. Gliding them up and down her midsection, my thumbs pressing higher on the wire of her bra.

"God, baby, you feel fuckin' amazing," I groaned into her ear, following her lead and kissing her along her neck.

She rotated her hips against my cock in approval, leaning her head back to give my lips more access to her creamy white skin. My mouth moved from her neck down to her collarbone, slowly, savoring the elevated heat of her body pressed up against mine. Getting hotter with each caress of my tongue touching her skin.

I nudged her nose with mine and she gazed adoringly into my eyes. I knew that look.

*She wanted me.*

I grabbed both sides of her face, closing the distance between us, colliding our lips together. Our tongues did a sinful dance, devouring each other. I bit her bottom lip, causing her to whimper. Her mouth was so fucking perfect and all I could picture was her plump lips sealed around my cock.

Kissing Aubrey was like coming home. It was like tasting Heaven for the first time and knowing you would never be able to find anything like it.

She was one of a kind.

*Mine.*

It never started off innocently. It always became it's own thing, something neither one of us could understand or deny. Something neither one of us could control.

The electricity…

The connection…

The intensity…

Was constantly right there. Wavering and waiting for either of us to make the move. All we had to do was look at each other and sparks fucking flew like the damn Fourth of July.

Her lips parted, I slipped my tongue into her waiting mouth. When she breathed out, her scent was all around us, consuming my desire to feel her wrapped around me.

It didn't take long for her lips to move against mine, demanding a response from me that only she elicited. Her tongue was smooth and felt like silk. Like fucking ecstasy all rolled into one. I started to lean forward. Flipping her onto her back. I wanted to feel her body beneath mine. The second I was above her, my hand started roaming. It started at her hair, tugging on the ends of it, which I knew she loved me to do to her every chance I got. It traveled to the nook of her neck, to bring her closer to me, to kiss her harder, faster, and with more determination.

Her breathing picked up, as did the scent of her arousal, engulfing me in nothing but my need to keep going and claim what I've wanted for so long.

*What I knew belonged to me.*

She writhed and moaned beneath me, only enticing me to go further. To seek how far this could really go. My hand moved to the top of her breast, and I could feel her nipple hardening through the flimsy cotton of her shirt and the bra she wore underneath. She pushed her breast further into my hand. I immediately gripped it harder, earning me another moan.

The best sound in the world.

I had copped a few feels here and there, but it wasn't enough anymore.

Not right now.

Not the way I was feeling.

I rubbed my hard cock against her pussy. My thin gym shorts and her cotton ones made it easy to feel the friction that ignited between us. It felt so fucking amazing that I did it again. She followed my lead pretty quickly and started rubbing up against me.

"Fuck, suga," I growled against her open mouth.

My dick firm to the point of pain.

My hand moved under her shirt, kneading her breast, feeling it swell beneath my touch. I pushed the cup aside and caressed her nipple with the palm of my hand, feeling it harden. Resisting the urge to lean down and suck it in my mouth.

"Please… don't stop… please…" she begged.

Her hips moved faster against my cock with much more momentum than before. I felt her hand creep down between us and delicate fingers wrap around my dick over my shorts. I was too caught up in the moment to stop her. She stroked me with a steady rhythm of an inexperienced hand, resonating the fear that harbored inside me. I kissed her one last time and instantly pushed off her, leaving her with the same need I felt in my shorts.

"You've got to be kidding me? Please tell me this is a joke?"

"My balls are so fucking blue they're starting to look like they're part of the Blue Men group, darlin'." I readjusted my cock as I paced around the room. "And you're askin' me if this is a joke?"

She sat up, pulling down her bra and shirt. "I wasn't the one who stopped, McGraw. How many damn times are you going to do this? We've been together now for seven months. Seven freaking months. Is it me? At least I don't think it's me, judging by the tent you're sporting." She sarcastically gestured toward my dick.

I sat back on the armchair and rubbed my temples in an effort to calm the migraine that was forming to no avail. I peered up, looking right into her eyes and stated, "You're a virgin."

I sighed, defeated. "So, what if I am?"

"That's not the problem."

He didn't move, his face remained neutral with no emotion at all, and I started to wonder if he had heard what I said. When he leaned forward, placing his elbows on his knees, his eyes barred into mine like he was calling my bluff without having to say a word.

"Then what? What's the problem?"

Silence.

"Are you just going to sit there? All stealth-like without one thing to say?"

There was something animalistic about the way he was staring at me. Almost like a lion before it attacked its prey, luring me with his eyes and his captivating demeanor. It started to make me nervous.

"What do you want, McGraw?"

"Only what you can give me. You give me what I want and I'll give you what you need. I want you but I want all of you, your heart, your body, your soul. I'm all in," he simply stated not budging for one second.

I lowered my eyebrows, my gaze going every which way, trying to figure out what he meant.

We locked eyes.

"Oh…"

He grinned.

"Well, lookie here." I tried to pull off my best southern accent and sound like him. "That's how you say it, right?"

He narrowed his eyes at me with a sexy arrogant expression that only Dylan McGraw could pull off.

"Hmm…" I purposely mused. "I just don't know if I can do it. You know what they say, McGraw, don't buy the car without testing it out first. And, what you've had to offer so far." I callously shrugged. "Well, it's not much."

He slowly, purposely nodded. "Is that right?" he drawled out.

"Mmm hmm… just keeping it real. I know how much you love honesty. God knows you never know when to shut up."

I knew I was testing his limits. Poking the bear, provoking him on purpose, but this was a power struggle I wasn't willing to lose.

"I mean, *just so we're clear,*" I mocked throwing his own words back at him. The same words he had used on me time and time again. He slid back in the chair. His legs were wide open in the expanding space that now seemed smaller with him sitting in it. His elbow rested on the armrest, as his thumb worked his bottom lip back and forth.

*Watching.*

"I think I feel something for you. Possibly those three little words that you're inkling for, but sex and… you know… foreplay and stuff, that's some important shit. I am inexperienced so the pressure to perform shouldn't be too bad for you. Because let's face it, boys that talk a big game, usually never deliver," I paused to let my words sink in. "And judging by how vocal you've been about your stellar… equipment." I gave him a sarcastic expression, allowing it to linger for a few seconds. "Yeah… it's not looking promising."

I held back a laugh that could lite up the entire room.

His eyes were brazen and dilated.

"I think it's time you put your money where your mouth is," I added.

He shook his head with a penetrating glare and rasped, "No."

"Fine." I stood up from the bed, ready to leave him.

"Sit down," he ordered.

I recognized that voice. I froze instantly, standing in place with my back to him. The tables were just turned.

"I won't ask again," he warned through gritted teeth.

I was breathless, my chest immediately heaving. "What if I don't want to?"

"I didn't ask what you wanted, did I?"

"Are you going—"

"Sit. Down," he ordered again, that time in a much rougher tone.

I contemplated disobeying him, pushing his buttons a little more but the look on his face told me he had reached his limit. He was in my face in three strides, as soon as he sensed my resolve, hovering above me in the way that made me weak in the knees and wet in my panties.

He cocked his head to the side, a silent request to follow his direction with a look that screamed this was my last chance to listen.

*I did.*

Not because I wanted to, but because I wanted to know what he would do next. My curiosity outweighed my defiance and the fucking asshole knew it.

He watched me for a few seconds or maybe it was minutes, time just seemed to standstill. My heart was in my throat and my pulse quickened with every fiber in my body. McGraw was calm, cool, and collected, displaying no emotion what so ever. I never understood how he did that, always so in control of his surroundings, manipulating people to do what he wanted without even trying very hard.

It was almost like the more severe and intense the situation, the better he was at remaining in control. That proved to be more than accurate throughout the years.

"Lay down," he demanded out of nowhere.

"Why?" I blurted out.

"Darlin', when I'm asking you a question, you'll know. Now, lay down."

I swallowed hard as I lay back onto my firm mattress that suddenly felt too damn soft. The sheets were cool on my already heightened skin. Our eyes stayed connected the entire time as he watched my every move, like he was trying to ingrain it into his memory.

He pulled my cotton shorts down, inch by inch, deliberately taking it slow. Before he gradually crawled his way up my body, lightly skimming his lips across my bare flesh, igniting tingles all over my skin. Awakening a craving deep within my core for the first time in my life.

He worked his way up from my thighs, lifting my shirt with the movement of his mouth to kiss along my torso, and all along the sides. Gliding his way up to my breasts, and then my neck, taking my shirt with him. He left me much more exposed than before in only my bra and panties.

His predatory gaze never left mine as he continued his assault on my body. Only stopping when we were face to face, and his body was perfectly placed on top of mine. With his nose he nudged mine. Brushing it all along my cheeks, my chin, and sliding it across my lips, gently pecking them in its wake.

"That feel good?" he breathed out, gently licking my lips, stirring my need for him to kiss me.

I nodded not being able to form words, lost in the sensation of Dylan.

"Do you want me to touch you?" he said in between kisses.

I sucked in air, and he grinned against my mouth with his fingers caressing the side of my face.

"Tell me," he urged, never stopping the torment of his lips against mine. "Do you know what it feels like to let go? Mmm..." he groaned, watching his fingers move from my cheek to my shoulder, sliding my bra straps down my arms. Leaving little kisses as he went. He removed my bra with one swift move, my breasts completely exposed and ready for him.

"Do you know what I could do to you, baby? How I could make you feel?" he continued, kneading my nipple and then sucking it into his mouth. "Do you want that? Do you want me to make you come?"

I moaned in response and his eyes glazed over as he went back up to my mouth,

"Where, baby, where do you want me to touch you?" He cocked his head to the side, still not moving his lips from mine. "Where?" He slid his fingers down my stomach, slipping them into my panties. I just about came undone and he hadn't even touched me yet. Another moan escaped my lips just from the anticipation of what he was going to do next.

"Here?" he taunted, touching my folds.

I didn't say a word. I could barely breathe.

He rubbed everywhere, except where I really wanted him too.

"Or…" He pressed his fingers against my clit. "Here?"

I loudly panted, which earned me a smile. He didn't even try to hide it.

I grabbed at the back of his neck for more leverage, I couldn't take it anymore, as he played with my clit in a side-to-side motion.

"Feels good, right?" he raspingly asked, as I continued to try to keep my fluttering eyes open.

"Yes," I finally whimpered.

He slid his finger in between my lips, running it from my opening, back up to my clit. I could feel my wetness pooling and I subconsciously turned my face into his neck from embarrassment.

"I love that you're so fucking wet. I can't wait to fucking taste you, darlin'," he growled as if reading my mind.

He continued his torture for a few seconds, enjoying the feel of my slickness against his callused fingers. When he eased his finger into my opening, I whimpered again and he shoved his tongue into my mouth at the exact same time. Savoring both the taste and feel of me, and how my body was completely his to command as he held me beneath him. I melted against him, and into his touch, taking everything he was giving me and wanting more.

"Oh, God, right there," I panted into his mouth, when his finger angled somewhere deep inside me. He slipped another finger in and worked my pussy, pushing in and out with a steady rhythm making me squirm.

Completely at his mercy.

"Right there?" he mocked, pushing harder against it and my back arched off the bed. Allowing him to suck my nipple into his mouth.

My body felt warm all over with the uncontrollable need for something to happen that would take away this ache that he was creating. When I felt his thumb manipulate my clit as his fingers continued to rub that sweet spot, I thought I was going to die.

Right then and there.

"I want you to come, baby, I want you to come so fucking hard that you squeeze the fuck out of my fingers."

The sound of his filthy words had my pussy pulsating. When he removed his fingers, I immediately felt his absence. He peered deep into my eyes and then licked his fingers clean. My mouth dropped open and before I could give it too much thought his fingers were back inside me as if they never left in the first place.

"You know what else I want, darlin'?" He kissed me with a much more heated look in his eyes. "What I want more than anything?" He kissed me again. "Is for you to tell me what I need to hear." He rubbed harder and faster, and my lips parted.

"Until you do. You don't get what you need."

And then the bastard stopped.

# DYLAN

I stood, leaning forward to grab her ankles. She gasped as I tugged her over to me until she was at the edge of the bed. Her eyes shuttered closed. I casually crouched down to the ground in between her legs, gripping the sides of her panties. I slid them down, never taking my eyes off her pretty, disheveled face, her chest rising and falling with every movement of my touch caressing down her legs. I brought her wet panties up to my face, and inhaled her sweet scent, then threw them to the side when I was done.

I devoured every last fucking inch of her body with my gaze for the first time, taking in her beautiful naked glory. Starting from her rosy cheeks, down to her perfect, flushed, voluptuous tits that looked better from where I squatted. Right where I wanted to look the most.

Her pussy.

Her legs were spread wide open. Her pussy was the prettiest fucking shade of pink. Her breathing was heavy and deep, and her skin was warm. Sweat glistening off her flesh. Her clit was so exposed that I could see the bright red nub from where I was. She shined vibrantly with the pre-glow of her impending climax that I didn't allow her to finish. The smell of her arousal was all around me, consuming me.

"Now is not the time to get shy, suga'. I know what your pussy feels like when it's about to come, and how your face gets flushed and your breathing gets heavy," I taunted, placing her legs on the sides of my shoulders.

I kissed along her knee, making my way down, slowly to where she needed me the most. Her breathing hitched when I reached her inner thigh, I roughly bit the soft tender area and she whimpered in response. I licked and nibbled around it to make it better.

I glanced up at her with a mischievous glare, making sure to lick my lips as I continued my way down. I kissed her pubic area where she had a landing strip, nicely trimmed.

"I fucking love that you have hair on your pussy, darlin'. I don't want a little girl."

I faintly kissed her clit, resisting the goddamn urge to lick her fucking clean.

She moaned and her head fell back.

I silently laughed as she gyrated her hips against the bed, a silent plea to keep going.

"Oh, trust me, baby, I want to." I tenderly licked her nub.

Exactly the way she wanted me to.

Exactly the way she would love.

"Oh my God," she purred, shuddering.

"I've barely licked you and you're legs are already shakin'. That what you want, darlin'? For me to eat your pussy?"

"Please," she begged.

"Here?" I murmured, sucking her clit into my mouth, enjoying the taste of her for a few seconds. Her legs tightened around me.

I stopped again, sitting back on my heels. She immediately looked up at me, bewildered and aroused.

"Oh my God!" she screamed out in frustration, but also in urgency. "You can't do this to me!"

"I believe I just did."

Her head fell back and I crawled up her naked body to get to her face. "You smell that?" I asked, against her lips, kissing her. "You taste that?" I kissed her again. "That's you."

Her eyes widened. Shocked by my forwardness.

"It's addicting. The taste of you, the feel of you, the *love* for you. I'm mad for you. You're mine."

A single tear fell down the side of her face.

"It's just you and me, darlin'. I'm not going anywhere, and trust me, neither are you," I stated in a possessive tone. "I'm yours."

Another tear fell and I kissed that one away.

"Promise?"

"Always."

She faintly smiled and whispered,

"I love you."

# Chapter fourteen

# Aubrey

We were halfway through the new school year.

Lucas and Alex barely said two words to each other and that happened only when we were all together. Something came between them. Cole Hayes managed the unthinkable. He drove a wedge between them and gave Lucas a run for his money. Half-Pint finally admitted to me what's been going on with her and Lucas for years. Since they were kids. I tried to call Lucas out on his bullshit behavior, for stepping into McGraw's old shoes and sleeping with anything that had a pulse.

There was a huge divide between them and I hated seeing Alex so torn up and hurt about it. Lucas, well Lucas just pissed me off. We were all young and stupid but little did we know they would spend years playing this cat-and-mouse game. The boys didn't help the situation either. Dylan calmed down a bit about it, but I think it was just because I influenced him as much as I could.

Though it wasn't much.

Jacob, well he was another story. He was probably one of the biggest factors as to why they stayed on different sides of the fence, fighting off their feelings that we all knew were there. He was as thickheaded as they come. Except, when Lily was around. I tried not to pay too much attention to it, just because she was still such a little girl.

Austin, I genuinely cared for that boy. It was hard not to. There were times where I swear he would look at Dylan and I, with jealousy in his eyes. Not because he had any feelings toward me other than friendship, but because he wanted the intimacy that came with a relationship. It wasn't the sex he craved, it was the emotional connection. Sometimes I felt as if he was as lonely as I was before I met Dylan. Maybe he was born that way too.

It made me sad for him.

I couldn't imagine standing in a room full of people who loved me and still feel so alone.

"You ready, darlin'?" Dylan asked, coming up behind me at my locker.

"It depends," I giggled as he tickled my neck. "Are you going to let me drive your Jeep?"

He smiled, as he spun me to face him.

"Not a chance in hell."

I frowned. "Why? I have my license. You were there when I passed. Remember, you wouldn't stop flirting with my aunt?"

My Aunt Celeste loved, I mean really loved Dylan. I couldn't blame her. He charmed the pants off her.

She never stood a chance.

McGraw got up at the butt ass crack of dawn, his words not mine, to witness this monumental event in my life. I was very excited to have two of the most important people in my life be there with me although I wished my mom had made it too. She was supposed to be the one to take me that Saturday morning, but at the last second she got called into the ER, for some head-on collision accident.

I would be lying if I said I wasn't disappointed and tried my best to hide it from both of them. Dylan and I watched Saturday morning cartoons instead, knowing it was one of my favorite things to do back home. When my doorbell rang not even five hours later and my Aunt Celeste was standing there with a great big smile on her face to take me to get my license, I jumped into her arms. I thought my mom called her like she had done so many times in California to fill her shoes.

*She didn't.*

Dylan had taken my phone without me realizing it when I went and cried in the bathroom for a few minutes. He called my aunt and she was on the next flight out.

I couldn't have loved him more than I did in that moment, and I privately thanked him later for it. We still hadn't had sex but we did everything else. I don't know how he resisted the urge. We came close a couple of times, but he never allowed it to go any farther than us just messing around.

He said I wasn't ready yet, and maybe he was right.

"Suga, that's just my Southern charm." He kissed me.

"Please! Can I please drive your Jeep? How am I ever going to learn how to be a good driver if I have nothing to practice on?"

My mom said I couldn't have a car until I got more experience, which was interesting seeing as though she was never around for me to gain it.

"Oh, you know how I love the beggin'."

I smiled.

"Hey, you guys ready?" Alex interrupted, holding her books against her chest.

"Yep! McGraw is going to let me drive. Keys *please*," I stressed.

Alex smirked, peering between us.

He placed his keys out in front of him, but then snatched them away from my hand when I tried to reach for them.

"What do I get?" he arrogantly demanded, tugging on the ends of my hair.

"A thank you."

He cocked his head to the side, waiting. Alex blushed and looked away.

I stepped toward him, standing on the tips of my toes and whispered into his ear, "I'll do that thing you like."

He nudged his nose on the side of my cheek, murmuring, "What thing?"

I sighed. "You just want me to say it."

"And yet I'm still waiting."

I got in closer to his ear. "I'll talk dirty to you while you go down on me."

"While I do what?"

I narrowed my eyes at him and he grinned.

"While you eat my pussy."

Just like that, he handed me his keys.

# DYLAN

Aubrey was one hell of a fucking runner.

The girl was like the speed of lightning. I thought she was fast when I saw her running down my street, but that was nothing. She said she was nervous to try out for the track team because she hadn't ran in months, and she usually spent months conditioning prior to the season starting back in California. I showed up at her house one morning when the sun was barely out and her mom was just getting home from work.

I told her I was there to help Aubrey get back in shape for track, since tryouts were a month away. She smiled, patted me on my shoulder and told me that I was one of the good guys and proceeded to ask me what I wanted for breakfast. Aubrey was sound asleep when I tiptoed into her room. It was cold that morning and she looked so warm and soft in her bed. I crawled in behind her and wrapped my freezing cold arms across her waist, tugging her toward me. She shrieked so damn loud I thought she might have woken up the neighbors.

She called me an asshole and tried to fight me off, which only made me hug her tighter.

But she got up.

And I got to cop a feel.

Time was going by so fast. It was February and Aubrey was well into the track season. She didn't have one problem making the team. Our morning runs paid off, she made varsity right off the bat. She was up for all-state champion that weekend and her aunt couldn't fly in for the competition. Aubrey said she wasn't going to bother her mom with it, she knew she was busy.

I knew the real reason.

She didn't want to be disappointed.

The team had been practicing late most days. Sometimes I stayed and watched. Other times I went and surfed with the boys, but I always came back to pick her up. I took her to and from school everyday.

I walked up to the nurse's station at the hospital.

"Hello, how can I help you?" the receptionist greeted.

"Hi, I'm looking for Dr. Owens."

"Oh, you're in luck." She looked away from her computer screen. "She just got out of surgery. She'll be in her office. Go past those double doors towards the ER." She pointed down the hall. "Once you get there take the elevator up to the fourth floor. Her room is 479."

"Thank you."

I made my way up toward her office, pausing for a minute before knocking on the door.

"Come in." She smiled when she saw me. "Dylan, what a nice surprise. Is Aubrey okay?" she worried.

"Yea and no," I honestly spoke.

She placed her hand over her heart and breathed out, "Have a seat."

I did, looking around her office. She had pictures of Aubrey everywhere, and I immediately wondered if Aubrey knew about it.

"So what do I owe the honor for this unexpected visit?"

I smiled. "I'm not sure if you knew that Aubrey made states for track."

She leaned her back against her chair, her happy expression quickly faded. "No." She shook her head. "I didn't. She didn't tell me."

"Yeah, she—"

"It's harder to keep tabs and know what's going on with her here," she interrupted out of nowhere. "Back in California I knew everything. Her dad or aunt would tell me everything. Sometimes Aubrey, but usually not," she informed.

"She needs you," I stated. "With all due respect, ma'am," I added.

She nervously chuckled. "I know." She fidgeted with her fingers for a few seconds. "I don't know why I'm telling you this, but you're a good young man. I like you, Dylan. My daughter is happy. I haven't seen her this happy in a long time. I guess, I don't know, maybe it's why I don't worry about her, as much I should. Since I know she has you. Thank you for taking her under your wing."

"It's been my pleasure," I simply stated.

She affectionately nodded. "It's hard to do this single parenting thing. I'm probably doing a really shitty job, huh?"

"I—"

She put her hand up in the air to stop me. "Don't answer that," she paused. "I've always been the provider. That was my role. Aubrey has never wanted for anything. It didn't matter what it was or how hard it was to get, it was hers. Her father and I used to fight about it all the time. The only reason I haven't bought her a car is because I'm scared," she admitted out loud for what seemed like the first time.

"I'm terrified something will happen to her. She's my whole world, Dylan. My reason for living. I love her. I love her more than anything in this world. Please know that."

"I do. So does Aubrey."

"You really are a good guy. Look at you lying to make me feel better." She looked down in her lap, thinking about what she wanted to say. "It's hard to be her mom in the way that she needs me. That's not a cop out, I swear to you it's not. I just don't know how. I tell myself everyday when I look in the mirror. I say today is going to be the day. I'm not going to work so much. I'm going to get to know my daughter. I'm going to be there for her. I'm going to do all those things I know she needs. All those things that I want."

Her eyes watered. "But I can't. I don't know how, and I'm scared of losing her. I failed my marriage, my husband, and I don't know if I could handle failing her, too." A tear escaped from her eye but she quickly wiped it away.

Here sat this woman I barely knew, other than through passing, and there she was sharing her deepest, darkest secrets with me.

"I'm not one to judge, ma'am. I love your daughter. I love her very much. I didn't know love like that existed. I hate seeing her sad or upset. That's why I'm here. It's why I came. I know she would really love it if you were at that meet tomorrow. Sitting in the stands cheering her on."

She nodded.

"It starts at seven in the morning and it will probably go till after lunch. It won't fix everything, but at least it's a start."

"Did she tell you about—"

"Yes, ma'am, she did."

"I figured as much."

I stood and she followed, walking me toward the door. At the last second I turned to face her.

"You know, everything you just said to me. You should say to her, because I'm positive she would love to hear it."

She nodded again.

"I hope she gets to see you tomorrow. Have a good rest of your day, ma'am."

I turned and left, not looking back.

"Dylan!" she shouted when I was near the elevator and I looked in her direction.

"Thank you."

# Aubrey

"What if I don't win?" I asked as he pulled into our school parking lot.

"Then you don't win."

"That was the worst pep talk ever. You're fired."

"You win some, you lose some, suga'. All that matters is that you tried."

"You should have led with that."

He laughed, tugging on the ends of my hair.

I warmed up on the track, getting ready for the long day ahead. The stands were quickly filling. Alex and the boys all showed up to show their support. Not going to lie, I was nervous.

I wanted to win.

To prove to myself that I was still that girl from back home, and even though my father left, it didn't have to define who I was. I could be happy again. Here in Oak Island with Dylan and my new friends who all quickly became my second family. I didn't feel broken or lonely anymore, I could have a fresh start.

When I heard the buzzer sound off for the first round of schools to start getting ready, I looked up back toward the stands. I found Alex and the boys, but no sign of Dylan. I peered through the crowd trying to find him. It didn't take long, he stuck out like a sore thumb with his long blonde hair and his large, stalky build. He was walking toward someone with his hands up in the air, and I followed his gaze.

*My mom.*

She had never been to one meet.

Not one.

There she was walking toward the boy that just made me fall in love with him a little bit more.

# DYLAN

"Just one more picture," Aubrey's mom requested very much to my annoyance, but I played nice for her. This was her daughter's first prom, and she was making an effort.

"Mom, you have like a hundred pictures already. If you take anymore we're not going to make it to Dylan's prom."

"I know, honey, just one more. Smile. Oh, come on, Dylan, smile!"

"I am smiling," I griped, not being able to take much more, my face fucking hurt from smiling so much.

"Okay, okay, we're done. You guys look so nice!"

She pulled Aubrey into a hug and kissed the top of her head. Ever since the track meet three months ago her mom really started trying to become more involved in Aubrey's life. I don't know how she worked it out with the hospital, but she was home at least two nights a week, eating dinner with Aubrey. Sometimes I would join them, but most of the time I left them alone. They needed that time together, to reestablish their relationship. To bond and shit. Aubrey was happy and at the end of the day that's all that mattered.

"I have to go into work. Be safe and have fun! I'll call you later." She kissed her head one last time and then smiled over at me. "Take care of my daughter."

"Always."

When the garage door closed I made my way over to Aubrey. She looked so fucking gorgeous. I had never seen her look more stunning. She was dressed in a light yellow gown that was perfectly fitted to her ridiculous body, hugging her in all the right places, reminding me how goddamn lucky I really was. Her hair was curled and tied up near the left side of her face. I had never seen her wear so much make-up before, but yet it was the perfect amount. The black eyeliner she wore just accented her bright green eyes even more.

She was breathtaking.

"How am I supposed to keep my hands to myself when you look good enough to eat, darlin'?" I caressed the side of her face with the tips of my fingers.

"That's the point, McGraw."

I looked deep into her eyes. "I love you. I just wanted you to know that."

She beamed with a gleam in her gaze, starry eyes that were new and unfamiliar. "I love you, too."

Hearing her utter those three words never got old.

I pulled her toward me by the nook of her neck and kissed her pink pouty lips. "Let's go show you off, suga."

Prom was incredibly cliché, from the streamers down to the balloons. There wasn't a place in the banquet hall that wasn't covered with confetti, ribbon, or a decoration of some sort. Aubrey tried to get us to take one of those traditional prom pictures with the photographer and I did it because it made her smile, even though I wanted to shove the camera up his fucking ass.

I wasn't much for dancing in a room full of people I barely liked, but when "With or Without You" by U2 came on through the speakers, I grabbed Aubrey's hand and took her out to the balcony where it was just the two of us. I spun her around in a circle, bringing her into my body, fitting her perfectly in my hold. I guided her arms to wrap around my neck, wanting no space between us. She laid her cheek against my chest and I placed my chin on top of her head, softly singing the lyrics of the song that became ours that night.

That moment with her had to be one of my favorites.

We left shortly after dancing to one more song. We were supposed to head over to Ian's to meet up with the boys, since none of their pussy-asses went to prom. That sure as hell didn't stop them from crashing after- parties though. The only reason I went was because when I mentioned it to Aubrey her face lit up like a goddamn Christmas tree.

"Shit! I forgot my cell phone back at my house. My mom might call. I don't want her to worry. Do you mind heading back over to my house before we go to Ian's?"

"I'm onto you, darlin', always leaving your 'phone' at home."

Her mouth dropped open.

"Close that mouth, darlin, unless you want me to stick something in it."

She shook her head. "Wow. You go from zero to a hundred in seconds."

I laughed. "It's part of my charm." I grabbed her hand, bringing it up to my lips.

"It's part of your something." She grinned as I kissed the palm of her hand and placed it onto my lap.

We drove the rest of the way to her house in comfortable silence. I followed her in to use the bathroom and to grab a water bottle from the kitchen, while she found her phone.

"Dylan!" Aubrey shouted from her bedroom upstairs. "I need your help with something!"

I made my way up the stairs and into her room, stopping dead in my tracks.

What I saw nearly knocked me on my ass.

I wasn't nervous.

Not even a little bit.

I took off my dress and hung it on the hanger, taking my hair down and letting the soft curls and waves fall around my face. My panties and bra were next, throwing them on the floor next to my bed. I pulled the comforter back to the end of the bed to just lie under the white sheet, barely covering myself before I called out Dylan's name.

I would never forget the look on his face when he walked into my room.

It was a memory I would take to the grave.

He leaned his shoulder against my doorframe, folding his arms over his chest and cocked his head to the side.

"Is it bedtime, baby?"

I smiled. "Why don't you come here and find out for yourself. I saved the best spot for you," I said, patting the bed.

He pushed off the doorframe, slowly taking off his suit jacket and then tie and throwing them on the armchair in the corner of my room. He walked over to me in four precise and calculated strides. Each one more alarming than the last.

He leaned forward, crawling toward me in the middle of my bed.

"Do you need me to tuck you in, darlin'?"

"Sleep isn't exactly what I had in mind," I purred in a seductive tone.

"Is that right?" he drawled out.

I determinedly nodded, softly kissing his lips. "No more talking, just be with me. Just you and me, right?"

"Always," he breathed out between kisses.

"Touch me, please."

I wanted to feel him in every possible manner.

"Where?" he groaned into my mouth.

I placed my hand over his heart. "Here."

He growled as he opened his mouth, slipping his tongue passed my parting lips. Working it in ways that had my legs spreading to wrap around his waist, my arms quickly followed, doing the same around his neck. He gripped the back of my neck, bringing us closer but still not nearly close enough. I wanted to be one with him. No space or distance between our ravenous bodies. His lips crashed into mine, kissing me gently, adoringly, fervently. Savoring every last touch, every last push and pull, every last movement of his lips working against mine. As if I was made just for him.

Only for him.

He pulled back a little, resting his forehead on mine to look into my eyes. To cripple me in ways I never thought possible. There was a hunger in his glare that I couldn't quite place, he wasn't even touching me and yet I still felt him all over. Both of us were panting, our breathing mirroring one another's, our hearts escalating higher and higher and beating beside each other.

So intense.

So consuming.

So mind-blowing.

In that second, in that minute, in that hour… I wanted him.

I wanted his touch, I wanted his kiss, I wanted his taste, I wanted all his movements, all his adoration and his love, all his devotion, his laugh, his smile, everything, anything.

Every. Last. Part.

*Him.*

I reached for the front of his shirt, unbuttoning it and pulling it away from his body and he let me. I touched the pulse of his neck, down to his heart, passed his taut abs until I reached his belt. The warmth and velvetiness of his skin made my sex clench and my stomach flutter. The butterfly feeling never got old. It was becoming one of my favorite feelings.

A feeling only he could ignite in me.

I gasped when he unexpectedly gripped my hand, stopping me.

"Are you sure?" he huskily rasped, my favorite sound in the world.

Before I could assure him, tell him what I felt so deeply in my heart, tell him how much he meant to me, how much I wanted to be his and only his, how much I wanted him to undo me.

Own me.

He hoarsely murmured against my lips, "Suga' once I start there will be no going back. I won't stop until I've explored every last inch of your flesh… until I'm etched so far into your heart that you'll never be able to touch your skin and not feel me."

With wide eyes I swallowed hard and breathed out, "Promise?"

"Always."

He let go of my hand and I unclasped his belt, next were his slacks, pulling them apart and lowering the zipper. Before I could touch him where I really wanted to, where I had been craving since the second I saw him in his black tuxedo, he slapped my hand away.

"This isn't about me. This is about you."

His gaze set me on fire, my heart kicked into overdrive. I loved having him look at me like that. Knowing I never wanted him to stop looking at me in that way, the way that made me feel like we were the only two people in the world, like I was the only girl in the world. He had my heart in his hands, to do what he pleased with.

I knew right then and there that I would never be able to go without him.

He licked his lips and leaned in to kiss me. The second his tongue touched mine, it turned into its own moment, its own creation, its own world. His body fell forward and mine backward, pushing me further into my mattress. My legs spread wider and he readily lay in between them, placing all his weight on his arms that were cradling my face. The room was dim, but I could sense him everywhere and all at once.

"You're so fucking beautiful, Aubrey. So damn beautiful," he groaned into the side of my neck as he placed soft kisses down to my cleavage and toward my nipple. He sucked it into his mouth as his hand caressed my other breast, leaving me withering beneath him. Chills running up and down my waiting body. My back arched off the bed, wanting more and he obliged. I could feel his erection on my wet core as he purposely moved his hips, grinding against my heat, creating a delicious tingling that I felt all over.

I sucked in my bottom lip to conceal the moan that was about to escape.

"Darlin', I want you to make every fucking noise possible. Do you understand me?"

I moaned in response and it earned me a forceful yet tender caress of his hand against my clit. He manipulated my bundle of nerves and within minutes my legs started to shake and I couldn't keep my eyes open. He effortlessly made his way down my body, pushing his fingers into my opening and sucking on my nub in a back and forth motion.

My hands immediately gripped his hair and he grunted in satisfaction. I couldn't take it anymore, the room started to spin and my breathing faltered.

"Hmm... ah... mmm..." I exhaled.

The next thing I knew, he was kissing me, and I tasted myself all over his mouth. It was intoxicating as much as it was arousing. He knew my body better than I did, spending hours upon hours exploring it until he memorized every last curve.

I heard a rustling of some sort and opened my eyes to see that he was opening a condom as he kicked off his slacks and boxer briefs. I watched with fascinated eyes as he rolled it up his big, hard cock, barely being able to contain my need for his body to once again be on top of mine.

He kissed me again, giving me exactly what I craved and placed the tip of his dick at my opening.

"I love you," he whispered in between kissing me.

"I love you, too. More than anything," I murmured, not breaking our kiss and eye contact.

I moved my hips, beckoning him to keep going. He still didn't move and I started to worry, but when I felt his hand move lower and toward my clit, I began to relax. His fingers played my over-stimulated nub and seconds later he slowly started to ease his way inside me. The sensations of his fingers replaced the uncomfortable feeling of his thrusts.

I was done for.

There would be no coming back from him.

I was his.

Exactly the way I wanted.

# DYLAN

"Are you okay?" I groaned into her mouth.

"Hmm…"

"You're so fucking tight, so fuckin' good. Your pussy was made for me, baby."

Nothing compared or even came close to the feeling of Aubrey, to the sensations that only she stirred within me. This was more than just sex, more than just two bodies coming together, more than anything I've ever experienced before.

This was her.

*Mine.*

I patiently move in inch by inch, taking her slowly and cherishing her like she deserved, like I had wanted to for so damn long. Her body was mine to do with what I pleased and my heart was hers for eternity.

Her back subtly arched.

"Almost there, baby." I thrust in a little more. "I love you," I reminded, wanting to give her a bit of comfort.

"Mmmm…" was all she could reply.

I took a moment when I was fully inside her, to savor the feeling, not stopping the friction of my fingers against her clit.

"Open your eyes. Let me see your eyes."

She did.

"There's my girl."

I moved my fingers faster, gradually thrusting in and out. She was so fucking tight, so fucking wet, and so fucking perfect. I kissed her, savoring the velvety feel of my mouth claiming hers. My thumb brushed against her cheek and she smiled. I kissed the tip of her nose, thrusting a little faster.

"You feel me inside you?" I growled into her mouth. "You feel that?" I thrust in harder, manipulated her clit with the sway of my hips.

I positioned my knee a little higher and her leg inclined with mine. Her breathing elevated and I knew I was hitting her sweet spot better from that angle. I gently grabbed the back of her neck to keep our eyes locked. My forehead hovered above hers as we caught our breaths, trying to find a unison rhythm, as I brought her lips to meet mine, pushing my tongue into her waiting mouth. My thrusts became harder and rougher, her body responding to everything I was giving. Everything I was taking… She was claiming me, too. Our bodies moved like we were made for each other.

Her eyes dilated in pleasure but also in pain. I immediately lapped at her breasts not being able to get enough of her.

"Dylan," she breathed out and I swear my cock got harder.

I moved back up to her face and our mouths were parted as we both panted profusely, not being able to control the thoughts that were wreaking havoc on our souls. Desperately trying to cling onto every sensation of our skin-on-skin contact, I felt myself start to come apart and she was right there with me.

"I love you," she repeated over and over, climaxing all down my shaft and taking me right over with her. I shook with my release and passionately claimed her mouth once again. She returned every ounce of emotion I was giving her.

We stayed like that for I don't know how long. I kissed all around her face, her neck, and her breasts before I got up to go to the bathroom. I turned on the shower and when I came back she was in the exact same position I left her, looking up at the ceiling with a glow about her I had never seen before.

I grabbed her ankle, tugging her toward me and she shrieked in response.

"What are you doing?"

"Taking care of what's mine."

I carried her into the shower and did just that.

# Chapter sixteen

# Aubrey

I wish I could tell you that things got better.

I wish I could tell you that nothing changed between us.

I wish I could tell you a lot of things.

But I couldn't.

*I can't.*

I never regretted the decision to give Dylan my virginity. I never regretted meeting him or being with him, I never regretted anything that ever happened between us, not for one second.

No regrets.

I loved him.

*I love him.*

The night we made love it changed so many things that I never expected to change. That I didn't even think would be possible, and that I sure as hell never contemplated for one damn second.

That it could change *everything.*

Every smile.

Every laugh.

Every touch.

Every. Single. I. Love. You.

For the first time in my life I realized what it was like to truly give yourself to someone. To open your heart to the possibility of love and happiness and everything that comes along with it.

All of the stuff that filled the spaces in between.

The good.

The bad.

The *love…*

It had been a few days since we made love and I was still riding the high feeling of bliss. Late one night when I was alone, an unfamiliar sound woke me from a dead sleep. I followed the noise down the stairs and found my mom crying to the point she couldn't breathe.

"Mom?" I called out as if I were a child, standing in the archway that led into the dining room.

She immediately wiped her face, trying to hide the evidence of her meltdown. It was no use her mascara ran everywhere causing black streaks down her face. Nothing could take away the vision of the strong woman crumbling to pieces before my very own eyes.

"I'm fine, honey, go back to bed," she spoke in between sobs.

"What are you doing home? Shouldn't you be at the hospital?"

She shook her head. "Aubrey, go to your room please. I'm fine."

"I'm not leaving until you tell me what's going on." I stepped closer, not backing down.

It was then that I noticed the open bottle of wine on the table. My mother never drank and it was blatantly obvious that she was drunk.

"Is dad... is dad okay?" I asked, with tears filling my own eyes, my mind running wild.

She immediately broke down, uncontrollably bawling. Her body shaking and shuddering so hard, I rushed to her side, bending down and closing her in with my arms, holding on for dear life. She shook even harder. I found it hard to breathe from the force of her crying. I would never forget what it felt like to try to hold my mother together while she fell apart in my arms.

"Shhh... it's okay, Mom. Feel me... follow my voice. It's going to be okay," I reassured her with the same soothing tone Dylan had used on me the day I told him the truth. Gently, I stroked her hair, rocking us back and forth, desperately wanting to give her any comfort that I could.

"No! It's not, Aubrey, it's never going to be okay! I'm so sorry. I'm so sorry that I ruined everything! It's all my fault!" she wallowed against me.

"It's fine, Mom, just try to calm down please." I begged and pleaded with her.

"I can't! Please forgive me! I'm begging you to please forgive me!"

"Of course I will," I replied with tears falling down my face. I couldn't hold them in any longer. "What's going on? You're scaring me. Please tell me what's going on?"

"I wish I could take it all back. I wish I could go back in time and make it all better but I can't. I will never be able to. He left me and he's never coming back. There's nothing I can do about it anymore."

"Dad? Mom he left—"

"I held him back, Aubrey! He wanted to do so much with his life and I just held him back to fulfill my dreams and to do what I wanted. I never let him have a choice. Not once. It was always about me. I was selfish, Aubrey. I loved him so much and he sacrificed everything for me. I could see it in his eyes. He wanted more out of life, out of what I could give him, but I didn't care. I made him choose me!" she uncontrollably wept.

"We were so fucking young. I didn't know any better. I thought our love could make it through anything, but I was wrong. He gave up everything for me, but he said he wanted to. He made me believe he did. I should have known. I just never thought it would ever get to this point."

"Mom, I—"

"He resented me, Aubrey. When I realized it, I tried to make it better. Why do you think he went back to school? I thought if he did something he loved, it would fix things, but it only became worse. Our dynamic changed. I wasn't the provider anymore and I didn't know how to share that with him. I felt like in his eyes I wasn't doing a good job, like I failed at that too. It was just too much to handle. All we did was fight all the time. I didn't know how to make it better, I didn't know how to be a wife or a mother, I didn't know anything anymore."

I pulled away from her, needing to look into her eyes. She looked so broken, so alone, even though I was right there with her.

"Mom, you didn't do—"

They say that everything happens for a reason. That your life could change in an instance, in one moment in time and you never even see it coming. There was no preparing for it. No battle to be won. I thought this was my moment.

I couldn't have been more wrong.

"I did, Aubrey. I failed at everything. I'm still failing. I was at the hospital working my shift and I got served with papers today. Your father wants a divorce. It's over."

That night changed everything for me.

There was no going back.

Only moving forward.

I held my mom in my arms until she passed out from the exhaustion of her tears. I stayed there all night with her mourning the cost of her mistakes. I finally put her to bed when the sun came up. I never told Dylan that my father wanted a divorce. My mom and I never discussed that night again either. There was no point, the damage was done.

For both of our lives.

Summer went flying by. I blinked and we were almost through Dylan's senior year of high school, my junior year. He had applied to several colleges all around the states and got accepted to most of them. He asked me my opinion on every last one, what I thought, what I wanted, where he should go, what was best for us. It was constant, over and over again. Every month became every week and soon it was a daily question. Each time he asked me my heart broke a little more, screaming at me to tell him what I needed.

*The truth.*

Except I never did.

I never could.

I smiled and told him that he had to choose for himself, that I couldn't make the decision for him. Which only led to us arguing, a lot. We fought more than we should about the little things because we couldn't fight about the big things. I couldn't confront the elephant in the room.

That he was leaving me.

Like my dad did to my mom.

Like my dad did to *me.*

I wasn't going to make the same mistakes as my mom. I wasn't going to hold him back, even if I wanted to and ask him to stay…

Would he?

I was afraid to find out the answer. He may not leave today, or tomorrow, but someday he would and the vicious cycle would repeat itself.

I know you're asking yourself why I couldn't just tell him that. Why I couldn't just open my mouth and be honest with him. Tell him what I felt, every last insecurity that was buried deep within my bones, harboring to the point of pain, what was really going on.

*See, love is a beautiful thing.*

It builds you up so high until you reach the end and there's nowhere else to go, but down. I was only seventeen, but felt much older. Mature beyond my years. It had always been that way for me, having to grow up fast and mostly alone. You don't realize how much of your childhood affects the person you become, the person you are. How memories shape your life, your feelings, and most importantly your *love*.

The struggle between the things we could change but didn't want too, versus the things we could change but didn't know how too.

I was terrified if I told him what I needed, he would leave me anyways. Except the inevitable would take much longer, like a ticking time bomb located in the center of my heart just waiting to go off and leave me broken. Days, months, years of getting closer and closer to him, building a life with him, for what? Eventually that love he had for me, for us, would turn into resentment for holding him back, not letting him accomplish his dreams and goals. Our love would die like a plant that I spent years and years showering with tender love and care.

I couldn't do it.

I'd rather him leave me now.

Then hate me later.

I would become my mother.

There was no way in hell I could go through that again. Once was enough. Twice would be unbearable. I also couldn't just walk away from him. I would love him until he left me because either way.

I would lose.

"What are you doing?" he asked, laughing as I straddled his lap on my bed with my phone in my hand.

We had just finished making love. We were doing that a lot more now. It was the only time my mind stopped spinning and I allowed myself to just feel.

*To be with him.*

I was wearing my bra and panties and he was only in his boxer briefs.

"Taking a picture of you," I said, looking adoringly in his eyes.

The eyes I wanted to remember.

"Why?" he asked, gripping my waist, rubbing his thumbs back and forth along my lower stomach.

"Just in case," I simply stated with a tone I barely recognized.

He noticed it immediately. There was very little that Dylan didn't notice and he often called me out on it, which led to us fighting. I squealed when he unexpectedly flipped me over instead, caging me in with his body and locking my arms above my head like he knew I loved.

He hovered above me and looked deep into my eyes and rasped, "Try to leave."

# DYLAN

Everything fucking changed.

The irony was not lost on me.

I went from having meaningless sex with every girl, to making love to the one girl that meant everything to me and it still went to shit. I couldn't catch a break. If I knew sex would have changed things between us I would have never been intimate with her. I was eighteen and about to graduate from high school. All I wanted to hear her say was that four letter word.

*Stay.*

We fought. We argued a lot.

Over nothing.

Over everything.

I pushed her and pushed her and pushed her and yet I still couldn't say what I truly needed to. The truth.

*"Ask me to stay. Please, just fucking ask me to stay."*

Pride was a very powerful thing, especially for a man like me.

"So, I hear Lucas and Jacob got accepted into Ohio State," Aubrey coaxed as we sat on a blanket at the beach. She was pressed under the nook of my arm, her head lying on my shoulder, snuggled in just the way she loved.

"Mmm hmm," I simply replied, trying to avoid another argument with her.

"When were you going to tell me that you got accepted, too?"

"Since when do you care where I go?" I retorted back at her.

She tried to pull away from me, but I held her tighter.

"Can we just sit here and enjoy the evening, Bree?"

I started to call her Bree more often, suga' and darlin' were few and far between. She didn't say anything, but she didn't have to.

"Do you want me to go to Ohio State?"

"I want you to go wherever you want. I've told you—"

"No shit, I have it fucking memorized now," I snapped.

She sighed and I glanced at her. "I'm sorry, okay?" I kissed the top of her head.

"I figured you wanted to be with your boys, Dylan. That's all. I mean you've never left this town. Ohio State seems like a great opportunity for you to explore."

"Explore what exactly? What do you think I'm missin' out on that I need to see, Bree?"

She shrugged only pissing me off further. She did that a lot, started an argument and would never finish it, leaving me to feel like the asshole for wanting to.

"What is going on in that beautiful mind of yours?"

She peeked up at me with defeat already appearing in her eyes.

"What do you want to do with your life, Dylan? You graduate in a few months and you've already missed several deadlines from your college acceptance letters. What are you waiting for?"

"Maybe I want to stay here. Would that be so bad?" I finally admitted.

"That's not what you want," she bit in a tone I didn't appreciate.

I roughly pulled my arm away, missing her warmth immediately.

"Jesus Christ, Bree, enough with the vague responses. I'm sick of this shit."

She stood, hovering above me. I placed my arms on my knees, looking out at the water.

"Just go! Go to Ohio State! That's what you want. Don't stay here for me! You know you don't want to."

Her bare feet kicked around the sand nervously, as her eyes looked everywhere but at me.

I snidely nodded. "It's fucking funny how you seem so damn sure of what I want, but you have not a clue what you want."

"What's that supposed to mean?" she yelled back, throwing her hands in the air.

"Nothing, fucking forget it."

My blood started to boil. I couldn't take much more of this conversation with her.

"What? Now I'm not worth an argument? Where's my asshole boyfriend, Dylan, huh? When did he get replaced with such a goddamn pussy?"

I stood so fast she never saw it coming, getting right in her face. She folded her arms over her chest, arched an eyebrow in a challenging gesture.

"If you fuck with the bull, sweetheart, you'll get the horns. Want to try that again?" I warned, taking another step into her personal space.

"For fucks sake, just go to Ohio State, Dylan. Go be with your boys. Leave me here. We can do the long distance thing and see what happens, okay? That's what I want. That's what you need," she answered in a neutral tone, shocking the shit out of me.

The force of her words, causing me to step back. "Is that right?" I gritted out.

"Yes, that's right, McGraw." She dug her finger into my chest, pushing me backward.

My head jerked back, stunned and I blurted out for the first time, "Promise?" out of nowhere.

She held her head higher, knowing if she said the following it would be the end. The decision would be made with or without my consent. She took a step toward me, her intense gaze never leaving mine and then whispered,

"Always."

# Chapter
## seventeen

# Aubrey

It was a lonely school year for me.

My world wasn't the same anymore and I felt like I was just going through the motions of day-to-day life. My parents were now officially divorced. I saw my mom less than I did before. She drowned herself in work, to appease her heartache. I talked to my dad here and there. He tried to be more active in my life, but it wasn't the same.

Nothing ever was.

Dylan, Jacob, and Lucas were all at Ohio State experiencing college life and Alex was going through her own shit, as was Austin. The school year was almost over and I had seen Dylan maybe three times. Each visit was only a few days long. He came back home for his nineteenth birthday, for my eighteenth birthday and then again for the holidays. We talked on the phone almost every other day, but the conversations were short. Texting became our normal way to communicate. I had applied to a few colleges including Ohio State and to my surprise I got accepted. I still hadn't told Dylan that bit of information. I didn't want him to think I applied there to follow him, or pressure him to be committed to me.

Our relationship changed, like most long distance ones did. I didn't know how to talk to him anymore or maybe I did and I was just scared. I spent most of my time by myself thinking, contemplating, and drowning in everything that was around me.

I was shocked as shit when Alex texted me saying she was going to one of Charlie's infamous parties with Austin. She never went to parties. In fact, the last one she went to, she ended up throwing up. I had to cover for her with the boys while Lucas took her somewhere to tend to her. I stayed home instead and watched television late into the night. When my phone rang bringing me out of a dead sleep, I realized it was only early morning.

"Hello," I groaned, wiping the sleep from my eyes.

"Aubrey," my mom's worried tone screeched through the phone.

I instantly sat up. "Mom. What's wrong?"

"Honey, a taxi is on its way to come get you, okay? I will tell you what's going on when you get here."

"What? No!" I panicked, jumping off the couch. "Tell me now, what's going on? Is everything okay?"

The line went silent except I could hear her breathing. She sighed. "I can't leave or I would come pick you up myself. It should be there in a few minutes. Come into the ICU."

"ICU? What's going on? Just tell me, please. Are you okay?" My heart was pounding out of my damn chest, anxiety coursing through me.

"I'm fine. Your father is fine. I'll see you in a little bit." She hung up.

I stood there in shock listening to the silence for a second. My mind was reeling, trying to grab onto something, anything. I ran upstairs, having fallen asleep on the couch. I brushed my teeth and threw on a hoodie with some jeans. By the time I was done the taxi was honking in my driveway. I sat in the back seat with my heart in my throat the entire ride to the hospital. What should have taken minutes, felt like hours.

I came barreling through the ICU doors.

"Where's my mom?" I yelled out to the receptionist who looked at me with sympathy.

*What the fuck is going on?*

"Aubrey," Mom called from behind me.

I ran to her side. "What's going on? You just hung up on me."

She looked all around the open room and then back at me.

"Honey, last night…" She rubbed her forehead and then at her temples. "There's been an accident. Austin and Alex have been in an accident."

My eyes widened. "Oh my God," I breathed out. "Please don't tell me…" I couldn't finish my sentence. My heart felt like it had

149

broken into a million different pieces, only being able to think of the worse.

"They're alive, but they're in bad shape," she explained.

"Are they going—" I stuttered, tears started rolling down my face.

"Austin is in much worse shape than Alex, he flew out the windshield. We had to put him in a medically- induced coma after we operated on his brain with the hope that it would help the swelling decrease. He's suffered severe trauma to the head, honey, with several broken ribs, burns and deep cuts on his face and chest from the airbag and windshield. He's going to need a lot of therapy, but it's not impossible."

My hand went to my mouth, my eyes filling up with tears.

"And Alex?" I asked, my voice breaking.

"Alex's brain was swollen from her head busting the window, but we didn't need to operate, it should go down on its own. But she's still in a coma and should eventually wake up. We just have to be patient, head trauma is very serious and both of them will be under close watch for a while. She had to get some stitches on her forehead and lip. Other than that, she suffered minor cuts on her face, her arms and around her body. She's bruised everywhere, along with a few broken ribs. I'm telling you all this because I don't want you to be surprised when you walk in and see them," she warned.

I shook my head not believing what was happening. "I don't understand. How did this happen, Mom?"

"Austin was driving drunk and he ran into a tree. His alcohol level was .092, and Alex's was .16, they're lucky to be alive. It's just a waiting game now. They have the best doctors taking care of them."

"Are the boys—"

"Yes," she interrupted.

I didn't know what hurt more. That my friends were both fighting for their lives or the fact that Dylan didn't even call to tell me. He obviously didn't need me here to support him and that was the hardest pill to swallow.

"Lucas is in Alex's room. He hasn't left her side and Dylan and Jacob have been going back and forth between rooms. I believe they're all in Alex's room right now."

"Is Lucas' dad—"

"Yes, Dr. Ryder is here. His wife took Alex and Austin's mom to get some coffee. They're in room 702."

I nodded. "Okay."

"Come on, I'll take you down there."

I nodded again not able to form words. I barely felt it when she wrapped her arm around me and we walked side-by-side to Alex's room. The boys didn't even notice that we were standing at the doorway. Lucas was sitting in a chair in the back corner, Jacob leaned up against the wall and Dylan was sitting by her bed holding her hand.

I cried harder, seeing them all torn up with my best friend lying on a hospital bed, nearly unrecognizable. I couldn't imagine what Austin looked like.

They all looked in my direction when they heard my sobs, Dylan didn't even bat an eye that I was there.

"I'm so sorry," I wept. I didn't know what else to say.

"She's going to be fine," Lucas stated with a stern tone, I don't know if he was trying to convince me or himself.

"Of course she is," I replied, hugging my arms around my torso, trying like hell to hold it together.

"I'm going to go check on Austin, honey, I'll be back. Talk to Alex, she can hear you even though she's not awake," Mom coaxed, trying to break the tension in the room.

"Okay," I replied, but stayed put in the doorway.

She left and I just stood there as if I was an outsider looking in and not one of them anymore. I wondered what Dylan had told them, what they knew.

Dylan stood, nodding toward me to come sit. I swallowed hard, my heart beating faster with every step I took. He gestured toward the chair not breaking eye contact with me. He didn't try to hold me or kiss me, nothing of what I expected him to do.

I sat, looking at the girl who I considered a sister, immediately feeling guilty for alienating her. I had barely spoken to her that whole year. She probably needed me the most this past year since she was just as alone as I was and yet I had shut her out. I had been too lost in my own mind and problems to care about hers. The thought that I might not ever be able to talk to her again, that

151

something could go wrong was too much to take and I broke down. My upper body gave out on me, and falling over to her side.

"I'm so sorry, Alex. I'm so sorry that I haven't been a better friend to you," I sobbed, holding her hand tight in my own. "I promise I'll make it up to you. Please just give me the chance," I cried so hard into her hand. My body shook with each sob.

It was then that I felt Dylan's strong hands press against my shoulders, rubbing at the tense muscles. I hadn't felt his hands on me in such a long time. I couldn't remember the last time we made love.

"She's going to be fine, suga'."

I also couldn't remember the last time he called me that and it only made me cry harder.

"Promise?" I murmured loud enough for him to hear.

He crouched down beside me, whispering, "Always" in my ear.

I don't know how long I stayed like that. My arms wrapped around her with his arms wrapped around me. It could have been seconds or hours. Time just seemed to stand still and from that moment on I knew I would hate fucking hospitals. I never wanted to see one again. Nothing good came from them. I had no idea how my mom could do this everyday. How she chose this over her family.

When Alex's mom walked back into the room, I let her have my chair. I hugged her tight before she sat down to hold her daughter's hand exactly how Dylan and I had.

"I'm going to take her to see Austin." Dylan put his hand out waiting for me to follow him toward the door.

They nodded, looking back and forth between us.

"It's good to see you guys. I miss you," I said out of nowhere, needing them to hear it.

Jacob pulled me into a hug and kissed the top of my head, Lucas quickly followed. It felt like old times but under horrible circumstances.

"He's not as strong as he pretends to be, Aubrey," Lucas whispered in my ear, catching me off guard. "He needs you now more than ever. Don't fuck with him if he's not what you want."

*What was that supposed to mean?*

I pulled away as our eyes locked, he smiled and kissed my forehead. Dylan grabbed my hand and I looked down at the ground not being able to face him after what Lucas just said. Dylan took me into Austin's room and I didn't have the same breakdown as I did with Alex. His mom was in the room and I wanted to stay strong for her even though I was massively hurting on the inside.

My mom went home to rest up for her next shift. When she returned to work, it was well into the night and she found me in the exact same place, as I was when she left. Sitting in the waiting room for something to change.

Any news.

I felt like I was getting in everyone's space, the boys, their parents, and the staff. I thought it would be easier if I sat in the waiting room to stay out of the way. Dylan came out a few times to check on me, but never stayed long, not that I expected him to. He had barely said more than a few words to me and as much as I tried not to take it personally, I couldn't.

Which only made me feel worse. I should have been thinking about my friends, but there I was thinking about my relationship.

*Proving that I am selfish.*

I really was my mother's daughter.

# DYLAN

We took the first flight out after our parents called. None of us even grabbed clothes. I thought about Aubrey the entire time. I wanted to call her and tell her I needed her, but every time I started to dial her number, I stopped. I knew her mom would take care of it and she would show up eventually. Things were tense between us. I didn't even know where we stood half the time anymore. All I wanted was for my friends to be okay. I didn't need any more problems than the ones that were already lying in comas struggling for their lives.

I was so pissed at Austin, I could barely fucking see straight. We all were. All we ever asked him to do was protect Half-Pint.

It was that simple.

Each one of us told him that he needed to step up and watch over her, while we were gone off at college. He looked all of us in the damn eyes and swore he would. I couldn't say one damn thing about how I felt, because that would only provoke Lucas more to walk into his room and take him off life support, if I did. Jacob and I kept our mouths shut, knowing that nothing between them was ever going to be the same after this.

Especially if…

I pushed the thought away from my mind before it even fully formed. Terrified it would take over and I would be the one walking into Austin's room. Although, Jacob was the oldest by a few months, I always felt like I was. These boys and Alex, they were my life. If I could trade places with either one of them, I would in a heartbeat. No questions asked. I couldn't help but feel responsible for both of them fighting for their lives.

I walked out of Alex's room needing to get some fresh air. I was starting to go stir crazy at the hospital and it had barely been two fucking days since the accident.

"Honey, you need to go home and get some rest. You can come back after you get a few hours of sleep. I promise I will have the cab there for you first thing in the morning," Aubrey's mom said as I walked up behind them stopping in the archway, to listen.

"I don't want to leave."

"Aubrey—"

"You don't understand. What if I leave and something happens, huh? What if I don't get to say goodbye. I can't do it again, Mom. I can't know someone might leave me and not get to say goodbye. Been there, done that already, remember? I can't go through that again. Please don't make me leave them," she wallowed, neither one of them knowing I was standing there.

I didn't step away. I was glued to the floor that felt like it was caving in beneath me.

"Oh, honey," her mom sympathized. "Is that what—"

"Please let me stay. At least if something happens, I can say goodbye this time. They won't leave me, too." She was on the verge of hysterics.

All the air was knocked out of my body. The realization hitting me harder then a ton of fucking bricks. That's why she wanted me to go, she would rather me leave on her terms.

*I'm such a fucking idiot.*

"Nothing is going to happen to them. They're going to pull through, sweetheart. Look at me, I promise you. I'm treating them myself and I know they're going to be just fine." She pulled her into her arms and Aubrey visibly melted against her mom as she repeatedly kissed the top of her head. "Baby, your dad didn't leave you. He left me. He divorced me. Not you, never ever you. You have to understand that. I'm so sorry it's taken me this long to say it to you. He loves you more than anything in this whole world," her mom declared, holding her at arm's length so she could see the truth in her eyes.

"It doesn't feel that way," Aubrey murmured. "It hasn't felt that way for a long time."

"Oh, honey. Give me a chance, okay? I'm going to be there for you. Things are going to change. I promise you. You have no idea how I felt when your friends came in. God, Aubrey, I didn't even know if you were with them. I swear I thought you were going to be pulled in next. My whole world flashed before my eyes. They're going to make it because I will do everything in my power to make it happen." She kissed her head again.

Watching such an intimate moment between them was something that I would take to the grave. Her vulnerability in that moment took me back to the time that I first fell in love with her. Back to a time that I didn't know I missed till right now, back to a time that my life seemed complete because I had her.

All of her.

Things became much clearer to me now and it took everything in me not to run to her and tell her how much I loved her. How I would make everything better, how much I thought about her, dreamt about her, how hollow I felt on the inside because she wasn't with me. How I debated so many damn times to transfer to Wilmington just to be near her again, just to see her smile every day. To tell her she was so damn beautiful, even when she was broken.

To promise her that I would never leave her, that she was mine.

"You can stay—" her mom was in the middle of saying as I walked up to them.

"I'll take her home, ma'am," I interrupted, both of them immediately wiping at their faces.

"You don't have to—" Aubrey interjected, but I cut her short.

"Suga', I'm taking you home."

155

I gave her a stern look that told her I wasn't going to back down on this. I wrapped my arm around her shoulder and tugged her into my side.

Her mom walked toward us, lovingly smiling. "Get some rest, too, okay? I'll hold down the fort. Your friends are going to be just fine," she reassured both of us.

"Thank you, ma'am."

She gripped my shoulder for a few seconds and then walked back towards Alex's room, leaving Aubrey and I alone in the waiting room. There wasn't anyone else around, but us.

"You don't have to take me home. I know you want to stay here." She looked up at me, with tears still in her eyes.

I tugged on the ends of her hair, I couldn't remember the last time I did that either.

"Dylan, what—" I placed my finger to her lips to quiet her.

"Not here." I grabbed her hand. "Come on."

We walked hand in hand out to my parents' car that was parked in the parking structure. We drove in silence both of us lost in our own thoughts. When we got to her house, she went straight up to her room. I followed after I splashed some water on my face and made us some sandwiches. I knew neither one of us had eaten all day.

When I walked into her bedroom she was sitting in the middle of her bed with her legs pulled up to her chest and her arms wrapped around them. Exhaustion was evident on her face.

"You heard what I said didn't you?" she asked, breaking the silence between us.

I set our plates on her nightstand and sat on the edge of her bed, resisting the urge to pull her toward me.

"It doesn't matter."

She glanced at me. "It doesn't?"

"No," I simply stated.

"And why is that?" she questioned not amused.

"Because I'm here now."

"For Austin and Alex. You're not here for me. You haven't been here for me this entire year," she blurted out. Her voice laced with nothing but anger and hurt.

"I know what you're trying to do, darlin', and I'm not falling for it. Not this time. Not ever again."

She needed to get that through her pretty little head. No more fucking games.

"You just know everything, don't you, McGraw?"

"When it comes to you, I do," I countered.

She scoffed. "I don't want you here. I don't need you here. You can go."

She was full of shit, but I didn't call her out on it.

"I'm not going anywhere."

## *Aubrey*

I couldn't take it anymore. The walls were caving in on me, my emotions suffocating me and burying me alive. I crumbled onto the bed, my body giving out on me.

"I can't do this anymore," I sobbed for what felt like the hundredth time that day. "Please just leave, Dylan, just leave me now because I won't be able to live through it later."

My body was shaking to the core.

My truths shattered all around me.

Dylan's arms engulfed me, laying me against his chest. Tears streamed down my face. It felt so good for him to hold me, to feel his love and devotion, to feel everything that I desperately tried to push away for the last year. It was then that I openly bawled. I sobbed like a baby. Big, huge, ugly tears.

He placed my hand over his heart.

Calm.

Steady.

Secure.

*Dylan.*

"Shhh... feel my heart. Shhh..." he repeated.

I placed my face near the hand that was over his heart, wanting to feel his love beat against my cheek.

"I love you and I'm not going anywhere." He kissed the top of my head. "Just you and me."

"Promise?" I found myself saying.

He didn't falter.

"Always."

# eighteen

## Aubrey

"Are you packed?" Dylan asked over the phone.

I giggled. "I told you I was like a hundred times now." I swore he had selective hearing sometimes.

"I know how you are with clothes. All I need is that pretty little smile, and lingerie. That shit's good stuff, too."

I laughed. "It's going to be cold at night. We're up in the Smokey Mountains," I reminded him.

I walked over to my dresser and pulled out the one piece of lingerie I owned, and stuffed it in the bottom of my bag.

"Suga, let me worry about how to keep you warm at night," he assured me.

It had been three months since the car accident. Austin and Alex pulled through, thank God. The judge charged Austin with a DUI, suspended his license for a year with a shitload of legal fines and community service. He was still going to therapy and popping pain pills like they were candy. I overheard Dylan and him in an argument about it a few weeks ago, but never said anything about it.

I had officially graduated from high school and I decided to attend Ohio State with Dylan and the boys since Austin got accepted as well. I was going to tell Dylan on our vacation that he had planned well over a month ago. He said we needed a fresh start to the year from hell and I couldn't have agreed more.

My mom kept her word, that night at the hospital was a turning point in our relationship. She was once again starting to become more involved in my life, like she had before my dad served her with divorce papers. When I told her I wanted to go to Ohio State to be with Dylan, she was over the moon excited for me. I talked to my dad more often now too, at least a few times a week. He seemed happy for some reason and I was content for him.

There was peace in my soul again, thanks to Dylan.

"What time does our flight leave?" I stopped pacing for a second to look around my room and make sure I wasn't forgetting anything.

"Six in the morning. It's why I'm spending the night. We need to leave at four to get to the airport on time."

"Oh, so that's why you're spending the night?" I teased.

"That's exactly why, you minx. I'll be over later tonight. I'm going to go check on Austin before we leave," he said with worry in his tone.

"Is something wrong with him?" I coaxed, hoping he would tell me what was really going on.

"Darlin', I wish I knew. I'll see you soon. I love you."

"I love you, too."

I hung up, and fell down onto my bed. The cool sheets felt amazing against my warm skin. I lay there staring up at the ceiling, thinking about the possibilities that lay ahead of us and for the first time in a long time I wasn't scared because I knew they included Dylan.

# DYLAN

"What the fuck, man?" I argued, grabbing the empty pill bottle on Austin's nightstand. "This shit just got refilled two weeks ago. You want to know how I know? I fucking drove you to pick it up from the pharmacy."

He rolled his glazed eyes at me like a fucking teenage girl. "What do you want me to say? I'm in fucking pain, man," he slurred.

"No. What you are, is playing with fire. Read the warning label, asshole. Take *two* tablets a day for pain. Do not mix with alcohol and I know I fucking smell weed in here."

"When the hell did you become my dad, McGraw? Jesus Christ, you act like you've never smoked weed before. What are you, to good for it now that you're so goddamn pussy-whipped? Maybe try and pull your head out of Aubrey's ass cheeks long enough—"

"You talk about Aubrey like that again, Austin, I won't hesitate to knock you the fuck out. I don't care how high you are."

"What the fuck do you want? What is this a 'Just say no' drug campaign? What are you going to do next, Dylan, fry me an egg and tell me that this is what my brain looks like on drugs?"

"Lay off the pain pills. This shit's highly addicting," I warned.

"So is pussy, but I never heard you fucking complaining."

I took one last look at him and left, already knowing that this wasn't the end.

It was only the beginning.

I drove to Aubrey's house later that evening. I hit the waves after I left Austin's place, needing to clear my mind before I saw Aubrey. I didn't want my sudden change in mood to affect how excited she was about our vacation. Things were great between us.

Better than great actually, and I wanted nothing or no one to ruin that.

We landed close to nine in the morning the next day. I rented a car and drove us up toward our cabin for the week in Pigeon Forge, which was known for being the center of fun in the Smokies. The higher we went the more breathtaking the view got. Aubrey was pretty excited to see some trails near the cabin she could go running on.

"Wow, McGraw," she admired, peering all around the cabin.

The fireplace was on and there was food in warming trays on the kitchen island that I had delivered just for us. I didn't want to share her with anyone the entire week, not even housekeeping. I spent a small fortune to have the reclusive cabin that was at the edge of the mountain. I had barely touched any of my college funds that my parents had started when I was born. Spending most of the last year at the apartment I shared with Jacob and Lucas.

The cabin was breathtakingly beautiful with a big open area that had stairs leading up to the master suite. The kitchen was placed directly underneath with barstools below the high granite tops. The thought of eating Aubrey as she sat on the counter immediately crossed my mind.

"Penny for your thoughts, McGraw?" She smirked as I backed her up into the counter, lifting her onto the edge.

"I'd rather show you," I groaned into her ear.

I got down on my knees, taking her panties with me and did just that.

We spent the next few days in the cabin by ourselves enjoying each other's bodies mostly. We had our own private hot tub on the deck that we christened a few times. We were all alone, no one around for miles. I purposely had meals delivered so that we wouldn't have to go anywhere, I had Aubrey and food, what more did I need?

By the fourth day she said we needed to do something other than eat and have sex. She wanted to do some sightseeing, walk around the cobblestone picturesque streets that were crowded with small stores and buy a few souvenirs for everyone. I took her to Dollywood and we rode roller coasters the entire day, screaming and laughing with each other. I literally threw Aubrey over my shoulder for a few rides because she refused to go on them with me. We stayed there till the park closed and then headed back to our cabin where I made up for being, "Such a fucking asshole."

The next day was mostly spent in bed, but since I promised her that I would take her downtown to shop, I had to get my ass up even though all I wanted was to spend the day buried inside her. We decided to shop around in some of the tourist traps then go grab dinner and barhop.

"My mom would love these!" she exclaimed, grabbing a pair of earrings from the fourth shop. "Do you think Half-Pint would like these?" She held up another pair of earrings to her ears.

"Darlin', have you ever seen Alex wear jewelry?"

She shrugged. "Exactly. She needs more than just that shark tooth necklace she wears all the time. I don't think I've ever seen her take it off. I'm going to get them."

She strolled to the next display, running her fingers across an antique jewelry box with a familiarity in her gaze as she smiled to herself.

"My mom used to have one of these. My dad gave it to her when they first started dating. It looked exactly like this. I remember when I was little I used to sit on her bed and watch her get ready for work, pulling out all sorts of shiny jewelry from her special box. My dad would buy her a piece of jewelry every year for their anniversary and he would hide it in her jewelry box. She would pretend to be surprised every time she opened it the next morning," she yearningly laughed.

"It's one of the best memories I have from childhood. Things weren't always bad." She opened the lid and a pink ballerina came to life, spinning in circles with a soft tune playing.

"It's 'Fur Elise' by Beethoven," she said out loud, answering the question in my mind.

"When things started getting bad and neither one of them were around very much, I used to go to her room and take the jewelry box back to my bedroom with me. I'd listen to the song until I fell asleep. For some reason it made me feel not so alone."

My eyes widened, surprised by her confession. She nervously glanced at me, shutting the box and placing it back on the shelf.

She smiled. "So, I think these are the winners," she announced, changing the subject and holding up the earrings.

I tugged on the ends of her hair and then kissed the tip of her nose. "I think those are perfect."

I paid as she went to the bathroom. I knew she needed a second to be alone. Aubrey would unexpectedly have these vulnerable moments almost as if she was reliving that time in her life all over again. Just as quickly as they would come, she would brush them back under her rug, which was filled with nothing but a pile of memories and feelings.

As soon as she walked out of the bathroom she was my girl again. Just like I knew she'd be.

We found a little dive bar that served food and had live music with karaoke. We sat at dinner for the next few hours talking and enjoying each other's company. I ordered us some drinks and the waitress didn't card us. I was going to be twenty soon and her nineteen, but I was often told I looked much older than I was. We took a cab that night so I indulged in the drinks, too. It didn't take long to realize that the alcohol was getting to Aubrey. I had never seen her drunk before and it was fucking entertaining. It only made me fall in love with her just a little bit more, if that was even possible.

"Suga', you're drunk."

She shook her head and closed her eyes with an adorable smile on her face.

"Nah uh," she giggled, making me laugh.

"You keep looking at your phone, McGraw. You expecting a phone call?"

"Something like that."

"Ah! Is the love of your life calling?" She grinned, wiggling her eyebrows.

"No, darlin', she's sittin' right in front of me."

She smiled, big and wide and I swear it lit up the entire room. "Well I'm expecting a phone call from my dad," she said, sipping her drink.

"Is that right?" I gave her a questioning look.

"Mmm hmm…" she replied with the straw still in her mouth. "He's away on business and I haven't talked to him in a few days. I guess my aunt told him we were away on vacation and he texted me earlier today to tell me that he would try to call soon."

I nodded.

"I'm going to go to the bathroom." She stood and started to walk away. "I'll be right back," she said over her shoulder.

I grabbed her wrist, turning her toward me. She squealed as I brought her lips to mine to kiss her. She was so fucking irresistible right then that if we weren't in a crowded bar, I'd take her right there on the damn table.

"Now, you can go to the bathroom," I said, dismissing her.

She rolled her eyes, kissing me again. She was taking her sweet ass time in the restroom and I was about to go looking for her when Etta James' "At Last" came on through the speakers.

I laughed because I just knew my girl.

I looked up on stage and there she was, standing pretty as fucking ever with a microphone in her hand. Swaying her body in the sexiest way I had ever witnessed.

My cock twitched.

The beat of the music came on and she effortlessly moved her hips, pulling up her hair from the nook of her neck as her hips began to sway faster. The lyrics came on and she gradually moved her hands from her hair to her neck, to her breasts, then down to her body. She sang, touching herself exactly the way I wanted to. I shook my head no and she understood my silent warning, hitting the high note. I had no idea she could sing that well.

She made her way over to me, slowly, making me wait. Teasing me further, her hands roaming her body. Doing a sultry dance, never once missing the lyrics of the song. When she finally made it to me, she lowered her body down my chest with the beat of the music. She moved to sit on my lap and provokingly rocked her hips against my already hard-as-shit cock. Licking her lips when she felt my need for her.

I sucked in my bottom lip and spread my legs, knowing that everyone was watching us and that we were probably going to get kicked out of the bar, but by that point I didn't give a flying fuck. My girl was on my lap and if she wanted to give me a lap dance in front of a bunch of strangers, who was I to deny her of that happiness.

She leaned back and rotated her hips like she was fucking me while the epilogue of the song was rising then she grabbed my hands to touch her breasts and then her waist, gliding her body on top of me the entire time. I couldn't take it anymore and gripped her hair, bringing her face to mine as she sang out the last lyric of the song.

As soon as she was done I plunged my tongue deep into her mouth, biting her lower lip to show her who she belonged to while not being able to get enough of her. The entire bar clapped and cheered. Aubrey got off my lap and took a bow for her sexy performance.

I asked for the check and we got the fuck out of there.

I honestly don't know what came over me. I wasn't much for being the center of attention, but when I walked into the bathroom I had an overwhelmingly strong urge to make him desire me in a way he never had before, I wanted to be the instigator. When I walked out into the bar area, I saw the girl who was just singing getting off the stage. That's when I knew I wanted to put on a show for him.

As soon as I saw the music selection, I remembered his love for blues music. I would never forget his face as I sang and danced for him, as if the bar wasn't full of a crowd watching my every move. It always happened when we were together. Everything and everyone just faded away and nothing else mattered but us.

The taxi ride to the cabin was interesting to say the least. Our poor driver definitely got a show while I was straddling Dylan's lap, as we heavily made out. Dylan threw some money at him before he carried me out of the cab with my legs wrapped around his waist and my arms around his neck.

"I want you," I moaned into his ear, kissing all along the side of his neck.

The second his lips touched mine he growled, parting them. His hands were all over me. He couldn't decide where he wanted to touch me the most. I leaned into every touch and sensation that he had to offer. Enjoying the thrill of what was to come. Dylan was always in control, but with the show I put on for him and the alcohol coursing through his veins, it was enough to make him lose all sense of reason.

Exactly how I did when I was with him.

I reached for his belt and he eagerly moved his hips against my hands as I worked his button and zipper. I couldn't get them off fast enough. I pulled out his long, thick cock and aggressively stroked it back and forth while he opened the door. Rushing in and kicking it closed behind him, he slammed me up against it.

It should have surprised me, but it didn't.

He tore open my blouse, buttons flew everywhere with the sound of them crashing onto the floor. My bra was off within seconds. I felt his strong, callused hands roughly kneading my breasts as he sucked and licked all around my nipples. My back arched, making me grip the back of his neck. I wanted him closer and yet he still wasn't close enough.

I whimpered when he placed my feet on the ground, but I didn't feel the loss of his touch for very long. He roughly shoved me up against the door again, taking off my skirt and panties in his wake. I didn't even have time to blink before his tongue was pushing into my folds, swirling it into my opening.

"Fuck," I panted as he placed my thigh onto his shoulders.

My hands instantly went into his hair, pushing it away from his face so I could watch. I loved to watch when his face was buried in my most sacred area.

The only place *he's* ever touched me.

As if reading my mind he opened his eyes to look up at me as he sucked my clit into his mouth, urgently moving his head in a side-to-side motion followed by a back and forth one.

"Ah!" I yelled out, trying to catch my bearings.

My chest heaved with every precise manipulation. His mouth literally eating me, like I was his favorite fucking meal of the day. I watched him push two fingers into my wet heat causing my legs to shake, which only made him finger fuck me harder and lick me faster. Bringing me so close to the edge of my release, I was going to have the most intense orgasm of my life.

Through hooded eyes, I saw him start to stroke his cock and that was my undoing. I came so fucking hard I saw stars. I didn't even have a second to recover before he picked me up, slamming me against door yet again and plunging deep inside me with one, hard thrust.

"Fuck," he loudly groaned against my parted lips. "You make me so goddamn crazy," was the last thing he said as he slowly pushed in and out of me.

Savoring the moment.

"Take me like you want," I raspingly demanded, licking his lips and scratching at his back. "Fuck me," I whispered close to his ear in a seductive tone.

I didn't have to tell him twice. He was never rough with me, we always made love, but I wanted him to own me.

To break me in every way possible.

Mentally.

Emotionally.

Sexually.

"Lean back," he huskily ordered,

I did as I was told. He placed one of his hands around my throat and his other on my hip, gripping hard. Applying ample pressure to both. I knew there would be markings all over my body when he was done having his way with me, but I didn't care. I wanted them.

Every. Last. One.

He forcefully and urgently made me bounce on his cock as he slammed into me with his own movements. I had never felt him that deep before and the pain along with the pleasure was enough to drive me to the point of no return.

I sucked in a breath. "Your cock feels so fucking big. I'm so wet for you."

He growled and clutched my hips harder, nothing turned him on more than filthy words coming out of my mouth. He angled my body in a way where I felt like I was going to fall.

"I got you," he breathed out, reading my body.

I nodded and he swiftly thrust back inside me, except this time his cock hit my sweet spot more forcefully.

"Fuck…" we said in unison as he roughly thrust in and out of me, holding my hips and body weight the entire time. My noises grew louder and louder the closer I got to my release.

"Oh my God, Dylan, I'm going to come so hard. I'm going to come so fucking hard. Please… please… please… make me come."

He fucked me harder and faster, mercilessly pounding into me, his balls drenched from my wetness.

"That's it, baby… squeeze my cock with your tight pussy. I can't get enough of it, I wanna fucking devour you."

The slapping sound of our skin-on-skin contact echoed in the room.

"Yes… yes… yes…" I breathlessly moaned.

My body shuddered, throwing off my balance from the intensity and overpowering orgasm that only Dylan could ever give me. No one would ever be able to touch me like he could and I knew that from the moment he first put his hands on me.

*I was his.*

He didn't stop, his hands moved to my shoulders as he continued to slam into me. I tried to keep his pace, barely done with one release before another hit.

"Fuck yes… do it, do it, do it," he urged. "Keep coming on my cock."

I fell forward, clenching onto his neck. He made this roaring sound from deep within his chest as we both came together. Panting profusely, trying to catch our bearings while he placed kisses all over my face, still not removing himself from deep inside me.

"I fucking love you. I fucking love you so much, Aubrey. I'm yours."

"Promise?"

He looked deep into my eyes and spoke with conviction, "Always."

# Chapter nineteen

# DYLAN

I woke up the next morning with Aubrey in my arms and I knew right then and there that I never wanted to wake up without her by my side again. I hugged her tighter and kissed the top of her head.

"I could get used to waking up like this, McGraw."

I smiled, she was thinking the same thing I was.

"Well, I guess it's a good thing that I'll be at Ohio State with you so the odds of us waking up like this every morning are looking pretty promising," she announced out of nowhere.

I sat up, taking her with me.

"What?"

She grinned and shrugged. "I've been waiting for the right time to tell you that I got accepted to Ohio State. I applied months ago when we..." She shook her head. "When I... was pushing you away. I'm sorry about that, McGraw. I never apologized for what—"

I placed my finger on her lips, silencing her.

"Darlin', it's in the past. I'm not one to dwell on somethin' neither one of us can change. I'm here now and that's all that matters," I said, stroking her cheek.

She nodded, throwing her arms around me. I pressed her closer to my body and it was then that I noticed the bruises on her back.

"Shit."

She immediately pulled away from me and I saw the bruises on her hips, her neck, and some bite marks on her breasts.

"Fuck," I roared, taking in the purple and black marks that I gave her. "Suga', why didn't you tell me I was hurtin' you?"

"What?" She peered down at herself and laughed. "I wanted those." She looked back up at me. "I wanted you. I think you and I both know I very much enjoyed it. Plus I bruise easily. We just had some rough sex, you're thinking too much into it."

I pulled the hair away from my face, holding it at the nook of my neck. "I shouldn't have drank that much," I revealed, suddenly remembering my fuck up.

"Dylan, please don't do that. I wanted it. I asked for it. I loved it."

"Darlin', we didn't use a condom," I stated, shaking my head.

Her eyes widened but she quickly recovered.

"It's fine." She smiled. "I'm not ovulating."

"And you know that how?"

"I have an app on my phone and it tells me stuff like that, but maybe I should get on the pill, huh?" she nervously asked.

"You don't have to do that for me."

"I know that. I want to do it for me. For us. I guess I didn't even realize that sex without any barriers would feel so different. I want to keep that going. I want to feel all of you, every time with nothing between us." She blushed, biting her lip, and covering her breasts with the sheet.

I tugged on the ends of her hair. "I've never gone raw before."

"Really?"

I shook my head no. "I've been tested, too. Before we got together. I wanted to make sure—"

She tackled me to the bed, kissing all over my face.

"I love you, I love you, I love you!" she repeated, and I flipped her over.

"Now, bring that sweet pussy over here suga', ride my face. It's fuckin' breakfast time."

And I did for the rest of the morning. It was afternoon when we finally left our bed. We showered together and ate some lunch. Our late night, early morning sex escapades left us both pretty damn hungry.

"I googled one of the trails, and I thought maybe we could go running. I want to try out for the track team at Ohio State, and I need all the practice I can get."

"Whatever you want," I simply stated, checking my phone.

"Wow. I could get used to you saying that."

I laughed, placing my phone back on the counter.

"It's a private trail, too. Everyone goes on The Cades Cove Loop or The Ramsey Cascades trail, so maybe we could... you know." She wiggled her eyebrows at me.

"Darlin', I'll be staring at your ass the entire time we're running. What do you think?"

She hopped down off the bar stool and took off towards our room. I put on my sneakers and grabbed two waters from the fridge. Aubrey came out in a yellow sports bra and white cotton shorts, her hair tied in one of those knots on the top of her head.

"You ready?" she asked, catching me checking her out.

"Lead the way, beautiful," I said, smacking her ass.

She grabbed my hand and opened the door, but I stopped when I heard my phone ring in my pocket.

"Shit." I answered it. "Hey, give me one second." I put my hand over the receiver. "I have to take this call." I gave her an apologetic look.

"Oh ok." She started to come back into the cabin.

"Just go. I'll catch up, darlin'."

"You sure?"

"Yeah. It's the trail that we saw on the way up here, right?"

She nodded. "Yeah it's just a straight trail. It won't be hard to find me, but are you sure? I can wait for you."

"No, it's fine. You go," I said insistently.

"Okay."

I kissed her and she turned to leave, she was about to close the door behind her.

"Suga'."

She stopped, walking back inside while I took off my shirt and threw it at her.

"Put some fuckin' clothes on."

She smiled, laughing loud while putting on my shirt.

"I won't be far behind you."

"Promise?" she teased.

"Always."

She kissed the air and she was gone. I looked at my phone, relieved.

"I've been trying to reach you for weeks. I'm so glad you're finally calling me back."

# Aubrey

I had my ear buds in, Dylan's blues playlist blasting and my water bottle by my feet as I stretched my muscles for a few minutes. It was then that I realized just how sore I truly was. I smiled to myself remembering everything that happened last night and this morning. The fluttering feeling in my belly still lingered. I shook off the sentiments as I jogged down the trail getting my body warm for the run ahead.

I couldn't help but think about Dylan and how much I loved him. How our relationship was genuinely the real thing now. The type you read about in books and watched in movies.

What fairy tales were made of.

I had never been happier in my entire life, and it was all because of him. He changed me in more ways than I ever imagined possible. The emotions, the feelings, the devotion, the adoration, and the love. I lived and breathed for him. It was real.

Sincere.

Consuming.

I thought about him when I was alone and even when I was laying in his arms. It didn't matter where I was, I always wanted to be near him. Nothing was ever enough. The thought alone that I would soon be moving, and we would be together everyday like we were before was all I ever wanted and needed.

Was for someone to love me.

Exactly the way he does.

I finally found *him* or maybe he found me, but all that mattered was the loneliness was gone, as if it was never there to begin with.

I ran faster, my body getting used to the pace and fast movement of my limbs. With each stride I felt lighter from the demons that haunted me. From the sadness that always felt like it was lurking just around the corner, ready to take me under.

I closed my eyes for a few seconds wanting to remember this moment. Etch it into my mind and secure it in my heart.

I gasped, almost losing my footing when I felt his strong arms come around me.

"Jesus, McGraw, you scared the shit out of me," I laughed, my heart racing from the running and his surprise attack. I took a few steady breaths waiting for him to say something and took off my ear buds.

Silence.

"Dylan?" I nervously chuckled, trying to turn around.

"There's no Dylan here, *baby*," a deep voice responded.

A voice I didn't recognize. The scent of whiskey assaulted my senses and panic set in. My heart immediately dropped, and I instinctively screamed bloody murder, trying to fight him off. He chuckled against my ear, pressing me closer to his chest.

"Do your best, bitch. No one can fucking hear you out here," he rasped in a menacing tone that made my body shudder. "I love to make them all scream," he added. His voice sounded muffled and I could hear some type of accent.

"No!" I whimpered, pathetically thrashing around my entire body, kicking and screaming at the top of my lungs. "Dylan, Dylan!" I repeated over and over again, hoping that any second now he'd come and save me from this hell. "No! No! No!" I yelled out to no avail, making him laugh.

The bastard fucking laughed.

His body shook against mine. I fought harder. I fought so fucking hard, trying to break free from the monster who was about to take my life away from me.

My thrashing feet connected with his shin, causing his arms to slack just enough to give me the illusion of freedom. I stumbled forward scraping my knee on the gravel, trying to escape, trying to run toward my happiness.

*Dylan.*

I wasn't fast enough.

"Where do you think you're going?"

He picked me up in the air as if I weighed nothing and body-slammed me face first onto the ground. Pain radiated throughout my body. I choked from the sudden loss of breath, the wind knocked out of me with his entire weight resting on my back. I sucked in air that wasn't available for the taking as he roughly gripped my hair, jerking my head so far back that I reeled in pain. My vision turned black, blinking away the white spots.

"Please, please don't hurt me," I groggily choked out. Pleading with him to let me go.

He pulled my neck back further, and I swear I thought he was going to tear my hair out.

"Please," he sadistically repeated. "Oh, *baby*, I want you to beg. I want you to beg me to fucking stop. It only gets my cock harder for that sweet little cunt that I'm about to rip to shreds."

He rocked his hips a few times against my ass. Grinding his already hard dick on me. I could feel him everywhere, his filthy hands violating me. Bile rose to my throat. The bile I was fighting back was making its way back up.

I instantly started bawling. Tears streaming down my face, my lips shaking and my teeth chattering.

"Please, don't do this! Please, please don't do this," I sobbed over and over again, my body convulsing.

"Shut the fuck up! You're going to enjoy what I have in store for you, and if you don't, I'll fucking do it again!"

He spit on my face and slammed my head into the dirt, smearing it back and forth like he was trying to bury my face in it. The dirt, leaves, and branches on the ground scratching my face even more.

I could feel every little stone cutting into my cheek. I cried harder and screamed louder, whipping my legs around. I screamed till my voice felt raw and my mouth dry. My throat burned and the sounds just faded away.

He pulled back my arm, lifting it higher up my back and I cried out in agony.

"Don't fucking move. I'll break your goddamn arm. But, *baby*, you can go ahead and try fighting me. It's only going to make me fuck you harder."

He let go of my hair and slowly, deliberately roamed his hand down to my waist.

"No! No! No! Please, please, don't hurt me! PLEASE!" I bawled, I pleaded, I begged. My tears so intense, so consuming I couldn't see anymore. I couldn't breathe, I couldn't move. "I'm begging you please don't do this! I'll give you whatever you want just don't hurt me!" I openly wailed, pleading with the man I knew was going to cause me pain.

He pulled the hem of my shirt over my eyes and nose leaving my mouth exposed. Taking away all my surroundings and engulfing me in nothing but Dylan's scent. My earplugs now closer to my face, Dylan's playlist my only solace while my soul was getting destroyed. I could dimly hear "Ain't No Sunshine."

"Mmm…" he groaned, causing me to cringe. "So much fucking better."

He touched all along my back with his dirty hands, slowly making his way down to my waist again, snapping my shorts and making me jolt.

"Let's get to the good stuff, shall we?"

I sobbed, choking on my own tears as he pressed his hand onto my hips, roughly ripping off my shorts and panties.

"No!" I shouted, kicking and fighting with every ounce of strength I could muster. His hand that was holding me down let up a little, and I pushed up ready to run. For a second he let me feel like I had a chance, for a moment I thought this nightmare was over. I was up on my hands and knees, my foot digging in the dirt to get up.

"Why you running? The fun's just getting started," he taunted, gripping my ankle, causing me to fall face first back onto the ground. Dragging me back to him. My stomach now being ripped by the dirt.

He was toying with me, I was his prey.

I struggled against him as I heard him lower his zipper, but it was no use. He was too strong for me. I never stood a chance and when that realization hit me, he coarsely flipped me over onto my back and slapped me so hard across the face that I immediately tasted blood. He didn't let up, he punched my stomach and ribs repeatedly, until there was no fight left in me, and all I wanted to do was die. I never thought there could be pain like that. When he restrained my hands with a zip tie, I knew there was no saving me.

My dying body lay limp in a pool of my own misery while he violated me. I heard what sounded like a switchblade and instantaneously started fighting him off once again.

"No! No! No! Please!" I pleaded in agony. My body was slowly slipping away, my soul dying, all while he violated me over and over again.

I felt the knife at my neck and I closed my eyes, thinking this was the moment that I was going to die. I was going to be killed seeing Dylan's shirt and engulfed in his scent that he gave me with so much love to protect me, listening to the music that made me fall in love with him.

He ripped down the center of my sports bra, leaving me much more exposed than before. The knife faintly grazed my chest with each flick of his wrist, and then he punched me in the stomach again. My head lay slack against the dirt, and I hazily felt his body get on top of mine before he finished killing me completely. Thrusting so hard inside me that my body jerked forward from the pain of his sudden intrusion.

*This isn't happening, this isn't happening. Dylan will save me. He will save me.*

"Fuck, you feel better than I thought you would," he growled against my face, gripping his hand around my neck and clutching his other hand on my hip, opposite side to where Dylan's hands had laid the night before.

I gasped for air, for tears, for my voice but nothing came out. The pain was too overwhelming, too strong, too crippling. I screeched out in agony with each rough thrust. He pushed in and out of me. I blocked out his voice and all the filthy shit that came out of his mouth about my pussy being so fucking tight, so fucking perfect, so fucking *his*. I closed my eyes silently praying to God that he would kill me, that I would die, and that he would take away the hurt that I felt in every last fiber of my body. The throbbing between my legs, the ache on my muscles, the bruises all over me, and the hole in my heart where Dylan used to be.

I checked out, I detached myself.

*Aubrey is gone.*

All that was left was the girl being raped.

Nothing would be the same after this.

Nothing…

I felt him come deep inside me. It was in that moment that I lost my faith in God, no hope, no light at the end of the tunnel.

Not for me.

Not ever again.

He shook with his release, grunting, as I resisted the urge to throw up. Soft tears slid out of my eyes, soaking Dylan's shirt. He sat up and buttoned up his pants, the sound of his zipper would forever haunt me. I kept my face to the side, my vision still blocked, falling in and out of consciousness. Each time I blinked a happy memory came into sight and instantly was ripped from me, one by one. I saw my mom, my dad, Dylan, the boys, and Alex, followed by nothing but darkness. The loneliness creeping back in as if it never left to begin with, as if my mind was showing me one last time what happiness was, because I'd never feel it again.

"Better than I thought it was going to be."

He threw what felt like my torn clothes on my chest.

"Don't pretend like you didn't like it, you dirty whore. I see those fucking bruises on you. *Baby* loves it rough, huh?" he scoffed, kicking what felt like dirt on me.

And that's when I died a little more.

He kicked me in my stomach one last time and I instantly recoiled to the side, holding my waist, once again choking for air.

"Until next time you little cock tease."

I gasped, wheezing for my next breath. Bringing up my knees to lay in fetal position, shaking, and suddenly freezing. I removed Dylan's shirt from my head, placing it on top of me, trying to find any warmth, any comfort, any solace that I could.

I felt nothing.

I was numb.

Not even Dylan's scent comforted me or the soft blues tune that I would never bear to hear again.

I don't know how long I stayed there, cold, broken, by myself with nothing but my despair and I closed my eyes wishing that I would never wake up.

When I heard a familiar voice yell out, "No!"

It was only than that I realized…

Dylan would die, too.

# DYLAN

I didn't expect to stay on the phone that long. A conversation that wasn't supposed to take longer than a few minutes lasted almost an hour. When I looked down at the time, I realized Aubrey should have been back by now. The hair on my arms stood up and an awful fucking feeling instantly took over.

I ran into the bedroom and grabbed the first shirt I could find from the drawer. Throwing it on over my head as I sprinted toward the door. I didn't even lock it behind me. I just took off, my feet moving on their own accord. The longer it took to find her, the worse the feeling bubbled up inside me. Soon, all I felt was panic and a deep urgency to see her. I pushed through, my feet hitting the dirt faster and faster, sweat pooling at my temples with my heart beating out of my chest.

The closer I got to her the more I sensed her around me. She had to be close by. The dreadful feeling built higher and higher, making it nearly impossible for me to remain calm.

*I shouldn't have let her go alone, I shouldn't have told her to go without me. I shouldn't have taken the damn call.*

Plaguing thoughts were assaulting my mind, one right after the other, turning inklings of fear into pure panic that something terrible could have happened to her and I allowed it to. The trail began to ascend, causing me to slow my pace. I knew I had to be close, I swear I could hear her. Right before the trail started to even out I saw one of Aubrey's running shoes and her white panties, lying in the dirt. Nothing could have prepared me for what I saw next.

Nothing.

Seconds before I came upon her unrecognizable naked body, I heard her whimpering in pain. Someone might as well have taken a sledgehammer to my heart right then and there. Some fucker left the love of my fucking life lying on the ground like a piece of trash that was thrown out as if she were nothing.

As soon as I saw her, I knew things would never be the same.

Our relationship.

Our love.

Our future.

*My girl.*

She was lying on the dirt, broken. Her once flawless skin now covered in bruises. Her face covered in scratches and her beautiful eyes looked empty now. Tears were rolling down her cheeks and she kept rocking herself while her hands were bound to her front.

I yelled out, "No!" I ran as fast as I could, falling to my knees before I even fully got to her. I ignored the shooting pain that screamed from my knees.

She flinched, recoiling away from me.

*From me.*

"No, no, no, no..." she repeated with a shaky voice I had never heard before.

"Baby, it's me."

She winced like it hurt her to hear me say that.

"Jesus Christ, I'm so sorry, darlin'," I pleaded not knowing where to touch her, hold her, comfort her. I needed to get her to a hospital right away.

With shaky hands I pulled out my cell phone, dialing 911.

"What are you doing?" she simply asked her voice void of emotion.

"I'm calling for help, Suga'."

I yearned to touch her and when I reached out for her again she retracted like a wounded child.

"Please, don't call anyone. Please," she pleaded in a tone that broke my fucking heart more than it already was.

I set the phone down next to me and put my hands out in the air so she could see them.

"Suga', I'm not going to hurt you. Do you understand me? You're safe now, I'm here," I pleaded with her.

She closed her eyes, a single tear falling down her bruised cheek.

"Baby," I muttered my voice breaking with my eyes watering. "Baby, please, let me touch you. It's me, Aubrey, it's me."

More tears slid down her beautiful face and I gently swept them away, but she still flinched from my touch. My face frowned and it took everything in me to keep it together. She needed me to be strong for her.

*For us.*

"Please, baby, open your eyes and look at me, see that it's me."

My walls were crumbling down. I took her blood-covered hands that were zip tied together and gently placed them on my heart. "Feel me, Aubrey."

She instantly pulled her hands away from me and winced in pain.

I took in all the bruises, the finger imprints on her neck and arms. I had to shut my eyes for a minute before I made my way below her waist, already knowing what I'd find. I opened them and immediately saw the dried blood on her inner thighs and the marks on her legs and skinned knees.

I bowed my head in such shame and remorse all at once, hitting me harder than anything I have ever experienced before.

"No, no, no… what did he do to you, baby? What did he fucking do to my girl?" I openly wailed, trying to catch my breath. "I'm so sorry, Aubrey, I'm so fucking sorry," I choked out hanging my head over her body.

My face drenched with nothing but guilt.

I sat up pulling my shirt over my head. "I'm going to sit you up so I can put this on you, and then I'm going to carry you and we're going to go to the hospital so that the doctor can check you and make sure—"

"NO!" she shouted, opening her eyes. "No fucking hospitals. I don't want to go! Please, please, please, don't make me go. I'm begging you, please—"

"Shhh…" I whispered, caressing her face with the knuckle on my hand. "Shhh… I'm still going to sit you up and carry you, okay? We can go back to the cabin, and I can check you. Alright?"

She didn't answer, but I took her silence as a yes. She whimpered in pain when I sat her up, and I quickly placed the shirt over her head and down her body. The zip ties not allowing me to pull her arms through the sleeves.

She turned away from me like the mere smell of me was painful.

"I'm going to carry you now. We can go as slow as you need, suga'."

"Just fucking do it," she replied in a harsh tone.

I picked her up into my arms like she was a baby, being careful not to hurt her. She cried the entire way back to the cabin. Each tear that fell from her face would forever be ingrained in my soul.

Every. Last. One.

I opened the door, trying like hell not to make any sudden movements that would cause her any more pain. I grabbed the scissors from the kitchen and gently laid her on the bed in one of the other bedrooms. I didn't want to take a risk carrying her up the stairs to our bed. I cut the zip ties, sick to my fucking stomach the entire time. She immediately scooted as far away from me as possible when she heard them snap, even though it caused nothing but more agony to her already broken body.

"Baby," I whispered, sitting on the edge of the bed, reaching for her.

She put her hands out in the air, stopping me. "Please, just go," she muttered, barely loud enough for me to hear.

"Go where, darlin'? Where do you want me to go? I'm not fucking leaving you like this."

She looked right at me for the first time since I found her with dead eyes. Not one ounce of love left in there for me.

"Away. Away from me," she gritted through her chattering teeth.

I violently shook my head, my fists clenched at my sides. "I can't do that. Aubrey, let me take you to the hospital. They can check you, and we can catch this guy. Something can be—"

"No," she sternly argued. "Can't you see, Dylan? It's too late, the damage is done. I'm already dead."

"Oh my God, don't say shit like that." I placed my hand over my heart, trying to hold it together. I got off the bed and paced back and forth, wanting nothing more than for her to let me hold her, show her she had life in her still.

Most of all, I wanted to take away everything that fucker did to my girl.

"Baby, you're right here," I cried, pushing my hands through my hair. "You're right fucking in front of me. You're not dead. You're right fucking here with me," I argued, pounding my fist on my heart.

"Just go! I don't want you here. Please just get out!" Her body shook from anger.

"If you're not going to let me take you in to get help, then please just let me look at you. Let me make sure—"

She crawled to the end of the bed, her body almost giving out on her. I reached once again to help her and she slapped my hands away. She slowly stood, pulling her arms out through the sleeves to hold her ribs and lean against the bed frame.

I stepped toward her. "Let me help—"

"Jesus Christ!" she yelled out, stopping me dead in my tracks.

We locked eyes.

"Look at me, Dylan! Fucking look at me! What more can they do for me? Nothing! What more can you do for me? Fucking nothing! The damage is already done. You can't help me! You can't save me! You're too fucking late!"

I immediately jerked back like she knocked me the fuck out. Fresh tears erupted from her eyes, and it took everything in me not to rush to her side and beg her to forgive me.

"Now leave!" she screamed at the top of her lungs, wincing once again from the pain in her ribs, I was sure were broken.

I stood there, glued to the goddamn floor that was caving beneath me. There was no coming back from this. It took one phone call to rip my happiness away, to take *my* girl away.

The irony was not lost on me.

"LEAVE!"

She fell to the floor in defeat and rocked back and forth. She shattered and this time I couldn't pick up the pieces.

I shook my head, bowing it in defeat and walked out of the room. I heard the door slam shut a few minutes later as I paced around the living room, tugging my hair at the back of my neck, wanting nothing more than to rip it the fuck out.

I was at a loss.

I didn't know what I could do. I didn't know what I could say. I didn't know one damn thing on how to handle this.

To handle her.

When I heard the shower start running, pure panic set into my bones.

*She was cleaning off all the evidence.*

"What the fuck, Aubrey?" I lamented out loud to myself, looking up at the ceiling. Silently praying to God that this was a nightmare I would soon wake up from. A God-awful dream.

Something…

Anything…

Than what was actually happening.

It didn't take long to hear her sobs, each one of them tore into my heart, my soul, my mind, as if I was the one crying. The longer I stood there, the louder they got.

"Please, God," I wept, looking back up at the ceiling again. "Please… help me, help her. Please… I beg you." I wasn't an extremely religious man, but I did believe in the power of prayer.

But at that moment I would have sold my soul to the devil if it meant it would take away her pain, undo what had just happened, and her memory of this day.

I couldn't take it anymore. I ran into the room, slowly walking toward the bathroom as if I was walking towards my execution. In a way, I was. With each step my heart pounded faster, it rang louder in my ears. I gripped the handle, leaning my forehead against the door for a few seconds. Praying once again she wouldn't push me away. I took a deep, shaky breath and gradually opened the door.

My stomach dropped.

My heart was now in my throat with bile rising, but I swallowed it back down. The glass shower doors so fucking foggy with steam immediately pouring out of the bathroom as if she couldn't get the water hot enough. Her skin bright red, which only accented all the bruises on the side of her stomach, her arms, and down her legs.

She was sitting in the middle of the shower with her legs pulled to her chest and her arms wrapped around them. Her face tucked in between, sobbing so fucking hard, her entire fragile frame shaking uncontrollably.

The memory of seeing her like this would forever haunt me. There wouldn't be one day where I wouldn't see her like that.

Falling apart in front of me.

Not. One. Day.

I didn't even bother to take off my shorts or sneakers. I opened the glass door and she never stopped bawling, if anything she just cried harder. I approached her with caution, terrified that she would push me away, but not caring if she did. I needed to hold her, to help her, to do fucking something. I crouched to sit down behind her, straddling my legs around her body.

I gently touched her back with the tips of my fingers, where more bruises and cuts had formed, instantly shutting my eyes remembering that I put some of them on her last night. I shook my head, feeling nothing but disgust towards myself. Her body shuddered when she felt me, but I didn't stop.

I couldn't.

My fingers moved to her sides, her stomach, and down to her legs. Wanting to transfer all the hurt and the pain that she was feeling to me. Wanting to remember that I did this. That I was the reason she was raped. That I was the reason my girl was gone.

*It was entirely my fault.*

I sucked in air, my chest heaving from my own sobs. She was hysterically crying at that point. I wrapped my arms around her, pressing her into my chest, and she let me.

As soon as she was in my arms I broke down.

"I'm so sorry, baby… I'm so fucking sorry… please… please… I'll do anything for you to forgive me… please…" I wallowed in her misery and my own. "I'm so fucking sorry…"

I don't know who was crying more. Steaming hot water rushed down on us as if it was cleaning off the mistakes that I would never be able to change. Never be able to make better, never be able to forget.

We stayed like that until the water was freezing and her skin started to turn blue. I shut off the shower and cradled her in my arms, grabbing a towel and laying it on her. I took her up to our bedroom, taking each stair with ease. I pulled back the comforter and sheets before gently placing her under them. She didn't move from the place I laid her, just stared up at the ceiling that I was praying to, minutes maybe hours before, and I wondered if she was doing the same thing.

I took off my shorts, grabbing a dry pair of boxers. I sat at the edge of the bed, looking at her for a few more seconds. I slowly gripped the seam of the towel and she immediately froze, holding her arms tightly around her torso.

"Shhh…" I whispered, placing her hand over my heart. "Shhh… feel me, suga', feel my heart beating for you." I placed my hand over hers and gently rubbed my thumb up and down.

She shut her eyes but still didn't relax. I carefully took off the towel, never letting go of her hand. Her face fell to the side the moment it was fully off her. My hand went straight to my mouth.

My sadness turned quickly into rage.

There wasn't a place on her torso that wasn't black and blue, what looked like a boot print etched near her belly button. I fell over, holding myself up with my hand on the other side of her waist. Breaking over my girl that was already broken. With my teeth chattering, I kissed her bruised cheek, her neck, her chest, her waist, her wrists, every place that I saw a mark, I touched it with my lips. Her body remained stiff the entire time, but she didn't stop me.

I would take what I could get.

By the time I made it down to her waist, I was shaking, closing my eyes to get the courage to look at her sacred area that wasn't mine anymore.

"Please, don't," she wept, reading my mind.

"Baby, I have to make sure you're okay. I'm not going to touch you," I replied with agony laced in my tone, not wanting to look but needing to.

She sniffled, sucking in air as I spread her legs, opening my eyes. I resisted the urge to fucking hit something when I saw the bruises on her inner thighs and her swollen folds. There was a tiny tear at her opening, and I had to look away unable to control the anger and remorse I felt burning inside.

She rolled over to her side, cradling her body in a fetal position. I scooted up toward her front and engulfed her in my arms. Her face now mere inches from mine with her dark dilated eyes, vacant, soulless, and dead.

"I love you. I love you so fucking much," I blurted, needing to have her hear me say it.

She just blinked with no emotion whatsoever.

"I'm so sorry, I'm so sorry, I'm so sorry," I repeated, over and over again like a broken record, kissing all along her face.

She tucked her face into my neck and cried.

I lay there trying to hold her together, knowing it didn't matter. She wasn't the only one who died that day...

I died, too.

# Chapter twenty-one

## Aubrey

I didn't sleep one second that night.

I barely remembered closing my eyes. Every time I did it took me right back to the moment my life was abruptly taken from me.

*When I died.*

I thought I hurt that day, but the pain the next morning was almost unbearable. There wasn't one place on my body that felt like mine anymore. I was a stranger in my own skin.

Dylan held me the entire night, refusing to let me go. I wish I could tell you it gave me comfort, or made me feel safe, loved, and cared for.

It didn't.

It made me sick to my fucking stomach.

*His scent.*

I resisted the urge to push him away and throw up all night. From the second he touched every one of my bruises in the shower, to the way he kissed over every one of them in the bed, down to the minute he looked in between my legs. I wanted to be sick.

*I let him hold me because what else could I do?*

I didn't blame him.

But I couldn't look at him either. Everything I loved about him was ripped away from me, his touch, his lips, his music, his smell.

*His love.*

Every single time I looked at him all I felt was hatred, hatred for the man that did nothing but love me.

He stirred a little when I moved away from him and I bit my lip hard to hold in the pain and not let it escape through my mouth. I didn't want to wake him. I didn't even want to be near him right now.

I don't know what time it was when I decided to give up on pretending to sleep. I winced the instant my feet touched the carpeted floor, holding onto my ribs that were definitely broken. I stood there for a few seconds, breathing through the agony that took over the body I didn't recognize. I slowly walked toward the bathroom, trying not to make a sound.

I wanted to be alone, I used to hate to be alone.

I wanted and needed to take another shower. To rinse away the filth that covered my entire body.

I could still smell him.

I could still hear him.

I could still fucking feel him all over.

When I finally reached the bathroom, I made sure to lock the door behind me. There wasn't a chance in Hell that I would allow Dylan to hold me again. Once was enough. I cringed at the thought. I leaned over on the counter, completely naked and alone. Desperately trying to hold up my frame that seemed to want to give out on me.

I peered up into the mirror, and I didn't recognize the girl staring back at me. Her eyes were bloodshot, glazed over, and hollow. Her cheek had a bruise right at the bridge. I brought my hand up to it and the image of him backhanding me across the face immediately flew through my mind. Her neck had finger marks and bruises. There wasn't any skin color left on her chest, ribs, and stomach- they were purple, blue, and black all over.

I touched the boot print near my belly button and shook my head, closing my eyes to block out the memory of him kicking me before he left me there to die. My hand moved down to my folds as if a string was pulling it, I hissed out in pain before I even got to my pubic bone. My gaze never left the mirror as I took in every last inch of my broken body. Gradually turning around to see my back that resembled my torso.

I scoffed in disgust when I thought about how much I wanted Dylan to mark me the night before. To leave bruises on me. To make me his.

*Did I ask for this?*

189

*Did I bring it on myself?*

Dylan's markings intertwined with *his* and I couldn't tell them apart. I didn't know which I asked for and which I didn't.

I didn't know anything anymore. I was a black hole of nothing.

I turned on the shower, setting it on the hottest temperature possible, stepping inside, welcoming the heat. Hoping that it would burn away my tainted skin, scorch away the feeling of his hands all over me, his body on top of mine. The hold I knew that would never go away, no matter how much I tried, how much I wanted it to.

My mind ran wild. I couldn't get it to stop, image after image of my brutal attack playing out in front of me. I was like a hamster on a spinning wheel with nowhere to go.

Round and round in circles with no end in sight.

I heard the rustling of the doorknob and then the knocking on the door.

"Darlin'," he spoke as I pressed my hands against the shower wall, leaning my forehead on the cool rustic tile.

"Baby, please," he begged, making me cringe with the simple word *baby*.

I closed my eyes and all I could see was *him*. The coward who hid behind a cloak of anonymity, the monster who raped me physically and killed my very being.

And all I could smell was *Dylan*.

I fell over, heaving down the drain.

"Shit! Aubrey, open the damn door!" He pounded.

I threw up again, holding my ribs that ached in pain. Protesting against my actions.

"Ugh!" I let out, hurling up some more. I spit, wiping my mouth with the back of my hand as I slid down the tile.

"Aubrey! Please! Please, don't do this!" he pleaded, beating on the door.

I instantly placed my hands over my ears, tuning out his voice, shutting out my own. I shook my head back and forth.

"Leave me alone! Please just leave me alone!" I shouted until my voice felt raw.

The banging on the door stopped.

Except the one in my mind had only just started.

# DYLAN

We stayed a few extra days, giving Aubrey some time before she had to face anyone back home.

I couldn't tell you how many showers she took, she would stay in there for hours upon hours, as I sat waiting for her to talk to me, to look at me, to acknowledge that I was even in the fucking room.

*She never did.*

She didn't raise her gaze to mine.

She didn't sleep in our room.

She didn't want to be anywhere near me.

She either showered or she lay in the room that I brought her to after I found her. The door stayed closed and locked.

I would knock to tell her I left food by the door, but I would come back hours later and the food remained on the ground untouched. The days went by like that with no change, no progress, nothing. I went to sleep every night praying that she would come to me, that she would crawl into my bed and let me hold her. Let me tell her how much I loved her and how sorry I was. How I would spend the rest of my life making it up to her. I held onto the hope that after some time she would let me back in. I barely slept, waking up in pure panic every night remembering how I found her lifeless and everything that happened after. Her dead eyes and broken body was the only image I saw of her now.

*My girl was gone.*

I woke up one morning, groggy as hell and looked over at the clock. It read almost noon. I shook off the sleep, surprised that I even slept in that late. The sleepless nights and overwhelming days must have caught up with me. I sat at the edge of the bed, leaning forward to place my elbows on my knees. I ran my fingers through my hair, pulling it away from my face and holding it at the nook of my neck.

I sat there contemplating and racking my brain for what I could do that day to make it different than the last. I gave up trying after a few minutes. I threw on some gym shorts and made my way to the kitchen to make us some breakfast, even though I already knew

Aubrey wasn't going to eat it. I stopped dead in my tracks when I saw that her bedroom door was open. I immediately ran toward it in hopes that she would let me see her.

That she was waiting for me.

When I reached the room it was empty, her bed untouched like she hadn't even been sleeping in it. I opened the bathroom door, and she was nowhere in sight.

"Aubrey?" I called out into the house to no avail. "What the fuck?"

I walked outside and peered around, calling out her name some more. The rental car still securely parked in the grass. I went back into her room and that's when I noticed her suitcase was gone. I opened the drawers and all her clothes had disappeared, too. I turned in a circle searching for something, anything, raking my hands through my hair, ready to pull it out.

"Jesus Christ," I muttered to myself.

*She left without saying goodbye.*

I called her cell phone and it went straight to voicemail. I texted her a few times and got no response. I waited for hours, worried sick. How could she do this, after everything? Our flight was supposed to leave the very next afternoon, but she couldn't even wait one more damn day to get away from me. I spent the entire day trying to call her and text her again and again, finally giving up around nine.

I called her mom.

"Hey, honey," she answered. "Are you as exhausted as Aubrey?"

I breathed a sigh of relief. "Something like that."

She laughed. "You kids had a good time, huh? Aubrey looks like she hasn't slept in days."

I nodded even though she couldn't see me.

"That was quite a fall though. I wish one of you had told me. I'm not very happy about being left in the dark."

"Fall?" I asked, confused. I had to sit down to hear this.

"Aubrey told me about you guys running through the trails and her sliding down a hill into a valley. She looks so beat up, Dylan, but she told me you took good care of her and she went to a clinic to get looked at. I understand that you guys didn't want me to worry."

I was instantly sick to my fucking stomach.

"Dylan? Honey, are you there?"

"Yeah, I'm sorry. I'm so sorry, ma'am." I cleared my throat, my voice breaking.

"Oh, it's okay. I know you would never let anything happen to our girl. I know she's safe with you. I understand accidents happen, just next time please let me know, so I'm not surprised when I see my daughter walk in with bruises and cuts on her body."

"Mmm hmm…" Was all I could manage to get out.

"Are you alright? Aubrey said she wasn't feeling good. She's been in her room all day in bed. She barely touched her lunch and dinner. You guys coming down with something?"

"Maybe," I simply stated.

"Well, get better, okay? I know Aubrey can't go more than a few hours without seeing you," she laughed.

"Yes, ma'am."

"Was there a reason you were calling?"

"Umm… yeah." I scratched my head. "Aubrey wasn't answering her phone. I just wanted to make sure she was alright."

"Awww, Dylan. You're a mothers dream for their daughter. I'll tell her you called."

"Thank you. Have a goodnight."

"You too."

I hung up with her mom. I was livid, for all I knew she could have been dead somewhere. My anger got the best of me. I took my phone and threw at the wall. I watched it break just like my heart had.

I went home by myself the next afternoon.

I drove to her house as soon as my plane landed. I barely had my Jeep in park before I opened the door to get out. I made it up her porch steps in three strides and knocked on her front door, but no one answered. I knew her mom would be at work. I stepped back and looked up at her bedroom window, it was dark and I couldn't see a thing.

I knew she was in there.

I could feel her.

"Darlin', please…" I shouted, praying that she would hear me and open the front door.

*She didn't.*

I sat on her porch with my back against the door for hours, knocking every few minutes. I realized she wouldn't answer, but I hoped that maybe her knowing that I was there, still waiting for her, would reassure her that I wasn't going anywhere, no matter what.

I nodded off a few times and woke up to my phone that I replaced that morning, pinging with a text message. I swiped over the screen.

*Please. Leave me alone.*

I didn't have to wonder who it was from. I replied back.

*Never.*

She stopped texting me. That was the last message I received, and I went home an hour later. Days of not seeing her, of not talking to her, turned into weeks. Not for my lack of trying. I was going fucking crazy, and there was nothing I could do about it.

Not one damn thing.

All I could was wait.

I was all out of prayers.

"Hey," Alex said, sitting beside me at her parents' restaurant. "Why aren't you surfing with the boys?" She gave me a worried look. It was out of character for me not to be surfing, but I wasn't up for anything lately.

I shrugged, looking out at the patio from the corner table.

"Are you okay?"

I shrugged again.

She picked up my arm, placing it around her tiny frame to lie against my shoulder. We stayed like that in comfortable silence for a while.

"The first time you boys started bringing girls around, I hated every last one of them. I thought you were replacing me with boobs and blonde hair."

I chuckled, and it sounded so foreign coming from my mouth. I couldn't remember the last time I laughed.

"You know I never felt that way with Aubrey. Not once. I loved her instantly. She is like the sister I never had, other than Lily of course."

I nodded, hugging her closer to me.

"I may not understand what you boys do."

I knew she was referring to Lucas, but I didn't call her out on it.

"At the end of the day you're a part of me, each one of you. A bond like that can never be broken."

I glanced at her, understanding her subtle metaphor and she smiled. I caught someone out of the corner of my eye, and that's when I saw her.

*Aubrey.*

I instantly stood up. Our eyes connected from across the room, as if she felt me. For the first time since I met her I couldn't read her. I didn't know what she was thinking, what she was feeling, what she wanted or needed. That scared me more than anything.

I stepped toward her and she stepped back, shaking her head no. My face frowned, confusion quickly taking over my entire body. I cocked my head to the side with wide eyes not believing what the fuck I was seeing, what the fuck was happening. She took one last look at me and turned to leave.

I booked it across the room, and roughly gripped her arm when I caught up to her. I didn't think before I acted. She flinched, her body locking up. I dropped her arm like she was on fire and her skin burned my hand. She shut her eyes tightly, hugging her torso, slightly shaking.

"Shit!" I instinctively reached for her but pulled back. "I didn't think, darlin', I'm sorry."

She bit her lip, lightly nodding.

"But how can you just run away from me like that?"

She stepped back, needing to get further away from me, like I repulsed her.

"What the hell?" I stepped toward her again, and she suddenly opened her eyes.

"Please, Dylan, please just give me some space, okay?" She moved back yet again.

"Jesus Christ, suga', you can't even be near me? Look I know what happened—"

"You. Know. Nothing," she gritted out with a hateful glare.

I stood there shocked, not recognizing the girl standing in front of me. Her bruises and cuts may have been gone, but so was *she*.

"I'm only here because my mom wanted some dinner from this restaurant. If it were up to me I would never leave my room again, but I can't do that. Now can I?" she sneered.

I jerked back. "Who do you think you're talking to, Aubrey?"

She turned, walking towards her mom's car, dismissing me. She opened the door and at the last second stopped to look at me.

"No one," she answered. "Not anymore."

She got in the car and left, taking my heart with her.

Leaving me standing there.

To die inside.

# Aubrey

"Thanks for your help, Aunt Celeste," I said into the phone. "Talk soon." I hung up.

Seventy-six days.

Ten weeks.

Two months.

Since I recognized the girl that stared back at me in the mirror.

She doesn't smile.

She doesn't laugh.

She barely talked.

She hardly moved.

The reflection peering back at me as I sat in front of my vanity was just a body. There was no soul, no life, a shell of a human being.

"I love you," I muttered so low I could scarcely hear it. "I love you," I repeated a little louder. "I. Love. You," I yelled out, emphasizing each word.

I reached for my heart but nothing changed, the beat still remained neutral, a complete lack of any emotion.

*Life.*

I stood up so fast, I knocked my chair over, raising my fist and slamming it into the mirror as hard as I could. It shattered all around my hand. Shards of glass cut through my numb skin.

*Still nothing.*

"I hate you!" I punched it again, the glass breaking wider. "I fucking hate you!" I yelled, smashing my fist into the mirror over and over again. Screaming at the top of my lungs, "I fucking hate you! I hate you! Do you hear me! I hate you!"

Dylan rushed into my bedroom out of nowhere, grabbing me tightly around my wrist.

*Too tight.*

*Too hard.*

*Too much.*

"What the fuck are you doing?" he roared too close to my face.

I shut my eyes, holding in my breath with his smell all around me.

"What are—"

"No! No! No!" I shrieked, roughly pulling away my arm, shaking my head back and forth.

He wrapped his arms around me, engulfing me in nothing but his scent and I couldn't breathe, I couldn't move. I was suffocating, drowning deeper in my despair, in the memories that haunted me when I was awake and when I tried to sleep. He closed me in tighter, and pressed me firmly against him, I could feel him everywhere and all at once.

"Don't fucking touch me!" I screamed bloody murder, pushing him as hard as I could and his back hit the wall. I didn't falter.

"FUCK YOU! I hate you! I hate you!" I repeated, hitting all over his face. He tried to block each and every advance, so I pushed him and hit him harder.

"Aubrey, calm the fuck down," he reasoned only pissing me off more.

That was it. I couldn't take it anymore.

"I hate you! I hate you! I hate you so fucking much!" I sobbed, hitting and shoving him the closer he tried to come toward me. "I fucking hate you! I hate you!"

My eyes blurred with nothing but tears, and my body twisted with the longing to break apart.

"I hate you! I hate you!" I yelled, talking to myself. I repeated it over and over to let it sink into my pores, drain into blood and make it become a part of me. Making me truly believe it, truly know that this was the end. There was no hope for me.

*For us.*

I shuddered to the ground, taking him with me as I sat on my knees with my body hunched over.

"I can't breathe, Dylan. I can't fucking breathe," I bawled uncontrollably. "I feel like I'm dying. I feel like I'm dying everyday. It won't go away! It will never go away! And I can't breathe!"

He pulled me into his lap and I let him, desperately trying to block out his scent that assaulted me all over.

"Shhh... it's okay, suga'... it's okay, I'm here," he sympathized, his own voice breaking.

I collapsed into his arms, emotionally, physically, mentally exhausted.

I was there, but I wasn't.

He placed my hand over his heart.

"Feel me, Aubrey, feel my heart."

I tried, I really did, but I couldn't feel anything because I knew...

His was broken, too.

# DYLAN

Summer was almost over.

I was leaving to head back to Ohio in a few days. Who knows, maybe the distance would be good to clear my head. I hadn't seen or spoken to Aubrey since the breakdown in her room a few weeks ago. I was just grateful that I remembered her mom kept a hidden key under one of the lawn ornaments by the flowerbed. I wouldn't let my mind ponder what Aubrey would have done to herself had I not heard her when I was by her front door. That dreadful day was the last communication between us. She wouldn't return any of my calls, answer any of my texts, and she refused to see me. I was either turned away by her mom or blatantly ignored when I knocked on her door. It's like she fell off the face of the earth.

Words couldn't express how surprised I was when she texted me that morning, wanting me to meet her at the beach. I jumped in my Jeep and headed there with hope in my heart.

She was sitting by the water, crying.

The exact same spot she was in when I first talked to her at Ian's party. She was thinner, pale, and lifeless, but God she was still so fucking beautiful, so breathtakingly beautiful. Her hair was down and flowing through the light breeze, it was the only part of her that moved with ease. She wore my favorite light yellow dress. I could visibly tell she was uncomfortable in her own skin. I walked slower the closer I got as I approached her. The last thing I wanted was to scare her away.

She flinched a little when I sat beside her, our shoulders barely touching, but to my surprise she didn't move away. The warmth that usually radiated off of her was missing. She was cold. Detached, lost in her own mind. I saw her painfully close her eyes and swallow hard for a few seconds before she opened them again to look out toward the ocean.

It was a beautiful summer day outside.

There wasn't a cloud in sight. The sky was calm with soft colors of blue for miles and miles, with no end in sight. The gentle lull of the ocean and the smell of water all around us seeped into our senses. I couldn't have asked for a more picturesque day.

My girl was sitting beside me except it wasn't *my* Aubrey, this person was an imposter.

She suddenly leaned into my shoulder, catching me off guard. At first I thought my mind was playing tricks on me. When she scooted towards me a little more I held back the desire to pull her into me, to place my arm around her and lay her in the nook of my arm like she loved. I didn't have to dwell on it too long because she did it herself. She moved my arm, setting it around her frail body. The body I didn't recognize anymore. The body that was no longer mine. Resting her head on my shoulder, she leaned her frame alongside mine.

I felt her take three, deep, steady breaths before she somewhat relaxed against me.

I fucking smiled.

I smiled so big for the first time in months, finally being able to breathe. I hugged her closer to me, kissing the top of her head. She let me, only tensing for a few seconds before calming once again.

We stayed like that for the rest of the afternoon in complete silence, watching the world revolve around us as if we were the only two people in it. The bright colors of the sky started giving way to nightfall, blending brilliantly in deep oranges to fire reds. Sunsets in Oak Island were always a sight to behold. Before panic could set in that she was going to end our time together and push me away once again, she stood, hovering above me. Looking down with an expression I couldn't place.

She reached her hand down in front of my face.

"Come on," she simply stated.

I grabbed her delicate hand and stood, she led us up the beach for a few minutes. I watched the way she moved, the way her body swayed with each movement of her feet, the way her hair smelled in the breeze, the touch of her soft skin against my rough hand. Not paying any attention to where she was taking us. We reached a house on the water that appeared to be abandoned. She steered us up the patio steps by the empty pool, opening the glass door into a house that was nearly remodeled, but it looked like it was left to sit and rot away like most homes in Oak Island.

When I closed the sliding doors and turned around I saw blankets, pillows, water, and food lying around the empty open space. Someone had been using it as their own. At first I thought it might have been squatters, but the stuff was way too nice for people living on the streets.

She peered around the room taking in our surroundings, still not letting go of my hand. Her eyes found mine again.

"Where did you find this place?" I questioned.

"Alex."

"What do—"

She placed her finger on my lips. "Shhh…"

I cocked my head to the side, confused.

"Shhh…" she repeated, stepping towards me without cowering for the first time in months.

She looked deep into my eyes intently, searching for something in my stare. Looking for some recognition of whom I was or maybe remnants of who she was when she was with me. I had never seen her look at me like that before.

*Longing.*

Using the finger that was already on my lips, she started gently swiping it back and forth against my mouth. Pulling my lips apart to rub along the inside where she could feel my breath. I didn't stop her, I let her do what she wanted, what she needed in hopes that it would bring back *my* girl.

She slowly moved her finger along the edge of my face, tracing my jawbone from one side to the other. Moving to my cheeks, then the bridge of my nose and up to my forehead. Just touching ever so softly along my skin, remembering my face. She made her way back to my lips, repeating the tracing motion once again.

Our eyes stayed connected the entire time. She licked her lips as she brushed her finger down my chin to my neck, stopping to caress my throat with her thumb. She made her way down to my chest, breaking eye contact, focusing on my heart, tracing her fingers along it, hardly touching me. Sending shivers that shook my core.

When she firmly placed the palm of her right hand against my heart, I saw a subtle smile appear on her face. It was quick, but it was there. She gradually joined our left hands and brought them up to her heart. Pressing her fingers on the backside of my hand to hold it in place. It was beating a mile a minute, nothing compared to my steady beat. She gazed up into my eyes with a glazed look in hers. They changed from what I saw only a few seconds before.

I waited for her next move, feeling her rapid heartbeat pounding against my hand.

She looked down at my lips and continued to where her hand was placed on my chest. Taking a deep breath, she stepped closer to me, leaving no space between us. She took away the hand that was over mine resting on her heart and moved it to the side of my face, tugging on the ends of my hair as I had done countless times to her. She slipped my hair behind my ear and we locked gazes.

Her hand settled on the side of my neck where my reassuring pulse was, and she faintly smiled yet again.

Standing on the tips of her toes with our eyes still locked, she leaned in to tenderly place her lips on mine. I had no time to register what just happened before she parted her lips, beckoning me to do the same.

I did.

I cherished every second that our mouths moved against one another as if they were made for each other, our mouths starving for affection. I hadn't kissed her in months.

I didn't understand the change of events, but I was grateful for them nonetheless.

When she suddenly stopped I resisted the urge to whimper as I opened my eyes. I found her still staring at me like she hadn't closed her eyes the entire time we were kissing. I watched her crouch down in front of me, taking my hand with her. I followed her to the blanketed floor where she laid down, guiding me to lie on top of her.

Her expression told me not to ask questions.

I slowly lay on top of her, being cautious of my movements. It was then that I noticed her hand was still on my chest, above my heart. She had never taken it off. I rested my arms by the sides of her face as I started to lower my frame on hers. Her heartbeat drastically accelerated, and I swear it echoed in the room.

I pushed off her to sit on the heels of my shoes.

"Suga', this isn't a good idea," I said, speaking the truth.

She took in my words for a few seconds and then sat up with me, her face void of any and all emotion. She reached for the hem of her dress, never taking her eyes off mine. I lowered my eyebrows, shaking my head no, but she still started to pull it up. I gripped her wrist immediately stopping her.

"Aubrey," I coaxed. "We don't have to do this. This isn't what I want." I lowered my hold.

She narrowed her eyes at me and then whispered, "I love you. Just you and me right?" Her voice laced with so much sadness, so much pain.

I nodded with so many emotions coursing through my body I couldn't find the words to speak.

"Promise?" she added.

"Always."

Her eyes melted before she raised her dress over her head and was left wearing only her panties. Revealing her once curvy body that looked so frail now. No matter what she looked like, I still fucking loved her so damn much. I peered back up to her eyes because it physically hurt me to remember why she was so small to begin with, and I didn't want to lose this moment that I prayed would lead to many more.

She looked down at my clothed frame, silently asking me to take off my clothes, and I obliged since it was what she wanted. In that moment I would give her anything her little heart desired.

When I was fully undressed she crawled over to me, resting between my legs and placed her hand over my heart once again, kissing me ever so softly. I didn't know what to do with my hands, I didn't know what was okay and what wasn't, but she must have sensed my resolve because she pushed me back to lie down with her hand that was over my heart. I kept my eyes closed the entire time, terrified that if I opened them this wouldn't actually be happening and I truly was dreaming.

We stayed like that for I don't know how long, I could feel her thoughts raging a war in her mind, but then I felt her straddle my waist, breaking our kiss to rest her forehead on mine.

"Please open your eyes. Please look at me," she murmured so low I could barely hear her.

I instantly did, and what I saw nearly broke my fucking heart. Her eyes were filled with unshed tears and that was my undoing, I couldn't take it anymore. I gripped the sides of her face.

"Suga', look at me. We do not have to do this," I breathed out against her lips.

"I need you. I need you to make this better. I need you to make it all go away. I need you to erase him from my body," she rasped, her voice breaking. "Feel me. Touch me." A single tear escaped her eye.

"Where?" I coaxed.

She pressed her hand onto my heart like she did the night she gave me her virginity.

"Here."

I kissed her lips, her cheeks, the tip of her nose, all over her face as I slowly moved my hand from the side of her face down to her neck.

"Tell me if you need me to stop," I urged and she nodded, claiming my lips with hers, our eyes still wide open.

I caressed along her smooth skin, trailing my fingers over her naked body. Her hand immediately clenched against my heart when I reached her pubic bone. Her expression told me to keep going, so I did. Gently, I pressed the palm of my hand alongside her folds, staying above her panties. Her body locked up instantaneously.

"I love you, darlin', I love you so fucking much," I soothed in between kissing her. "My life didn't begin until the day I met you, Aubrey. Do you remember that strong, take-no-bullshit girl?" I coaxed, looking deep into her eyes with an intense stare.

She nodded, resting her forehead on mine as I slowly moved my hand back and forth, caressing her the way I used to. How I knew she loved. Wanting to bring back the affectionate time between us.

"Do you know what I first noticed about you?"

She sucked in air, my tender touch getting to her.

"The way you love, darlin', protecting the people you care about. I knew right away that I wanted you to love me like that."

She hazily smiled, her tense hand against my heart relaxing as I glided my hand on her clit a little faster, a little harder, her wetness seeping through on my fingers.

My heart surged.

"I knew that smile, that laugh, those eyes were going to be the end of me. I wouldn't ever be able to get enough." I pecked her lips and her mouth parted, my persistent rubbing visibly satisfying her.

"You're all I ever wanted but never knew I needed," I breathed out as she breathed in. It was like we were breathing for one another.

"God, Aubrey, you have no idea how much I've missed you. How much I love you."

My words were getting to her, too.

Her back subtly arched.

"I'm yours," I whispered in her ear as I took it in my mouth.

She was coming undone.

"Ah," she exhaled into my mouth, her body trembling, causing me to smile.

"There's my girl," I groaned, sliding her panties to the side. I positioned myself at her opening and she followed my lead, easing down my shaft.

"You can go as slow as you need, I'm not going anywhere," I reminded, loving the feel of her wrapped around me, trying like hell not to get lost in the sensation of her.

I took a moment when I was fully inside of her, paying close attention to the expressions on her face and the responses of her body. I always did, but this time it was so different.

Blinding and consuming.

All or nothing.

I caressed the side of her cheek and she leaned into my touch as she gradually rotated her hips.

"Jesus, suga', I love you so much. I will spend the rest of my life taking care of you, loving you. You have to know that. Whatever it takes. I'm here, and I'm not leaving. We're in this together, just you and me."

I closed my eyes and kissed all along her face again, savoring this precious moment between us.

"I'm sorry, I'm so fucking sorry, Dylan, I'm so sorry," she wept, breaking down on my chest, stopping her movements.

"Shhh... Shhh..." I wrapped my arms around her, wanting her to seek the comfort she needed in my arms. "Aubrey, I'm the one that's so fucking sorry. I promise you that I will spend the rest of my life making it up to you. We can go to therapy. I don't care as long as we're together. Do you understand me? Do you hear me?"

I wiped away all her tears and kissed every last inch of her face as I placed my body completely on hers like I knew she loved, and caressed her cheeks that were flushed and warm. My torso touching her chest and my legs firmly locked beside hers.

"Is this okay?" I had to ask. "God, I just want to hold you. I just want to love you," I whispered, gazing intently into her eyes. "I promise I will make everything better. We will go back to Ohio together, just you and me."

I needed her to understand how much it meant to me that she was letting me back in, and that she was giving me another chance, *us* another chance.

"What's wrong?" I questioned, trying to read her expression. Searching her face for an answer.

She shook her head and closed her eyes as she gripped onto my back tighter, like she was trying to mold us into one person.

She kissed me, and I took it as her silent request to move inside her. I loved to feel her wrapped around me, inch by inch, taking her slowly and cherishing her like she deserved. Wanting to wipe away every memory of that fucker's hands on her, and remind her that this was me.

*Us.*

Every time I would thrust inside her, she could feel the mass of my body movement, inching her a little higher each time. I softly kissed her, taking my time with each stroke of my tongue as it entwined with hers. Savoring the velvety feel of my mouth claiming hers. I pushed in and out of her before I pulled away needing to look into her eyes.

I loved seeing every emotion I felt through her gaze, it mirrored every feeling that was displayed inside of my heart. To a degree I never quite understood, but I didn't care because it was there.

It was for me.

Just for me.

I was always so in tune with her eyes, and in that moment they were indescribable, but I didn't care because I was inside her. We were together and that's all that mattered. The rest would come with time. My thumb brushed against her cheek and I kissed her slowly once again, thrusting a little faster.

"I love you. I love you so fucking much. Thank you, suga', thank you for coming back to me."

She would never fully understand what this meant to me, but I would spend the rest of my life showing her what it did.

My forehead hovered above hers as we caught our breaths, trying to find a unison pattern.

When her delicate fingers caressed the sides of my face, I was at a loss for words. I grabbed her by the nook of her neck and brought her lips to meet mine, pushing my tongue into her waiting mouth. Something took over me, this primal urge that had never happened with her before and our kiss turned passionate, completely moving on its own accord. There was something agonizing about the way we were making love.

Desperate and desolate.

Urgent and demanding.

All consuming.

Both of us giving what the other needed.

We couldn't get enough of one another, both of us wanting more.

Wanting everything.

Our bodies moved like we were made for each other. There weren't any of our demons in the room.

*It was just us.*

For the first time in months.

Our mouths parted and we were both panting profusely, unable to control the thoughts that were wreaking havoc on our souls. Desperately trying to cling onto every sensation of our skin on skin contact.

I shook with my release and passionately claimed her mouth once again. She returned every ounce of everything I was giving her. There was no holding back, and I couldn't thank God hard enough.

"My girl," I groaned in between kissing. "I love you so much, *baby*."

She roughly pulled her face away from my hold, turning her head to the side.

"Get off me," she snapped with a cold and detached voice, making me jerk back like the wind was just knocked out of me. Like I took a low blow right to the stomach.

"What?"

"Get. The. Fuck. Off. Me," she gritted out through clenched teeth her body instantly rigid.

When I didn't move fast enough she shoved me with her hands, scooting out from under me. Leaving me frozen on the ground, staring at the place we just made love.

She threw my clothes at me.

"Get dressed. I can't stand looking at you fucking naked."

*What the fuck just happened?*

I sat up with a stunned look on my face as I watched her throw her dress on. She looked at me like I was a goddamn idiot when I still hadn't moved, so I stood and put my jeans on, not bothering with my shirt.

I stepped toward her. "Baby, what's—"

She cringed, stepping away from me. "Fuck!" she sneered, shaking her hands out in front of her. "Don't call me that! Don't ever fucking call me that again!"

I opened my mouth to say something, anything.

"No! Don't fucking talk. It's over! It's so fucking over, Dylan. It makes me sick to even be around you. We're done! Do you understand me? Done!" she screamed hysterically.

"You've gotta be shittin' me? This is a joke, right?" I reached for her and she knocked my hand out of the way.

"No." She violently shook her head. "You want to know what's a joke? That you actually believe that we just made love and that I was miraculously cured. When in fact, the entire time I was praying that I wouldn't throw up because the mere smell of you makes me fucking sick," she spewed, causing me to step back.

"I know what you're doing. I know what you're fucking doing, and I'm not going to let you push me away! Not after all this!" I argued, pointing my finger at her.

"Fine, then I'll leave."

She turned but she wasn't quick enough. I gripped her wrist, holding her in place in front of me.

"You're not going anywhere. Not until I say you can and, darlin'... I won't."

"Fuck you!" She crudely tore her hand away from my grasp. "You don't know anything! Not one damn thing! You need to go now! What more can I say to you! I don't want you here! Go back to Ohio! Leave me alone!" she screamed the last part.

"I'm not going anywhere. I fucking love you, Aubrey."

She winced like it hurt her to hear me say it.

"I. Love. You," I emphasized each word, needing her to understand, needing to get through to her.

She scoffed. "What do you want, McGraw? This wasn't love making, this wasn't me coming back to you. This was me fucking you."

"Stop," I roared, becoming livid with her rant.

"Stop what? The truth? Dylan, this was goodbye, nothing more. I'm leaving for California! I'm not going with you! We have no future. So, get that through your goddamn head."

"Bree," I forewarned. "You don't need to do this. I know, darlin', it's okay. Let me be here for you. I'm not going anywhere," I pleaded with her.

"I'm sick of your shit! This is your fucking fault! You let me go by myself! You let me get raped! You let me fucking die that day!"

She turned away from me and headed for the door. I was over to her in one stride, grabbing her shoulder to turn her to face me, pulling the hair away from her face to look deep into her eyes.

I spoke with conviction, "Please, don't do this! Please, don't fucking do this," I urged, hanging on by a thread. "You don't have to do this, please!"

"Let go of me! Do you hear me?"

I did and she immediately started to walk around the room. When I heard the rattle of her keys I didn't think twice about it, I just acted. She was about to take my whole life with her.

I threw myself on my knees in front of her and wrapped my arms tightly around her waist, holding her as close as possible. The side of my face lying against her stomach.

"Please, don't do this. I am fucking begging you on my knees, please!"

I could sense her resolve breaking, and I couldn't take it anymore. I bawled. I sobbed for the first time since I found her broken body on the trail.

"My hands are tied, Aubrey. Isn't that what you wanted? Me on my knees. Me on my goddamn knees, waiting for you! Well here I am, pleading with you not to do this," I cried like a newborn baby. "I'm so fucking sorry, darlin'! I didn't save you then, but please let me do it now."

She didn't waver. "I don't love you anymore. I can't love you after what happened, it's too hard. I just can't. My love for you died the day that I did. Love isn't supposed to hurt this much."

I shook my head. "No one said that love was easy."

She didn't falter. "Yeah... But no one said it was going to be this hard either."

I hesitated for a few seconds, silently praying that she wouldn't reply with what I thought.

"Promise?" I asked the one word that would take all of her away from me.

"Always," she simply stated as if it meant nothing when it meant everything.

It was then I finally understood.

She tried to fuck me out of her heart.

And I would spend the rest of my life…

Trying to fuck her out of mine.

My heart was breaking, lying on the floor next to his.

This was the only way he would ever leave me alone. The only way he would ever let me go. I knew if I made him believe that we still had a chance, if I allowed him to have hope, allowed him to touch me, allowed him to make love to me, feel my heart, and reach my soul… then he would never forgive me for breaking him right after.

Except I didn't pretend.

I made love to him, too.

Everything he was saying was true, every last word. I almost couldn't go through with it, apologizing profusely and crumbling on his chest like it would suddenly excuse what I was about to do to him. Like it would suddenly make it all go away and all that would be left was our love.

The one that I wanted back so badly, so profusely, so intently. But when I felt his strong arms come around me, and the sick feeling in the pit of my stomach creeping back in from his scent, I realized it didn't matter anymore, nothing ever would. I wasn't that girl anymore. The one he fell in love with. She was gone. She died the day he found me broken in that godforsaken forest.

I needed to set him free.

He didn't deserve this.

*Me.*

What was left of me.

I dug my fingernails as hard as I could into the palms of my hands to keep from giving in to every last promise he made. Every last word that fell from his lips.

I couldn't do this to him anymore.

I needed to end it, knowing that all it would take was a few simple words.

I swallowed hard and with the coldest, detached voice I could muster, I said, "I don't love you anymore. I can't love you after what happened, it's too hard. I just can't. My love for you died the day that I did." Tears fell down the sides of my face, one right after the other. Waiting for him to respond with what I already knew was coming.

*The end.*

"Promise?" he simply wept.

I closed my eyes and pictured that day.

*His* hands…

*His* lips…

*His* thrusts…

And whispered, "Always." Hammering the final nail in the coffin.

I pushed him off of me like he disgusted me, and I knew he could feel it. I walked toward the door, looking back one last time to find him on his hands and knees, bowing his head in defeat as I bowed mine. I never meant to say all the hateful things that came out

211

of my mouth. I didn't think it was his fault. Not for one second. I was just trying to add fuel to the fire of our now tainted love.

I wanted one last time with him, I was planning on breaking his heart by walking out, I needed to set us free from each other, we had become toxic. But when he called me baby… Dylan was gone and the faceless man was in front of me. The two men became one and a volatile feeling took over.

I left him there, broken.

Knowing that he would never look at me the same.

Knowing that what we had was gone.

Knowing that he would now know that, too.

He would hate me, and the thought of that alone made my body shudder to the point of pain. I walked back to my mom's car numb, cold, and alone.

I drove the entire way home in a fog of my own doing. I parked the car in the driveway, taking a deep breath before I turned my face to see what was in the passenger seat.

And then…

I fucking lost it.

I sobbed for hours upon hours, days upon days, months upon months.

Years to come.

Clutching on to the only love I've ever known who gave me the same jewelry box that made me feel not so alone because he knew that it would…

*Undo me.*

# Chapter twenty-three

# DYLAN

I was halfway through my junior year in college. I hadn't seen or talked to Aubrey in almost two damn years. I wish I could say I forgot about her, but I'd be lying. I would see her in just a few short hours, since we promised Half-Pint we would come and visit her on spring break. Her and Aubrey shared an apartment in California, both attending UCLA. They still remained close. I didn't allow Alex to be caught up in our bullshit, it had nothing to do with her. She was halfway through her freshman year of college and Aubrey was a sophomore.

I knew Alex needed us now more than ever since she was going through so much shit with Lucas knocking someone up. He was going to be a father in just a few short months. Another bomb was dropped on us, Lucas' mom had stage three breast cancer.

We all took the news hard, but that was fucking life.

"What is that?" she asked, pulling me away from my thoughts and nestling closer to my torso, with one arm over my chest and her leg draped over mine.

"None of your goddamn business." I grinned, trying to lessen the blow of my direct response. Placing my keychain back on the dresser.

She melted in my arms the exact way I knew she was going to. Women were predictable beings. It didn't matter how I said something, anything. All that mattered was the way it was delivered.

With a grin, always a grin.

"Am I going to see you tonight?" she questioned, trying to mold her body closer to mine, making me hot.

"Highly unlikely," I put it to her bluntly.

"Aren't you going to miss me?" she purred into my chest.

She was my professor's daughter. I had met her a few times in passing and each time she saw me, she eye-fucked the shit out of me. Spring break had officially started yesterday, and I decided to start it with a bang. The professor was a prick, always busting my balls about one thing or another, so I decided to put them in his daughter's mouth.

"Probably not," I grinned again and hastily pulled myself away from her.

This pussy was getting way too attached for my liking. If there was one thing I hated most about women, it was their neediness. It wasn't an attractive quality to have, and trust me, men didn't fucking like it.

Especially a man like me.

"When will I see you again?"

I sighed, annoyed with the constant questions and badgering. This chick couldn't take a goddamn hint. I didn't mind being an asshole.

In fact, I fucking preferred it.

"Darlin', does it look like I'm the type of man to make promises?"

Her eyes widened, shocked.

I stood up from the bed. I had my fun, and now it was time to go. I pulled my jeans on, zipped them, and stepped into my sandals, never taking my eyes off of hers.

"We had a great time, but let's call a spade a spade. I'm not the first man you've brought home." I shrugged and nodded toward her. "And let's be honest, I'm not going to be the last," I chuckled.

Her eyebrows lowered, making her eyes appear smaller. "You fucking asshole!" she yelled.

Women's moods changed faster than their goddamn panties.

"I call it like I see it," I stated with a big smile.

At least she was amusing.

"Fuck you!" she roared.

I nodded. "I did that. Twice to be exact, but if I go by how many times I made you come… I would say closer to five… maybe six."

Her jaw dropped.

I rolled down my shirt and raised an eyebrow. "Don't keep your pretty little mouth open like that unless you want me to stick something in it. Or is that your plan? Do you want me to fuck your face? Because all you had to do was say please," I crudely mocked.

She scoffed in disgust. "You're unbelievable. I'm not that desperate," she challenged, and it instantly made my dick hard.

"Is that right?" I cocked my head to the side and narrowed my eyes, biting my lower lip.

I walked to the edge of the bed and her eyes glazed over. I leaned forward and grabbed her ankles, tugging her over to me. She gasped as the sheet effortlessly fell off her naked body. I casually massaged her foot as I crouched down to the ground. She was leaning up on her elbows and her chest was rising and falling with every movement of my body.

She knew what I was going to do. She wanted it. Which is probably why she was provoking me. Women like her knew exactly what kind of man I was, that's why they wanted to fuck me in the first place.

*The more things change, the more they stay the same.*

Pleasure was a powerful thing.

"So, tell me again? What were you saying? Hmmm…" I taunted, spreading her legs to the sides of my shoulders. I kissed along her knee and made my way down, slowly. "Something about not being desperate?" I repeated, wanting her words to sink in.

Her breathing hitched when I reached her inner thigh. I roughly bit the soft, tender area and she whimpered in response. I licked and nibbled around it to make it better. I glanced up at her with a mischievous glare, making sure to lick my lips as I made my way down to where she wanted me the most.

Her pussy.

I kissed her pubic area, she was trimmed and I appreciated the effort, although hair didn't bother me much.

Pussy was pussy.

"That feel good?" I provoked, faintly kissing her clit that was still exposed from our last session.

She moaned and her head fell back.

I silently laughed as she gyrated her hips against the bed, a silent plea to keep going. "Because…" I tenderly licked her nub.

Exactly the way she wanted me to.

Exactly the way she loved.

"From where I'm lapping…" I murmured, sucking her clit into my mouth, enjoying the taste of her for a few seconds as her legs tightened around me.

"I can smell…" I added, shoving my tongue into her opening, pushing it in and out a few times before suddenly moving away.

She immediately looked up at me, bewildered and aroused.

I nodded toward her. "The desperation is all fucking over you," I viciously spewed, kissing the air and standing. I turned and grabbed my keys and headed toward the door.

"Oh my God!" she screamed out in frustration but also in urgency. She was like a bitch in heat. She wanted me to treat her like a play-toy.

*They all do.*

I turned and grinned. "Not God, darlin', Dylan," I stated, winking at her one last time and getting the fuck out of there. Women could turn violent real quick. I got in my car and sped down the road faster than a bat out of Hell, making it back to my apartment with plenty of time to spare before our flight left that afternoon. She didn't live far from campus, *Daddy* wanted to keep her close.

I walked into my apartment that I still shared with Jacob, except Austin was our new roommate since Lucas moved back to Oak Island. He wanted to step up and help raise his son, Mason. I for one commended him for it. Plus, he wanted to help out with his mom and Lily, who was now a sixteen-year-old young woman that Jacob couldn't stop playing this cat-and-mouse game with. It was only a matter of time before he wouldn't be able to keep his dick in his pants.

Despite my not so subtle warnings.

"You're such a fucking asshole." *Speaking of the devil, Jacob.*

I put my hands in the air. "What the fuck did I do now? I just got here."

His friend Troy was on the couch with his girlfriend sitting beside him. I never told Jacob, but she came on to me the last time they were here. When he and Troy left to go buy more beer, I let her suck my cock. It was none of my goddamn business, and if Troy couldn't see what a slut she was, then that was his problem not mine. At least I didn't fuck her, even though she begged me to.

Austin was lying on the other couch, and he looked high as shit. God knows what the hell he was taking now. He was never the same after the car accident and we all knew it, especially me.

Jacob followed me into my bedroom.

"How was last night?"

I smiled.

"You know that's probably going to come back and bite you in the ass, right? I mean fucking the professor's daughter. That's quite a stupid move, even for you."

I shrugged. "I'm not worried about it." I wasn't.

"Of course, you're not. Was it at least worth it?"

"Nothin' to call home about." I zipped my duffle bag.

He laughed. "You're such an asshole. I have no idea how you score as much pussy as you do. Everyone knows you're a dick."

"And that's exactly why. I don't give a fuck what people think, especially women."

"You're worse than you were in high school. You're aware of that, right? Isn't college supposed to make something out of you?"

I chuckled. "It made something out of me, I'm just not quite sure what that is yet."

He sat on the edge of my bed. "You all packed?"

"Mmm hmm."

"So, you ready for this week? You know Alex would understand if you stayed back. You sure—"

"I'm sure."

He nodded, understanding. "You know this probably doesn't make a difference, but Aubrey was fine with us staying at their apartment. Half-Pint even said she seemed somewhat excited."

I narrowed my eyes at him and scoffed. "You're right, it doesn't make one damn bit of difference. How many times do I have to tell you, Jacob? She was just a girl I used to fuck."

He sighed, not believing my poker-face. I barely believed the shit that spewed out of my mouth when it came to her.

It didn't matter how many women I had been balls deep in since her.

I. Always. Saw. Her. Face.

# Aubrey

Their plane landed forty-five minutes ago.

They would be here any second.

I tossed and turned all night. I couldn't fall asleep to save my life, not that I ever slept well anymore to begin with. I couldn't remember the last time I slept more than three or four hours straight, or didn't wake up from a nightmare.

I paced around the living room anxiously waiting. Alex was in her bedroom with Cole. Yes, that same Cole that made Lucas' life a living Hell in high school now kept Alex warm at night. I couldn't blame her. Lucas fucked up royally. She was just moving on with her life. It only took nineteen, almost twenty years for her to finally do so.

I liked Cole.

He was good to her.

But he wasn't Lucas, and I knew that as much as she did.

"Alright, darlin'," Cole said, walking into the living room.

I internally cringed every time I heard him call her that.

"I'll see you later." He kissed her. "See ya, Aubrey." He nodded toward me and left.

"Cole doesn't want to make best friends with the boys before he leaves?" I teased, sitting on the couch, placing my legs under me.

Alex was as perceptive as they come. She already knew I was freaking the fuck out without even witnessing it.

"Hardly," she chuckled, sitting the same way I was on the armchair. "By the way, the boys don't exactly know that Cole and I are," she hesitated for a few seconds, debating on what to say, "dating."

I grinned. "Now, why is that, Half-Pint?"

She cocked her head to the side, arching an eyebrow. "Is that the third or fourth outfit you've changed into?" She eyed me up and down.

I stopped smiling.

"I'm just kidding. I'm sure Dylan will appreciate whatever you're wearing, Aubrey."

"Alex, Dylan and I haven't spoken in almost two years. That's the only reason I'm nervous to see him. Don't read too much into it," I sternly advised.

"I don't want to fight, okay? I love both of you, but I'll never understand why you're not together. You haven't been with anyone since him. Aubrey, you barely leave our apartment, so you're obviously not moving on for a reason. Why don't you ask yourself what that is?"

I shook my head. "Half-Pint, don't talk about things you don't know about."

"Then tell me so I do," she challenged, placing her hand on her hip.

I was about to say something when there was a knock on the door. My heart dropped. Alex took in my pale face but didn't say anything. She got off the couch to open the door. Every step she took I felt my resolve crumble a little more.

*I can't do this.*

I got off the couch to rush to my bedroom, but I wasn't quick enough. She opened the door, and I stopped dead in my tracks in the entrance.

"Half-Pint!" Jacob greeted, making her squeal when he picked her up off the ground.

My heart was beating out of my chest, echoing in the room. The room began to close in on me. I tightly shut my eyes, trying to catch my bearings. My skin felt cold and clammy, I thought I was going to pass out. I heard Austin's voice next, waiting for Dylan's.

As if reading my mind, Alex asked, "Where's Dylan?"

"Oh," Jacob muttered. "Umm… he had some shit to take care of or something. He will be here later."

I instinctively turned, locking eyes with Jacob. Austin lightly backhanded him in the stomach.

"Why you lying? Half-Pint, you know how Dylan is, he has pussy in every zip code. He's with some chick who picked us up from the airport, he'll be back once he's done with her."

Jacob's face frowned and his shoulders hunched over. He closed his eyes for a few seconds, shaking his head.

I swallowed the lump in my throat and faintly smiled. "Some things never change, huh?"

Austin glanced over at me like he just realized I was standing there and remorse spread throughout his entire expression.

"Shit, Aubrey, I didn't—"

"How was your flight?" I interrupted Austin, wanting nothing more than to change the subject.

They recovered quickly, but for the few moments they all looked at me with pity. I hated myself a little more.

"It was great," Jacob chimed in, pulling me into a hug.

I despised being touched, but I let him because what else could I do? Austin was next. They both lingered with their arms around me for far too long. Which only made me want to shower again.

"So," I breathed out, trying to steady my nerves from their hands being on me. "What do you guys have planned?"

"I thought I would show them around," Alex chimed in. "Want to come?"

I shook my head. "Nah, I gotta study. Finals and stuff are coming up. You guys have fun though. We'll catch up later."

Alex nodded, and I left to go to my room. The last thing I wanted was to see the look on their faces, once was enough. I took another hot shower and changed into some cotton shorts and a tank. The only time I ever wore revealing clothing was when I was by myself in my safe space. I threw the stupid yellow dress I bought in the farthest end of my closet and studied all day, locked in my room.

I yawned, reading the time on my phone, seeing it was almost one in the morning, and I hadn't heard anyone come home yet. My stomach rumbled, so I set aside my textbook and got up to go to the kitchen to find something to eat. I rummaged through the upper cabinets, trying to decide what I wanted, when the door opened.

"Half-Pint, do you know where my cereal is?" I asked, stepping higher on the tips of my toes searching the back.

"Still eating Lucky Charms?"

I froze.

*Dylan.*

I felt him come up behind me, the smell of him muffled by the stench of a woman's cheap perfume. My breathing hitched when the warmth of his chest pressed against my bare back, my eyes falling to his strong hand resting against the counter.

*Why did he have this effect on me, still?*

He reached up behind me, skimming my shoulder to grab my Lucky Charms and set it in front of my face.

He leaned in close to my ear, his breath hitting the side of my neck causing shivers to course through my entire body. He chuckled when he noticed the hair on my arms standing up.

"I didn't know we were havin' a slumber party, darlin'." He softly caressed along my arm where my hairs were standing at attention. "Although, I did always prefer it when you slept naked," he groaned, igniting a tingling feeling deep within my belly.

*God, I hadn't felt that in such a long time.*

The front door opened again and he moved away from me rather quickly, taking my cereal with him. I turned around and our eyes connected immediately. He bit his lower lip and looked me up and down, making me feel naked.

*Damn, he looked good.*

His hair was blonder than I remembered, and he had it tied up in a high bun on his head. His eyes were a soft color of honey with a glossy glare, which I assumed were the after effects of alcohol. I had never seen him with facial hair before, all sorts of blonde and brown mixed along his upper lip and along his chin. He was wearing a tight white shirt that accented his defined arms that were a lot bigger since the last time I saw him.

*My boy grew up.*

He was a man now, a devastatingly handsome man, in a rough and rugged kind of way.

He grinned, taking pieces of my cereal to his mouth, purposely licking his lips when he realized I was looking him over.

"Dylan!" Alex exclaimed, breaking my trancelike state.

He set down my cereal on the counter next to him and picked her up off the floor. I yearned for him to do the same to me.

After everything…

I still loved him.

I still loved him so much.

He didn't take his eyes off of me as he held Alex in his arms. I wondered if the same thoughts were going through his mind.

"Half-Pint, look at you all grown up," he stated as he took her in.

"You say that every time you see me," she giggled, looking back over at me. "I see you've been reacquainted."

He narrowed his eyes, waiting for me to say something.

"Hey, McGraw," was all I managed to get out.

He flinched, pushing off the counter with my cereal in his hands, stopping when he was right in front of me. I gripped the counter, my legs suddenly feeling weak.

He cocked his head to the side, tugging on the ends of my hair. He leaned in like he was going to kiss my cheek.

"I remember when you used to grip my cock that hard," he rasped, gesturing to my hands white knuckling the counter.

I gasped, taken aback. I didn't realize I was holding on so tight. I released the counter and warmth took over my cheeks. He handed me my cereal, letting his grasp linger, mimicking the hold he still had on my heart.

He left me standing there in shock.

For the first time in years, I had no idea who he was anymore.

# Chapter twenty-four

# DYLAN

We had been in California for almost a week and had one day left. I hadn't seen or spoken to Aubrey since that night in the kitchen. I avoided her like the plague.

As far as I was concerned, there was nothing left to say to her.

"You're such an asshole," Jacob stated.

I grinned. "Why, whatever do you mean?" I asked with a smartass tone, pulling some random pussy to my side.

"How many girls do you plan on fucking while we're here? Are you trying to make your way through the sorority house or just continue to piss off Aubrey?"

I laughed. "This has nothing to do with her."

"It has everything to do with her. She's staring at you right now. The hurt look on her face pains me, Dylan, and I have nothing to do with it."

I rolled my eyes. "She should have thought about that before she left me."

"Why don't you try talking to her? Maybe hear her out?"

"That would imply that I actually gave a fuck about her."

I pulled another random girl to my other side, and Jacob shook his head, walking away from me. We were at Cole's fraternity party, and as much as Alex tried to hide it, I knew her and Cole were together. I caught the looks that they gave each other and the way she would touch him when she thought no one could see them. I didn't understand why she was trying to hide it from us. I didn't care who she dated as long as she was happy, and Cole seemed to treat her right.

The night took a turn for the worst when Alex came running up to Jacob to tell him that Austin was high on ecstasy. I wasn't surprised in the least. The boy had a fucking death wish. After Jacob and I found him in the park and tried to help him, all it led to was our friendship going to Hell in a hand basket. Shit was said that could never be taken back, and my disappointment in both Austin *and* Jacob at the moment was enough to send me spiraling down a bottle of rum.

I took a swig out of the bottle as I made my way down to the beach. The fiery liquid burned with delight. I wanted to forget. I wanted to pretend like the last fucking hour didn't happen. I ended up on the beach that was within walking distance of their apartment and I knew that was Aubrey's doing.

She loved the beach.

I wanted to imagine that I didn't see her fucking face in front of me, the same face that I desperately tried to forget over the years.

All of it, every memory and emotion hitting me in the face, back to back. Taunting me. Making me feel like the piece of shit I knew I was.

I didn't want to feel anything.

I didn't want to remember anything.

I didn't want to know anything.

I felt as though I was reliving it all over again — the rape, her leaving me, the demise of my life and our love. Falling on me like a ton of fucking bricks, and I couldn't breathe. I was suffocating. My adrenaline was pumping through my core, and I could feel the sweat pooling at my temples. I walked out into the water, the bottle already half gone. I was numb. I was always numb. Except when I wasn't.

*Women.*

*Fucking.*

"You know there are sharks in there, right?"

I spun to find a brunette standing there and just like that it was gone. I could breathe. "No shit, is that right?"

She laughed. "Aren't you scared of sharks?"

"Sharks don't come to the shoreline, darlin'." I took in her figure, a small waist and big tits. She was wearing a cover up over her bikini, easy access.

"I know, but why risk it? Anything can happen."

"Anything?" I grinned.

She blushed.

"Isn't it a little late for you to be walking the beach by yourself?"

"I'm not alone. You're here," she warranted.

"Exactly."

"My name's—"

"I don't care what your name is," I interrupted, walking toward her.

"Well, I know your name. Dylan," she sassed.

"Is that supposed to impress me?"

Her eyes widened.

"Your lips." I reached out and rubbed my thumb back and forth on her bottom lip. "They're already doing that."

Her breathing hitched.

"I want to see what else they can do." I pushed my thumb into her pouty mouth. "Do you?" I questioned with conviction.

She sucked on my thumb like a damn pro and reached for my belt, unbuckling it.

"Good girl," I praised, removing my thumb and bringing her closer to me by the nook of her neck. "Pull out my cock," I groaned into her ear, and her skin immediately warmed my hand. I softly kissed down her neck, taking in her sweet smell of sunscreen.

I did recognize the girl. She was one of the sorority girls or some shit.

All the faces blended together, all but one.

I didn't know her name and I didn't care, I wasn't lying about that. If she had followed me out here then she would definitely do anything for me.

And I wanted her on her knees.

She did as she was told with unsteady hands.

"Stroke it. Harder," I ordered as I continued to kiss down to her breasts, making sure to rub my facial hair along the way. Women loved that.

"Like this?" she breathed out.

I groaned and cupped her breasts into my face. "Yeah…"

She was so responsive and that's what I enjoyed the most about women. I jerked her head back and she moaned, pulling her onto the ground till she was on her knees. She took her hand away and I placed my own around my shaft, pumping myself up and down in front of her face as she looked back at me with hooded eyes.

When she realized what I was doing, her eyes glazed over like she had never seen a man stroke himself before. Or it could have been the size of my dick.

Either way it turned me on.

I looked down at her. "It's not going to suck itself, sweetheart," I huskily urged.

She didn't have to be told twice, and her soft, wet, hot mouth took me in. I continued to jerk myself off while she sucked on the head of my cock until she started to move her mouth down toward my shaft.

"Deeper," I demanded.

This girl followed directions quite nicely, but when she didn't take me as far as I would have liked, I did it for her. She gagged when I felt the back of her throat, making me growl and her wet.

"Pull down your bottoms, put your hand on your pussy and play with yourself. I want to watch you come."

Again she followed my orders perfectly, manipulating her clit, slow at first then faster and more demanding. I gripped onto the sides of her face, moving her mouth on my cock the way I wanted.

The way I craved.

Her hand once again stroked me, and I quickly found a rhythm that had my head leaning back.

"Good girl, such a good girl," I groaned, staring up at the moon.

Thinking of someone else as I fucked her mouth.

I enjoyed the feel of her lips wrapped around me, but I was drunk as shit. I wasn't going to come. When I looked back down at her she wasn't who I wanted her to be and that pissed me off. I roughly removed myself from her mouth, tucking my cock back in my pants.

"What the hell?" she snapped.

"I should ask you the same thing, darlin', with lips like yours, I thought you'd be a goddamn pro."

I left her there yelling obscenities, tuning her out.

By the time I made it back to their apartment, my drunken haze lingered but I started to sober up. I used the key Alex gave me knowing no one would be home yet. It was still fairly early by college standards. It was pitch dark when I walked inside. I must have left the bottle somewhere since it was no longer in my hand. I made my way toward Alex's bedroom wanting to pass the fuck out on her bed till she got home.

I opened the door and Aubrey gasped, spinning around to face me with her arms over her naked chest.

I immediately smiled, gripping the door handle. Cocking my head to the side to take in her gorgeous fucking body that looked like the Aubrey that I remembered.

*My girl.*

"Jesus Christ, McGraw, don't you knock?"

"Ain't nothin' I haven't seen before, suga'."

She rolled her eyes. "You're drunk."

"You're beautiful."

She shook off my complement. "Were you raised in a barn? Shut the damn door."

"Well, I'll be damned, darlin, you don't have to ask me twice." I shut the door, leaning my back against it with my arms crossed over my chest.

"I meant get out," she scolded.

"But I really want in," I countered, peering down her body.

"You're vile. How many girls have slept in your bed in the last two years, McGraw? Better yet, how many girls beds have you slept in the last week?"

I snidely smiled. "Bree, you lost the right to ask me about my bed when you decided you didn't want to be in it anymore."

She jerked back, stunned. "Get. Out."

I raised my eyebrows. "Truth hurts, don't it?"

"You're such a—"

"You stole my heart and never gave it back."

Her eyes widened.

I sighed, walking towards the bed to sit against the pillows by the headboard. I beheld the ceiling for a few seconds before tossing my arm over my eyes to allow her to change. I don't know how long I sat there until I felt the bed dip next to me.

"That's not fair," she announced out of nowhere.

I moved my arm and pulled back my hair, glancing at her sideways. "For who?"

She wore cotton shorts with a top similar to the one she was wearing the first night I saw her. Her blonde hair had gotten long, descending all the way down to her waist. Her bright green eyes still had the power to bring me to my knees all with just a simple look. She wasn't wearing any makeup but she never needed it, she was always naturally breathtaking. The women I slept with didn't even come close to her.

She looked older, and I hated the fact that I missed all that time with her. There was something in her eyes that told me that she wanted to say so much, and I would sit there for the rest of my life if that's what it took for her to open up to me.

The past was still lurking right around the corner like a goddamn shadow I couldn't get away from. All I wanted were a few moments in time where it didn't haunt us anymore. Where it wasn't right there for the taking.

She broke my heart, and yet there I was willingly waiting for her to do it again.

She caressed my cheek with the knuckles of her delicate fingers as if she knew what I felt, what I thought, what I wanted.

I leaned into her hand and it fell onto the back of the headboard. I used it as a pillow as her other hand played with my hair, pulling the longer pieces away from my face.

"I can't believe you kept your hair like this," she murmured as if it hurt her to say it.

"You loved it," I simply stated the truth.

My face turned into the palm of her hand and I softly kissed it, waiting for her to pull away like she always did before she left me on my knees, begging her to stay.

When she didn't, I slowly placed tender pecks up her arm, brushing my lips back and forth to enjoy the feel of her skin against my mouth.

She was so soft.

So warm.

I made it to her shoulder and moved her hair to the other side of her neck, never stopping my caresses on her skin. I could feel the effect I was having on her and she hadn't stopped me, yet.

"Dylan," she lightly stirred, her body tensing.

My heart sped up. "What, suga'?" I was getting closer to her neck.

"You need to stop."

"No, I don't."

Her chest lifted with every movement of my lips getting closer to her mouth.

"We can't do this."

"Yes, we can."

I grabbed the side of her face, beckoning her mouth to mine and she let me. Her eyes were tightly shut, and she smelled like everything I ever wanted.

"You're so fucking beautiful," I groaned, desperately craving to take what I needed to be mine.

Her mouth parted as I brought her over to me. The smell and feel of her were making me dizzy, and all I wanted was to kiss her. It was such an innocent gesture, such a simple desire.

I wanted to capture this moment and hold onto it for as long as I could. I wanted to remember her just this way.

For me.

*Mine.*

"I know a part of me will always be waiting for you. And I want to hate you for it, but I can't," I murmured, getting closer to her mouth.

She shook her head unable to find the words.

"I'm going to kiss you now."

She licked her lips beckoning me to do it.

"You've ruined me for every other woman, Aubrey, every last one," I found myself saying.

She immediately opened her eyes and looked right into mine. "Promise?"

I didn't falter. Not for one damn second. "Always."

The front door slammed open, and it was like a bucket of ice cold water was briskly poured on top of her. She jumped back and away from me after the sudden intrusion.

"You need to go," she ordered.

She wasn't done breaking my goddamn heart.

# Aubrey

"That's not what you want," he replied.

"You don't know what I want, McGraw."

"That's where you're wrong, darlin', I've always known. It's you that hasn't."

I held my chin higher, trying not to let the truth falling off his lips affect me.

"Someday you're going to find yourself and wish you hadn't."

"What do you want from me?" I breathed out.

"Everything," he simply stated. "But right now I'll settle for holding you."

I shook my head no, scared that if I opened my mouth my response would be different.

"Let me hold you, darlin, just for tonight. Tomorrow you can go back to pretending that you don't love me."

"Dylan…"

"I'll sleep on top of the blankets like a good ol' boy."

"I can't."

"Try."

I knew what I was doing to myself but the memories already held me captive, and I wanted so desperately to feel anything other than the hatred that lived inside of me.

Even if it was for one night.

I pulled the covers back and got under them, turning away from the face that I couldn't bear to lie to anymore and waited. He flipped off the light and the darkness immediately took me under. I never slept with the light off. I was about to open my mouth and tell him that I couldn't do this.

As much as I yearned to.

When I felt his arm come around me, just his arm. He didn't tug me toward him, he didn't move me from the place I lay and he didn't scoot over closer to me. All he did was place his arm over my stomach as if he knew it was all I could take, and I think I fell in love with him all over again.

But too much had happened.

Things that I couldn't forget.

Mistakes that I couldn't change.

Regrets that I couldn't take back.

I closed my eyes and to my surprise it didn't take long for me to start to fall asleep. Except before I did, I heard him whisper,

"I love you. I'll always love you."

I slept the entire night for the first time since the day I died with the man who promised he could save me.

# Chapter twenty-five

## Aubrey

"Right, I know, Aunt Celeste," I lied.

"Are you eating? Sleeping? Taking care of yourself?"

"Mmm hmm…"

"Aubrey," she coaxed.

"How is she? Is she doing okay?" I asked out of nowhere.

"Of course she is. I would tell you if she wasn't."

I nodded even though she couldn't see me.

"I got to go though, Jeremy is on his way. I'll check back in soon."

"Call your mom, okay?"

"I will."

"I love you, honey."

"Me too." I hung up.

It was my senior year of college, and I was twenty-two years old about to graduate with my bachelor's degree in fashion and design in a few short weeks. I didn't have a clue what I would be doing with it, but I would have it nonetheless.

The front door slammed open.

"Aubrey, where the fuck are you?"

I jolted off my bed.

"Nice to see you too, Jeremy," Alex greeted as I rushed out of my bedroom.

He immediately smiled, his demeanor changing drastically from the man who just barged through my front door.

"Alex," he coaxed. "I didn't see your car outside."

"I left it at Cole's. He dropped me off this morning, he's waiting for me outside."

"Hey, baby," he acknowledged, reaching for me and pulling me to his side. He kissed me and then looked back at Alex.

I had met Jeremy at one of Cole's fraternity parties at the beginning of the school year. He was alumni having graduated three years prior as vice president of the fraternity like his father before him and so on. His family was high profile, and they were generations upon generations of politicians. Jeremy worked for his father, running his office and handling the behind the scenes campaign needs.

He hated it.

He traveled all the time, and each time he came back he was worse than he was before he left.

"Aubrey, can I talk to you for a second? Alone."

I nodded, glancing over at Jeremy. He wearingly eyed me before excusing himself to go into my bedroom.

Alex gripped my upper arm, tugging me into the kitchen, further away from my room.

"What are you doing with him, Aubrey? He's a jerk."

"So was Dylan," I simply stated, regretting the words as soon as they left my mouth.

They were nothing alike.

Nothing.

Alex shook her head, disappointed that I was even comparing the two. I couldn't hate myself more for it, there wasn't any extra room left for me to feel that. I hadn't seen or spoken to Dylan since the night I slept with his arm around me. The last time I had a good night's sleep was over two years ago, so much had changed but yet not enough.

"Dylan wasn't—"

"I know, Half-Pint, I don't know why I said that."

"Why are you doing this to yourself? It makes no sense that you're with him when you know Dylan is—'

"Not everybody gets their happily ever after, Alex," I harshly responded.

She stepped back. "What happened to you, Aubrey?"

"I grew up."

"Let me—"

"Mind your own business, that's what you need to do. You can't save me anymore than you could save Lucas."

She jerked back, hurt.

"I'm sorry. I didn't mean that."

"No, Aubrey, I think you did." With that she turned and left.

I took a deep breath as remorse and shame washed over me. I spun around to walk back into my bedroom and before I could take my first step, Jeremy backhanded me across the face so fucking hard I fell to the ground.

"You, stupid bitch!" he roared, hovering above me as I clutched my cheek.

I wish I could tell you that Jeremy wined and dined me, that he made me fall in love with him and his charming personality. That I didn't know he was a monster. That he tricked me, made me believe he was something that he wasn't before he showed me his true colors.

He didn't do any of those things.

I knew what I was getting myself into. I knew what kind of person he was, and what kind of demons were sitting on his shoulders. Waiting for me.

I knew it all.

From our first talk to our first date to the first time he ever laid his hands on me. I knew what he was capable of, and I wanted it. I looked for it.

Those moments when his fists did the talking or his mouth was spewing degrading and hateful words were the only times that the hurt I felt in my heart.

The ache that lived in my soul.

The anguish that consumed my body and mind.

Every. Single. Day.

Was numb for a few precious minutes.

I relished the feeling of the pain that he inflicted, even if it was just for a few minutes. It took away the memories of the person that I had become.

"Fucking look at me!"

I did.

"You don't defend me to your stupid fucking friend? What kind of a girlfriend are you? A piece of shit one! You're good for nothing but that pussy between your goddamn legs."

He kicked me in my stomach and I recoiled in pain, gagging hysterically.

"Get the fuck up, you weak pathetic excuse of a girlfriend!"

I gasped for air, seizing onto my stomach.

"GET THE FUCK UP, AUBREY! You do not want me doing it for you!"

I sat up on my hands and knees, breathing through the pain.

"Aubrey, I'm not going to tell you again," he warned through gritted teeth.

I hissed through my discomfort, standing hunched over. Blinking through the white spots in my vision as he crudely gripped my chin.

"Dylan is better than me, huh? He's still waiting for you, isn't he?"

Silence.

"Answer. Me."

"No," I simply stated.

"Tell me you love me."

"I love you," I whispered with a lack of emotion in my voice.

"Tell me you know you're a worthless piece of shit. Tell me that I'm better than him, that I'm better than your Dylan, and you're lucky to have me."

I could take the hitting, the physical abuse. It was mild compared to the verbal assault his words inflicted inside me. Like a knife carving my already wounded body. The sting much more intense than anything his hands could ever do to me.

"Look me in the eyes and say it like you fucking mean it. If you don't, I'll hurt you until you make me believe that you do."

I swallowed hard, clenching my ribs where he just hit me so that it would numb the words that were about to come out of my mouth. Each lie that would fall from my lips.

I peered deep into his eyes and murmured, "I'm a worthless piece of shit."

His eyes dilated, I could see the high my words were giving him and I hesitated for a few seconds.

"You're better than him and I'm lucky to have you."

"Better than who, Aubrey? Who am I better than?"

I pressed my ribs harder, wincing through the pain that I wish were from my ribs.

"You're better than Dylan," I stated, holding back the tears and my voice from breaking.

He snidely smiled. "Who loves you, baby?"

"You."

He let go of my chin and tapped on his cheek like he always did after he hit me. I kissed it.

"You know I love you, don't you, baby?"

I nodded.

"Tell me you know."

"I know you love me."

"Only me, baby, only me."

He pulled me into his arms, wrapping them around me.

"I do this for you. I am what you deserve."

If only he knew how true his words were.

# DYLAN

"I'm coming! Hold on!" I yelled out, wrapping a towel around my waist. I opened my front door to find my mom standing there.

I smiled. "Hello."

She rolled her eyes. "Dylan, I have been calling you all morning."

I nodded, stepping aside to let her in.

"And I've been ignoring you all morning, but at least you knocked this time, much better than last time."

She shook her head. "Well, I think catching my son having sex once is enough in a lifetime for any mother."

I laughed, bracing myself up against the front door and folding my arms. "Oh come on, Ma, it hasn't just been one time," I joked.

"Don't remind me, Dylan," she stated in an exaggerated breath.

"Awww, Ma, you've seen me naked before. Don't blush," I teased.

"It's not about your wiener, darling, I used to change your diapers, and I'm fully aware of what it looks like. It's the fact that I saw it in some girl's mouth that caught me off guard."

I smiled high and raised my eyebrows, amused. "My wiener?" I repeated while laughing. "Only you refer to it as a wiener, Ma, and besides she was a nice girl, she swallowed."

Her face frowned as she put her hands up in the air in a stopping motion. "Enough, Dylan, don't think I don't know what you're doing. You're trying to distract me from the reason I'm here. I don't want to hear any excuses. You're going."

"I have plans," I answered not needing to know the question.

"Cancel them."

I pushed off the door and walked toward my kitchen with her right behind me. "I'm not arguing with you today, Ma."

"Good, seeing as I have no intention of arguing. You're going," she ordered again.

I grabbed two bottles of water from my fridge and handed her one. "I'm not a kid, you can't order me around anymore."

She scuffed. "Right, because you listened so well when you were a child, huh?"

I twisted the cap and took a sip, placing it on the counter to face her. "I'm not going. There is no reason for me to be there."

She pulled out the barstool and sat on it. "Yes, there is," she replied, already prepared for every rebuttal I was about to throw at her.

"What?" I questioned, genuinely curious about her response.

"It's important to Lucas' mom. You know the woman who's like a second mother to you."

"Oh, well, thank you for that guilt trip. Mission accomplished. I'll meet you there," I sarcastically stated.

"Dylan, do not take that tone with me."

I gripped the back of my neck, annoyed.

"You need a haircut. How about I schedule one for you? Darling, don't you want to cut your hair? It's too long. Only girls have their hair that long, honey, you don't want to look like a girl, do you?"

"It's never been an issue for me. I don't have a problem getting pussy, Ma, if that's your concern."

"Dylan!" She stepped toward me.

I put my hands out in front of me, surrendering. "What? You started it."

She placed her hand on her forehead and took a deep breath. "Oh my God, you're giving me a headache. Your hair is past your shoulders and have you never heard of a razor? Your face, you're covering your handsome face with nothing but facial hair."

"Again, it's never been a—"

"Enough. I do not want to hear about your bed hopping ways. I know you're on the police bureau and about to be promoted to Detective here in Oak Island," she beamed even though she was trying to reprimand me.

"Only after working on the force for three years since you graduated from college," she added with nothing but pride laced in her tone, stepping toward me again like she was going to hug me, but at the last second she smacked me upside the head. "By the way I don't care if you're twenty-six years old or fifty years old. You do not talk to me like I am one of your boys or colleagues. I raised you better than that, Dylan Anthony McGraw, do you hear me?"

I rubbed at my head where she just hit me. "Yes, ma'am."

"I know, honey. I know Aubrey is going to be there with her boyfriend. I know it's been years since you have seen her. I know you still—"

I sighed and we locked eyes. She knew I hated that she was bringing this up again, knowing I wouldn't discuss it with her.

I wouldn't discuss it with anyone.

She lovingly smiled, reading my mind. "This is not why I'm here. It would mean a lot to Lucas' mom if you were there for her Christmas Eve party. She wants everyone together. We don't know what's going to happen, Dylan. She's getting worse, and I know you see it. This might be her last..." she stopped, unable to finish her sentence.

"I know, Ma. I'll be there."

She stood and walked over to me. "Thank you, honey. Everything is going to be okay. You'll see."

I silently prayed she was right.

I sat at my vanity, peering at the woman in the mirror.

"I love you," I whispered, barely being able to hear it over the melody coming from my jewelry box. The one that Dylan had left for me in my mom's car all those years ago.

Holding on to the only thing I had left of him.

*Of us.*

Her eyelashes were long and covered in mascara.

Her eyelids were coated in grey eye shadow with thick black eyeliner.

Every inch of her face was coated with concealer, foundation, and powder. Blush creeping along her cheekbones.

Her mouth was bright red.

Her blonde, silky hair laid on the right side of her face, a bow shaped clip placed strategically in her hair that matched her lips.

Her red silk blouse and black pencil skirt hugged the curves of her body. She finished the disguise off with black sky-high heels.

She looked so flawless, so beautiful, so put together and perfect, exactly the way he wanted. Not a hair or stitch of make up out of place.

No one would think that this woman was broken. No one would know that bruises covered her face and body. No one would know that she spent hours fabricating her impeccable appearance so that people would think she was happy.

She was loved and cared for.

My family and friends wouldn't know the truth that lied under the façade. Not even the man that put all these marks on her could tell.

"I love you," I repeated, desperately wanting to believe it but knowing I never would.

Taking one last look at the woman staring back at me through the mirror and then I let my eyes travel to the necklace around my neck. My fingers touched the silver heart that lay on my chest and traced the words. *Always. Promise.*

It took years for me to open the jewelry box that Dylan gave me. The first time Jeremy hit me I didn't cry, I didn't weep, I didn't even make a sound. I went home that night and grabbed the jewelry box that I kept hidden in the back of my closet where I locked away my truths. I placed it on my vanity, looking into the mirror at the sharp bruise on my cheek still not feeling anything.

With trembling fingers I opened the box. Music and a delicate ballerina dressed in a white tutu was sitting in the fourth position, came to life. It was then that I realized there was a piece of jewelry hidden in it.

It was only then…

That I cried my heart out.

# twenty-six

# Aubrey

We were all at Lucas' mom's Christmas Eve party. The good ol' boys were all back together again, with the exception of Austin. He took off after their visit from spring break. Alex told me they all got postcards from him every so often, but no one knew where he was or what he was up to.

They all worried nonetheless.

I watched from afar as a random girl I didn't recognize flirted with Dylan. She wasn't even trying to hide it. She was all over him and of course, McGraw was enjoying her advances. Not batting an eye that I was in the same room. He'd never pass up an opportunity to get his dick wet, and I'm sure it was much worse now that he was somewhat of a hometown hero.

This was supposed to be a family function. It was the only reason I came. Alex pressured me into it, saying Lucas' mom was getting worse by the day and this may be her last Christmas. She told me that being there would mean the world to her. I would be lying if I said I wasn't completely caught off guard by how sick she looked. I hadn't seen her in years. She looked nothing like the strong woman she was when we were in high school. It broke my heart seeing her in that state of health. I immediately felt bad for Lucas and Lily for what was obviously going to happen.

It was only a matter of time.

Dylan and I stayed on opposite ends of the room the entire night, though it didn't matter, I could sense him anywhere.

It wasn't just that night.

It was all the time.

We didn't get close to each other the whole evening, but that didn't stop me from watching him work his magic on the girl who was coming onto him so damn hard. Dylan didn't look my way once. He never acknowledged my presence. I silently hoped that it was because of Jeremy. He wouldn't leave my side, playing the part of the perfect, doting boyfriend. He refined that act in the last three years. We lived together in California, and for an outsider looking in I had the picture-perfect life. My boyfriend took care of me and I didn't have to work. I was a kept woman and he provided for me in every sense of the word.

Some may say he spoiled me.

Except when he would come home at night or after days of being away dealing with his father, I was the one who took the brunt of his violence. I was the one who paid the price for the unhappy life that he led. I was to blame for the sacrifices he had to make, so he could give us the ideal lifestyle he was trying to provide for us.

*For me.*

I knew Dylan had moved back to Oak Island after his graduation from Ohio State, Alex offered the information in passing. His whole life was there. I wasn't one bit surprised when he joined the police force and was working his way up rather quickly. It was who he was.

Always so damn determined.

Deep down I knew his choice of career was partially because he couldn't save me all those years ago. Maybe it gave him peace of mind that he could save someone else.

Jeremy excused himself, saying he needed to take a phone call. Whenever he did that, he always took a while to return. It could have been his father or the random women that he slept with when I wasn't around. I found a pair of panties after one of his business trips when I was doing his laundry. Which was my job, I took care of him and the household. Always having to please him, waiting on him hand and foot. If I didn't do it the way he expected, the way that was good for *me*, he'd make me pay.

Lessons learned he called it.

I waited up for him that night with the panties lying firmly on my lap. He took one look at me, grabbed the panties and said, "Thank you, baby, she was looking for those." That was the end of the conversation that never even started. He backhanded me across the face the next morning, reprimanding me for being so fucking nosey.

When Dylan walked towards the garage, my feet moved on their own accord as if an invisible string was pulling me. Before I knew it I was closing the door behind me, the sound making him turn to face me and actually look at me. We hadn't been face to face in four years. I missed his eyes on me.

The boy I once knew was gone, but the man that I was still in love with was very much there, standing in front of me looking as handsome as ever. His hair pulled up high in a man-bun, his build broader, wider, more defined, making me long to have him hold me. To touch me. Wrap me in his arms and never let me go again. More than anything, I wanted him to take my hand and press it against his heart and whisper to me to feel him.

I opened my mouth to say something, anything, but I didn't know where to start. There was so much to say, so many explanations and apologies to be made but not nearly enough time to do so. By the look on his face he felt the same way, or maybe it was just my wishful thinking. I hoped for the latter.

I was frozen in front of him, picturing what life could have been.

The years of memories, mistakes, and regrets came rushing over me. Piling on top of me, their weight suffocating me.

*The first time I met him.*

*Our first talk on the beach.*

*Our first date.*

*Our first kiss.*

*The first time he told me he loved me.*

*The first time we made love and every time after that.*

Our love…

That was taken away so harshly, so violently, so unfairly.

My eyes filled with tears, my lips trembled, and whatever little piece of my soul that had mended over the years, now just crumbled around me. My heart started to race at the memory of that day, the day that ended our future.

I let go of the door handle and walked toward him, he watched every step as if his whole world was making its way back to him again. I couldn't take it anymore. The overwhelming desire was almost unbearable. I don't know what came over me, as soon as I got to him, I didn't think twice about it.

I placed my hand over his heart.

The stable, steady heart that remained beating just for me, as if no time had passed between us. We stood there for I don't know how long, both of us lost in our own thoughts, consumed by our own desires. With an intense stare he extended his hand, I thought he would place his hand over my heart, replicating my action.

*He didn't.*

Instead his hand traveled upwards and his thumb gently rubbed back and forth on my cheekbone, and I flinched when he started wiping off my makeup, a move so unexpected it threw me off my axis. I immediately shut my eyes, scared of the ramifications of his action, of what he was about to see.

*My truths.*

He sucked in air and roared deep within his lungs, "I'll fucking kill him," he breathed out with nothing but agony in his tone.

I instantly opened my eyes and the glare on his face almost brought me to my knees.

The irony was not lost on me.

"How long, Aubrey?"

"Dylan, I—"

"How fucking long, Aubrey?" he repeated with a much deeper voice.

"You don't understand," I pleaded with him.

"You have five seconds to make me understand or I'm going inside and laying him the fuck out for putting his hands on you," he violently spewed.

"Stay out of it, McGraw."

He shook his head, understanding my simple yet pungent statement. "Jesus Christ, Bree, you're ok with this? You want this?"

I bowed my head in shame. "You have no idea."

He stepped away from me, moving my hand off his heart. It took everything inside me to not grab his hand and place it over my heart so he could see what it was doing to me.

I didn't want to lose his love, his warmth, his comfort.

"Why? Why are you doing this after everything? You know, I'm still fucking here. Right here, I'm not the one who left. I'm not the one who walked away from our love. I still fucking love you! I love you so damn much. I can't even breathe when I think about all the years we've spent apart, Aubrey."

"Please, don't—"

"WHY?" he yelled, making me jolt.

"You know why," I replied even though I didn't mean it. I couldn't tell him the truth.

"Un-fucking-believable. You blame me for that day, and yet here you are with a man that fucking hurts you. You gotta be fucking shittin' me, Bree." He paced back and forth, making me even more anxious.

I didn't know what to say, so I didn't say anything.

"I can't even look at you right now. Do you have any idea how much that kills me? I haven't seen you in four years, four goddamn years and yet you're still the first and last thing I think about every single day. I'm reminded daily of what I lost."

Tears slid down my face. His words were like a double-edged sword, causing me pain and euphoria simultaneously.

"I can't tell you how profusely fucking sorry I am, Bree. How I have to live with the fact that *I* urged you to go by yourself. That *I* let that son of a bitch take away what was mine. What fucking belonged to me. *I* was the one who allowed him to do all that, Bree, *I* failed to protect you!" He slapped his chest. "I hate myself for what I let happen to you. I have to live with that guilt and without you for the rest of my life," he hesitated, letting his words linger.

"Are you punishing me, Bree? Is that what you're doing? Trying to rip my fucking heart out... again? Cause if you are, it's workin'."

"No," I whispered loud enough for him to hear.

He got close to my ear and murmured, "Then why does it fucking feel that way?" he gritted out through clenched teeth.

His warm breath lingered there for a second, sending shivers straight to my core. I loved and hated the effect he still had on me. Then he turned and walked away from me, slamming the door behind him. The entire garage rumbled, making me jump.

I stood there, *waiting*.

It didn't take long for *my* punishment to come.

# DYLAN

I went to the bathroom, sick to my fucking stomach.

Alex told me time and time again that Aubrey had changed since she got with Jeremy. I assumed the real reason was the rape, that it finally took its toll. I couldn't have been more wrong. When I saw her that night she was still so breathtakingly beautiful, but it wasn't *her*.

It didn't matter how many times Jeremy held her, whispered in her ear, showed her any kind of affection or love. She would press her nails into the palm of her hand and her eyes would lower to the ground. At first I thought I imagined it, but when he casually gripped her arm and she winced in pain I had to leave the room. The confirmation of my suspicions was too much to bear. I was going to fucking kill him if I didn't walk away.

I never expected her to follow me out to the garage.

I never thought she would blatantly admit it.

I never imagined that my nightmare would play out in front of my very own eyes and I couldn't do one thing about it.

I left her there before I lost my temper and took it out on the wrong person.

I stayed in the bathroom for how ever long it took to calm the fuck down, ready to walk back into the garage and have it out with her. Even if it meant I had to throw her over my goddamn shoulder to get her the hell out of there and away from that asshole of a boyfriend and sorry fucking excuse for a man.

As soon as I walked out, I heard what sounded like yelling, but I couldn't make out what was being said due to the loud music that was playing in the house. Adrenaline coursed through my entire body as I ran as fast as I could back into the garage.

"Shut your goddamn mouth, little girl," Jeremy snarled.

"Fuck you!" Lily shouted and my heart dropped.

I opened the door, stopping Jeremy mid-action. He was about to go towards Lily. She was on the ground with Aubrey lying in her arms, that was hunched over and reeling in pain. It reminded me of when I saw her on the trail. Memories of that day came flooding back, only infuriating and consuming me further. I shut the door behind me. No one was going to take away my chance to fuck this motherfucker up before I brought him in and locked him the hell up.

The rage took over and I charged him, knocking him over with my entire body, both of us falling to the ground. We wrestled around for a few seconds, but he wasn't strong enough for me.

"Please… please… stop," Aubrey pleaded for I don't know who.

I straddled his chest and the pussy immediately blocked his face. I hit him anyways, gripping a chunk of his hair and slamming his head as hard as I fucking could into the concrete.

"You piece of fucking shit!" I yelled out, hitting him anywhere I could, over and over again. "You like to beat women, motherfucker!" I punched him repeatedly, slamming his head once again onto the concrete.

"Lily, he's going to kill him," Aubrey spoke.

"Who cares, he was hurting you," Lily argued, only pissing me off further because she had to defend me from the son of a bitch lying in front of me.

"I'm fine. Please, Dylan, please stop!" Aubrey begged.

"You sack of fucking shit," I ignored her, my fists beating all over his face.

"Please, Dylan, if you ever loved me… please stop!" she screamed out with pure desperation in her tone.

I instantly stopped, standing up to spit on his face. What happened next shocked the shit out of both Lily and I.

Aubrey went to him.

She went to Jeremy.

Choosing him over me.

For the third time in my short life I felt like I took a bullet to my goddamn heart.

"What are you doing?" I seethed, gripping her arm.

She roughly snatched it out of my grasp. "Mind your own goddamn business. Leave!" she ordered, her demeanor quickly turning callous. Nothing like the woman I was just in here with.

"Have you lost your fucking mind? Get the fuck up, Aubrey! I'm taking this piece of shit in." I grabbed my phone from my back pocket, but she knocked it out of my hand, causing the screen to shatter on the floor.

"What the fuck is wrong with you? Why are you defending him?" I argued.

"You know why. Leave. Leave now."

"You can't be serious?" I shook my head. "You think I'm really going to leave you with him? Give me some goddamn credit, Aubrey."

*She's lost her goddamn mind.*

"If you don't leave, Dylan, I swear I'll never let you..." she hesitated, but I understood her subtle warning.

*She was going to throw that in my face, now?*

She blamed me for what happened and there was no taking that back. As much as I wanted to, as much as I prayed I could.

"Un-fucking-believable. I loved you. I still fucking love you and you stand there and defend this piece of shit?"

She swallowed hard her resolve breaking.

"I guess I really never knew you at all," I bit.

She shut her eyes. I could physically feel her pain in the distance between us. I took one last look at her before kicking Jeremy in the stomach, peering down at him with disgust.

"Mark my words, motherfucker, one day I'm going to fucking kill you," I snapped, barely being able to hold back the desire to do it right then and there.

I grabbed Lily's hand and led her out through the side door. She halted as soon as we were a few feet away.

"What are you doing? We can't leave her in there. We have to tell someone. You have to arrest him. Go back in there, Dylan!" She was hysterical.

I clenched my teeth. "I don't have a choice."

"Why?"

"Lily, just pretend you didn't see that tonight. Do you understand? For me. Do it for me," I pleaded, looking in her eyes.

"You can't ask me to do that."

"I'm not asking," I lightly warned.

"Dylan, I—"

"Lily, you know I love you. Don't make me say it. We both know what I'm talking about. I've kept my mouth quiet, now it's time for you to return the favor."

She was taken back by what she knew I implied, Jacob and their secret of whatever the fuck they were doing behind everyone's backs for the last few years. The last thing she wanted was for Lucas to find out or anyone else for that matter.

I nodded, feeling bad, and kissed her forehead. I didn't stay around to see the confused and hurt look on her face. I had too much plaguing my own thoughts and emotions that I could barely fucking see two feet in front of me. I went straight to the bar and took four shots of bourbon, one right after the other. Welcoming the warm burn it left in its wake. I poured a drink and walked into the backyard. I needed to get myself together before I went around anyone. By the time I made it back inside, Aubrey and Jeremy were just leaving. They said their goodbyes and I watched every single step Aubrey took, praying that she would turn back and run into my arms. Hoping that I would see some recognition of the woman she used to be.

*Nothing.*

# twenty-seven

# DYLAN

It didn't take long for the inevitable to happen.

Almost a year later Lucas' mom lay on her deathbed, surrounded by her loved ones. Family and friends flew in to say their last goodbyes. I tried to be there for Lucas and Lily. I could tell he was barely hanging on by a thread, and she rarely left her mom's side. Not that I could blame either one of them. I dealt with things differently, I always had. I still dreaded the afternoon when it was my turn to have my time with her.

To say goodbye to a woman who had been like a mom to me.

I was always the strongest among us boys. It was the role I took on as a child, but I felt anything but that when I walked into her room to say my last goodbye. Nothing could have prepared me for the emotions that surged through my body, heart, and mind.

"Dylan-fuckin'-McGraw," she rasped, making me laugh.

Bringing me back to the day she washed my mouth with soap when I was eight after she heard me say fuck to the boys.

She lovingly smiled, patting the side of the bed for me to sit. I took a deep breath, taking in her frail body where she lay about to say her last words to me.

"You have always been such a good boy and now you're an even better man."

"Yeah..."

"You know, Dylan, sometimes in life things happen that we can't control. That we don't understand. But it doesn't matter because it still fucking sucks," she drawled, trying to talk like me.

I chuckled.

She never spoke to me like that before, but I knew she was just trying to make me comfortable and make light of our goodbye.

"You were the first boy to start trouble, start cussing, picking up girls, the first at everything. You were also the first to take the blame when it wasn't yours to take, defending the boys when they needed defending, protecting Alex the most when she never asked for it to begin with. And look at you now, baby, you're a narcotics Detective. Do you have any idea how proud I am of you? I never worried about you, Dylan. Out of all you boys, you were the least of my concerns. I knew you would always lead with your heart, as much as you try to mask it with women." She shook her head, frowning.

"It's not who you are. It's who you think you're supposed to be. Like right now, you want to cry. You want to break down so badly, but you won't because you're strong. You've always been so damn strong for everyone else, even when you're hurting inside."

I swallowed hard.

"There's a time and place for everything. Sometimes it takes us longer than we hoped, but that doesn't mean that it will never come. It'll just mean that much more when it finally does."

I nodded, taking in her words.

"I'm going to be watching from Heaven, smiling and cheering you on, because no one deserves it more than you do."

I bit my lip, my eyes watering.

"I prayed last night. I prayed for the first time in a long time, Dylan. For patience, strength, and courage. For love. Not for me… I'm not scared of dying. I'm terrified of what I'm leaving behind. My kids, you boys, my friends, and the love of my life. It's you guys that will suffer. I'm going to a better place because it's my time to go, but that doesn't mean that you won't feel me." She placed her hand on my heart. "Here."

I peered down at her hand, lost in what she was saying.

"I don't have to tell you to watch over my kids. I know you will. You've been doing it your entire life."

I blinked away the tears, unable to hold them back any longer.

"Dylan-fuckin'-McGraw, I love you and one day you're going to love yourself again too."

I leaned in and hugged her unable to form words.

The next few days felt like they were zooming by, yet at the same time, standing still. All of us waited for the expected. Her heart started to give out one evening, and it was time for their dad to make the decision to take her off the machines that were keeping her alive. The pain she was feeling was noticeably unbearable. We could all see it in her eyes, she wanted to go, but was holding on for us.

After he made the decision that it was time to leave her in God's hands, he came into the room. I stood with Lily in my arms and Lucas sitting next to me. Their dad bent down by her, holding her hand in his. She had maybe spoken five words all day. He looked down at her with tears filling his eyes and remorse for what he just decided.

He begged, "Please, tell me you love me, please, baby, tell me you love me."

She pried open her heavy lids and whispered, "I love you."

He then kissed her forehead and cried, "Good, because I love you, too."

I had just witnessed one of the most beautiful, but painful moments of my life.

It was then that I bawled.

For a love that I yearned for, a love exactly like that, and finally realized that I might never get to have it.

# Aubrey

"You, stupid fucking bitch." He backhanded me across the face so hard that I saw stars. "Fuck! I hate this goddamn town. Why? Why did I listen to you and move here? To fucking Oak Island?"

We relocated back to Oak Island four years ago when Lucas and Alex got married. Jeremy hadn't let me live it down since. The only reason he agreed to move with me was he thought he wouldn't have to deal with his father as often. Unfortunately, it backfired on him, and consequently, on me. He traveled all the time back to California and who knows where the hell else.

We had a "don't ask, don't tell" policy. Except when it came to me. That was a whole different story. I had to ask and tell him everything, or I'd pay for it.

Lucas and Alex got married almost a year after Lucas' mom lost her battle to cancer. After everything they had been through they still found their way back to each other, and I was thrilled for them.

They were meant to be together.

I went to the wake and the funeral, but Dylan and I didn't say one word to each other. He was in so much pain and there wasn't anything I could do for him.

*Not anymore.*

The last time I saw him was a year ago for Lily's twenty-third birthday in Nashville, but the truth was that Dylan had been trying for years to talk to me and help me. Always sending emails that I had to keep deleting out of fear that Jeremy would find them, always trying to call even though I never picked up, always offering help, lists of shelters and ways to help myself.

I always ignored him.

Lily just took off one day and moved to the Music City in Nashville. She had been living there since her mom died. She worked at a bar as their entertainment. Which didn't surprise me, Lily was always singing, a talent way beyond her years. To my surprise Jeremy said we could go, but I should have known better. He never did anything for me, even though he claimed everything he did was for me.

We were late for our flight since he was hungover from the night before. He proceeded to blame me for it. Screaming at me like a damn kid that I didn't wake him up early enough, that I didn't give him an ibuprofen the night before. Hell, he blamed me for the heavy traffic. Alex and Lucas were getting suspicious. I lived ten minutes down the road from their house and hardly ever saw them. That's one of the reasons why Jeremy agreed to go in the first place. Like the stupid woman I was, I jumped at the chance to see him.

*Dylan.*

Which was a waste since we didn't talk at all. Jeremy wouldn't let me out of his sight for more than a few seconds, making it nearly impossible to talk to anyone that much. Lily followed me into the bathroom at her bar to have a word. What she said would forever haunt me.

*"Not everyone gets their happily ever after, Lily." I tore the paper towel from her hand and looked back at the mirror, wiping the blood from my lip. Another wound from Jeremy's handiwork for not paying enough attention to him.*

*"You're wrong, Aubrey," she stated, washing her hands in the sink next to me.*

*I looked at her through the mirror.*

*"You couldn't be any more wrong. I hope by the time you realize that… it won't be too late," she spoke with conviction. She didn't beat around the bush.*

Hearing her say that was a tough pill to swallow.

I was still trying to get it down one year later.

At the end of the day I don't know why we went. It was a huge mistake on my part.

The time wasn't completely shitty for everyone. After three years of trying, Alex finally got pregnant that weekend. I couldn't have been happier for them. Her blissful vacation was my very own hell.

They gave Alex's stepson Mason a brother three months ago and named him Bo, her childhood nickname for Lucas. The day he was born I was getting ready to go to the hospital, but Jeremy put an end to that. He punched me so hard in the stomach. I spent the entire day in bed from the consequences of him not being happy with how I made his breakfast. He blamed it on me being in a rush to go meet my best friend's newborn son.

Alex was so hurt that I wasn't there for her. She hardly talked to me these last three months. I couldn't blame her, I was an awful friend. When we got the invitation in the mail for a party at Alex and Bo's house to celebrate the birth of Bo, and Jacob and Austin moving back to Oak Island, I was relieved that she still included me in her life.

"Jesus Christ, baby, I barely fucking touched you," Jeremy said, reaching his hand up to my face.

I flinched when he caressed my cheek.

"Go get dressed so we can go to this stupid party. Do you see how much I love you? No one loves you like I do. No one."

Bile rose up my throat.

I nodded as he tapped his cheek for me to kiss. I did, resisting the urge to fight back.

Which had been happening a lot more lately.

# DYLAN

"Jesus Christ, man. If you want her so fucking bad, then just tell her," Jacob argued.

I glanced at him. "What the fuck are you talking about?" I asked, knowing damn well what he meant, but I wanted him to say it.

"You're staring at Jeremy like you're ready to kill him. They've been together for years, bro, I don't know if you have a chance anymore, but you're never going to know unless you try."

I cocked my head to the side with a shit-eating grin. "Oh," I mocked. "So now that you're permanently attached to Lily's pussy, you're an expert on relationships, are you?" I busted out laughing.

He jerked back, stunned that I was calling him out on what no one had yet to figure out. "I'm a Detective Jacob, I read people for a living. You do remember that right?"

"How long have you known?"

"Since she was ten?" I laughed again. "Always knew you liked little girls, I should arrest your sorry ass," I chuckled, nudging his shoulder.

He scoffed. "You're such a fucking dick."

I laughed harder, I couldn't help it. "Being in a relationship is making you soft, Jacob. Do I need to worry about your feelings now, too? Awww, I'd hate to make my best friend cry. Do you guys sit around and braid each other's hair and shit?"

"This coming from the man whose hair has been down to his shoulders since he could walk? Who's the one that grew a fucking pussy, huh?"

I shrugged. "You are what you eat."

"But it tastes so damn good," he rasped, and I clinked my beer with his.

"Touché, motherfucker, touché. When are you telling Lucas?"

"Soon."

"Good thing you're a lawyer, Jacob, because he's going to need it after he tries to kill your ass."

He took a deep breath.

"And you?"

"And me what?"

"You're okay with it?"

"What other choice do I have? I love that girl. Even when she was a kid and annoying the shit out of me with her guitar early in the morning."

He nodded, chuckling.

"Don't hurt her again. It's good to see her smiling," I gestured towards Lily who was giggling with Half-Pint, looking so happy.

They locked eyes from across the room.

"I love her, Dylan. I love her more than anything. I always have."

"No shit. If Lucas weren't so far up Half-Pint's ass since she could walk, he would have noticed it, too. But, I'll tell you something."

He looked at me.

"You hurt her again and I'll be standing right there with Lucas while he buries your body. We clear?"

"Crystal."

I patted his back. "Good talk, bro."

It didn't matter how many times I had been in this house it still felt like I had never left, as I gazed at the exact spot where I was on my knees begging Aubrey to stay.

We locked eyes from across the room.

As if she was thinking the same thing I was.

"I'm taking off," Austin interrupted, rubbing his nose.

"What the hell are you doin', man?"

He rolled his eyes. "Not this shit again. Give me a fucking break."

"Wipe your nose a little better next time and maybe I won't ask you."

He bowed his head, sniffling and cleaning at his nose again.

"Get out of my fucking sight before I search you," I warned.

He took a deep breath like he wanted to say something, but at the last second changed his mind, turned and left.

There was only so much I could take. I had to get the fuck out of there. I went to work instead. I had just gotten this undercover case and decided that now was as good as any to start. I sat in my car outside the shithole bar on the other side of town, waiting to see if anything would go down. I'd been sitting there since eleven and it was past two in the morning when all of a sudden I saw Aubrey stumbling out of the bar.

"What the fuck?" I said to myself, getting out of my car to follow her down an alley. "Have you completely lost your goddamn mind?" I yelled out from behind her.

She instantly stopped.

"What are you doing here at this time of night by yourself?"

She spun to face me. "Trying to forget," she simply stated.

"And what exactly are you trying to forget?"

"You, McGraw. I have spent the last ten years of my life trying to forget you."

"Then that makes two of us, darlin'."

"Right? Because you've spent so much time thinking about me," she snapped.

"Lets get one thing straight, Bree, you asked me to mind my own fucking business and even though it went against everything I am and all my principles, I backed off, hoping that one day you would wake up. I was hoping those emails and phone calls would one day give you the push and strength that you needed to get out of this toxic relationship. Let me ask you something, Aubrey, how much do you truly know about your boyfriend, other than the fact he likes to use you as his goddamn punching bag?"

She jerked back.

"What? You don't think I can tell? You think I buy the whole bullshit story of how good he is to you? How you try to pretend your life is so perfect? Come on, Bree, you know me better than that."

"I don't know you at all. Not anymore," she yelled, pushing me away. I grabbed her by the wrist, stopping her from leaving.

"Is that right?"

She nodded not backing down.

"I wasn't the one who left with that son of a bitch that night in the garage. I wasn't the one who turned their back on me, time and time again. I was the one who's been trying to help you for years! Jesus Christ, Aubrey, I've been your goddamn puppy, waiting with my tail tucked between my legs for ten fucking years. After that night I couldn't do it anymore. The back and forth bullshit that you keep doing to me like I'm a fucking pussy at your beck and call is over." I got up in her face, my adrenaline pumping hard.

Her chest heaved.

"But just because you haven't seen me doesn't mean I don't know everything there is to know about you. At the end of the day, I'll always be here looking out for you. I don't know how to be any other way. So, let me ask you again… what do you know about your boyfriend?"

She opened her mouth but quickly shut it.

"That's what I thought. Did you know that he was accused of rape in college and that Daddy the rich politician paid a shit-ton of money to save his little boy's ass? How about the fact that he handles all the shady shit his father is involved in? Daddy keeps his hands clean by dirtying up his sons?"

"You're lying." She shook her head. Disbelief was written all over her pretty little face.

I scoffed. "I wish I was, darlin'. Here's a good one, did you know that he has pussy in every fucking area code that he visits?"

She winced.

"Oh, so you are aware of that, and yet you're still with him." I shook my head. "Ten years, Bree, ten fucking years of your life you have spent existing. I know that you think you died that day on the trail, but no, suga', you've been slowly killing yourself every single day since. How does it feel? Huh? What are you punishing yourself for exactly? I'm the one that fucked up, not you."

Her eyes watered.

I dug a little deeper, inch by inch she was crumbling.

"I stayed away because I can't see you hurt yourself anymore and know that you don't care. Why are you protecting him? He's nothing to you. It doesn't matter how much damn makeup you use, Bree, the scars are already there, and I'm not talking about the bruises and cuts. You need help and I can't help you unless you are ready to help yourself first."

It was time for me to be the man I was supposed to be and get Aubrey back. I would make her mine once again no matter what it might cost me. Words always seemed to fail us so maybe I needed to give her a physical reminder. I needed her to remember what we used to share.

Our love.

I used the only weapon I could.

"When was the last time you were touched, Aubrey?"

"What?" she replied, taken aback.

"Kissed, loved? When was the last time someone made you come?"

She lowered her eyebrows. "You can't talk to me like that. Who the fuck do you think you are, McGraw?"

I grinned. "That long, huh?"

"I'm not having this conversation with you."

"Great, seeing as I don't plan on talking." I looked her up and down with a predatory regard. "Let me give you what you need," I paused to let my words linger and then groaned, "Let me fuck you right, like old times. Let me fuck him out of you."

"What?"

"Did I stutter?"

"You can't just come here and-"

"And what? Tell me, darlin', what can't I do?"

"Dylan, please…"

I was over to her in three strides her back hitting the wall. I tugged on the ends of her hair and placed my hand behind her neck before she even saw it coming.

"Okay, only because you asked so fucking nicely," I drawled out.

I kissed her.

For the first time in ten fucking years, I kissed the woman who belonged to me. And she didn't stop me. I grazed her cheek with the tips of my fingers and placed a fallen piece of her hair behind her ear. My touch alone made her shutter.

The simple gesture made her lips part.

"Fuck, Aubrey," I murmured in between kissing her. "Tell me to stop, push me away, tell me to go. If I keep kissing you, feeling you against me like this, I'll never be able to let you go again."

She opened her eyes and looked deep into mine.

"Promise?"

"Always."

I purposely trailed my fingers down her neck. I lightly brushed my fingertips against the top of her heart, her rapid breathing causing her breasts to rise and fall every few seconds. Our eyes once again connected and for the first time in over a decade I finally saw what I longed for every day and night.

*My girl.*

Her eyes showed me everything that I so desperately wanted to hear. They spoke for her. When my hand reached her heart it was beating so profusely. I pulled her closer to me by the nook of her neck.

"I love you," I whispered close enough to her mouth that I could feel her breath upon my lips.

"I know. I've always known," she murmured, brushing her lips against mine.

I smiled against them. "What do you want, suga', I'll give you whatever you fucking want. Just say the words, I'm yours."

"You. Touch me. Please, touch me."

There was silence again.

I gripped the front of her neck, my thumb and index finger clutching her pulses. "I know what you feel like when you come, suga', I know how your face gets flushed. I know you stop breathing just slightly before your pussy starts to pulsate so fucking tight that it pushes my fingers out of it." I bit her bottom lip and then kissed her softly. "I know what you taste like."

She swallowed the saliva that had pooled in her mouth. Her breathing elevated, showing me that I was getting to her. I moved my hand from her neck down to her inner thigh, pushing aside her panties and slowly caressed her soft bare folds.

"But most importantly, I know what it feels like to be inside you."

She gasped when my fingers rubbed against her like I knew she loved. I pecked her lips as I played with her clit, getting her nice and wet.

"And I'm not talking about this." I pushed two fingers inside as I pressed my hand against her heart.

"Here."

She tilted her head back slightly and kissed me, soft at first, testing the feel of my mouth around hers. The way her lips claimed mine told me she wanted me to keep going, keep taking what was still mine.

Even after all these years.

I savored both the taste and the feel of her, how her body angled perfectly beneath mine, and she melted against me, taking everything I was giving her and wanting more.

Wanting everything.

"Do you want me?" I whispered in her ear, as I continued my assault down her neck. "Do you want me to make you come?

Silence.

"Tell me…" I urged, pushing my fingers deeper into her sweet spot.

She moaned, "Right there."

"Where?" I cocked my head to the side, not moving our lips apart. "Here?"

"Yes…"

"Tell me."

"I want you," she finally panted, gliding her tongue into my mouth as her walls tightened around my fingers so close to coming undone.

"Oh my God," she panted.

"What? Oh my God, what, suga'?"

Her eyes rolled to the back of her head and her legs trembled. I instantly removed my fingers and she whimpered at the loss. I kissed her one last time, slowly leaning away from her. She followed until she couldn't anymore, opening her eyes with a questioning stare.

"You don't get my love again until you're fully mine."

Her eyes widened in shock.

"I'm always here for you. No matter what, I'm always fucking here. When you're ready to move forward, call me."

I tugged on the ends of her hair and then left her standing there in the alley. As much as it killed me, it was time to show her tough love.

All I could do was hope it was enough.

"Where the fuck have you been?" Jeremy roared when I walked through the door.

I violently shook my head, clenching my teeth. "What are you doing here?"

"What am I doing here? This is my fucking house!" he yelled, making his way over to me. I didn't cower.

He gripped my hair so hard that I thought he was going to tear it out. Getting right up in my face. He was seething with anger. I'd never seen him so mad.

"You fucking whore," he gritted out. "You smell like fucking men's cologne. You stupid, stupid slut!"

He let go of my hair, but I didn't get a moment to breathe before he punched me in the stomach. I doubled over in pain, but that didn't stop him. He backhanded me across the face and I crumbled to the ground.

"After everything I have done for you!" He kicked me in the stomach and I finally screamed. Which only made him kick me again, and that time I heard my ribs crack under his boot.

I hated those fucking boots.

I gasped for air, trying to block my body with my arms. He clutched my hair by the nook of my neck and my hands instantly went to where his were, clawing at his fingers. He dragged me by my hair to the kitchen. My legs flailed behind me, trying to gain control to stand up. I didn't know if I was crying or screaming. I didn't even know if I was going to live through this.

"Look at the kitchen! Look at this fucking kitchen!"

He slammed my head against the fridge and I immediately saw stars. I vaguely remember him pulling out the drawers and throwing them all around the room.

"You can't do anything fucking right! The spoons are where the forks are supposed to be, you put the oven mitts and dishtowels in the same goddamn drawer! Why the fuck do I buy you nice things if you can't keep them organized? Are you fucking stupid? Answer me, you fucking bitch."

He kicked me in my side again.

"I'm sorry," I whispered so low he couldn't hear me.

He grabbed me by the collar of my blouse and slapped me across the cheek, my face whipping back so hard I thought he was going to break my neck.

"Look at me! Fucking look at me, you useless whore!"

"I can't," I whimpered, unable to move.

He let go of me and my lifeless body fell to the floor once again.

He crouched down close to my face. "I came home early for you. I do everything for you and this is how you repay me. Spreading your legs to whom, Aubrey? Dylan? That piece of shit who doesn't love you. I'm the only man who will ever love you, your daddy doesn't even fucking give a shit about you."

"Why do you hurt me?" I breathed out between sobs, needing to know. "Why do you hurt me so much?" my voice was only a whisper. I could barely breathe, let alone talk.

"Because I fucking love you. That's why."

The next thing I knew he punched me in the face.

Everything. Went. Black.

# Chapter twenty-eight

# Aubrey

"God, Aubrey, I've been so busy with Giselle, I didn't even realize what was happening to you. I had no idea Jeremy was putting you through Hell. How did I not know this?"

"I kept it a really good secret, Aunt Celeste, but I can't do it anymore."

I thought about Dylan the entire way home that night. What he said, how he touched me, how his hands and words affected me, all of it. I hadn't been touched like that in years. The last man to ever give me an orgasm had been Dylan. Jeremy never took his time with me. Not once was it ever about my needs or me.

In every aspect of our relationship.

Everything Dylan said was right and knowing that he blamed himself for what tore my life apart was too much to take. I didn't know why I was hurting myself anymore. Nothing made sense.

Everyone had moved on.

Including Dylan.

The fact that he was moving on without me shook me to the core. I guess I always thought he would be there, waiting. Knowing that he was done with me was a thought I couldn't even bear. Dylan was right I needed to get help. When I woke up the next morning in a pool of my own blood, it was the wake up call I needed. Jeremy was nowhere in sight the next four days.

He was going to kill me.

And I was going to let him.

It took weeks for me to heal from the beating I received that night. It had been a little over six months since I started seeing a therapist behind his back. I finally found the courage to start sticking up for myself. I'd been taking some self-defense classes, and tonight when he went to slap me I instinctively blocked it, almost knocking him on his ass. He didn't say one word to me. It was like I had slapped him across the face for once and I waited for the attack that never came.

He just left.

"Aubrey, I'm flying out right now," my Aunt Celeste stated.

I don't know why I told her. I was scared and I just wanted to talk to someone. Have them listen to me for a change.

"No," I sternly stated. "I don't want you or Giselle around Jeremy. I'm fine. I have this taken care of. I promise."

"Honey, you can't just expect me to sit here and wait not knowing if you're ok."

"I'll call you first thing tomorrow. Let me just figure things out, okay? Try to set something up."

"Aubrey, you can come here. You could go home to your mom, too."

"I know. I just need to do this for myself, okay? Can you please understand?"

"Yes. I don't like it though. I don't like this one bit. If you don't call me first thing tomorrow morning, I'll call the cops. Do you understand me?"

I nodded even though she couldn't see me.

"Aubrey."

"Yes."

"I love you. I'm here. I don't care what time it is."

"I know."

She took a deep breath and hung up.

I paced around the living room with an eerie feeling in my stomach. I decided to make myself some tea to try to calm down, debating on whether to call Dylan or not. I knew he would come for me, but I was being honest when I said I wanted to do this on my own. I was sick of feeling weak and out of control. I needed to help myself, save myself, and stop expecting everyone to do it for me.

I sipped my tea, debating on whether or not to lock myself in the guest bedroom. If he wanted to hurt me, he would have already done it when he had the chance. He wouldn't have just left like he did. It made no sense. I contemplated what to do for what seemed like forever until I couldn't take it anymore and decided it was best to go lock myself in the room.

I was safer that way.

I made my way into the guest bedroom and gasped, when I felt his arms come around me. I didn't even hear him come in through the front door.

So many bad memories came rushing back to me. To this day I hated being snuck up on.

"Jeremy," I coaxed, my heart racing. The smell of whiskey instantly assaulted my senses as if he bathed in it. I resisted the urge to throw up.

"*Ain't no sunshine when she's gone,*" he sang against my ear, swaying his hips behind me. I could feel his erection digging into my back.

My heart stopped.

"Jeremy, what are you—"

"Shhh… shhh…" he whispered, my body locking up. "No more talking. I'm done hearing your goddamn mouth. So, you think you can leave me?" He spun me around to face him, and continued to sway his hips to the non-existent music.

"I never said that. I'm not—"

"Shut the fuck up!" he roared too close to my face, making me jump. "It's okay, baby, I'm not going to hurt you. *Ain't no sunshine when she's gone. It's not warm when she's away.*" He spun me out then roughly pulled me back into his chest, our bodies colliding together like we were slow dancing. I had never seen him so fucking drunk before.

He suddenly let me go.

"Turn around, I can't stand the sight of your fucking face right now."

I slowly moved on shaking legs. He watched my every move. I felt his hands go to my thighs, slowly working their way up my sides. Singing the words of the song to me. He abruptly stopped, removing them from my body. Standing there, I could still feel his stare on the back of my head. I don't know how much time went by before I looked behind me only to find predatory eyes on me. I instantly turned and started running up the stairs as fast as I could go.

"Where are you going? The fun's just getting started!" he laughed, grabbing my ankle.

I fell face first onto the steps, but I didn't falter. I couldn't. I flipped over and kicked him in the stomach.

He barely wavered, making my escape nearly impossible. His eyes lit up like a goddamn Christmas tree. He gripped my ankle once again, tugging me toward him, slamming my body down the stairs. I kicked and screamed bloody murder.

"Well, lookie, lookie here, someone's been a busy little cunt!" he shouted, slapping me across the face and tearing open my robe.

"No! No! No!" I violently shook my head

"Baby, I want you to fucking beg," he gritted out, gripping onto my chin, making me look at him. Eye to eye with nothing but evil in his and fear in mine.

He spit in my face and smeared it all over like he was branding me.

"You're mine! You're fucking mine! Do you hear me, you little whore? No one leaves me, get that through your fucking head."

He grabbed my shoulders, lifted me up and connected my head with the stairs. My vision blurred.

When he roughly placed his hand over my throat, my eyes widened. Pure panic coursed through my body as he ripped my shirt open and then tore off my panties, squeezing my throat harder when I tried to resist.

Jeremy had always been a bastard, but he never tried to rape me.

I closed my eyes. I was reliving the first time I thought I died. I couldn't go through that again. I wouldn't survive it this time. As if reading my mind, he took his hand off my throat. I took a few steady breaths, trying to regain any composure I could muster.

"Open your eyes. Open your goddamn eyes."

I did, my teeth chattering and my body shaking.

He deliberately roamed his hands from my neck down my stomach.

"You don't have to do this," I pleaded in a tone I didn't recognize.

It was like I was there, but I wasn't. I watched everything unfold in front of me as if I was having an out-of-body experience.

He cocked his head to the side and narrowed his glossy eyes at me.

"I don't?"

I shook my head, trying to form words. "No. You don't."

"And, why is that?"

"Because you love me," I reminded, hoping that it would grant me some mercy.

"Mmm…" he groaned, causing me to internally cringe.

"What about you, Aubrey, do you love me? Or are you just using me like a fucking whore would do?"

I choked back the tears. "Of course I love you."

He smiled and for a second I thought everything was going to be okay, for a moment I thought this nightmare might be over.

I was wrong.

It had only just begun.

He leaned over, his entire body hovering above me. I heard him lower his zipper and that's when I mentally checked out. My mind protecting me from what he was about to do. My face fell to the side, as my tears started flowing. My body jerked forward when he thrust into my dry opening. The edge of the stairs dug into my back. Causing me even more pain.

"Fuck, you feel better than I thought you would," he growled against my face. I breathed through the throbbing.

He drove in and out a few times, each movement worse than the last. When I didn't fight back, he started to fuck me harder. The stinging becoming almost unbearable, but I wasn't going to give into him.

*Not this time.*

"Fucking scream!" he demanded through a clenched jaw.

I didn't say anything, I didn't even move.

"I want to hear you fucking cry! Fucking beg me to stop."

Silence.

He slapped me and I instantly tasted blood.

"What the fuck?" he snarled, backhanding me across the face again.

When I didn't make a sound, he mercilessly pounded into me with much more strength and determination.

"You're good for nothing, you piece of shit!"

He thrusted in a few more times and unexpectedly pulled out. Standing to look down at me with disgust spread across his face.

He jerked off instead.

"You're mine. I won't ever let you leave me! Do you understand? MINE!"

He came all over my chest and face, laughing the entire time as he buttoned up his pants.

"Don't pretend like you didn't like it, you dirty whore. I know you like it rough. Now get the fuck out of my sight."

He roughly pulled my body off the stairs, throwing me into the wall. I stumbled to my feet, my legs felt numb and my pussy raw.

I didn't have to be told twice.

I ran all the way up the stairs, blocking out what I already knew in my heart.

# DYLAN

They say when you love someone you can feel them even if you're miles apart.

I woke up from a dead sleep that night, sitting straight up in my bed, gasping for my next breath. I immediately grabbed my phone off the nightstand. No missed calls. I tore the covers off of me. My skin burned and my heart pounded. I went into the kitchen to get a bottle of water and tried to calm the fuck down.

I took a few swigs when the keychain on the key rack got my attention. Trying like hell to shake off the unease that I felt in the pit of my stomach. I lay back down on my bed, staring up at the ceiling for what felt like a lifetime. I must have passed out sometime during the night. I woke up the next morning with the keychain held tightly in my grasp and I couldn't remember bringing it back with me.

I spent the entire morning in my office, pretending like I was fucking working when all I was thinking about was Aubrey. I counted down the hours until Lily's twenty-fifth birthday party that evening, needing the distraction from the feeling I just couldn't shake.

I was on my way home to change and head over to Alex's restaurant for the party.

When my cell phone rang, I swear that I just knew. I knew that something horrible had happened.

"Aubrey," I answered, taking a sharp U-turn and obstructing traffic to detour back to her house.

"I'm sorry. I'm so fucking sorry, Dylan..." she sobbed into the phone.

"Calm down, darlin'. Where are you?"

"Home," she wept, barely getting the words out.

"I'm on my way. I will be there in five minutes. Just hold on, suga', okay?"

"Okay," she bawled.

"Aubrey, darlin', don't cry. I'm coming for you."

"That's what I'm afraid of. Dylan, I'm so sorry, you have to know that. Please, please, forgive me."

"Suga', there's nothin' to forgive. I love you. I will always love you."

"I love you, too. I never stopped. I swear to you I never fucking stopped," she cried.

My heart soared. I had waited almost eleven goddamn years to hear her say that to me again.

"Please forgive me. Please... promise... no matter what you'll forgive me..."

"Always, Aubrey, always."

She whimpered into the phone as if it caused her pain to hear me say that and I didn't understand.

"Darlin', there is no me without you. Don't you understand that?"

She wept harder.

"Where's my girl, huh? Where's my tough girl? I need you to take a few deep breaths, in through your nose and out through your mouth."

"I don't know anymore. I have spent the last year trying to find her."

"It's okay, we will find her together. Just you and me, just you and me," I repeated, needing to get through to her.

I pulled into her driveway, opening my door before I had the car in park. I ran up to her door, slamming it open with her still on the phone.

"Aubrey!" I yelled out into the foyer. "Aubrey, where are you?" I asked into the phone.

"In the guestroom closet."

I placed my phone in my back pocket and pulled my gun from my holster just in case the motherfucker was still in the house. I ran to the first door that was closed that could have been a bedroom. She wasn't in there.

"Aubrey?" I shouted, running up the stairs, taking three of them at a time. "Aubrey! Answer me, darlin'!"

I heard sobs coming from one of the bedrooms and when I went to open the door it was locked. She cried louder and harder, I didn't think twice about it. I stepped back and kicked the door open.

I sprinted toward the closet, slamming the sliders open. What I saw nearly brought me to my knees.

She was sitting in the back corner with her knees pressed against her chest, her arms tightly wrapped around them. The jewelry box that I had given her was clutched securely in her lap, with the music playing. She held a filet knife so fucking tight in her hand that her knuckles turned white.

"Jesus Christ," I breathed out, taking in the bruises all over her face, her busted lip and her left eye almost swollen shut.

She hadn't looked at me once, hysterically crying. I holstered my gun and placed my arms out in front of me, scared shitless that I would frighten her.

She was in shock.

"Darlin', it's me. It's Dylan. Can you hear me?" I crouched down beside her, immediately grabbing her hand and to my surprise, she let me.

I placed it over my heart. "Feel me, Aubrey. Feel my heart. Feel it beating for you."

She sucked in air and turned to look at me as if she just realized I was in there with her.

"Dylan?" she frowned, her lip trembling and it took everything inside me not to cry right along with her.

271

"Yes, suga', it's me."

"You're really here?"

"Where else would I be?" I shook my head.

"I'm so sorry… I'm so fucking sorry…"

"Shhh… shhh…" I soothed, prying the knife out of her hand, and setting it beside me.

"You're my girl. You'll always be my girl," I coaxed, tugging on the ends of her hair and down her cheek.

She leaned into my hand and it was then that I noticed she was wearing the necklace I left in the jewelry box for her years ago. I beamed even though my heart was torn in two seeing her in the state of distress she was in.

"Darlin', I'm going to pick you up, okay? We're going to get you washed up and pack some clothes. I'm taking you home."

"Home?" She peered into my eyes, lost and desolate.

I nodded. "My home. It's where you belong. Just you and me. I'll protect you, darlin'."

"Okay." She nodded.

I picked her up like a baby and sat her on the counter of the bathroom, turning on the faucet to wet a rag. I gently pressed it against her face and she hissed upon contact. Her hand never left my heart and for the first time in my life I actually had to concentrate on keeping it steady for her.

The rage and adrenaline that pumped through my veins was searing to the point of pain.

"I'm here now. I'll take care of everything, don't you worry."

She nodded like she believed me. I picked her up again, carrying her in my arms. I took her into her bedroom, sitting her on the bed and she instantly stood up.

I didn't have to wonder why.

"Darlin'."

I brought her attention back to me.

"Can you help me grab some things for you? We could get out of here a lot faster if you helped me."

She shook her head no. "I have everything I need," she stated, clutching the jewelry box closer to her chest and holding the charm on the necklace tighter.

I smiled for the first time that day, stepping toward her when the front door crashed open.

She froze.

"Aubrey, look into my eyes right now. I'm not going to let him hurt you." I placed her behind me, as he trampled up the stairs.

He shook his head when he walked into the room not fazed in the least that I was standing there.

"You, fucking whore! I knew you were fucking him behind my back."

He charged me and Aubrey screamed, moving out of the way as he slammed me against her vanity. Glass shattered everywhere. He punched me in the face and then in the stomach. I growled, shoving him with so much force into the wall that he tore threw the drywall.

"I'm not Aubrey, motherfucker!" I hit him in the face a few times and then in the stomach. "Not so fucking tough when it's not a woman you're beating on, are you?" I snarled, kneeing him in the ribs when he hunched over in pain.

I pushed him on the ground, kicking him a few times before finally stepping away. I wiped the blood off my mouth with the back of my hand. I looked back toward Aubrey who was standing in the corner of the room with her eyes so dark and dilated I couldn't see the familiar green in them anymore.

"Darlin'." I stepped toward her.

Jeremy laughed, sitting up against the wall, getting ready to stand up. Holding onto his stomach.

"You're with this piece of shit." He spit blood onto the floor. "The man that didn't protect you. The very man that let you go out all by yourself."

"Shut the fuck up!" I roared, getting ready to lay him out again. I wanted nothing more than to kill this motherfucker.

Aubrey shook her head back and forth. "No, no, no, no, no," she repeated, placing her hands over her ears like she knew what he was going to say next.

*What the fuck was going on?*

"*At last... my love has come along... and my lonely days are over...*" he sang and I jerked back, the realization hitting me like a ton of fucking bricks.

"God, I loved you then. You were so goddamn beautiful. Everyone in the bar wanted to fuck you, right then and there. What kind of man lets his woman provoke men like a fucking whore? Any guesses? I'll tell you, one that knows that is exactly what she is."

"Please… please… stop…" Aubrey panicked, whipping her body all around the room. I felt her slipping away from me, again.

"Oh, now, you want to beg me," he viscously mocked. "I followed you home that night. I watched you fuck her up against the door. I pulled my own cock out and jacked off the entire fucking time. The slut loved it rough and that's when I knew. I knew she was mine."

That night flashed before my eyes.

Every last second of it played out in front of me.

"I waited. I waited until I had my chance. It didn't take long." He snidely smiled. *"Ain't no sunshine when she's gone…"* he sang again. "I watched her run and I couldn't wait to fucking chase her down. She thought I was you," he sadistically laughed. "I cleared that up for her real quick though. See… Dylan, I made her fucking hate you. It's the only way I could make her truly mine. I placed your shirt over her face as I fucked her seven ways till Sunday. She smelled nothing but you while I ripped into her tight fucking pussy that I still can't get enough of."

I couldn't breathe.

I couldn't fucking breathe.

All that time… All that goddamn time. That's why she wouldn't come near me. She couldn't stand to smell me. It brought her back to that moment.

I shut my eyes, reliving that day all over again.

The image of her lying there broken, beaten… dead.

As if we never left.

"Please, Jeremy, please, fucking stop…" Aubrey pleaded, crying her eyes out.

I went to her and she actually held out her arms for me.

"Oh, Dylan, what a damn fool you are," he spewed, stopping me dead in my tracks.

"No!" Aubrey screamed loud enough to break glass.

"See, I never forgot about the girl who stole my heart. It didn't matter how many other girls I raped, I always saw Aubrey's face. Her pussy is so fucking addicting, huh? It's like she was made just for sex."

"Shut the fuck up." I came at him and he surrendered his hands out in the air.

"*Baby*," he ridiculed. "Why don't you tell Dylan here about Giselle." He shrugged. "Maybe he should hear it from you. I can't wait to see the hatred in his eyes. Go ahead, baby, rip the man's goddamn heart out."

I looked back toward Aubrey and her face turned white.

"Giselle?"

She fiercely shook her head. "I'm sorry... I'm so fucking sorry, Dylan... please forgive me... please let me explain... please..." She immediately started bawling again.

Jeremy sighed, bringing my attention back to him.

"Aubrey is a goddamn liar. It didn't take long for me to find her. The first time she let me fuck her I noticed she had a little scar."

"Shut up! Shut the fuck up!" she yelled out uncontrollably.

"Want to guess where it is. Better yet, why don't you take a look for yourself?" He gestured towards her lower stomach.

Her body shook as my feet moved on their own accord.

"*And... life is like a song... oh... at last... and here we are in Heaven...*" he continued to sing.

"Please... please..." she begged, pleading with me as I pulled down her cotton shorts.

"Oh my God," I breathed out in disbelief.

"*For you are mine... at last...*" Jeremy hissed. "She gave up your daughter even after she knew it wasn't mine."

I would remember the next few seconds for the rest of my life.

It all ended with a...

BANG.

# twenty-nine

# DYLAN

**Six years later**

I walked out of the gates of Hell.

The boys and Alex were all waiting for me on the other side of the fence, as I passed through the prison walls that I called home for the last six years. I was supposed to serve ten years for the manslaughter of Jeremy Montgomery, but got out after six for good behavior.

They all looked so goddamn happy to see me. I gritted my teeth hardly being able to tolerate it.

There was nothing to be excited about.

Not one fucking thing.

"Dylan," Alex beamed, throwing her arms around my neck. "I'm so happy you're out. I've missed you so much," she wept, breaking down.

I didn't hug her back. I grabbed her arms from around my neck. She froze, immediately frowning when I pulled them back down. Still perceptive as always, except this time I didn't give a flying fuck.

The boys didn't pay her any mind. They were too caught up on the fact that we were all together again. Me? I wanted to get out of there faster than a bat out of Hell.

And I wasn't talking about prison.

"Let's go," I rumbled not bothering to hug any of the boys.

I opened the passenger side door and got in the SUV. I was thrilled about the fact that it wasn't a car and I didn't have to sit close to anyone. After sharing a cell with three other guys who wanted to fuck you over in more ways than one, you learned to appreciate some personal space when you could get it.

"How does it feel to be out, brother?" Austin asked, slapping me on the chest as he drove.

I didn't falter. "I will definitely miss the ass raping going on around me and especially the fucking food. I'm sure one day you will experience all of it first hand… brother."

No one spoke after that.

I shut my eyes, leaning my head against the headrest, already dreading what was to come.

I held the invitation in my shaking hands.

"Aubrey, you've come such a long way. I'm so proud of you," Dr. Wexler stated.

She was the therapist that I had been seeing for the last seven years.

"They wouldn't have invited you to Dylan's welcome home party if they didn't want you to go."

"His mom invited me. Not Dylan."

"I'm sure he knows."

I shrugged. "I wouldn't know that. I haven't seen him since the trial."

I went to visit him once a month for the last six years and was denied visitation each and every time. He refused to see me, not wanting anything to do with me. I couldn't blame him, but it still hurt nonetheless.

"Aubrey, you're not that person anymore. The broken woman that came to me is long gone, sweetheart. She's not even in the same vicinity as you anymore. You're strong, independent and most of all you learned to love yourself again. You can overcome anything and you have."

I took a deep breath. "I know." And I did.

"So, you're going to go?"

I nodded. "Yes."

"Great. I can't wait to hear about it next week."

I drove home with a heavy heart. I knew he was getting out. It was all over the papers. During the months of his trial and then after his sentencing all you heard and read about was how Detective Dylan McGraw was behind bars for the murder of Jeremy Montgomery, son of the highly respected politician Bill Montgomery. Our families and close friends knew what I went through with Jeremy, but it didn't matter. There were no police records for any of my so-called allegations of the years and years of abuse I endured from him.

Jacob said he was lucky that he was a Detective and had closed several cases saving peoples lives or else he would have been looking at twenty plus years versus the plea bargain that he had to take for only ten.

It didn't matter how many times I tried to write him, all my letters were returned unopened. I kept them all in hopes that one day he would forgive me and read them.

The celebration of his release was being held at his mom's house tomorrow afternoon. I would have to go to the home that held so many of my happy childhood memories. Come face to face with my truths.

I was going to go.

It was time to face my demons.

Most of them I had already conquered, especially the one smiling at me as she opened the passenger side door.

"Hey, honey, how was school?"

"Hey, Mom." She kissed my cheek.

She was the sweetest girl with the sharpest tongue, much like her daddy. After the night Jeremy left me in the kitchen to die, I started to see Dr. Wexler, I told her that my biggest regret was turning my back on our daughter.

My Aunt Celeste came to see me a few weeks after the rape, nine to be exact. I could never lie to her. She was always very perceptive when it came to me, making it nearly impossible to slip anything past her. I broke down one night and told her about the rape. She held me in her arms the entire time, comforting me the only way she knew how. The next morning we went into my mom's office at the hospital and she proceeded to tell my mom everything that I shared with her the night before.

Knowing there was no way in hell I could utter the words again. My mom cried for what felt like forever. Then they both took me down to the lab so that my mom could test me for every STD under the sun.

Except she took one test that I never even considered a possibility.

A few days later we found out I was pregnant. I was nineteen and knocked up, but the question at the time was whose baby was I carrying?

Dylan's or my rapists?

I refused to tell anyone about it, which my mom and aunt understood.

Two days after that my mom and Aunt Celeste decided that it would be best for me to leave Oak Island and spend the duration of my pregnancy living with my Aunt Celeste. I attended a community college near her house, lying to everyone that I was at UCLA.

The following day after the decisions and plans were made, Dylan found me in my room having what my therapist referred to as a nervous breakdown.

"School was great. So, when can I meet my dad?" She bounced in her seat with excitement.

Another one of Dylan's qualities that I had been dealing with for the last six years, his daughter didn't beat around the bush.

She said what she meant and meant what she said.

"Honey, I told you. I need to see him first."

She rolled her eyes. "That's so stupid. I'm his daughter and I'm super adorable and loveable." She shrugged. "He's going to love me instantly."

I laughed. She was also cocky like him.

Giselle knew everything that happened to me. My Aunt Celeste never kept it a secret from her. I always knew what was going on in her life. I just wasn't involved in it until I got her back when she was ten. The first time I met Giselle was only a few months before she came back to me. Our daughter loved hard, exactly like her father. She forgave me, saying she had been waiting for that moment all her life, and she knew in her heart that I would make my way back to her.

We belonged together.

"Why can't I go to the party?" she asked. "Gammy and Papa invited me, too. They told me, Mom. Besides, my name is on the invitation, which in my book means I should be there."

"Honey, I promise. Let me see him first and then you can meet him."

She frowned, disappointment clear across her face.

"You're right."

She glanced over at me as I parked the car in our driveway.

"You are super adorable and loveable. Your daddy is going to fall in love with you instantly."

She beamed. The same honey colored eyes tore into my heart, exactly how her dad's used to.

"Fine, but take a picture of me, just in case. You know, just to seal the deal and stuff."

I nodded, silently wishing I had her confidence.

# DYLAN

"What the fuck are you doing here?" I roared, taking in the woman I never truly knew.

I didn't want this party.

As far as I was concerned there wasn't anything to celebrate, thanks to the bitch standing in front of me. I woke up in my teenage bedroom. I was thirty-seven years old and officially living back home with my parents. I couldn't even rent my own goddamn apartment, seeing as I was a convicted felon fresh out of prison.

I was outside on the porch, needing to get some air before this godforsaken party, that I never asked for or wanted to begin with, started when I saw her.

"I won't fucking ask you again, Bree, what the fuck are you doing here?"

She peered all around the open space and then back at me. "I... I was invited," she stammered. "I came early to help set up and hopefully talk to you."

"You gotta be shittin' me? You have quite a set of brass balls on ya, don't you? Who the—"

"I... no... I just—"

I loomed over her. "Do not interrupt me! Don't you fucking dare interrupt me," I seethed.

She shook her head. "I'm just trying to explain. If you could give me—"

"If I could give you what? What else do you need me to give you? My fucking life? Oh, no, you already took that away from me on more than one occasion."

"Dylan, I—"

I placed my finger over her mouth, quieting her. I was done hearing her goddamn mouth and pitiful excuses. The old pussy whipped McGraw was gone. I kicked his sorry ass to the curb the day I found out she was a fucking liar. Everything I ever felt for her vanished as if it ceased to exist in the first place.

"I don't want you here. Do you understand me? The mere sight of you makes me sick to my fucking stomach. I spent half of my life loving the shit out of you, and I lost everything in a matter of seconds because of you. Everything! My career, my freedom, and my fucking daughter. You took away my choice to be a father by hiding her existence from me for ten fucking years. As far as I'm concerned you fucking died the day Jeremy did."

She gasped.

They say that vengeance doesn't make you feel better. Well, that was a lie.

It felt fucking amazing.

"I'll never forget you, although I'll spend the rest of my life trying."

Her eyes widened, immediately watering. I saw her cry so many damn times that I could drown in a sea of her crocodile tears.

"Is that why you never read my letters? Or let me visit you in prison?"

"No, Bree, that's not why." I leaned in close to her lips and her breathing hitched.

I spoke with conviction, "On *that* day you just turned into another girl I used to fuck."

She shattered. Her glass house breaking as she ran away from me. I held the hammer firmly in my hand ready to use it again, when needed.

"Dylan Anthony McGraw," Mom snapped from behind me.

I spun around, facing her as she came toward me. "Don't even go there, Ma. Don't even try to fucking go there with me."

"Oh my God! I am so ashamed of you right now, I can't even look at you."

"Good," I barked. "Then turn your ass back around so you don't waste my time with this fuckin'—"

Her hand was up in the air, connecting with the side of my face before I even got the last word out.

"Oh, Dylan, I don't care where you just got released from. I don't care what you may have seen. I don't care what you have gone through or who you think you are now, but if you ever," she gritted out through clenched teeth, shaking the sting off her hand that I felt on my cheek.

"Ever, raise your voice or talk to me like that again, boy, I will not hesitate to remind you who it is you're talking to. Do you understand me? Or do you need me to remind you again?"

"Yes, ma'am," I forced out, holding my cheek.

"Oh my God. Where is my boy? Where is my son? Because I have not seen him since you walked through these doors yesterday afternoon. I raised you better than this."

"Yeah, Ma. You raised me so damn good and I still ended up in prison."

She shook her head. "Whose choice was that? Yours! No one else's but yours. That girl has been through enough and she doesn't need your shit on top of everything else. She is an amazing mother to that young girl."

I jerked back. "What?"

"You heard me."

"Obviously not clear enough."

"She has Giselle. She's had her for the last six years, and has done nothing but include us in her life. I know my granddaughter because of her. That girl is exactly like you, and up until a few minutes ago, I was proud of that fact."

"I... I didn't..." I stuttered.

"Now, you get your act together before your guests arrive. The one's who are so excited and relieved that you're finally home. Go take the stick out of your ass and find *my* son. When you do, have *him* come find me." She spun, walking back inside.

"Jesus Christ, six years, Ma! Six damn years. You couldn't have told me that when you visited! You couldn't have let me know that Aubrey had Giselle, that she was raisin' her. I have spent the last six years thinking of nothing but my daughter! No one had the decency to tell me that!" I yelled, stopping her and making her turn to face me.

"What good would that have done? You were behind bars. The last thing we wanted to do was cause you anymore pain. You know, as well as I do that seeing Giselle and not being able to hug her and kiss her would have torn you apart. Hell, maybe if you would have accepted Aubrey's visitations or read her letters, she would have told you. If I would have known this—" she gestured at me, "—would have walked out, trust me, Dylan, I would have told you. Your sourpuss mood while you were in there was understandable and never stopped anyone from visiting you. But you're out now. It's time to put on your big boy pants and deal with the fact that this is your life now. Hopefully the Dylan I used to know, the boy I raised to have manners and respect others, will still come out on top and figure out something meaningful to do with his life, instead of tearing everyone to shreds for his own decisions."

"I don't know how to anymore, Ma," I honestly spoke.

"Then figure it out before you really lose everyone that you and I know damn well, you still love."

# Chapter thirty

# DYLAN

I was more lost now than I was three weeks ago when I was released from Hell. I never thought getting back to the real world would be such a huge adjustment and drastic change. I didn't know which way was up or down anymore.

I went for a walk to try to clear my head and ended up where my childhood existed, Alex's restaurant and the beach. Maybe I just needed to talk to Alex. I walked into the restaurant for the first time in six years, spotting a very pregnant Lily.

"Hey," she greeted, walking up to me, rubbing her stomach.

I nodded.

"I would hug you, but I'm pretty sure I'm growing a wrestler in my belly, and he will more than likely kick you."

I nodded again.

"Did you become a mute behind bars, Dylan?" She cocked her head to the side.

I shook my head. "No. Just don't have much to say, I guess."

"Well, then you came to the wrong place. The kids are surfing, Alex is out there if you want—"

"Kids?" I interrupted.

Her eyes widened. "Umm… yeah. Shit. I suck."

"Lily?" I gave her a questioning glare, wondering what she wasn't telling me.

She sighed. "See, the kids are kinda all friends. So… you know, they all hangout together and stuff. They love surfing. I mean Giselle is only a year older than Mason, and they're like two peas in a pod."

"Giselle? She's out there?" I pointed towards the beach. My heart began to beat harder. The daughter I never met was right outside.

"Well, yeah. But if someone asks you who told you that, you never saw me, okay?"

I left before she got the last word out, walking toward the beach.

"Dylan," Alex announced, stepping out in front of me. "What are you doing here?"

"I need an invitation now?" I snapped.

"No. Of course not. It's just umm…" She glanced at the water.

"My daughter is out there," I stated, finishing her sentence for her.

She wearingly nodded, pointing. "She's the furthest one out. You can't miss her. Her hair is almost white from the sun and salt water. She's beautiful, Dylan."

I took in my girl for the first time in sixteen years, desperately yearning to run out into the water to meet her, hold her, and tell her how much I loved her.

"Does Aubrey—"

"Fuck her," I gritted out.

"Dylan, that's not fair." She reached up touching my shoulder in a comforting gesture.

I scoffed, taking my eyes away from my daughter that already owned my heart.

"Half-Pint, do I look like I'm in the mood to be fucked with right now?"

She put her hand on her hip, cocking her head to the side. "Dylan Anthony McGraw, you need to take a step back and realize that I'm not like the boys and I won't take your crap. You're better than this. Aubrey has been through hell—"

"And what about me, Alex, what I have been through?" I countered.

"I know. Trust me, I know. But Aubrey has done nothing but try to make amends with you and everyone that she's hurt. It's taken her a long time to get to this point in her life. She's come such a long way, and I won't let you ruin that for her."

"Well, I'll be damned, Half-Pint. Here I thought you were *my* friend."

"You know I am. But if you don't forgive her, Dylan, then you're never going to be able to move on. Aubrey spent ten years of her life unable to forgive herself and it got her nowhere. This vicious cycle needs to end. For everyone's sake, especially your daughter's."

"She has nothing to do with this."

"She has everything to do with this. She lost ten years with her mom and sixteen with her dad. You think that girl wants to see her parents' fighting? See her dad hating her mom? Do you think that's fair to her!" she yelled, pointing to Giselle.

I jerked back, opening my mouth to say something, but quickly shut it.

"Exactly," she simply stated, saying it for me.

"Half-Pint, I'm not like you. I can't forgive and forget that easily."

"Dylan, don't you think I know that? Lucas put me through hell, but at the end of the day I always knew he loved me. There was never a question about that. I forgave him because I couldn't live without him. After all this time, after everything you guys have been through. Can you honestly look me in the eyes and say you can live without her?"

"I don't know who I am anymore, Alex. Me. Of all people, you have to know how hard that is for me. I lost everything. Everything that's ever meant anything to me because of her. I don't know how to move past the fact that she ruined my entire life in a matter of seconds."

She frowned. "Dylan, she lost everything, too. Don't you see that? You need to give her a chance to explain. You owe her at least that much."

"I owe her absolutely nothing. Not one fucking thing, Half-Pint."

"See, that's where you're wrong. She's the mother of your child. You owe her everything."

I stood there shocked as shit. I never thought about it that way. Before I could contemplate more, I felt someone walking up to us, and I didn't have to wonder who it was.

I turned to face my daughter for the first time in sixteen years. I actually fucking gasped at the sight of her. She was breathtakingly beautiful, exactly like her mother, except she had my eyes. She had freckles on her face and bright blonde hair from the sun. She wore a black bikini that I would be burning and never allowing her to wear again. She was shaped just like her mom.

She nervously smiled. "You probably don't know who—"

"I know who you are, darlin'," I interrupted, tugging on the ends of her hair.

She beamed. "Mom says you used to do that to her. She's told me all about you. All about your love and relationship. How you guys met and what you went through. How you were always there for her. How much you loved her and saved her. How much she loved you. She tells me I'm just like you! I've probably looked at the pictures she has of you about a million times. I've wanted to meet you for a really long time now. Mom never let me go to your visiting hours with her because she said you didn't want to meet me under those circumstances. You didn't want me to see you like that. But she said that you talked about me all the time. That you loved me so much and that you couldn't wait to finally meet me. I fought with her every time she told me she was going to visit you. I'm so happy right now! She told me you hadn't come to meet me yet because you were trying to find the perfect time. I know this probably isn't that time, and I know I'm all wet from the ocean, but can I hug you? Please."

I blinked away my tears and cleared my throat. "I would love that more than anything."

She jumped into my arms and it was the first time in six years that I truly embraced someone back. I closed my eyes and held her as tight as I could against me, trying my best to hold it together. I couldn't believe Aubrey lied to her. I couldn't believe she included me in Giselle's life all those years as if I was right there with them. With just a few words my hatred towards her lessened in a matter of seconds.

As if it wasn't even there to begin with.

Giselle was the first to pull away, and I resisted the urge to pull her back toward me and never let her go.

I locked stares with Aubrey when I opened my eyes. She was hugging herself in a comforting gesture, with tears in her eyes. I actually took her in that time and she appeared as if she hadn't aged a day, if anything she looked younger.

She wore a soft yellow dress that hugged her in all the right places, and after all those years it was still my favorite color on her. Her blonde hair was long, down to her waist. It was lighter than I remembered. That only told me she must have spent a lot of time on the beach.

"Mom!" Giselle greeted, hugging her and looking back at me.

Our eyes never wavered from each other.

"Can Dad come over for dinner?" she asked, instantly bringing my attention to her. "Oh, I mean... can I call you Dad? Is that alright?" She looked up at me, waiting for an answer with nothing but love in her eyes. Her mom used to look at me the same way.

"Darlin', I'd be honored."

"Good." She nodded. "Now, that you're out we can finally be a family!" She shouted, jumping up and down.

"Giselle," Aubrey cautioned.

"What? You told me yourself you're still in love with him."

I grinned and it seemed so foreign coming from me. I couldn't remember the last time I smiled.

"Giselle! Go get your stuff. Now!"

She frowned. "Why? I'm only repeating what you've told me for the last six years."

"Giselle, I'm not going to tell you again."

"Fine. Dad, can you talk some sense into her?" she questioned, rolling her eyes before she left. She was definitely my kid. I almost felt bad for Aubrey having to deal with a mini-me.

Aubrey looked annoyed, and Half-Pint couldn't wipe off the huge fucking smirk on her face. She didn't even try to hide it.

"I'm going to leave you two alone," she declared, leaving.

Aubrey shook her head as I stepped toward her until we were face to face, only a few inches apart.

"I'm sorry. Giselle doesn't have a filter. She doesn't think before she speaks. Want to guess where she gets that from?"

I laughed. I couldn't remember the last time I did that either.

"I didn't know you'd be here," she said.

"You and me both. I sort of just ended up here."

"Oh."

"I'm glad I did," I said, nodding toward Giselle.

She nervously licked her lips, folding her arms over her chest. Making me look down at her breasts that were now pushed up with the necklace I had given her all those years ago.

A soft blush crept along her face when she realized I was staring at her chest. I gazed into her eyes. She swallowed hard, and I fought back the desire to tug on the ends of her hair.

"You lied to her," I stated, breaking the silence between us.

She grimaced, probably thinking I was going to attack her again.

"Thank you," I added.

She instantly relaxed. "You can see her anytime you want, McGraw. We can work something out so you can get to know her. Although, what you see is definitely what you get with her. You have more in common with that girl than you'll ever know."

"I want joined custody."

I jerked back. "What?"

"You heard me."

"Dylan, we don't have to do that. I won't keep her from you."

"I want it to be official. Legal. Documented. I don't trust you. I'm sure you can understand why."

It was like he kept dropping bomb after bomb over my head. Not giving me anytime to seek shelter.

"I also want her to carry my last name. She's mine as much as she is yours. I want it—"

"Already done," I blurted, cutting him off.

He narrowed his eyes at me in disbelief.

"I'll show you the paperwork I filled out when I got my parental rights back. She's carried your last name for the last six years, McGraw. I wanted her to know where she came from. Which is why she knows everything about you. Except, I didn't tell her one thing."

He cocked his head to the side.

"How much of a fucking asshole you are!"

I turned to walk back inside, but he grabbed my arm, stopping me. The mere touch of his hand made my belly flutter and my heart pound. I peeked up at him through my lashes. I could tell he was fighting an internal battle with how to respond to that.

How to deal with me.

That was the hardest pill to swallow.

"I'm going to be in her life. Which also means I'm going to be in yours. Get used to it, because this *asshole*, isn't going anywhere," he bit.

I tried to pull my arm away, but he wouldn't let me.

"What happened to you?" I blurted, needing to know.

He reached out and touched the promise, always charm dangling from my neck. For a second I thought he was going to rip it off.

"You, Aubrey. You happened to me." With that he let go.

Leaving me with nothing, but the hold he still had on my heart.

# DYLAN

It had been six months since I was released from prison. A few days after the beach, Jacob filled out all the paperwork in his office for us to share custody of Giselle. After we signed the papers I wrote Aubrey a check for child support to cover the last sixteen years. She fought me tooth and nail, claiming she didn't want it or need it. We finally came to an agreement weeks later. She would open a separate bank account where all money concerning Giselle would go. A place I could deposit future child support checks that Giselle could use for college.

I was civil towards Aubrey, but to be completely honest we only spoke when it came to Giselle.

And I damn well preferred it that way.

Since Lucas was a general contractor he was able to work out something with one of his realtors for me to be able to rent a house near Aubrey's in South Port. I wanted to stay close to Giselle. It was a two bedroom, two and a half bathroom colonial style that had been upgraded with modern finishes and fixtures. It had a huge back porch with a pool and outdoor kitchen.

Giselle immediately started decorating her room as soon as I got the keys. My baby girl loved purple. We spent a whole weekend painting her room a deep shade and buying furniture for her room and the entire house. I had always been good at saving money and smart with investments that were still earning me income during my time in prison. I didn't have to work for years to come, so it allowed me the liberty to try to get whatever was left of my life back on track, without worrying about finances.

I got Giselle every other weekend and one day during the week. Aubrey and I each got our own holiday, switching back and forth every year. Giselle stayed with me every summer.

Aubrey was right about one thing. My daughter was exactly like me. Strong willed, stubborn as all hell, cocky as shit, and said what she felt, not caring about other peoples feelings.

She was perfect in my eyes.

She sat on the couch when I walked in from the grocery store.

"Darlin', can you help me with the groceries?"

She got up and walked out into the garage without saying a word to me, which wasn't like her at all.

"I'm sorry I'm late. I got stuck in traffic, but I bought everything you like."

She nodded, walking back into the house. I grabbed her arm, stopping her. Obviously something was bothering her.

"Talk to me."

She shrugged.

"Giselle," I coaxed.

"I put away our laundry while you were gone."

"Okay…" I let go of her arm to lean against the counter.

"I just wanted to do something nice for you."

I tugged on the ends of her hair, trying to get her to smile. It usually worked, but today it didn't.

"What's wrong—"

"I'm fine!" she yelled in my face.

She left to go into the garage, leaving me standing there stunned by the turn of events. She never acted that way toward me before. We spent the entire weekend together and she barely said more than a few words to me. I swear one morning she looked like she had been crying all night. I paid extra close attention to her for the next few days, calling and texting her more often and most of the time she ignored my efforts.

"Hey, what's up?" Aubrey answered her phone.

"Hey, how are you?"

"I'm good. I just got off work."

Aubrey had gone back to school to get her certification in counseling. She was now helping battered women who were going through similar situations she had gone through. She said it helped her heal.

"How are things over there?" I asked, catching her off guard.

"What do you mean?"

"With Giselle. How is she actin' with you?"

"I guess she's been kinda quiet these last few days, but that's normal, Dylan. She's a teenage girl."

"I think there's more to it than that. She's blowing me off, and I don't fucking like it."

"Hmm…"

"Say it."

"I'll talk to Giselle. I'll see if I can get anything out of her. Better?"

"Much."

"God, McGraw. It's always a pleasure," she sassed like the old Aubrey I once loved, and then hung up on me.

I was meeting Jacob for drinks at Half-Pint's restaurant later that night. Lily was still the entertainment there and Jacob was just as pussy- whipped as he was before I was put away, waiting for her to get off to drive her home and shit.

"How's the little man at home?" I questioned.

"Exhausting," Jacob replied, peeling off the label from his beer.

I nodded toward what he was doing. "Damn, Jacob, been that long? Sexually frustrated, huh?"

He chuckled, "You prick. My sex life is on point. More than I can say for you. Haven't seen any pussy around you since you been out. Makes sense though. I guess Bubba would be hard to replace."

I grinned. "Jacob, you watch too many goddamn movies. Bubba doesn't exist, but Yolanda, my counselor. I tore that shit up."

"Wouldn't put it past you, bro."

I took a few swigs of my beer.

"Don't worry about me, Jacob. I don't have a problem getting pussy. How do you know I'm not seeing someone right now and I just don't want your sorry asses' to meet her until I'm sure I want to keep her around."

"How's Giselle?" he asked, ignoring me.

"Going through some hormonal shit that I apparently don't understand."

He nodded. "And Aubrey?"

I shrugged. "Don't ask, don't care." I placed my beer back on the table.

"So, if she was seeing someone that would be okay with you?"

I played off the impact of his words, instantly hating how it stirred up old emotions inside me.

"Jacob, I don't care who she's spreading her legs for now. That ship's been sailed too many times. Been there and fucked that."

His eyes widened. "You may want to reconsider talking about her like that, asshole, she's the reason you're out four years early."

I jerked back like he hit me. "What the fuck are you talking about?" I said a little too loudly.

He took a deep breath, shaking his head. "Nothing. Forget I said anything."

"The fuck I will."

"Listen, it's not my place to say anything."

"Not your place as what, my lawyer or my friend?"

He narrowed his eyes at me. "Her friend."

I slowly nodded. "I guess some things do change."

"Or they stay the same. You've been playing this role for the last sixteen years, Dylan. It must be getting a little old. You gotta be getting a little tired."

"The only thing I see that is old and tired here is you, but being pussy-whipped will do that to a man."

"I'm not the one going home alone, dick." He stood up. "You want to know the truth so bad then ask her. But prepare to eat your fucking words for ever thinking or talking about her like that."

And with that he left.

"Hey, honey," I said, walking into Giselle's room. She was lying on her bed reading a book.

"Hey," she replied, sitting up and scooting over for me to sit beside her.

"Good story?"

"Mmm hmm."

"How's school?" I asked, glancing at her.

"Fine."

"Your friends?"

"The same."

"Mason?"

She blushed, shrugging.

It was obvious to both Alex and I that Mason and her had a thing for each other. They never left one another's sides since the day they met. I couldn't blame her, he was as charming as Lucas was. We didn't get involved, but if something were to happen between them, it was more than okay with us.

"So, it's Mason that has you all quiet?"

She shook her head, playing with the seams of her tank top.

"Your dad says you've been ignoring him."

She shrugged again.

"Honey, you gotta give me more than that."

She took a deep breath, contemplating what she was going to tell me. "I was putting away our laundry at dad's house the other day. I wanted to do something nice for him."

"Okay…"

"I wasn't snooping. I mean not entirely."

I smiled, waiting for her to say she found a condom or a dirty magazine. That would have been typical to find with Dylan.

Nothing could have prepared me for the next words that came out of her mouth.

Not one damn thing.

"I found a black, velvet, ring box hidden in the corner of his sock drawer."

All the blood drained from my face. My body instantly turned cold.

"I didn't even know he was seeing anyone. Did you?"

I shook my head unable to form words. My mind was instantly spinning in circles, trying to form coherent thoughts.

"I guess… I don't know. I just guess I hoped you guys would find your way back to each other. Like Uncle Lucas and Aunt Alex or even Uncle Jacob and Aunt Lily."

*I did, too.*

I sucked back the tears that so badly wanted to surface. I had to be strong for her, even though I wanted to break down and hate myself all over again for what I did to us.

*This was all my fault.*

"I'm sorry, Mom," she wept, snapping me out of my daze.

I pulled her into my arms, laying her head on my lap to play with her hair.

"You have nothing to be sorry about, honey. It's normal for kids to want their parents together," I said, trying to keep my voice steady.

She sniffled, tears still falling down her face. "But you still love him."

"Giselle…"

"You told me all the time when he was away. Just because you haven't said it since he's been out, doesn't mean it's changed."

"There's always going to be apart of me that loves your father. That's never going to change, even if I'm with someone or he is," I explained, dreading the words that came out of my mouth.

"I'm so mad at him. I'm so mad that he didn't even let me meet her. Like my opinion doesn't even matter."

"Honey, I'm positive it's not that. I'm sure he's just waiting for the right time."

"There's never a right time to break my heart, Mom," she cried.

"You're so young. There's so much you don't understand."

"What if she hates me and then she takes him away from me? I don't want to lose him again when I just got him back."

I wiped the tears away from her face. "That could never happen. He's your dad, and that's a bond no one can ever break."

"Promise?"

I closed my eyes. Remembering every single time I said that to Dylan. Every. Single. Memory. Hitting me hard. Leaving me drowning in a sea of nothing but mistakes and regrets.

"Always," I whispered loud enough so she could hear me.

"I'm sorry, Mom. I'm so sorry you didn't get your happily ever after," she bellowed for me.

Taking the words right out of my mouth.

I spent the night with her head on my lap as I comforted her the only way I knew how. I let her cry for as long as she needed I let her cry for me, because I knew that if I cried for myself.

I may never be able to stop.

I spent the entire night mourning the loss of something I never had. Our love had been gone for years. After every unopened letter that got returned, after every time the guard came back and told me he didn't want to see me, every hope, every wish, every maybe simply turned into never.

Vanished in thin air.

Giselle finally passed out from the exhaustion of her tears and the next morning I made the phone call that kept me up all night.

"We need to talk," I said.

"Yeah, we do," Dylan replied.

"Are you busy with someone tonight?" I snapped, regretting my words immediately.

He was quiet for what seemed like forever, and I waited on pins and needles for him to just tell me he was getting married to a woman that wasn't me.

"Come over at eight."

"Okay," I breathed. "I'll see you tonight." I hung up before he said anything else.

Terrified that he would change his mind and that I would have to tell him goodbye without us being alone.

One. Last. Time.

I knocked on his door right at eight and I swear a part of me feared that a woman would be there, too. That he was going to introduce us. When he called out to come in, I made my way inside. I couldn't breathe the entire thirty steps it took to walk into his kitchen.

I knew because I counted.

It was the only way to keep me from passing out from the emotions that I couldn't control for the life of me.

He was sitting on a barstool at the kitchen island, paperwork scattered in front of him.

"Hey—"

"Do you care to explain to me how my record is sealed?" he asked not taking his gaze from the papers in front of him.

"What?" I asked, taken aback.

We locked eyes.

"I haven't tried to look for a job, I haven't had any need or desire to be told I'm a convicted felon and can't do jack shit with my life. According to Jacob I need to ask you why I got out of prison four years earlier than I was supposed to. Patience has never been one of my goddamn virtues, especially when it comes to your bullshit lies. I pulled up my record and it's been sealed. Now, are you going to tell me how the fuck that is possible? Or am I going to have to lose the bit of patience I do have left when it comes to you and make you fucking tell me."

"Dylan, I've been trying—"

"You haven't been trying shit. You want to know how I know? Because I still don't know the fucking truth!" he roared, making me jump.

"Are you for real? I spent six years trying to talk to you. Trying to see you. Trying to explain. Six fucking years!" I screamed at the top of my lungs.

He was over to me in three strides, knocking the stool over. He was in my face before I even saw him coming.

"Do I look like I want to be yelled at? Do I seem like I want to be fucked with? If you really want to start throwing out numbers, Bree, how about we start with the number ten! Ten years I waited for you! Ten years I was left on my goddamn knees with your back turned to me! Ten years of hell! For what? For nothing! For your fucking lies! Ten years you lied to me! Kept me away from my daughter!" he yelled in my face.

"That's not—"

"Oh, that number's not good enough for you? How about sixteen, huh? That number better? Sixteen years I've been away from my kid!"

I shook my head not knowing what to say to make it better. To make him see reason.

"Still not good enough? How about six then?" he rasped so close to my face that I could physically feel his hate toward me.

My eyes widened, my heart beating profusely with what he was about to say. I didn't think I would be able to live through it.

I stepped back, and he stepped forward.

"Six years I stayed locked up behind bars!"

Another step.

"Six more years away from my daughter."

Another step.

"Six years away from my family and friends."

Two more steps.

My back hit the wall, and I instinctively placed my hands on his chest. My left palm right over his heart and it was the first time that I ever felt it beating as fast as mine.

He leaned in close to my lips and spoke with conviction,

"Six years rotting in prison for you, for a crime *I* didn't commit."

# DYLAN

"I never asked you to do that," she murmured.

"You didn't have to. When you took the gun out of my holster and shot Jeremy straight in the fuckin' head you made the decision for me."

"Dylan, I... God, I barely even remember that day. I already knew it was Jeremy before he ever walked into the bedroom that day. Jesus Christ, Dylan, he raped me the night before. That's when I knew but he had been dropping hints the whole time. I had to relive that nightmare over and over again. Why the hell do you think you found me in the closet with a knife?"

I leaned back, stunned.

"I tried to tell you. I spent six years trying to tell you the truth. Everything happened so quickly. One minute, I was in the closet praying that day wouldn't be my last. The next minute you were there, then you were fighting, and... fuck... hearing him talk about that day. The rape. As if it were nothing but a goddamn bedtime story, I just, God, I don't even know. I can't even begin to tell you what was going through my head when I pulled that trigger. I had a moment of weakness, and I wasn't going to let him win that time. I couldn't. It was like I was there all over again, on that trail, being torn to shreds. I couldn't even catch my bearings before he told you about Giselle."

I stepped away from her, pulling my hair back away from my face, holding it at the nook of my neck.

She continued, "I was hanging on by a very thin thread at that point, and all of a sudden I snapped. I didn't stop for one second to think of the consequences. All I wanted to do was to shut him up. To stop him from talking. To stop him from continuously ruining my life. You took the gun out of my hand so fucking fast, that I didn't even realize what I had just done. All I remember was you telling me not to say a word until Jacob was present. Fuck... Dylan, I watched you clean the gun. I saw you put your fingerprints all over it. I witnessed you staging it all, wiping his blood on your clothing and it still didn't click that he was dead."

She shook her head in disbelief. The agony was clearly written across her beautiful face. As if she was reliving the day all over again.

"I stood there and watched the blood draining from his body, terrified that if I looked away, he would get up and hurt me. He wouldn't have thought twice, he would've ended my life. You took me into the kitchen and sat me on the counter and I swear everything just went in slow motion after that. The phone call to 911 where all you told me to say was "help" into the phone and hang up. The moment you told me to tell the cops you were at Alex's restaurant and to not say one other word."

I swallowed hard. The bile rising in my throat.

"They took me to the hospital. I remember them asking me questions, and all I wanted to do was go to you. Find you. But you were already gone. You just left me there, and I didn't understand why." Tears formed in her eyes.

"I woke up the next afternoon and Jacob was already there. He had been there all morning next to my hospital bed. He told me that you were placed under arrest for the murder of Jeremy. He told me you admitted to doing it. He told me he spent the entire night with you and you told him over and over again that you killed him. I swear for a few minutes I thought he was right. I thought he was saying the truth."

"Aubrey—"

"But then I remembered, the whole scene played out in front of my eyes. I told Jacob you were lying to protect me and that I did it. I pulled the trigger. He told me he knew the truth. He finally admitted that you told him everything, but it didn't matter because your mind was set and I needed to keep my mouth shut. That you made him promise that he would make sure I never told the truth. I did what you wanted. You wouldn't even look at me throughout the entire trial, and it took everything inside me not to scream out to the judge that it was me! That I killed him!" she yelled, walking toward me and it was my turn to step back.

"You never let me see you. You never gave me a chance to explain. You fucking hate me for what I did to you! For lying! When all I did was listen to you and kept my mouth shut. Why did you take the fall for me? Please! Tell me why?" She openly sobbed.

"Aubrey, you were in shock when I got there. Fuck, you were in shock the entire time. Especially after you pulled the trigger. The whole fucking time you were repeating 'Giselle, Giselle, Giselle, how am I going to get her? What did I do?' I asked you where she was? Where our daughter was? And all you said was Aunt Celeste. It didn't take a genius to put two and two together."

"That doesn't explain anything."

"I told you I kept tabs on you. I knew you were getting help. I knew you had started seeing a therapist. When you called me, I was expecting it. I was waiting. Jesus, Aubrey… I went to prison because I figured that it was only a matter of time until you could get Giselle back, especially if she was with your aunt. She needed a mother. She needed you. So, I had no choice in the matter."

Her eyes widened in realization.

"I did it for her. My daughter. No one else."

"Your family knows the truth. I told them the truth. My family, the boys, Alex. They all know that you're innocent."

I nodded. "I know, but that doesn't change anything. It doesn't give me back everything I've lost because of you. You've ruined my life, and all I've ever done is try to save yours."

"Don't you think I know that? Don't you think it kills me? I love you. Do you hear me? I fucking love you."

I closed my eyes. I had to. I wouldn't allow her to see my truths. She didn't deserve them, not now.

"I went to Jeremy's dad."

I immediately opened them, glaring at her.

She didn't falter. "I was at my wits end. You wouldn't see me. You wouldn't read my letters. It had been almost six years, and I couldn't deal with the fact that there was still four more to go. One afternoon Giselle and I were at your mom's house visiting. I went into your room to have a few minutes to be close to you. To feel you.

I laid in your bed and it smelled like you. I used to hate your scent. I despised it and in that moment I wanted to drown myself in it. I laid there for I don't know how long, savoring you. When I got up I went into your closet to take home one of your shirts. To bring something back with me, but then I remembered that you kept all your t-shirts in your drawer, so I went in there to find one. I pulled them all out to choose the best one and there before my very own eyes in a zip lock bag, was the shirt you gave me the day I was raped. I lifted the shirt up and my blood covered cotton shorts from that day, fell at my feet." She shook her head trying to pull herself out of the bad memory.

"I kept them in case you decided to try to find him someday. I hoped that you would change your mind and that maybe keeping the clothes would help with finding the motherfucker who took you away from me."

She nodded in understanding. "I took them straight to Jacob asking him if there was something that could be done with them, some sort of proof for the DA to show that Jeremy was a violent bastard. Any evidence that would take away some of your sentence. He told me no. Flat out told me there wasn't a chance in Hell that it would hold up in court."

I lowered my eyebrows still not following.

"I racked my brain for days. I had to do something. I woke up one morning, grabbed the clothes, packed a suitcase, and took the next flight out to California. I showed up at Jeremy's parents' house and threw the clothes on his dad's desk," she chuckled.

"He didn't bat an eye, Dylan. I remembered you told me that he was accused of rape in college and his dad bought the people off. I told him that if he didn't have you released from prison, I was going to press charges. I would go to anyone that would listen and air all his dirty laundry on national TV and any magazines that would give me a chance. That I wouldn't stop until everyone knew the truth. He was up for re-election. The scandal would destroy his entire career, and he knew it." She took a deep breath, walking back and forth telling me her story.

"I told Jacob what I had done, and you were released from prison eight weeks later. Your record had to be sealed. That was another condition for me to keep my mouth shut. You kept the clothes to save me, McGraw, but they ended up saving you."

# *Aubrey*

"I have been trying to tell you that since you were released from prison, but you've barely said two words to me that weren't in reference to Giselle. I figured that eventually you would apply for a job somewhere or you would need your record pulled up for something. When the time came, you'd seek answers from Jacob and he would lead you to me."

"Jesus Christ," he rasped overwhelmed with everything I revealed to him. "So, what, Aubrey? What do you want now? A thank you? Is that what you're looking for? Or do you want me on my knees again?" he viscously spewed. "This doesn't change anything. You made the decision to hide my daughter from me. My kid! I got no say in the matter. Not once did you ask me what I wanted. I have missed sixteen years of her life, and for what? After everything I did for you, after ten years of trying to save you from your own demise, that's how you repay me? You knew! You fucking knew that I would have raised her. That I would have been there for her with or without you. No questions asked. You had every chance to tell me the truth! Every fucking opportunity under the sun to let me know I had a child! Nothing! Not one word!" he roared, pacing the room and pulling at his hair like he wanted to tear it out.

"I used to wish it was dead," I blurted out the truth. It had been haunting me since the day I found out I was pregnant.

He stopped dead in his tracks and looked at me with an expression I had never seen before. One of pure hatred so thick I could almost choke on it.

"The day I found out I was pregnant, I wanted to kill it. I wanted to have an abortion. I wanted nothing to do with the mistake growing inside me, it was a constant reminder of my rape. I bawled my eyes out for two days straight trying to convince my mom and aunt to let me go through with it. They wouldn't. They told me that I didn't know if it was *his*."

"You're not helping your case, sweetheart. Now, you're telling me they knew the entire time, too? How was I not informed by at least your mom? I could have-."

"Jesus, Dylan! What did you think was going on when you found me in my room? What did you think I was doing, smashing my fists into the mirror? What do you think I was going to do if you hadn't barged in when you had?"

He winced. It was quick, but I saw it.

"Exactly. I couldn't be near you. That day in the abandoned house you weren't the only one left on your goddamn knees, McGraw! I was, too. I've been there the last sixteen years!"

His chest heaved.

"I went to live with my aunt for the entire pregnancy. I was going to give the baby up for adoption. I swear to you on Giselle's life that I thought it was *his*. Not for one second did I think it could be yours. Not one!" I shook my head, hating the next thing I was going to admit out loud for the first time.

"I thought it was a monster growing inside me, and I can't fucking tell you..." I whimpered, my voice breaking. "How many times I contemplated doing it myself. Falling down the stairs, taking a coat hanger..." I shut my eyes, the shame eating me alive. "I wanted it dead. I wanted it dead so fucking bad, I couldn't breathe. I used to pray that I would miscarry or that it would just disappear. How fucked up is that? The entire time I was pregnant I thought about *him*. His hands on me, his body over mine, his voice in my ear. Every single day I went through the rape all over again. I was positive it was *his* child, and there was no telling me I was wrong. I wouldn't listen. I hated the thing living inside me! There were days where I would go without eating, where I wouldn't take my prenatal vitamins, where I would miss doctor appointments, in hopes that it would die," I cried, uncontrollable tears fell from my face.

"Finally my aunt took charge and forced me to do everything I had to while I was pregnant. Pretty much dragging me in the car for the visits, making sure I was eating every day, and taking my vitamins. She barely let me out of her sight to use the bathroom, in fear of what I would do. I went to bed one night and woke up to a pool of blood in between my legs. I actually contemplated letting it die even if it meant killing me with it."

His eyes widened.

"But I couldn't do it. I woke her up and she rushed me to the emergency room. I was four weeks away from my due date, and they had to do an emergency C-section because I was hemorrhaging. I guess my efforts paid off. It all happened so fast. They took it out and all I remember was hearing it cry before I drifted in and out of sleep. I didn't even know the sex. I didn't even care to find out. They shouted 'her heart's going into distress' as chaos filled the room and they whisked it away. I didn't care. I was left with my aunt and my racing thoughts. My mom hadn't made it in from North Carolina yet, so my aunt stepped in. I laid there, still hoping it wouldn't survive."

"Jesus, Bree," he breathed out.

"The next morning I woke up to my mom sitting by my bed, crying. My aunt was doing the same. I thought they were going to tell me she had died. That there was nothing they could do, and she didn't survive." I took a deep breath. "The nurse brought in a wheelchair and I knew what they were trying to do. I said I wasn't going. I told them I didn't care to see her. I didn't want her. They made me do this. I told them that I hated them." I sucked in air that wasn't available for the taking.

"They forced me to go, pushing the wheelchair for me, bringing me to a room where there were incubators everywhere." I wiped my face. "They didn't even have to tell me where she was. I knew the moment we went into the room. She looked exactly like you, McGraw," I paused to let my words linger.

"That's when I realized I almost killed *our* baby."

# DYLAN

Tears fell from my eyes.

"I thought I hated myself before, but it was nothing in comparison to what I went through in that second. They wheeled me toward her and she looked so tiny," she sobbed, making me relive it with her. I felt like I was there.

"She had tubes coming out of her everywhere, it was heartbreaking. They let me stick my hand through one of the holes. I got to touch her soft skin. I got to feel her for the first time. I loved her immediately, but I didn't deserve her. She was there because of me. My mom said she would help me raise her, that we could tell you and that she knew you would be there for me. For us. That you would help in anyway that you could, and deep down I knew she was right, but I was fucked up, Dylan. I couldn't raise her after everything I did, after everything I felt, everything I prayed for. My aunt said she would take her, that all I would have to do is sign over my parental rights. She promised me that if I ever changed my mind and wanted her back, she would be mine as long as I got help and dealt with all the emotional trauma."

I nodded in understanding, silently encouraging her to continue.

"I didn't think twice about it. I handed her over to someone that I knew would do right by her. My aunt never lied to her, Giselle always knew what happened and I always kept tabs on her. I just wasn't in her life. Why do you think I ended up with Jeremy?"

The realization hitting me like a ton of fucking bricks.

"You were punishing yourself for giving up our child," I answered, shaking my head in disbelief.

"Don't you think I deserved it? After what I wanted, after what I prayed for?"

"I don't know what I think anymore," I honestly replied, my heart torn in two.

She nervously chuckled, "Well, that's what I've been trying to tell you for the last six years, and if you would have allowed me a visit or read any of my letters, you would have known."

I peered up at the ceiling, emotionally spent and then looked back at her.

"Come on," I said, leading her down the hall.

She followed me into the kitchen and I handed her a beer, chugging down mine in four swigs. Opening another right away. She excused herself to go to the bathroom and I sat on the barstool, hunched over with my arms propping up my head. A splitting headache was forming and I welcomed the distraction from the pain I felt in my heart.

"I guess it's a good thing you're moving on, McGraw," she announced, walking back in the kitchen. "Maybe this is the push I need to also move on from you. To move on from us. There's no more secrets or lies. No more demons lurking in the shadows. We're both free now."

I glanced up at her. "Moving on?" I replied confused.

"Giselle." She rubbed her forehead, leaning against the cabinet in front of me. "It's why she's been acting so funny toward you. It's actually why I came here to talk to you. She found the ring."

I jerked back, stunned.

"When were you going to tell her? I mean not that it matters, but we would like to meet her. I know Giselle's really hurt that she had to find out that way. I tried to explain to her that you were probably looking for—"

"It's yours," I simply stated, catching her completely off guard.

"What?" She looked at me with confusion and hurt in her eyes.

"It's yours, Aubrey, the ring, it's yours."

She lowered her eyebrows. "I don't understand. When…"

"Well, fuck. Might as well get everything out in the open, huh? Why the fuck not." I shrugged.

"Dylan, what are you—"

"I was going to ask you to marry me."

"Oh my God, no, please don't tell me—"

"Yeah, darlin', when we went away to the cabin. I was going to propose, I had it all planned out. The only reason I didn't was because I couldn't get a hold of your dad. I had been trying for weeks, leaving messages, texting him that I needed to talk to him. It's why I was constantly checking my phone the entire week. I was hoping he would call me back."

Her face paled and she looked like she was going to be sick. She already knew what I was going to say next.

"He called as we were heading to run on the trail. It's the reason I told you to go by yourself. I didn't want you to overhear our conversation. I needed some privacy so I could ask for your hand in marriage."

Fresh tears slid down her beautiful face. It took everything in me not to pull her into my arms and tell her I still loved her.

"Do you honestly think I would have let you go alone, Bree? You know me. I've had to live with that regret for almost half of my life. I didn't think the call would take that long. Ten minutes tops, so I let you go. Your dad was so excited, and he wouldn't stop talking. Catching me up on his life, giving me marital advice, ironic, considering how he failed his marriage but fuck… I was trying to be polite. The last thing I wanted was to be rude to my future father in law. I thought about you the entire time. As soon as we got off the phone and I realized almost an hour had gone by and you still weren't back. I fucking knew. I knew something bad had happened to you. I could feel it. The worse part was I allowed it," I paused to let my words linger and then spoke with conviction,

"All I wanted was a future with you, and one bad decision ended up costing me that."

# Chapter thirty-three

# Aubrey

A year went by since that night of clarity at his house.

There wasn't much more to say after that. We exorcised our demons and the truths were finally told. We were both emotionally drained, and at that point we agreed we needed some space from one another. To reflect on years of regrets that neither one of us could change.

Dylan told Giselle about the ring the next time he had her for a weekend. She couldn't wait to tell me all about it when she got home a few days later. Saying that she was right and he did still love me. We're meant to be together. He wouldn't have kept the ring all those years if he didn't want to be with me.

I wanted so desperately to believe her, but too much had happened.

We had broken each other too many times to count.

I explained to her that sometimes it's better for two people to walk away from each other rather than keep hurting one another. I reassured her we'd always love her and be devoted parents to her for the rest of her life. It didn't appease her, if anything it agitated her. She said I didn't know what I was talking about and our love could surpass anything.

That it already had been proven time and time again.

Now it was time that we found our way back together.

It's where we belonged.

A lot had changed since that night. Dylan was nice to me now, well, in his own Dylan way of course. We hung out with the boys,

Alex, and sometimes it felt like old times, except we weren't together.

We were friends.

It was nice to have him in my life again, even if it wasn't in the way that I once hoped for.

Dating was a lot harder than I remembered.

I had gone on a few dates and not one of them kept my interest.

Half-Pint said Dylan wasn't dating anyone. She hadn't seen any women around him, either. I found that hard to believe. He couldn't go long without some sort of interaction with his dick. I think she was trying to keep me in the dark when it came to his sex life.

"Mom, you think this looks okay?"

I nodded, looking at Giselle in the mirror. She was dressed in a blue gown for her junior year prom.

"Honey, you're breathtakingly beautiful," I beamed as I took her hand and made her spin for me.

"What the fuck is she wearing?" Dylan roared, making me shake my head.

Giselle and I both turned around to find him leaning against the doorframe in that McGraw sort of way. After all these years that look still made my panties wet. His arms crossed over his chest, one leg draped over the other with the biggest grin on his face. The man could be sinfully sexy even when he was being a complete asshole.

He started to make himself more at home in my house, not knocking on the door when he came in, staying for dinner without being asked. He even crashed a few times in the guest bedroom. Giselle was always with us. There were very few times that we hung out alone without the boys or Alex.

"Oh my God, you don't like it?" Giselle panicked.

I glared at him.

Her Daddy's opinion topped everyone else's. She had him wrapped around her finger and she knew it.

"Where's the rest of it?" he asked, looking her up and down.

She followed his gaze. "What do you mean?" she said, holding her dress out, swaying side to side for him.

"I mean…" He gestured toward his chest. "What's up with this?"

I shut my eyes, silently laughing.

"They're called boobs, Dad."

I had to turn around to hide my laughter. She was going to give him a heart attack.

"No shit. Why are they out?"

She looked at him like he had grown two heads. "I can't really do much about that. I got them from Mom. You should know that, I catch you staring at them all the time."

I blushed, clearing my throat. "Giselle—"

"I don't like this. I don't like this one fucking bit." He pushed off the door and left.

Her eyes widened.

"Honey, you know your Dad, he's just… well… he's just kind of an asshole."

"Tell me about it. He threatened Mason about tonight. He warned him that if he didn't keep his you-know-what in his pants that he would shoot it off."

I wasn't surprised, I actually thought it was pretty tame for Dylan.

"Reminding him that he's already been to prison for killing someone so if he hurts me in anyway, he'd get one of his prison buddy's to 'take care' of him. Mom, who's Bubba?"

I busted out laughing. She wasn't amused.

"Let me talk to him, okay? You have a great time tonight."

I made my way downstairs and into the kitchen. Dylan was leaning against the counter with a beer in his hand and an empty bottle beside him.

"Dylan—"

"Don't even fuckin' try me, Bree," he warned.

"She's seventeen and she's going with Mason. You know, Mason, your best friend Lucas' son?"

"Exactly. Do you remember what Lucas was like at Mason's age?"

I bit my lip.

"How about what I was like?"

My eyes widened. *Oh shit.*

"Should I keep going?" He pushed off the counter to stand in front of me. "What about what happened *after* my junior prom?" he asked, cocking an eyebrow.

"Oh my God! She's not going."

"I'll go tell her," he said over his shoulder as he walked away.

I gripped his arm. "I'm kidding! Stop! She's fine. I trust her. I trust Mason. He's good to her. And let me remind you that Lucas was also good to Half-Pint, it was you boys that fucked everything up for them."

"Debatable."

I laughed. "You gotta let her grow up. She's graduating next year. Who knows where she will want to go to college."

"Fine. Then give me another one," he simply stated, almost knocking me on my ass.

"What—"

The doorbell rang and I jumped. Dylan didn't even bat an eye. He starred at my hold on his arm and I instantly let go.

"I'm going to... the door... umm... yeah that," I stammered, leaving to go answer the door.

I took thousands of pictures of our baby girl and Mason. It brought me back to the time when my mom had done the same thing to us. I made a mental note to tell her about it later. Dylan lurked in the back corner of the living room like a creeper, literally burning holes into Mason the entire time. Poor boy never stood a chance. We kissed Giselle goodbye and told her to have the time of her life. I held back the tears when I saw them get into the limo and drive off.

I walked back into the living room and McGraw had made himself at home, sitting on my couch with a beer in one hand and the remote in the other.

My heart pounded with every step I took, and at the last second I decided to sit in the armchair. My legs tucked underneath me as I stared into the TV, feeling his intense stare on the side of my face.

I glanced over at him. His eyebrow was arched and he was grinning like a fool.

"Why so far away?" he asked, cocking his head to the side. "I don't bite, darlin'."

I took an audible breath, taking my time to walk over to the couch before settling beside him. He reached out and tugged on the ends of my hair. He hadn't done that in years.

"You wearing yellow for me?" he asked, playing with the hem of my dress.

I shook my head no.

"Is that right?"

His hand slowly moved to caress the side of my cheek, and I resisted the urge to lean into his touch.

"What is this about?" I blurted, needing to know.

He smiled not answering, sliding his fingers down my face to my neck. Touching the charm on the necklace he gave me.

"Are you just trying to get laid? Is that what this is about?"

He raised his eyebrows with a predatory regard.

"You and I both know that I don't have a problem scoring pussy, suga'."

He also hadn't called me that in years, and it still stirred emotions in me.

"You know I bought that necklace as a gift for our wedding day. I was going to put it in your jewelry box for you to wear down the aisle."

My mouth parted and I swallowed hard.

"I had that charm made when I bought the ring."

He let go of the necklace, and I almost whimpered at the loss of his warm touch. Reaching into his pocket, he brought out his keys. He took off a keychain and threw his keys on the coffee table. It had a series of numbers engraved on it with a heart cut out on the side, like it was missing a piece.

"I had this made that same day. It's the coordinates to the beach by Ian's house. The beach where I realized that you belonged to me."

He brought the keychain up to my necklace and placed my heart charm inside the cut out.

It was a perfect fit.

"See, darlin', you've always had my heart and I've always been your home."

"Dylan…"

"I am your soft place to fall."

The air was so thick between us that I found it hard to breathe, not knowing where he was going with this.

*Hoping.*

"After Giselle was born my aunt asked me if I wanted to name her. To have her carry a part of me, a part of us even though she was going with her."

He narrowed his eyes at me not understanding what I was getting at.

"Giselle means promise."

He beamed. "Well that explains a lot, doesn't it?"

I nodded.

"She gave me your letters."

I jerked away only to have him pull me back in by the nook of my neck.

"I asked her to. I read every last one. Word for word. I didn't stop until I read them all. Every time the guard would come to my cell to tell me you were there, I already knew it. I felt you. A huge part of me didn't want you to see me like that. I didn't want you to see the man that I had become. The man I hardly recognized anymore. I was a miserable bastard the entire time I was locked up. I barely spoke to anyone. I kept to myself. I purposely started fights so that they would put me in the hole and I didn't have to be around anyone and I could get lost in my own thoughts. Memories. Of you." He laughed, his thumb rubbing back and forth along the pulse of my neck.

"I should have known better when they said I was getting out early for good behavior. I was anything but."

He looked deep into my eyes for a few seconds, contemplating what to say as I waited on pins and needles.

So when he said, "I hated you."

I felt all my wishful thinking come apart.

# DYLAN

"But mostly… I hated you because I couldn't stop loving you."

She visibly relaxed.

"This last year I've done a lot of soul searching. For the first time in my life I was lost. I tried to find that man. The one that you met. The one that you loved. The one that was made just for you. I couldn't find him. The more I searched, the harder it was to accept that I might never be him again. The more time we spent together, the more I started to laugh, I started to smile, I started to feel like I was alive again. It was then that I understood that you could save me, too."

She finally leaned into my touch. I yearned to feel her. Wanting her to give me anything she could.

"I couldn't forgive you, suga', until I forgave myself," I sincerely spoke.

She closed her eyes, taking in my words. As if she wanted to remember them forever.

To remember this moment for the rest of her life.

I leaned in close to her lips, resisting the desire to claim her mouth, the urge to make her mine once again.

"I love you, Aubrey," I breathed against her mouth. "I have never stopped loving you. I belong to you. Just you and me. You're my girl."

She didn't hesitate, "Promise?"

I smiled along her lips before I softly pecked her. I kissed her slowly, wanting to savor this moment as much as she was.

"Always," I murmured, parting my lips, beckoning her to do the same.

She did.

We kissed for the first time in what felt like an eternity.

My chest rose and fell with each deep breath I took. I placed my hand over her heart and it felt like it beat for me and only me.

Like it never stopped.

With my hands framing her face, I kissed her again. Slower, more delicate, and defined this time. Less frantic, and desperate, but with the same intensity and passion.

"Dylan," she panted.

I bit her bottom lip and stood up bringing her with me. She wrapped her legs around my waist. I wanted to take my time with her. Remembering every last inch of her gorgeous body.

The layers of all our regrets were stripped away and all that was left was *us*.

I couldn't stop kissing her. Not for one damn second. I set her against the wall and her eyes immediately widened. My hands lightly grazed up and down her thighs.

Her eyes were different, yet I had seen them like that before.

We gazed into each other's eyes as I claimed her mouth the way I wanted to. Her breathing labored and I waited for the words that never came. I leaned away from her, putting some space between us. Her eyes dilated, knowing what I was going to do next. I moved my hand tortuously slow down to her soft bare folds, feeling her wetness seep through her panties onto my fingers. I proceeded to make circles around her clit, my techniques continued to become more persistent and demanding. Her legs started shaking, her eyes closed, and her head fell back against the wall.

"Don't close your eyes," I ordered.

She watched through a hooded gaze as I manipulated her bundle of nerves.

"What, darlin'?" I teased, rubbing faster and harder.

She moaned so loud that it shook her entire body. She came with such force. I had never experienced that before.

"That long, huh?"

She laughed still trembling. "Asshole."

"I want to fuck you against this wall."

Her eyes widened, listening to my filthy words that always did things to her.

"After I'm done coming so fuckin' deep inside you, there will be no chance in hell that we didn't make a baby on another wall," I growled, biting her bottom lip. "Then… I'll take you into *our* bedroom and make love to you all night long, because, suga', I haven't had sex in almost eight goddamn years. I will have no mercy on making you mine all over again."

"You're lying," I stated.

His eyes gleamed, and I knew he was telling me the truth. When the shaft of his cock slid up and down my slit, I came once again, lathering up our sacred parts with more of my wetness.

"Jesus, Dylan. Just fuck me already," I begged, wanting to feel his hard cock deep inside me.

"Ahhh…" he captured my mouth with his as he forcefully thrust into me. Giving me exactly what I just asked for. My back arched off the wall and he put his arms under mine, holding me close. My legs curled around his waist and my arms around his neck. He stayed inside me, just holding me and kissing me.

I rocked my hips, trying to get him to move because I was growing anxious and impatient with all the emotions and sensations he was creating. With each kiss and caress, he made his way deeper into my heart.

He grabbed the sides of my face and looked deep into my eyes. He was searching for something, I knew only I had the answers he was looking for. I kept his gaze as raptly as he looked into mine. It was as if we were absorbing our way back into each other's blood streams, where neither of us could function without the other.

Never taking his eyes off mine, he started to move, it was slow, loving, and passionate. His hand reached for my neck and he softy pressed down on it. It was a move that I was familiar with. He always wanted to feel my pulse against his fingertips. I did what came naturally and placed my hand over his heart, making him groan upon contact.

I moaned and my pussy pulsated. He started to pump faster into me and the nerves in my lower abdomen throbbed for release.

"Fuck, suga'… do you have any idea what you do to me? Tell me… tell me what you're thinking. Tell me what's going on in that beautiful mind of yours?"

"I'm going to come," I breathed out, thinking he wanted me to talk dirty to him.

He kept hitting the same spot, more aggressively than before.

"Do you feel me inside of you?"

"Yes," I panted.

"Give me what I want, Bree," he rasped. "Tell me what I want to hear."

I moaned, closing my eyes as I arched my back.

"Let me see your eyes."

I opened them and looked intently into his. I could feel he was close to losing it, because his thrusts were becoming faster.

"I fucking love you," he groaned, taking me over the edge just as he was.

It was then I screamed out.

"I love you, too."

He took me back to my bed and made good on his *promise*. Deep down in my heart, I knew it would *always* be that way.

# Aubrey

"Whoever said babies were exhausting, wasn't kidding."

Lily shrugged. "You're old now."

My mouth dropped open.

"Older! I meant you're older now."

It didn't take long for Dylan—in his words—to knock me up. I'm not sure if we conceived on the wall or the next month that he pretty much lived inside me.

We named her Constance, it meant always.

I was a high-risk pregnancy because of my age, but thank God I didn't have any complications. This only encouraged Dylan to want to make more. We talked about getting married a few times during my pregnancy, but honestly, we had waited that long, and the last thing I wanted was to walk down the aisle with a big belly. Constance was almost five-months-old now and still no proposal or ring on my finger.

Giselle was attending Wilmington University because she wanted to stay close to Mason, who was a year younger than her. They officially started dating after prom much to Dylan's disapproval, but she still lived at home with us, so that he approved of.

He said he loved having all his girls under his roof. It made him sleep better at night. We bought a house shortly after I found out I was pregnant, right on the beach. We literally lived within walking distance from Lucas and Alex, and that alone made Giselle want to stay at home. Of course, she didn't tell her Daddy that.

"How's my girl?" he cooed over the baby monitor, and Lily and I grinned at each other.

"Daddy missed you today. Let's not tell Mama that I woke you up."

I shook my head.

"Jacob did that with Riley and Christian. Get used to it. They don't understand that you shouldn't wake up a sleeping baby."

Not even a second later we heard her cries.

"Told you," she added. "I'm going to get out of your hair. Have fun with that."

I chuckled. Dylan had just gotten home from work. He went back to the police force, and as much as I worried about him, I knew it was a part of him. He promised he wouldn't take on hard cases now that he was a Detective III. So far it hadn't been that bad. He was home every night for dinner and weekends. He reassured me he spent most of the time in his office. He was assigned this case a few months ago, and I could tell it was wearing him down.

"Oh, by the way. Have you seen Austin lately?"

"Yeah. He came over the other day," I replied.

"Okay."

"Why?"

"Jacob mentioned something about him and Briggs officially breaking up."

"They've been together and breaking up for years. I stopped trying to keep up with them along time ago."

She nodded. "Good point. I'll see you later. Give Constance a kiss for me and Giselle my love."

Lily hugged me and left.

"Shhh... shhh... baby girl, feel my heart. Feel Daddy's heart. Shhh..."

Just like that she whimpered for a few seconds and stopped crying.

"Unbelievable," I said to myself as I made my way into our bedroom.

I stopped working once I got pregnant and that's what ultimately made Dylan want to start back at the force again. I wanted to stay home with Constance and be the mother I never got to be with Giselle. She was a great older sister and jumped right on board with Dylan on giving her more siblings. My doctor said women were having babies well into their fifties now and my thirty-nine years of age wasn't as much of a big deal as it used to be.

I would give Dylan whatever he wanted.

If he wanted a house full of his girls, who was I to deny his desires.

After everything he ever did for me.

I owed him…

*Us.*

That much.

"Daddy loves you so much, baby girl, but if you keep crying like that every night and not lettin' me have my way with your Mama, then how am I going to give you another sister?"

I laughed.

Dylan was the first man I'd ever met who didn't care if we had a boy. He said he wanted to stay the man of the house and protect what was his, and that he was more than enough of a man to deal with all of his girls.

I sat at my vanity looking at my reflection through the mirror, finally happy with what was staring back at me. I touched the charm on my necklace, sighing contentedly. I took off my earrings and opened my jewelry box, 'Fur Elise' by Beethoven immediately assaulted my senses. I placed my earrings in their usual spot, but there was something already there.

I looked over and my heart dropped.

"Oh my God."

"That's not the answer I was hoping to get, suga'."

We locked eyes through the mirror.

"Is that—"

"What do you think?" he walked over to me and picked up the ring that was shining brightly against the lighting in the room.

"I'm waitin'."

I cocked my head to the side. "So am I," I challenged.

He grinned, getting down on one knee and peering deep into my eyes.

"Marry me."

It wasn't a question.

I tackled him to the ground for it.

# DYLAN

There wasn't a place on Aubrey's body that I didn't kiss, touch, or suck. There wasn't one moan, pant, or I love you left for her to say after I thoroughly made love to her the way she wanted.

I had everything I ever wanted.

Everything I ever hoped for.

I didn't care how long it took us to get to that place because all that mattered was that we were there.

Together.

Forever.

"Mmm…" she groaned, her eyes fluttering open as I licked her pussy the next morning. "Jesus, McGraw, how do you want back in already?"

"I want another baby girl," I simply stated.

She smiled big and wide.

"You think you could do that for me?" I asked, sucking her clit into my mouth, moving my head side to side. "Hmmm…" I hummed.

"Ask your boys," she sassed in reference to my come.

I gently bit down and she squirmed.

"My boys do just fine, darlin'."

I pushed two fingers into her warm, wet pussy and her back arched off the bed. Hitting her sweet spot while I fucked her with my mouth.

"That feel good?"

Her breathing hitched and her legs trembled.

"What?" I pushed harder and sucked faster.

Her legs tightened so fucking hard around my head as she came all the way down my face. I savored the taste against my tongue, swallowing all her juices like she was my favorite goddamn meal. I kissed her clit one last time and made my way up her body, stopping when I was fully on top of her. Enclosing her with my arms and positioning my cock at her entrance.

I would never be able to get enough of her sweet, sweet pussy. *Mine.*

I thrust all the way inside her in one swift movement. Her eyes rolled to the back of her head. I kissed along her neck and down to her breasts.

Her heart pressed against mine.

Where it belonged.

"Do you feel me inside you?" I growled into her mouth.

"Yes."

"Give me another baby girl."

She smiled.

I slammed into her, shoving my tongue in her mouth. "God, suga', I fucking love you."

"Promise?"

"Always."

"I love you, too."

"Prove it."

I angled my leg higher, making her leg incline. Our mouths parted as I roughly took what's mine. We were both panting profusely, desperately trying to cling onto every sensation of our skin-on-skin contact. I felt myself start to come apart, and she was right there with me. I came deep inside her, her pussy squeezing my cock so fucking tight.

I kissed her one last time and looked deep into her eyes.

"There's my girl."

She beamed and announced,

"I'm pregnant."

I had been trying to find the right time to tell him, and that seemed as good a time as any.

"You're fuckin' with me?"

I shook my head no. "I found out three days ago."

"Well, shit, darlin', looks like you have a short time to plan a wedding. There's not a chance in hell I'm waitin' another nine months."

I smiled, nodding.

As if on cue Constance cried over the monitor.

"I'll go get her."

He kissed me one last time, flipping over to let me up. Spanking my ass as I put on my silk robe.

"Hey, baby girl," I greeted, picking her up from her crib and rocking her in my arms, as I took her into the kitchen.

"I told Daddy the news, and he's very excited."

She cooed like she understood what I was saying. I warmed up her bottle for a few minutes, talking to her as if she knew exactly what I was saying.

"Let's go lay you down with Daddy, so Mama can make some breakfast before him and your sister turn into not so nice people. You know how they get angry when they're hungry."

I stepped back into the room and Dylan looked as if he had seen a ghost with his phone gripped tight in his grasp that his knuckles had turned white. Nothing like the man I just left a few moments ago.

"Oh my God!" I rushed to his side, sitting down in front of him as I fed Constance.

He didn't say a word, staring out in front of him in a fog of whatever was tearing him apart.

"Dylan, what's wrong? You're scaring me!"

He instantly snapped out of it, looking at me then down at the baby. He caressed the side of her cheek like he needed to feel her soft skin to calm himself from what he was going through and about to say.

"Dylan, tell me," I let out not being able to control my nerves that were on edge and a sick feeling sitting in the pit of my stomach.

"Briggs just called," he whispered so low I could barely hear him.

"Okay..." I coaxed, anxiously waiting for him to tell me what was going on.

He took a deep breath and hesitated for a few seconds before he said...

"It's Austin. He's in ICU in critical condition. He OD'ed last night, and they don't know if he's going to make it."

# THE END.

For Dylan and Aubrey.
It's only the beginning for…

Austin and Briggs.
(The last installment in The Good Ol' Boys Standalone Series)
Coming May 10th, 2016
Pre-Order Now!

AMAZON

**Website:**
www.authormrobinson.com

**Like my Facebook page:**
https://www.facebook.com/AuthorMRobinson?ref=hl

**Join my VIP Group on Facebook:**
https://www.facebook.com/groups/572806719533220/?fref=nf
I share EXCLUSIVES & hang out with my readers

**Follow me on Instagram:**
http://instagram.com/authormrobinson

**Follow me on Twitter:**
https://twitter.com/AuthorMRobinson

**Amazon author page:**
http://amzn.to/1Vafa0s

**Sign up for my newsletter:**
http://eepurl.com/beltYj

**Email:**
m.robinson.author@gmail.com

28422409R00180

Made in the USA
Columbia, SC
12 October 2018